Growing

WITH MY Cousin

MOSAICA PRESS

Growing with my Cousin

WITH MY

A TALE OF LOVE, LIFE, AND LAND

ESTER KATZ SILVERS

Mosaica Press, Inc.
© 2018 by Mosaica Press
Designed and typeset by Brocha Mirel Strizower

ISBN-10: 1-946351-13-X
ISBN-13: 978-1-946351-13-5

Published and distributed by:
Mosaica Press, Inc.
www.mosaicapress.com
info@mosaicapress.com

To my friends
who have become family

She'arim
COLLEGE OF JEWISH STUDIES FOR WOMEN

June 4, 2017
10 Sivan 5777

Ester Silvers is a very sincere *yirat Hashem* who has raised a beautiful Torah family. She has a story to tell, a story of personal growth and growing commitment to Torah, a story of interpersonal relationships and aliyah to Israel.

Ester has written a novel about a young Jewish woman's journey from a small town in Middle America to building a life in Israel, in a small close-knit settlement. The journey includes a transition from a non-observant life to building a family of Torah-true values.

This journey is the backdrop to personalities, tragedies, personal failings, and rebuilding broken lives. In her novel, we discover a world outside of the big city Jewish centers, a world where Torah observance must be fought for, earned, and owned.

Although the novel is not autobiographical, it reflects some of the transitions Ester herself has experienced. As such, it rings true to life.

Rebbetzin Pavlov
Director, She'arim

Rebbetzin Holly Pavlov, *Director*

Mrs. Miriam Shaul, *Administrative Director* ♦ Mrs. Sandie Freishtat, *Registrar* ♦ Mrs. Ariela Sher, *Financial Director*
Rebbetzin Malka Kaganoff, *Educational Coordinator*

Agassi 23/2, Har Nof, Jerusalem, Israel   Mailing Address: P.O. Box 34629, Jerusalem, Israel 9134601
Tel.: 972 - 2 - 651-4240   Fax: 972 - 2 - 651-8370   E-mail: shearim@shearim.com

Letters of Recommendation

Thank you for sending me the manuscript of your book, *Growing with My Cousin: A Tale of Love, Life, and Land*. I found it enjoyable and inspiring. It gives one an awareness for important nuances of life and relationships. I recommend it as a positive reading experience.

Sincerely,
Rebbetzin Rivkah Leff

Ester Katz Silvers has written a beautiful novel that will touch every one of us in some way. *Growing with My Cousin* is a very interesting read, and I had a hard time putting it down. It left me with a lot of food for thought and discussion.

It is a story of loving cousins, friends, and communities, who struggle to succeed and grow in the face of adversity and challenge, with joy and friendship. Ester weaves in conflicts and challenges that people face, and every reader will be able to identify with at least one of the fictional but so realistic characters.

The reader will be inspired with this moving story of friendship, unity, and commitment to Torah and Am Yisrael.

I highly recommend this book.

Rivka Segal
Noted lecturer and teacher

Family is not a sanctuary. It needs loving input from all its members to make it work. In *Growing with My Cousin*, Ester Katz Silvers shows us the strength and weaknesses within a family—one that is facing challenges like intermarriage and aliyah, and the redemptive love between cousins Sondra and Lisa. How will they handle the ultimate trauma of Kobi's disappearance? Follow their story in this absorbing novel of family life.

Dvora Waysman
Israeli author of The Pomegranate Pendant, Seeds of the Pomegranate, In A Good Pasture, Esther, Searching for Sarah, and nine other books

Prologue

"Is this the Chazon family?" Sondra asked uncertainly in Hebrew. She'd checked her watch before dialing the number. It was almost eight in the morning in Israel, not quite ten o'clock in the evening in Phoenix.

"Yes." She didn't recognize the voice at the other end of the receiver.

"May I speak to Lisa?"

"Who's calling?"

"Her cousin, Sondra. I'm calling from America."

"Just a minute."

It was more like five.

"Hello?" Lisa's voice was thick, as if she'd just woken up.

"Lisa, are you okay?"

"Yeah, I'm fine." She didn't sound fine.

"Listen, I have some bad news from here." Sondra cleared her throat nervously. "I think it's something you should know."

"Yeah?"

"Shaindy's husband was killed in a car accident Saturday night."

There was a brief silence and then Lisa mumbled half to herself, "Well, at least she knows where he is."

1

Horrified by her cousin's inappropriate response, Sondra cried out, "Why would you say such a thing?!" But as she spoke, she realized the line was dead. She redialed the familiar number with a trembling hand. This time Lisa picked up.

"Lisa." Not wanting to wake any of her children, Sondra struggled to keep her voice low. "Are you okay?"

There was a long pause before Lisa responded. "Sondra," she said carefully, "Kobi's disappeared."

Sondra gasped. "What happened?" She heard her younger cousin sobbing. "Lisa?"

"I'm here." Lisa struggled for control. "Sunday morning he went to work and never came home. Yesterday the police told me that he'd been on a flight that landed at JFK, but that's all we know."

"Oh my gosh!" Sondra rose from her seat and began pacing the den, trying not to get tangled up in the long phone cord. "Oh my gosh!" she repeated. "Do your parents know?"

"I just found out yesterday." Lisa was crying again. "There's a lot to sort out."

"Did he leave a note?"

"Nothing."

"Oh, Lisa, I wish I could help you. Is there anything I can do from here?"

"Find Kobi!"

"I wish I could." Sondra recalled how Lisa had met Kobi at her apartment at the first Seder she and Danny had made. "I can't believe he walked out on you!"

"He's been depressed ever since the murder." Lisa's voice was flat.

"Yes, that was awful, but that's no excuse!" Sondra grew angrier as she absorbed Lisa's news.

"You're...Just a minute...Sondra, someone's at the door. I need to hang up."

"Okay," Sondra answered reluctantly, "but I'm calling you again in the morning, my time."

She replaced the receiver and sank down into her chair, her thoughts awhirl. If it hadn't been for her, Lisa might never have met Kobi. Of course, she reminded herself, if it hadn't been for her, Lisa might have converted to Catholicism and married a goy.

That had been such a long time ago. Winter 1975. Over eight years. She'd been a young bride living in Los Angeles and Lisa had been a freshman at Arizona State University in Tempe. So much had happened since then...

CHAPTER
One

Only Doc was around when Sondra Klein entered the kitchen in her in-laws' exclusive condominium in Arizona that morning. He put down the newspaper he was reading and invited his daughter-in-law to join him at breakfast.

"I just got back from rounds at the hospital." He pulled out a Chinette paper plate, plastic silverware, and a linen napkin. "Is Danny still at morning services?"

"He should be back soon. Where's everyone else?"

"Shirley never gets up before ten on Sundays, but Dorothy and Stan's Chicago flight leaves in the early afternoon, so I expect to see them shortly." He opened the refrigerator and took out the containers the kosher caterer had packed for them after his birthday party the night before.

"Bagel with cream cheese sound good?"

"Great! Is there any noodle-cottage kugel left? It was delicious."

"There sure is." Doc set the plate in front of her. She rose to wash her hands before beginning to eat.

Doc poured her a glass of juice and then piled some sliced fruit on a crystal platter. "Danny said cold glass is okay."

"Thank you." Sondra had liked Danny's father immediately when she first met him, barely a year earlier. He was an older version of her husband. Both were tall, with unruly black hair and kind eyes.

"Were you really surprised?" she asked him. Her grin revealed a dimple in her left cheek.

Doc chuckled. "It was enough of a surprise to have my children show up unannounced, and so nice to have Danny and Dorothy together again like when they were kids. I didn't need the party, but I have to say I enjoyed it. I just hope the drive wasn't too much for you."

"It was fine." Sondra smiled. In truth, the seven-hour drive from LA to Phoenix, finding a substitute to teach for her on Friday, and Danny missing some of his medical school lectures had been anything but easy. Spending Shabbos in her in-laws' house, three miles away from the synagogue, was also a big challenge, but she didn't want Doc to know that. "We really appreciate Shirley making the party kosher for us. I hope she was happy with the caterer."

"Yes, she was." Doc rose to pour himself a cup of coffee. "He was just as elegant as the caterer for our Dorothy's wedding."

Sondra shifted uncomfortably in the chrome chair that matched Shirley's dinette set. She and Danny had gotten married in Kansas City, an hour's drive away from Lincoln, the small college town where she'd grown up. Their wedding had been held in the social hall of the synagogue where Sondra had first become observant, and it had been anything but elegant.

Noticing her discomfort, Doc hastened to qualify his statement. "Your wedding didn't make the society page like Dorothy's did, but it was a lot of fun. I thought that separate dancing would be really strange, but it made a big difference. No one had to wait for a partner to ask her to dance. Everyone just joined in. We had a great time."

"So did we," Sondra said. It hadn't been the Jerusalem wedding at Danny's yeshiva that she'd dreamed of, but getting married in America meant that most of their relatives were able to attend. Sondra loved turning the pages of her wedding album and remembering the special day.

"Tell me," Doc took a sip of his coffee, "are you feeling okay?"

"I'm fine," Sondra answered a bit defensively, putting down her half-eaten bagel and pulling at the ends of the headscarf she'd brought back from Israel. She was almost at the end of her first trimester, and she and Danny weren't planning on sharing their news with anyone, even their parents, until she reached the second, especially since her first pregnancy had ended in a miscarriage. No one else had known about that except her doctor, and she was glad she hadn't had to endure anyone's pity.

"Are you eating right and getting enough sleep?"

"How do you know?" Sondra blurted out, flushing with embarrassment.

"My dear," Doc said kindly, "I haven't been an obstetrician for twenty years for nothing."

"Danny told me you wanted to be a doctor from the time you could walk." Sondra smiled fondly at him.

"That's why they call me Doc! My father was a wonderful role model. I'm sorry you didn't get to meet him."

Sondra nodded.

"Now tell me, are you happy with your doctor?"

"Yes," Sondra answered and she found herself telling him all about her bouts of nausea and even, to her surprise, about the miscarriage.

"Miscarriages are not that uncommon during first pregnancies," Doc reassured her. "Listen to your doctor and this one should be fine." He drained his coffee cup. "When do you two plan to head back?"

"Probably right after lunch. We both need to start early tomorrow morning, but I'm kind of hoping to see my cousin before we leave. She's studying at Arizona State University. Would it be okay to call her once I finish eating?"

"Of course. Use the phone in the den. You'll have more privacy that way."

Sondra *bentched* quickly. Eagerly, she entered the den and removed Lisa's dorm number from her pocket. She hadn't seen her cousin since the summer, when she and Danny had visited her parents in Lincoln.

"Sorry," the voice on the other end of the line responded to Sondra's inquiry. "Lisa isn't back from church yet. Mass should be over soon. Who should I say called?"

Church?! Sondra's stomach clenched. *What in the world is going on?*

"Uh, never mind. I'll call back later."

She hung up, her stomach queasy. What was her Jewish cousin doing at Mass? She sank into the easy chair near the phone, wondering what to do next. Would Danny be back soon?

The clock ticked loudly as she waited, but it was only five minutes later when she heard Danny's voice in the kitchen greeting his father. She considered getting up to join them, but she knew her face would betray her, and this was definitely not something she wanted to share with Doc.

Fortunately, Danny came to find her. Seeing her sitting listlessly in the den, he knew at once that something was amiss. "What's wrong, honey?"

Sondra told him about the phone call. "Danny, I need to go see her. I need to ask her what's going on."

"I'll drive you," Danny offered at once. "I know the way and I know the campus. I'll talk to my dad and we'll go."

Ten minutes later, they were in the car after promising to be back before lunchtime to say goodbye to Dorothy and Stan. During the forty-five-minute drive, Danny cautioned Sondra not to jump to conclusions, to stay calm, and to listen to what Lisa had to say. Sondra knew he was right, but she was a bundle of nerves when they pulled up in front of the tall dorm building. Although she was an only child, she considered her cousin almost a sister.

"I'll park over there." Danny pointed to a shady spot next to a grapefruit tree. "Come get me if you need me. Good luck."

CHAPTER

Lisa Apfelbaum had already slipped off her heels in the elevator. As the doors opened onto the sixth floor of Manzanita Hall, she was unzipping her shoulder bag. Hearing the blast of music from room 624 made her smile, and she abandoned the search for her key. The song on the radio ended just as Lisa opened the door and the news started blaring. Lisa made a face as she changed from the pleated skirt and matching blouse into her jeans and peasant top. Nixon had resigned four months earlier and still the newscasters droned on about Watergate.

"Thanks for the outfit." She tossed the clothing onto her roommate's bed.

"No problem." Carol Garcia put her finger in her book to hold her place and tossed her black bangs out of her eyes. "You had a phone call."

"Who?"

Lisa's roommate shook her head. "Some woman."

"Did she leave a message?"

"She said she'd call back after church. How was Mass?"

"Did you tell her I was at church?" Lisa demanded.

"Don't worry. She didn't have a German accent."

Lisa sighed with relief. Her mother had spoken to Carol several times, and her roommate was always amazed at how Irene Apfelbaum's perfect English syntax combined with such a strong accent.

"I'll have to call home this evening," Lisa announced. "I think it's snowing in Kansas. It would be cool to tell them I went swimming in February. Do you want to go to the pool with me?"

"Okay. Just let me finish this chapter. I have a test this week."

"You're so good," Lisa teased. But she picked up a yellow highlighter and the marketing textbook off her desk and began studying too. Both girls tuned out the rock music and concentrated on their studies to such an extent that they barely heard the knock at the door. It came again, louder and more insistent.

"Who's there?" Carol called out.

"Sondra Klein. Is Lisa back from church?"

Lisa groaned. She let her book fall and hid her face in her hands. Sondra was the worst possible person for Carol to have told about her being in church, far worse than her mother or father or even her Oma.

As she reluctantly got off her bed to answer the door, she couldn't help remembering the time Sondra had caught her smoking when she was in tenth grade. At that time, Lisa had decided that the best defense was a good offense and she'd been nasty to her cousin. Even so, Sondra hadn't said anything to her parents. Three days later, Lisa and her best friend had decided that sneaking around behind their parents' backs wasn't worth the risk. They made a pact to stop smoking and lying, and to protect each other from the ridicule of their other friends. That had been three years ago. Lisa had no intention of resorting to a strong offense this time, but she didn't know how she was going to face Sondra.

Petite and dark like her mother, Sondra bore little resemblance to Lisa, who was stately and blonde like hers. It was their fathers who were brothers, but their mothers were best friends. Despite their differences, there was a strong bond between the two cousins, and Lisa reached out to hug Sondra as soon as she opened the door.

"Is there somewhere we can talk?" Sondra asked diplomatically after Lisa introduced her roommate.

"Make yourselves comfortable here," Carol spoke graciously as she gathered up her books. "I'm meeting a friend at the library."

"Do you like it here?" Sondra sat on the desk chair Lisa had pulled out for her.

"I do." Lisa nodded emphatically. "Especially the weather."

"You never liked the snow."

Lisa shook her head. "I have memories of Mom bringing Howie and me out to your farm and your mother urging us to go play in the snow. She probably wanted us out of the house so the two of them could gossip their hearts out. We were always supposed to be making a snowman, but all I remember is you and Howie pelting me with snowballs, and being cold."

"Poor you!" Sondra managed to laugh. "Howie and I really tortured you when we were little, didn't we?"

"It wasn't until I hit junior high that you both stopped treating me like a pest." Lisa sighed. It felt good to talk with Sondra about her brother, who'd been killed in a car accident four years earlier.

Sondra also felt the solidarity. She definitely remembered how she and Howie had changed their attitude toward Lisa. Although she never knew what Howie's motivation was for the change, hers was simple. She'd hoped to influence all of her cousins to become observant, as she was. When she realized that probably wasn't going to happen, she began concentrating on getting Lisa to not date non-Jews. That hadn't worked either.

"Um, Lisa." Sondra felt her face flush. "When I called to say hello, your roommate, uh, Carol, told me you were at church — I guess a Catholic one 'cause she said Mass. What's going on?"

"You're not going to like it," Lisa mumbled.

"What is it?" Sondra didn't take her eyes off her cousin's face.

"Tim broke up with me right after winter break." Lisa bit her lip and avoided Sondra's eyes.

"Yeah?"

"He told me he'd been doing a lot of thinking about religion, and you know his family's Catholic." Lisa sniffled. "He told me he felt bad that he'd slipped away and he was going back to it." The tears started. "He said he couldn't go out with me anymore because I'm not Catholic."

"Oh, Lisa," Sondra said softly, remembering all the admonitions Danny had given her.

"We were so close," Lisa sobbed. "I picked Arizona State because he was going to the University of Arizona. We didn't want to be on top of each other because we knew we'd never study, but we were seeing each other every weekend — until after Thanksgiving. You wouldn't believe all the excuses he found not to get together."

Lisa controlled her sobs and her voice became hard. "Sure, we both had finals, but I studied during the week. And yeah, gas is expensive, but he has a good allowance." She began bawling and Sondra awkwardly patted her back.

"So you're going to Mass because of him?" she asked.

It took a few minutes before Lisa could answer. "I was so devastated. I couldn't eat or go to class or anything. I wanted to die if Tim didn't want me anymore. Carol was worried about me, so she suggested that I convert." The tears started again.

"You converted?" Sondra was horrified.

"Not yet." Lisa blew her nose. "I spoke to Tim and he said if I became a Catholic, he'd take me back, so Carol took me to the priest and he said to come to Mass for a month and then we'd talk. This is my third week."

Sondra could no longer sit still. "Has this guy given up anything for you or are you the one making all the sacrifices?" She jumped up and began pacing.

Lisa lowered her eyes. Ruefully, she remembered how she'd been dreaming of going to the Grand Canyon for Thanksgiving break, but Tim had wanted to go gambling. They'd ended up in Las Vegas. That was before he'd gone back to being Catholic.

"I didn't say I was converting. I said I was thinking about it." This was said with dignity.

"I hope you think about it a lot. Do your parents know anything about this?"

"Are you crazy?"

"What!" Sondra threw her hands in the air. "You're going to become Catholic and keep it a secret from them?"

"Well, no..."

"Maybe you don't remember how upset everyone was when Brenda married out, but I do. Marrying out is nothing compared to this."

"Sondra, you don't understand." Lisa grabbed a tissue and blew her nose. "You were lucky. You fell in love with someone who was Jewish. I didn't."

"Of course you didn't," Sondra said softly. "You never went out with anyone Jewish."

"Who was I supposed to go out with?"

"You could have waited till you left Lincoln, like I did."

"I'm not you." Despite Lisa's tears, Sondra could hear her resentment.

"No, you're not." She sat on the bed and put her arm around her cousin. "You are you, but part of who you are is that you're Jewish. Your parents didn't leave Nazi Germany so their daughter could become a Catholic."

"What do you expect me to do?"

"Call it off with Tim. Try and get over him."

"That's so easy for you to say! Would you call it off with Danny?"

Sondra wanted to tell Lisa that her relationship with her husband was a mature commitment, not some leftover high school romance, but she knew that wasn't the right thing to say at this moment. It wasn't the time to explain the Torah's view of courtship either. Instead, Sondra decided to tell Lisa about her high school friendship with Roger and how her parents wouldn't let her date him. Before she could start, though, she felt an uncomfortable twinge.

"Lisa..." Sondra moaned and clutched her stomach, "it's not the same at all. I can't explain it now, though. I — I just don't feel very well."

"What's the matter?" Lisa wiped away her tears. "Can I get you something?"

Sondra shook her head. "I'll use your bathroom and then I just want to get back to Danny's parents and lie down. I...I'm sorry. I'll call you later."

CHAPTER
Three

Oanny hadn't seen Sondra coming and only looked up from his Gemara when he heard the car door open.

"Sondra, you're as pale as a ghost!"

"Danny," Sondra struggled to keep her voice in control as she got into the car, "I think I'm having another miscarriage."

"Oh, no!" Danny looked at his wife compassionately. "I'll stop at the gas station and call my dad's partner. He can meet us at the hospital."

Sondra nodded and nervously played with her seat belt as Danny started the car's engine...

"How far's the hospital?" she asked in a shaky voice once they had crossed the bridge that separated Tempe from Phoenix.

"Ten minutes, even less with Sunday traffic. You know, Sondra," Danny turned to his wife at the stoplight, "this might not be a miscarriage. Think positive."

Sondra took a deep breath. "I don't think I ever told you that my mother had six miscarriages."

Danny changed lanes. "Your mother survived the camps, Sondra. She was lucky to have had you."

Sondra's bottom lip quivered as she tried not to cry. Danny kept up a running monologue and concentrated on the road. Sondra barely heard him.

Fortunately, Dr. Taylor was waiting for them when they arrived and she immediately went into his office to be examined. It didn't take him long to find the baby's heartbeat, and as they heard it over the fetal monitor, Sondra began to breathe more normally.

"You need bed rest for now," the doctor instructed her.

"We're supposed to drive back to LA this afternoon," Sondra said. "Do you think it would be okay if I just lie across the back seat of the car?"

"What kind of car do you have?" Dr. Taylor asked.

"A Ford Pinto."

The doctor burst out laughing. "You may be petite, young lady, but there's no way you're going to be able to lie down and keep your feet up in the back seat of a Ford Pinto. Your in-laws have a comfortable guest room and Shirley will be happy to have you."

Sondra wasn't so sure about that. Nor was she certain Shirley would be pleased by her news. Just the night before, she'd overheard her mother-in-law telling a friend — rather emphatically, she thought — that she was too young to be a grandmother. Then, as that friend showed off pictures of her new grandson, Shirley took out a picture of her daughter Dorothy with her cats. So Sondra was totally unprepared for the greeting she received from her mother-in-law.

"Sondra!" Shirley hugged her warmly. At five foot one, she was just a fraction of an inch taller than Sondra, but that was where their similarities ended. From her hair-sprayed coiffure to her stylish heels, Shirley was a contrast to her modestly-clad daughter-in-law.

"Ed already explained everything to Doc," she gushed. "I don't want you to worry about a thing. Do you want to lie down in front of the TV in the den, or should we move the portable into your room?"

"Mom," Danny spoke up, "Sondra's not a real TV watcher. And I think she should have a nap now. I'll get her settled."

"Okay, but Sondra, don't hesitate; if there's anything you want, ask. Dorothy and Stan send their love. Don't worry." Shirley anticipated what Danny was going to say. "We didn't tell them a thing. They're sorry they missed you. They left for the airport not five minutes before you came. They waited as long as they could."

"I hope they weren't insulted?" Sondra worried.

"No, they knew you went to see your cousin. Don't worry. And Sondra," Shirley called to her daughter-in-law's retreating back, "make a list of books you'd like me to get from the library."

"Thank you." Sondra turned and smiled warmly at Shirley. Maybe the next few days wouldn't be so bad.

Later, though, when Danny was packing up to leave, she couldn't help feeling as if she was being abandoned.

"Sondra." He sat down on his bed and faced his wife. "I know you're not that comfortable with my mother and staying here without me is hard for you. Maybe Hashem's made everything happen here so you and my mother can get closer."

"Maybe." Sondra was uncertain.

"You never told me what happened with Lisa."

"Danny, you don't want to know." Sondra repeated the entire conversation.

"Do you think she'll go through with it?"

"The conversion?" Sondra played with her wedding band. "Who knows? She has a lot of mixed feelings. I wish I'd finished talking with her."

"You can call her." Danny motioned to the phone between the two beds.

"I know." Sondra sighed. "But a conversation like this should really be face-to-face."

"You're right," Danny conceded. After sharing some soft words with his wife, he left her opening a book on Jewish history. Before leaving the house he made a quick call to Lisa's dorm room from the kitchen phone. Then he said goodbye to his parents.

"Don't worry." Shirley hugged him. "You're leaving your wife in good hands. I already spoke to Betty and we'll have the mah-jongg game here tomorrow instead of there. I'll only leave Sondra alone if Carmen's here, and she's coming Tuesday so I can still go to the library."

"The library?"

"Your mother tutors a young Indian woman." Doc's voice was proud.

"Wow, Mom," Danny said with respect. "That's great."

Shirley's smile was both pleased and embarrassed as she watched her son leave.

CHAPTER

Four

"*No esta aqui,*" Lisa struggled with the few Spanish words her roommate had taught her. "*Egresa la llamda.*" She hoped Carol's mother understood that her daughter wasn't there and would call her back later. Unlike her own mother, Carol's hadn't learned much English in the twenty years she'd been in America. Of course, the Spanish speakers in Florence, her small mining town, far outweighed the German ones in Lincoln, Kansas. Hanging up the phone, Lisa picked up her marketing textbook once more but had only read one page when Carol returned.

"How was the library?"

"Wonderful." Carol laughed. "I ran into Bill there. We studied and then took a walk and got a bite to eat — better than going to the pool. How's your cousin?"

"Okay." Lisa hesitated. "She left in a hurry and her husband called later. She's sick and he had to go back to LA, so she's staying by his parents and I'd kind of like to visit her..."

"Yeah, public transportation's a drag." Carol pulled off the turquoise earrings she was wearing and handed them back to Lisa. "But

Bill's going into Phoenix tomorrow afternoon. Maybe he'll give you a ride."

"Really! That would be great!"

"Do you mind if I smoke?" Bill asked as he pulled his Corvette onto Black Canyon Freeway.

Lisa shook her head. Even if the smoke bothered her, she wasn't going to object. Bill was doing a big favor for her.

"What are you doing in town?" He changed lanes.

"I'm visiting my cousin. And you?"

"Also relatives. My aunt and uncle are here for a convention. They're taking me out for dinner. Carol was supposed to come too, but she chickened out."

Lisa couldn't miss hearing the annoyance in Bill's voice.

"She has a big test tomorrow."

"Carol always aces her tests. She didn't need to study." Bill impatiently stubbed out his cigarette. "No, Carol's not coming because she's afraid my aunt and uncle won't like her because she's Hispanic."

"Would it matter to them?"

"It doesn't matter to me."

"Does your family know about Carol?" Lisa asked.

"They know I'm seeing someone seriously."

"Do they know she's Hispanic?"

Bill considered Lisa's question. "You know, I don't know."

"You never told them?"

"I'm not sure. Being Hispanic is part of who Carol is, just like her shoe size."

"Would they be upset if they knew?"

"I don't think so," Bill answered honestly. "Carol's the one making a big deal out of it, not me."

"Do you think you guys will get married?"

"Good chance." Bill smiled.

Lisa swallowed and looked at her hands. "What about her family?"

Bill sighed. "No one said love was easy."

"You can't become Hispanic for them," Lisa said matter-of-factly, "but you could become Catholic. They might trust you more if you did."

"No way!"

"Why?"

"I love Carol because of who she is and I expect the same from her."

"But shouldn't we try to improve ourselves for the one we love?"

"Improve, fine." Bill headed to the exit ramp. "Listen, Carol hates the smell of cigarettes. I'm trying to stop smoking, both for her and for me. But I'm not going to make myself into something I'm not for any girl, no matter how fantastic she is."

He turned on the radio, ending the conversation. For Lisa, it was a relief to let the music envelop her as she tried not to think about Tim or conversions or parents or cousins.

"Lisa!" Sondra's face registered pure pleasure when Shirley ushered her surprise visitor into the den. Sondra was propped up on the couch knitting. There were several books and an empty plate scattered around her.

"Danny called yesterday," Lisa explained.

"Let me get you something to drink," Shirley offered. "And then I'll leave the two of you alone until dinnertime. You're staying for dinner, aren't you? We're having steak."

"Steak?" Lisa questioned Sondra once Shirley left.

"The barbecue's kosher." Sondra grinned. "One day it's grilled chicken, the next steak, and then lamb chops. How'd you get here?"

Briefly, Lisa explained about Bill. "How long are you going to have to stay in Phoenix?"

Sondra took a deep breath. "I have a doctor's appointment Thursday and I think he'll tell me I can go home."

"You'll be glad to get back."

"Yes, I will."

There was a long silence. Sondra knew what she wanted to say, but wasn't sure how to begin. Lisa was self-conscious, well aware of what was on Sondra's mind. It was Lisa who spoke first.

"I decided not to go through with the conversion."

Sondra smiled as tears rolled down her face. "I'm sorry," she apologized and reached for the box of tissues. "I cry so easily now."

"It's okay."

"What did Tim say?"

"I haven't talked to him. I just decided on the way here," Lisa said simply.

"What made you change your mind?"

Lisa took a few minutes to form her answer. "There were a couple of things. I think you were right when you asked me if I was the only one making sacrifices for the relationship. And then Carol's boyfriend was telling me that if you love someone you love who they are and don't need to make them over into something they're not. I may not be a fanatic like you about Judaism, but it's always been part of me and I'm not ready to let it go."

"What about Tim?" Sondra queried gently.

"The ball's in his court." Lisa grabbed a tissue and wiped away her tears. "I miss him. Maybe he'll miss me enough to decide I don't have to be Catholic."

CHAPTER

Five

The smile on Sondra's face as she entered the waiting room was all Shirley needed to know that the appointment with Dr. Taylor had gone well.

"So Ed said you can go home?"

Sondra nodded happily. "And he said I can go back to teaching, just not to stand for more than an hour, and not to lift heavy things or run or," Sondra laughed embarrassedly, "wash the floor."

"I guess Danny's capable of that," Shirley replied. "Let's head home. I'll call the travel agent and see if she can get us flights already today."

"Us?" Sondra asked uncertainly as they entered the elevator.

Shirley looked at her. "I can't imagine putting you on a flight and then chewing my fingernails waiting to get the call that you're home safe and everything's okay. I thought I'd go with you and make sure you get settled in all right."

"Thank you." Sondra was touched. "Maybe," she said impulsively, "you'd like to stay on? We can make you a nice Shabbos."

"You know, Doc's on call all weekend." Shirley looked pleased with the invitation. "It might be nice, but I don't want you cooking anything yet. I'll buy the food from one of the kosher restaurants there."

In the end the only thing Shirley bought was challah, since Sondra's neighbors had sent in enough food for several days. Shabbos went well. Shirley didn't complain once about the simple food or not being able to smoke, although she did slip out after lunch to see the famous Farmers Market. When she came back she definitely carried the odor of cigarettes, but Danny and Sondra ignored it. So it was on a good note that the three of them left for the airport Sunday afternoon.

"Well, Mom," Danny said as he made the turnoff to the airport, "you survived having a real Shabbos with us, right?"

"Yes, I did."

"Maybe you and Dad would like to come for the Seders?"

"Oh, Danny," Shirley exclaimed, "what a lovely idea! Do you think Sondra will be up to it?"

"I'm already better now," Sondra said shortly. She plastered a smile on her face and thanked her mother-in-law for all her hospitality. While Danny checked his mother's bag in curbside, though, she fumed silently to herself. And as they left the airport she turned to her husband angrily.

"How could you invite your parents for Pesach without even asking me?"

"Oh." Danny put a hand to his mouth in consternation. "I didn't think. I'm sorry."

"Who do you think is going to be doing all the cooking anyway?" Sondra struggled not to yell. "And it's three days this year!"

"Sondra, I'm so sorry," Danny repeated. "I just know my parents want to be with us for both Seders. We can't go there, and we owe them big time."

There was silence from his wife.

"You know, Sondra, my mother skipped her beauty shop appointment to bring you home."

"I know. And I appreciate everything she did." Sondra smoothed the fabric of the maternity jumper Shirley had bought for her. "But you should have checked with me first." She blinked back tears of frustration.

"You're right. You know, I'll be helping you with everything."

"Yeah, with all your free time between classes and studying." Her voice was sarcastic.

The ride home from the airport was not the upbeat one they'd enjoyed on the way there.

"I'm going to return the chicken pan to Tamar," Sondra announced as they entered their apartment. "Enjoy studying."

With angry strides, she made her way four doors down and knocked on her friend's door.

"Hi, Sondra. You shouldn't have troubled yourself to bring that to me." Tamar Glinker smiled down at her friend. "You should be resting."

"Right, rest. Pesach's coming in six weeks and I'll have a slew of guests to prepare for. I better get used to not resting."

Her friend looked at her quizzically. "Would you like to come in and talk about it?"

Sondra followed Tamar inside, and they sat down at the Glinkers' cluttered kitchen table with glasses of juice in front of them.

"You're nervous about Pesach?" Tamar asked.

"Kind of," Sondra admitted. "Aren't you?"

"You bet! And I'll be working up until Seder night."

"Won't the dentist give you any time off?"

"Not really." Tamar tucked a strand of her blonde hair back under her headscarf. "I'll need my vacation days for actual *yom tov*. And we're certainly not going home to our parents."

"No?"

"You know Eliezer's a convert."

"Yeah?"

Tamar looked down at her lap. "Didn't I tell you that my father's a Reform rabbi?"

Sondra shook her head.

"Apparently it never occurred to him, even in his wildest dreams, that when he sent me to Israel for the summer with the Reform youth group, I'd end up going to the Kotel and being invited to a religious family's home for a Shabbos meal, or he never would have sent me. He thinks that my becoming Orthodox is a rejection of him. So my parents won't come to us for Seder. I'll be lucky if they come for the bris if I have a boy."

Sondra looked at Tamar meaningfully and Tamar nodded. "I'm due in September."

"I'm the end of August," Sondra said. "Do you think everyone here knows?"

"I think they suspect that's why you stayed on in Phoenix without Danny. I had no problem getting people to send in food for you."

"Thank you for taking care of that," Sondra said. She sipped her drink thoughtfully. "You know, I think Danny's parents are coming to us for the first days of Pesach. It would be really great if you and Eliezer would join us."

An hour later, Sondra returned to her apartment. She faced her husband rather shamefacedly as he put down his textbook.

"I'm sorry I got so angry."

"You're right. I should have asked you first."

"I didn't ask you when I invited your mom for Shabbos," Sondra mumbled.

"That's true."

"But I want to make things nice. I invited Tamar and Eliezer to come to our Seders and she's going to help me."

"Great." Danny smiled and refrained from mentioning that Sondra hadn't asked him first. "Listen, right before she went into the airport, Mom told me to get some cleaning help, on her. Let's get someone in right away."

"That sounds good. It was really nice of her."

"Uh-huh," Danny concurred. "Maybe you'd like to invite your parents for the Seders too?"

"I can," Sondra said. "But I don't think they'll come. They won't want to leave Oma and she's not well enough to make the trip. I would like to invite Lisa, though."

"Go for it!" Danny was relieved his wife's anger had passed so quickly. "She can come with my folks."

CHAPTER

Six

Around the same time that Sondra was apologizing to Danny, Lisa received a phone call in her dorm room.

"Lisa?"

Her heart began racing at the sound of Tim's deep voice. "Tim, I...I've missed you."

"I've missed you too." Lisa could imagine his confident smile. "I wanted to know how it went with the priest today."

"The priest?"

"This was the fourth week." There was a drop of impatience in his voice. "What did he tell you?"

"I didn't go," Lisa whispered.

"You didn't go?" He was incredulous.

"Tim, I can't convert."

"You said you care so much for me that you'd do anything."

"I still care." Somehow Lisa was able to keep her voice calm. "But I can't change my core. Being Jewish is part of who I am."

"Then it's over," Tim said flatly. "Bye."

"Wait!" Lisa cried out. "Remember how good it was with us," she pleaded. "Don't break up with me! Think it over! Call me tomorrow! Please! I'll be waiting for you. I'll wait for you forever!"

Then she hung up the phone before Tim could hear her tears. They'd dried by the time Carol returned from her afternoon date with Bill.

"I'm famished," she declared. "We didn't have a chance to eat. You want to go to the cafeteria with me?"

"No, I'm waiting for a phone call. But it would be nice if you'd bring me a bowl of soup."

"Sure thing."

The next day Lisa was still sitting by the phone and she asked Carol to bring her a sandwich. She did the same on Tuesday, but on Wednesday, Carol snapped at her.

"I'm not your delivery boy. Get up and go to the cafeteria yourself!"

With a glance at the phone, Lisa reluctantly joined her roommate, ate quickly, and hurried back to her dorm room. On Thursday, she came back from class to find a notice about programs being offered at the Jewish Student Union that Carol had clipped and set on her desk. She threw it in the trash. Friday she turned down Carol's suggestion for a double date with one of Bill's friends. By Sunday, Carol had had it.

"You know," she confronted Lisa, "if Tim really wants to talk to you and you're not here, he'll call back."

Lisa shrugged her shoulders.

"Start living your life and do something besides going to classes and waiting for Mr. Jerk to call you!"

Before Lisa could reply, the phone rang and she lunged for it hopefully. Her face fell as she heard Sondra's cheery hello, but she listened patiently to her cousin's Pesach invitation.

"I don't think so," Carol heard her say. "Okay, I'll think about it... Thanks for thinking of me."

"What was that about?" Carol demanded.

"My cousin wants me to come to LA for the Passover Seders."

"Why not go?" Carol picked up a hair clip and began pulling her long hair into a ponytail.

Lisa toyed with a pencil, trying to frame an explanation.

"If anyone calls for you," Carol said gently, "I'll give them your cousin's number."

"You don't understand," Lisa said. "They don't answer phones on the holiday!"

"They don't?" Carol frowned. "Why not?"

Lisa took a deep breath. "My cousin and her husband are Orthodox Jews; they're really fanatic. On our Sabbath, that's Friday night and Saturday, and on the holidays, they won't go in a car, or use electricity, or answer a phone."

"That sounds really medieval."

Lisa gave a small smile. "It's not quite as bad as it sounds. A couple of years back, when Sondra was still at home in Lincoln, we had the first Seder at my house and she slept over. I walked her home the next morning. Her farm is three miles away, but it was good weather and something different to do. She made a nice holiday lunch and taught me a few things. That evening, everyone came to her house for the second Seder, and when that ended, I got in the car with my parents and rode home. One day of religion was enough. This year, Passover runs into Saturday, so it will be three days of restrictions!"

"Okay, I get it," Carol said.

❋ ❋ ❋

The following week, Carol broached a serious subject.

"Lisa, I think I want to move into an apartment next year."

"In Sin City?" Lisa was referring to the blocks of prefab apartments adjacent to the campus.

"Yeah, are you interested?"

"Maybe."

"The only thing is...," Carol hesitated, brushed her hair out of her eyes, and plunged in, "I want a roommate who's a friend."

"I'm a friend!" Lisa was indignant.

"Not lately," Carol said. "You're more like a monk holed up in our room, leaving only to go to class or the cafeteria."

"What do you want me to do?"

"Listen," Carol took her hand, "I'd like for Tim to call you, but it doesn't seem like he's going to." She stroked Lisa's shoulder to take the sting out of her words. "If he would, though, I think it would be great for him to find you're not here. Maybe that way he wouldn't take you for granted."

"You really think so?"

Carol nodded adamantly. "Go to your cousin," she said gently. "It'll do you good to get away from here. Come back ready to live, and we can begin looking for an apartment. Sound good?"

"I guess so." Lisa sighed. Later she wrote a letter to Sondra accepting the invitation. For six weeks, she kept hoping for the call from Tim, but it never came.

As Danny finished checking for any sign of leaven in their home, Sondra proudly put the finishing touches on their table. It was set for nine. Danny's parents and Lisa would be leaving Arizona first thing the following morning. Shirley had informed Sondra that she was bringing a carton full of Manischewitz gefilte fish jars, macaroon tins, and matzah meal cookie boxes.

Tamar had invited them for dinner that evening. She'd made a huge pot of soup for the Seders and promised a couple of salads; her husband, Eliezer, had bought and delivered all the wine.

Their neighbor Mrs. Steiner stopped by with two sponge cakes. She had followed her only son and his family to Los Angeles ten years earlier, and when his work transferred him back east in the summer, she decided she was too old to move again.

"I can't tell you how much I appreciate your invitation for the Seders," she told Sondra for the sixth or seventh time. "I'll miss my son and his family, but I can't manage flying anymore. This way I won't even have to leave the building. Thank you so much!" She grabbed Sondra in a hug.

"You're welcome." Sondra smiled, rather embarrassed.

"Now don't forget," Mrs. Steiner called over her shoulder, "I'm checking all the romaine lettuce we'll need in the morning."

Danny completed his search and Kobi Chazon, the dark, handsome Israeli who'd come into their lives a couple of months earlier, knocked on the door.

"Here's all the hand-baked matzah you ordered."

"Thanks! Let me get my checkbook."

"Danny," Kobi objected, "we had an agreement. You'd host me if I didn't go home for Pesach and I'd pay for the matzah."

"Okay." Danny shook his friend's hand.

Sondra watched the interchange with a smile. Kobi had shown up in shul one Shabbos morning and Danny had invited him for lunch. An Israeli from a traditional family, he was in California studying electrical engineering. The following week, he again showed up in shul and again Danny invited him for lunch. Sondra wasn't sure if Kobi was motivated by the shul or by her food, but now he was keeping strictly kosher, learning with Danny on Shabbos afternoons, and going to a weekly Torah lecture at the shul.

"I put the chicken in Tamar's fridge," Kobi informed Sondra. "Twenty pieces enough, do you think?"

"Wonderful. Danny has the roasts ready to go in the oven first thing in the morning. The turkey's coming out in about an hour."

"We won't go hungry," Danny announced.

"With a cook as good as Sondra, we certainly won't!"

Sondra laughed with pleasure. Kobi was such a charmer! And he was helpful too. He schlepped the extra chairs from Tamar's, and during the Seder, he served the soup. Afterwards, he shooed Sondra and Danny out of their kitchen.

"Lisa and I will do the clean-up," he announced.

As he cleared and she swept, he teased and she enjoyed his attention even though she didn't take him seriously. Once back in Manzanita Hall, seeing that there had been no messages from Tim, she tried comforting herself by remembering how Danny's Israeli friend had found her interesting.

CHAPTER

Seven

As the temperature at ASU rose to triple digits, Lisa finally admitted to herself that Tim wasn't going to call her back and she made some decisions. She informed Carol she'd love to meet Bill's friend. She started going to the Monday lunches at the Jewish Student Union. And she asked her parents if she could stay in Arizona for summer school. To her relief, they had no objections. The long weekend she spent in Lincoln before summer classes began only reinforced the wisdom of her choice. It seemed as if everyone she met wanted to know what had happened to her and Tim. She was evasive with all of them except for Cathy, her best friend from high school. Cathy was no longer with her old boyfriend either. Theirs has been a mutual break-up, though.

"We just felt," Cathy confided as they sat cross-legged on her bed, "that if we kept on, we'd end up living our parents' lives. Who knows? Maybe if we see the world a bit we'll decide to go back to each other, but it won't be because we're in a rut."

Lisa thought over Cathy's words during the flight back to Arizona. Would a year or two without her change Tim's perspective on their relationship? She banished those thoughts from her mind and resolved to concentrate on the four classes she was cramming into ten weeks of study. At the end of the courses, she and Carol moved into a two-bedroom apartment. Lisa had just returned from throwing out another box of trash when Carol handed her the phone.

"It's your cousin," she said.

It wasn't Sondra, but Danny. "Mazal tov! Sondra had a baby boy."

"Mazal tov!" Lisa exclaimed. "Is Sondra okay? The baby?"

"Everyone's fine, thank G-d! The baby was born on Shabbos, so the bris is this coming Shabbos and we really want you here. You can come with my folks and we'll put you up at Tamar's again."

"I'd love to be there," Lisa didn't hesitate. "Where will you be doing the bris?"

"In our apartment. It will be crowded." Danny laughed happily.

The living room was filled to overcapacity with Danny's and Sondra's many friends from the synagogue and the handful of relatives who'd come for the ceremony. Oscar, Sondra and Lisa's middle-aged cousin, was given the honor of announcing the baby's name. He pronounced Zvi Chaim in a loud, clear voice.

Lisa, standing close to the door, found herself squeezed in beside Kobi. She felt the tears running down her face and she had no tissues to wipe them away.

"They say that the baby doesn't really feel it," Kobi whispered gently.

"I know." Lisa wiped at her cheeks with the back of her hand. "It's the name. I shouldn't be surprised that Sondra named her baby after my brother."

"Your brother?"

Someone shushed them, so Lisa just nodded. Later, at the meal for family and close friends, Lisa again found herself next to Kobi.

"Your brother's name was Zvi Chaim?" Kobi asked as he reached for a plate of coleslaw.

"His Hebrew name," Lisa answered. "His English name was Howie. He was three years older than me, a month older than Sondra, and they were really close." She took a deep breath. "He and his girlfriend and another couple were killed in a car-train wreck their last year of high school."

"That must have been really tough."

"It was." Lisa bit her lip and concentrated on her plate.

"You know," Kobi offered after several long minutes of silence, "I lost my brother when I was in high school too."

"You did? A car accident?"

"The Six Day War."

"I'm sorry. How did your family cope with that?"

"It's part of life in Israel," Kobi answered shortly. Clearly he didn't want to discuss his brother.

"Is that why you moved to America?"

"I did not move to America." Kobi shook his head emphatically. "I came here for an education and maybe some work experience, but I'm going back."

Before Lisa could reply, Danny stood up and cleared his throat, obviously ready to make a speech.

Later, after they'd helped stack the last trash bag in the corner of the kitchen, Kobi invited Lisa for a walk. More than a little flattered, she agreed. As they strolled past the Farmers Market, Lisa couldn't help but remember the first walk she'd taken with Tim.

It had been after football practice and there had been no invitation. Tim had simply said, "Let's go to the Dash Inn for a Coke."

Lisa had been thrilled. She'd had her eye on Tim for months. There'd been no getting-acquainted conversation, since they'd been in the same school from seventh grade. It was different with Kobi.

"What made you choose ASU for college?" he asked her.

"It has a good business program." She chose not to mention that Tim was attending a nearby university.

"What kind of business are you interested in?" Kobi ignored the noisy traffic passing by and focused on her.

"Retail! My great-uncle Simon founded Apple's, a department store in Lincoln. It's the biggest store there. Of course," Lisa laughed a little self-consciously, "it's not Macy's, but it serves our needs. Most of the family has worked there at one time or another. Some of them didn't enjoy it, but I loved it."

"Does your father work there too?"

"No." Lisa laughed at the thought. "He's a rancher. He has over a thousand head of cattle." Kobi heard the pride in her voice.

"It must be so neat to live on a ranch!" Kobi's brown eyes sparkled.

"We don't. We have a nice house in the newer part of Lincoln. Did you know that Sondra grew up on a farm?"

"Really?"

"Uncle Julius, her father, works at the store and also has a dairy farm. He has a dozen cows he milks by hand and sells the milk."

"I didn't know there were any Jewish farmers outside of Israel. So," he asked casually, "are you going back there after you graduate?"

"I don't know." Once, that had been Lisa's dream — to move back to Lincoln and take over as assistant manager in the store. That was before Tim dumped her.

"Where are you from in Israel?" she changed the subject.

"Beit She'an."

"Where's that?"

"Have you ever been to Israel?"

Lisa shook her head.

"It's near the Jordanian border, one of the hottest areas in Israel."

"Do you like the heat?"

"It's okay." Kobi grinned. "There's a lot of warmth there of all kinds. All my family, both sides, settled there when they came to Israel in 1948."

"So your parents were immigrants too?"

"From Morocco. Your parents weren't born in America?"

"They came from Germany, just like Sondra's parents did. Except for her mother, everyone got out before the war."

"They were fortunate."

Lisa nodded and they walked together in silence for a few minutes. "You know," Kobi said, "my father opened a grocery store after he'd been in Israel a few years. It wasn't as big a venture as your uncle's department store," Kobi chuckled, "but through the years, most of my cousins worked there. And when my grandfather was alive, he went to 'work' there every morning."

"Why do you say it that way?" Lisa stopped to shake a pebble out of her sandal.

"What way?"

"You sounded sarcastic when you said he went into work every morning."

"Oh." Kobi waved his hand dismissively. "All my grandfather did was give advice and annoy my father. Then he would sit in the corner, drink tea, and learn Gemara till lunchtime."

"Your grandfather was religious?" Lisa refastened her sandal.

Kobi nodded as they resumed walking.

"And your family?" Lisa asked.

"Sort of. My father and I went to *beit knesset* some mornings, and on Shabbat we made *Kiddush* and ate a nice meal, but that was it."

"Did you keep kosher?"

"Of course. Did you?"

"Yes, that was about all we did. Except I did have a bat mitzvah. I went to Wichita, an hour's drive each way, every week for months to take lessons with the rabbi. My Torah portion was…"

Kobi stopped walking and stared at her. "You read from the Torah?!"

"Uh-huh." Lisa was puzzled by his reaction.

"I guess it was at a Reform synagogue."

Lisa shrugged her shoulders. "It was kind of a mishmash. We used the chapel at Lincoln State University and had services once a month on Friday nights and on the holidays. The only people who came were my relatives and some professors and students. There were never very many. But we did have a Torah."

"You did?"

"Yeah, Cousin Oscar, the one who named the baby, brought it from Germany with him when he came to America. His little brother had rescued it from the synagogue's rubble right after *Kristallnacht*. Everyone thought Kurt would use it for his bar mitzvah, but he didn't get out."

"That's sad."

"It is." Lisa nodded. "You know, from the stories our Oma's told Sondra and me, I know my family was religious back in Germany. Now there's just some remnants of that left in Lincoln."

"Even in Israel a lot of Moroccan families have stopped being observant."

"I never gave it much thought, but Shabbos here at Sondra's is a lot different from back home," Lisa spoke wistfully. "There's something really nice about it."

"I've felt that too," Kobi smiled. Then he added, "I've decided to make the commitment to be *shomer Shabbat*."

"What's that?"

"To keep Shabbat according to the laws of the Torah."

"Oh." Lisa wasn't really sure what he meant, but she nodded as if she did.

CHAPTER

Eight

Zvi Chaim began sleeping eight hours a night when he was just a month old, which was fortunate since Sondra went back to teaching right after the holidays. During her last months of pregnancy, she'd arranged for Mrs. Steiner to babysit in their apartment and Sondra had filled her freezer with meals. Now, after her baby was born, nothing was as easy as she thought it would be.

"How're you going to manage when you get home?" she asked Tamar, who was cradling her newborn daughter in the hospital bed when Sondra visited.

"I have six weeks off and then I'll leave relief bottles."

"The La Leche handbook makes it sound so simple," Sondra complained as she cuddled Zvi Chaim, "but it's not for me."

"You'll get used to it," Tamar soothed. "Everyone does."

Instead of finding her friend's words encouraging, Sondra left feeling that there was something wrong with her.

Mrs. Steiner noticed that Sondra was dragging home from school each day. Without saying a word, she began doing all the light housekeeping that she was capable of. There was still plenty left to do, though, and when Danny found Sondra crying over a burned pot, he decided they had to make some changes.

"I know I'm not helping you enough," he apologized ruefully, taking the pot from his wife.

"You don't have any time for anything," Sondra sobbed. "You have to study."

"That's true." Danny made a face. "But you're going to have to do less."

"What do you want me to stop doing?" Sondra sniffled. "Sleep?"

"I'm going to ask my mother about getting the cleaning lady back."

Sondra just played with her ring.

"And no more fancy meals and Shabbos guests."

"What about Kobi?"

"Maybe Kobi," Danny conceded, "but no more families. If you don't take it easy now, we'll pay for it later."

Sondra managed a half smile at her husband's doctor voice and agreed reluctantly to his suggestions. Yet she felt she was moving on automatic pilot most of the time and never knew what made her lose hold of the pot of boiling soup when she took it off the hot plate the following Friday evening.

Kobi was the only one at the table with them that night. Sondra's shriek when the pot fell filled the apartment and spread through the building. Danny jumped up from the table so quickly that he knocked over his chair. He grabbed his wife, pushed her into the shower, and turned on the cold water, drenching her.

"Call an ambulance," he screamed to Kobi, who was already at the phone.

"You're going to be okay, you're going to be okay," Danny repeated over and over to Sondra.

Silently, Sondra heeded her husband's instructions to undress. Somehow her body did not feel the horrific pain it was in. Zvi Chaim woke up crying and neighbors began knocking at the door. Kobi was relieved to turn the baby over to Mrs. Steiner as he thanked the others for their concern and tried to turn them away.

One neighbor didn't accept Kobi's assurances that everything was under control. "You don't want to wait for that ambulance, man. Let's get her to the hospital now. My car's right out front."

With second-degree burns down her stomach and upper thighs, Sondra was admitted straight into the hospital from the emergency room and given pain pills. She never did remember much of that Shabbos. Sunday, however, she began asking about Zvi Chaim.

"Don't worry," Danny reassured her. "Mrs. Steiner's watching him. Are they treating you okay here?"

"I guess so."

"Maybe we should call my father and ask him to consult with the doctor."

"No." Sondra shook her head adamantly. "If you tell your parents, I'll have to tell mine."

"Maybe I should call them too."

"I don't want my mother to worry." Sondra began crying.

Not wanting to agitate his wife further, Danny dropped the subject.

Monday she begged to see her baby. Danny brought Zvi Chaim over in the evening, but Sondra couldn't find a comfortable position in which to hold him.

Tuesday she was alert enough to feel the humiliation of being undressed while her bandages were changed and the blisters drained.

"Did your soup have onions in it?" one of the nurses asked sociably.

"Yes." Sondra's eyes were shut tight as she tried to remove herself from the situation. "Why?"

"I can smell them."

It was said in a friendly manner, but Sondra turned her head away and blinked back tears of mortification.

When Danny came later that evening with Zvi Chaim, her eyes were still red-rimmed.

"Are you in a lot of pain?" Danny asked in concern.

"The pills help," Sondra answered, "but they make me feel so weird. I want to go home."

"You will soon," Danny soothed.

"When?"

"When the doctor says you can."

"When's that going to be?" Sondra asked, knowing she sounded whiney, but unable to stop herself.

"Sondra," Danny handed the baby to his wife while he sat down on the hideous orange plastic chair next to her bed. "The burns are open wounds and you're in danger of infection. It will take some time until they heal."

"What'd they say at school?" Sondra patted Zvi Chaim, trying to quiet his fussing.

"They found a substitute until you come back. Don't worry about it."

"I won't get paid for the days I'm missing." Sondra tried moving Zvi Chaim to find a comfortable position for them both, but he continued to whimper.

"You have some sick leave. Don't worry," Danny responded patiently. "Here, let me take Zvi Chaim back."

"I want to feed him."

Danny handed her the bottle, but Zvi Chaim refused to take it from his mother and only cried. Danny saw the disappointment in his wife's eyes and his heart ached for her. She read the emotions that crossed his face, but took no comfort from them.

"I'm such a burden to you," she whispered.

Danny didn't know whether to laugh or cry. Between med school, caring for his infant son, and worrying about his wife, he'd had no time to feel sorry for himself. Trust Sondra to do that for him!

"We're in this together, sweetheart. You'd do the same for me if I was in your place, right?"

"Right," Sondra mumbled.

"And we're getting a lot of help from a lot of good people."

Sondra nodded.

"Your job is to get better. And while you're at it, you can work on your *emunah* and not worry so much."

"You're right." Sondra felt chastised. She handed her son back to his father and tried to smile.

* * *

Wednesday afternoon the pain was somewhat better. She was drifting in and out of sleep when she heard footsteps enter her room. Expecting Tamar, Sondra opened her eyes and turned her head toward the hallway.

"Lisa!" Sondra's face broke into a smile. "What're you doing here?"

"Thanksgiving break starts tonight, so I cut classes today and came."

"How'd you know I was here?"

Lisa blushed. "Kobi called me." She kissed her cousin and settled in the plastic chair. "Why'd you think I wouldn't know you were in the hospital? Haven't you told Aunt Helga and Uncle Julius?"

"No." Sondra avoided Lisa's eyes.

"That's what I thought! When I called my mom and told her I was going to LA to see you, she wanted to know what the occasion was."

"What'd you tell her?"

"That since I wasn't going to be home for Chanukah, I wanted to be with you."

"I forgot," Sondra said wryly. "Chanukah starts Friday night."

For years, Lisa's mother had always made a family party on the Sunday afternoon of Chanukah. Sondra never could smell a latke without picturing herself in her Aunt Irene's family room and all the relatives gathered around exchanging stories, half in German and half in English.

"I wanted to make Zvi Chaim's first Chanukah special, like your mother always made ours."

"Sondra, Zvi Chaim isn't going to remember a thing about his first Chanukah. What he's going to remember is whether his mother is well or not."

"I know that." Sondra waved her hand impatiently, exasperated with all the implied rebuke she was getting about being a good patient.

"Okay." Lisa smiled. "I won't lecture you on patience. But I am going to lecture you about telling your parents."

Sondra shook her head adamantly. "No, they have enough to worry about — finding a retirement home for Oma, Mom's busy grading finals at the university, and the holiday season's starting at the store. I'll call them when I'm home from the hospital."

Lisa shook her head just as firmly. "If they find out from someone else, which they probably will, they'll be really hurt. What did Danny say when they called Sunday?"

"They went to Kansas City for the day and weren't planning on calling."

"Sondra, I know you want to protect your mother, but she deserves to know."

Sondra groaned. "My mother's suffered enough. She doesn't need to worry about me."

"The Holocaust is over." Lisa shook her head and continued, "Don't treat your mother like a child."

"You don't understand." Sondra changed the subject. "How'd Kobi get your number?"

"I gave it to him."

"When?"

"After the bris."

"He's called you before?"

Lisa nodded with a pleased smile.

"Do you talk a lot?" In her excitement, Sondra leaned forward in her bed.

"Every Saturday night." Lisa lowered her eyes demurely and added, "At least."

"Wow!" Sondra sank back into her pillow.

What Lisa didn't tell her was that following the positive Shabbos experience at Zvi Chaim's bris, she'd accepted a Shabbos invitation from Rabbi Frankel, a teacher at the Hebrew Day School in Phoenix who also gave classes at ASU. She'd gone back to his home several times and had also accepted another Shabbos invitation from a different family in the religious community. Last week, though, she'd stayed in the dorm and realized that she missed the whole atmosphere of a real Shabbos.

"Kobi made arrangements for me to stay at Tamar's this weekend. I'm looking forward to another Shabbos in LA."

"You are?" For the first time since she'd dropped the soup, the sparkle was back in Sondra's eyes.

* * *

It wasn't Sondra's parents who found out about her accident by chance, but Danny's.

"Irv, how was the conference?" Doc clasped his friend's hand at the entrance of St. Vincent de Paul's soup kitchen in downtown Phoenix. Every year they and a group of friends helped dish out Thanksgiving dinners to the city's poor.

"It was great, but the beach was even better."

"The corals are gorgeous," his wife chimed in. "You have to come with us next time there's a convention in Hawaii."

"I'd love that," Shirley declared, and everyone chuckled.

"We came back by way of LA," Irv told Doc, "so we could see Bruce."

"How's your son's residency going?"

"Good," his friend said with pride. "He saw your little daughter-in-law yesterday morning and she's going to be fine."

"That's good." Doc nodded, poker-faced. He caught Shirley's eye and raised his hands subtly, hoping she wouldn't begin asking embarrassing questions. She didn't disappoint him. But later, in the car on the way home, she unleashed a tirade.

"What did he mean by 'our little daughter-in-law is going to be fine'? What's the matter with her? Do you think everything's okay with the baby? Why didn't Danny tell us anything? Maybe this is why no one answered the phone Sunday. We've tried so hard to treat that girl as if she's our own daughter. Is this the thanks we get? What do you think happened?"

Doc let her talk herself out until she stopped to light a cigarette. Although he was worried about Sondra and felt distressed at the lack of communication from Danny, he spoke calmly. "We'll call Danny as soon as we get home. There's got to be a reasonable explanation for everything."

* * *

Lisa and Kobi had come to the hospital half an hour earlier and sent Danny home to do some sorely neglected studying. The open textbook did little to interest him, though, and he was just nodding off when the phone rang. Hearing his parents' composed hello, he didn't have a clue that they were dangerously close to becoming hysterical.

"Happy Thanksgiving, son."

"Happy Thanksgiving," Danny answered. "Are you back from the soup kitchen already?"

"Yes." Doc hesitated for just a second. "Dr. Peters was in LA this week. His son informed him that Sondra was going to be fine. I didn't ask him what he meant, but I'm asking you. What's wrong?"

"Oh, Dad," Danny groaned. "Sondra has second-degree burns down her front, but the doctor's really optimistic."

"Danny," his mother gasped, "what happened?"

His parents listened quietly to his account of the accident and then Shirley spoke up.

"Why didn't you call me to come take care of the baby?"

"Uh, I didn't think about it," Danny answered honestly. "Mrs. Steiner is staying longer hours."

"What about Sondra's mother?"

"Well..." Danny hesitated, decidedly uncomfortable. "I didn't tell them either. Sondra doesn't want them to worry."

"I don't believe it!" Shirley exclaimed. But inside she felt a certain satisfaction that Sondra had treated her and Doc no differently than her own parents.

"Danny," Doc spoke with authority, "you call your in-laws right now and tell them everything or they won't ever trust you in the future."

"No," Shirley interjected, "call them from the hospital so they can speak to Sondra. Use our credit card number."

"Your mother's right," Doc concurred. "And do you mind if I place a call to Sondra's doctor?"

"No, Dad." Danny felt relieved. "That would be great."

❋ ❋ ❋

Friday morning, after the bandages were changed, Sondra's doctor came to see her on his rounds, wearing a big smile on his face. He nodded hello to Lisa and settled down in the orange plastic chair that she'd just vacated.

"I see you're down to one pain pill in the evening."

"That's right," Sondra replied.

"How would you like to go home today?"

"Can I?" Sondra's eyes shone at the idea.

"If you follow my conditions."

"Okay!" Sondra nodded eagerly.

"I want you to stay in a prone position, only getting up to use the bathroom. You must come to my office daily to have your bandages changed. I'll give you pain pills for the night. If you feel you need additional medication, don't hesitate to call me. Any questions?"

"When can I leave?"

"As soon as you get the discharge papers."

"Thank you!" Sondra beamed at the doctor.

After he left, she smiled at Lisa, her left dimple deepening, and then she made a face.

"What's the matter?"

"I knew I should have waited to call my folks till I got out."

"Were they really upset?"

"Let's put it this way, the whole conversation was in German."

Lisa understood. No matter how long their parents had been in America, when they got emotional, they reverted to their mother tongue. "Why don't you call them now and tell them you're going home?"

"That's a good idea," Sondra hesitated, "but I don't want to use my in-laws' credit card at the most expensive time of the day."

"Talk fast and tell them you'll call again Saturday night."

"Okay," Sondra decided.

Only her mother was home and it was a quick call, long enough for Sondra to hear the relief in Helga's voice. Two days later, Helga and Julius made a quick overnight trip to Los Angeles. There couldn't have been a worse time for them to get away, but they had to see their daughter with their own eyes to be sure that she was going to be okay. The trip was important for Sondra too. It was like a tonic to eat her mother's special streusel and watch her father bounce Zvi Chaim on his knee and sing the old German rhyme he'd sung to her when she was young.

CHAPTER

Nine

Eighteen days after she dropped the soup, Sondra's bandages were removed and the itching began. There were nights when it seemed the only thing she could do to keep from digging at her healing skin was to lie in bed with her hands buried underneath her. She was healing, though. Every day, as she took her shower, she gazed with thankfulness at her fading scars. Hashem had indeed given her a miraculous recovery, and she was grateful. She was also grateful to be able to go back to the classroom.

"They had a cake for me in the teachers' room my first day back," she told her parents during their weekly Sunday call.

"I'm sure they're glad to have you back again," Julius said with pride in his voice.

"Yeah," Sondra laughed a little self-consciously. "And the kids all made me get-well cards while I was home. I thanked each of them individually."

"That's nice. How's Zvi Chaim?" her father asked.

"He's adjusted well to the bottle." Sondra sighed. "And there are advantages to being able to leave for longer periods of time." She sighed again. "How are your classes going, Mom?"

"Everything's fine," Helga replied shortly.

The following week, it was again her father who did most of the talking, and Helga's letters every few days began dwindling to one a week or less. In May, when the end of the school year was in sight, Sondra began longing to fly to Kansas for a visit. Danny didn't like the idea.

"I'm sorry, Sondra. We can't afford the plane ticket now."

"We can take a free loan," Sondra pleaded, "and once you're a doctor, we'll be able to pay it back easily."

"Do you know how many loans we have to pay back?" Danny exclaimed. "Wait until I'm a doctor and then you can visit your parents as often as you want."

"That's not fair!" Sondra cried out.

"What's not fair?"

"You don't understand! Your folks come here at the drop of the hat whenever your dad can get Dr. Taylor to cover for him. Zvi Chaim cut his first tooth — they're here. He learned to sit up — they came. He started crawling — they're here again. My folks haven't seen their only grandchild since December."

Danny bit his tongue to keep from retorting that if her parents really cared, they could come for a visit too. He knew his in-laws didn't have the income and the flexibility that his parents had. He also understood that Sondra needed to see her parents, but he didn't want to take on any more debt.

Sondra didn't say anything else on the subject, but there was a sadness about her that Danny hadn't seen before. One evening, he came home later than usual from evening services.

"I talked to Rabbi Frimer and he explained to me that the connection between a mother and daughter is very important and that you went through a big trauma this year — actually two, between giving birth and the burns. So I'll go tomorrow to ask for a loan."

Sondra's eyes shone with tears, but they were tears of relief, and Danny understood.

* * *

Three weeks later, Sondra settled Zvi Chaim in the crib she'd slept in as a child. Her father had taken it out of the attic and assembled it in the spare room. She gazed lovingly at her sleeping son and tiptoed out onto the landing. Feeling undecided, she stared down the steep stairs and then at the door of her old bedroom. Should she go back downstairs and be sociable or finish unpacking and have some time to think?

Nothing was going quite as she'd expected. Her parents had both been at the Wichita Airport to greet her, and their hugs were as loving as usual, but her mother had been unusually quiet during the hour drive back, leaving the conversation to Sondra and Julius. Once home, she asked to hold Zvi Chaim and happily rocked and sang to him until he needed a diaper change.

"Give me his things," Helga instructed her daughter. "I will give him a bath and he can be all clean and tidy for supper."

Supper was the usual — bread, salad, eggs, and cheese — but Helga had bought chocolate chip ice cream for dessert.

"Mom, my favorite!" Sondra exclaimed.

"It was on sale," Helga explained.

Julius smiled slyly. "Your mother made a double batch of streusel for your homecoming."

Helga waved her hand dismissively and rose from her place. "We have a present for Zvi Chaim." Proudly, she took out a shape sorter. "Let's see if he likes it."

Zvi Chaim did. Helga settled down next to him on the rug in the living room and they played together until it was his bedtime. She was so absorbed with her grandchild, she barely noticed her daughter. Now, remembering how she'd been ignored, Sondra still felt uncomfortable. With a shrug, she opted for her old pink and gold room. How she loved the furniture she and her mother had picked out together. But why, she wondered, was her mother acting so distant?

She glanced at the Princess Phone resting on the nightstand between the twin beds. Her parents had bought it for her birthday when she was in high school. She longed to dial her home number and talk to Danny, but he wouldn't be there yet. Besides, after all the fuss she'd made about seeing her parents, she didn't think it prudent to complain to him about the visit. Should she ask her father about her mother's strange behavior? Would that be *lashon hara*? Maybe, she tried to comfort herself, things would be better if she went downstairs now without Zvi Chaim to capture her mother's attention.

As she put her foot on the first step, however, the shrill ring of the phone spread throughout the farmhouse. Two rings and two steps later, Sondra heard her mother's voice.

"Sondra, it's for you!"

"I'll get it up here!"

She scrambled up the three steps and into her room, wondering if maybe it was Danny. Instead of her husband, though, she heard her Aunt Irene's cheery voice.

"Welcome, dear! How was the flight?"

"It was good," Sondra spoke more brightly than she felt. "How are you and Uncle Herbert?"

"We're fine, dear. Listen, I know your mother has a staff meeting tomorrow afternoon, so I'd like to come get you and have you and the baby just to myself. Would that work for you?"

"That would be wonderful!"

Sondra had always admired Lisa's mother, her fashionable Aunt Irene. It was strange. Helga, who couldn't care less about style, seemed to be the opposite of her sister-in-law in so many ways. Yet the two women talked to each other daily and each considered the other her best friend. More than once Irene had helped Sondra work out some snarls in her relationship with her mother.

The house where Lisa had grown up, in the new section of Lincoln, was light and modern. Sondra and Irene settled into the conversation nook that looked out onto Irene's flower garden, with Zvi Chaim and some toys at their feet. Although Sondra had expected the conversation to be about her mother, Irene was far more interested in what Sondra had to say about Kobi.

"Lisa told you she's dating him?" Sondra was pleasantly surprised to hear her aunt mention their Israeli friend.

"Yes." Irene nodded. "Only it sounds like more than dating. From what she's told us, Herbert and I get the impression that they're going to announce their engagement soon."

"Really!" Sondra squealed. She picked up Zvi Chaim and hugged him ecstatically.

"I take it you approve," Irene said dryly. "Is this Kobi a good man?"

"Yes, I think so." Sondra thought fondly of their regular Shabbos guest. "He's kind and helpful and he's not afraid to work."

"And you think he's right for Lisa? You're not just happy because Lisa's becoming religious like you?"

Sondra took a sip of lemonade and weighed her thoughts carefully.

"I think," she spoke slowly, "that a Torah lifestyle's a wonderful life-style and Lisa seems a lot more comfortable with herself since she made a commitment to keep Shabbos. Does it bother you that she did?"

This time it was Irene who paused before she answered.

"Before Howie was killed in the accident, I remember we gave you a hard time about not eating meat out, and we thought it was a shame that your parents didn't let you date non-Jews, which meant no dating in this small town. The last few months before he died, though, we were so worried about how serious it was getting between him and Patty. We were so scared he was going to marry out. We even began wishing that he cared as much about going to Friday night services as you did. If he had, he wouldn't have been in that car Friday night and he'd be alive today."

Irene bit her lip as the tears trickled down her face.

"Oh, Aunt Irene." Sondra hugged her aunt and blinked back her own tears.

It took Irene just a few minutes to get back in control.

"Back to Lisa." She smiled resolutely. "No, we're not sorry that she made that commitment. I hope it works out for her as well as it's worked out for you." She held out her hands to Zvi Chaim, who happily crawled to her.

"He's adorable, Sondra. Your mother must be eating him up."

Sondra smiled politely, but averted her eyes.

"It's not going so well at home?"

Sondra shook her head.

"I was afraid of that." Irene sighed and put Zvi Chaim down. "I might be telling tales out of school, but I think I should explain something to you."

"Yes?" Sondra sat forward on her chair.

"I don't have to tell you that after losing all her family in the Holocaust, your mother worries inordinately about the little family she has left."

Sondra acknowledged the truth of her aunt's words.

"Before you got those burns, your mother tried to assume that everything was always fine and no news was good news. But after you kept your injuries hidden from her, well, that burst her bubble. Now she's constantly worried that something's wrong and she'd love to call you every day to check that nothing's happened, but she knows she shouldn't."

"And I guess she's kind of angry with me for making her worry." Sondra fiddled with the couch cushion. "I just wanted to protect her!"

"You did the opposite." Irene's voice was gentle.

"What do I do now?"

"Talk to her," Irene said softly. "Just talk to her."

Helga was already home when Irene dropped Sondra and Zvi Chaim off.

"Good luck." Irene smiled and kissed her niece.

With her baby in her arms, Sondra opened the back door of the farmhouse and entered the cozy kitchen. Uncertain as to what to do or say, she smiled weakly at her mother, who sat at the table grading papers. Helga smiled back.

"Mommy," Sondra cried out and began speaking in German, "I'm sorry I didn't tell you right away about my burns."

"Me too." Helga nodded, pushing her papers away.

"I didn't want you to worry." Sondra set her baby down and wiped at her cheeks.

"The first week after you got burned, before you called us..." Helga picked up Zvi Chaim and bent her face over his curly hair, "I was terribly agitated. I was anxious about something, but I did not know what. Once we heard the news about you, though, I knew it was maternal intuition."

"Aunt Irene said you worry all the time now," Sondra mumbled.

"I do."

"I won't keep any more secrets like this from you, I promise."

Helga grabbed Sondra's hand and held it to her cheek. No words were necessary.

On Sondra's last night in Lincoln, all the relatives gathered at the house to say goodbye since she would be leaving for the Wichita Airport early the next morning. In the five days she'd been in Lincoln, she had managed to find special time with everyone except for Oscar. Her father's cousin suggested that they take a walk, something they'd always done together ever since she was a little girl. The sun was setting as they strolled across the pasture, and the sky was a beautiful shade of pink.

"I bet you don't see anything like this in Los Angeles," Oscar commented.

"I don't," Sondra agreed. She didn't think she would miss the smog-infested city when she moved to Phoenix in July. Although she did have apprehensions about Phoenix, she kept those feelings to herself. Instead, she concentrated on telling Oscar about the half acre of grazing land and several cows that were a block from the shul in her new community.

"That sounds promising," Oscar approved.

They had reached the back door when he abruptly slipped something into her hand. "Buy something to make your new apartment nice," he instructed and was already in the living room before she could thank him. She stuffed the bills in her pocket and, later, as she did her last-minute packing, she drew them out and counted four one-hundred dollar bills.

Gasping in surprise, she realized she'd be able to pay back the free loan for her trip right away. Not only that, but when she got home, she'd be able to tell Danny about Lisa and Kobi's hopefully imminent engagement. She couldn't wait for her plane to land the next day.

*   *   *

Once back in Los Angeles, Sondra began concentrating on their upcoming move. She'd been decidedly disappointed when Danny was only accepted at his third choice, Atkins Memorial Hospital in Phoenix, for his residency, but she saved her grumblings for her friend Tamar.

"I know I should be thankful for what Phoenix does have," she admitted. "There's a shul, a *mikveh*, a kosher butcher and bakery, and a day school."

"Are you going to teach there?"

"I'll be teaching second grade, thirteen kids. It's a mixed class. The boys and girls are together through eighth grade."

"It'll be okay," Tamar soothed. "Your in-laws must be thrilled that you'll be living so close."

"Yes, and they're good grandparents. I can't complain. They don't give a lot of advice and they're very happy to babysit once in a while. It's just that I'd like to be in a real community."

"Like here?"

Sondra shook her head. "I like the choice of shuls and classes and restaurants, but I hate living in such a big city."

"You're not going to find a thriving community anywhere but in a big city unless you move to Israel," Tamar told her.

"I know," Sondra replied. She swallowed hard and returned to packing up the Shabbos china.

CHAPTER

Ten

While Sondra was spending the month of June packing, Lisa was again in summer school at ASU, spending most of her time studying. Her most productive time was spent at the kitchen table in the apartment she shared with Carol, but after going over her advertising textbook for two hours straight, she desperately needed a break. She went straight to the junk food drawer, the only part of the kitchen that she and Carol shared.

Her roommate had been a good sport when Lisa announced that she wanted to start keeping kosher. She'd taken the left side of the kitchen and Lisa the right. Just as Lisa opened a bag of Fritos, the phone rang. She grinned in delight when she heard Kobi's voice.

"You're the perfect person to take a break with!"

"Excuse me?"

"Carol's out and I'm sick of studying and need to talk to someone."

"I'm glad to help out," Kobi said. "Guess what!"

"What?"

"Guess."

"I don't know." Lisa felt a tightening in her chest. "You're moving back to Israel." She tried to sound upbeat.

"Not yet." Kobi laughed. "But I'm moving. Do you want to know where?"

"Of course," Lisa replied nervously.

"To Phoenix."

"To Phoenix!" Lisa squealed with delight.

"Yeah, Intel came through with a great job offer."

"That's fantastic! When are you moving?"

"I have to start July 1. Danny starts his internship the same day, so we're sharing movers."

"We're really going to save on phone bills." In her excitement, Lisa spilled half her chips, but she didn't care.

"That's for sure," Kobi chuckled. "Where are you for Shabbat?"

"Probably the Frankels."

"Do you think they could feed me too?"

"I imagine so." Lisa smiled. "You're coming this weekend?"

"I want to see you." Kobi made it sound so simple to jump in his car and drive the seven hours to Phoenix.

"Okay, I'll call the Frankels. Should I ask the Weins to put you up?"

"Sounds good. I'll be seeing you in about forty hours. We'll talk then."

It wasn't forty hours. Kobi overslept and didn't get the early start he wanted. There was a lane closed on the freeway near Anaheim and he was stuck in traffic for an hour. Then, between Blythe and Indio, he got a flat tire. He reached the Weins a half hour before candle lighting and had just enough time to call Lisa, take a shower, and dress for Shabbos. Lisa didn't see him until he walked in from shul with Rabbi Frankel.

Since Rabbi Frankel was a teacher at the day school, he and his wife, Rena, often had students at their Shabbos table. This Shabbos was no exception, and between their two toddlers and the three high school guests, it was quite an active meal. Although Kobi and Lisa didn't stop smiling at each other across the table, there was no opportunity for a private conversation. As soon as the meal was over, Kobi announced that he wanted to go for a walk.

"Let me help clean up first," Lisa said.

"Don't worry," Yechiel Frankel spoke up. "I'll help Rena. It'll give *us* a chance to have some time together."

Without a second thought, Kobi and Lisa left the house and headed toward a little park outside a nearby apartment complex. More than once, the two of them had spent Shabbos afternoons sitting on the bench in the shade there, sharing their thoughts. This time they sat side by side, Kobi leaning back with his legs spread out in front of him and his arms dangling at his sides. He was unusually quiet and Lisa sat up straight with her hands clasped in her lap, trying to think of something to say.

"I think I did well on that test I was studying for when you called," she finally offered.

"Uh-huh," Kobi answered, but added no more in the way of conversation.

"Carol's going to use me as a guinea pig for her next paper."

There was just a nod from Kobi.

Confused, Lisa stopped chattering and her smile faded. Had she said something wrong? Why was Kobi so subdued? Suddenly, her memory of her last date with Tim when he broke up with her came to mind. Maybe Kobi's excitement about moving to Phoenix had nothing to do with her, just that he was pleased to have a job with Intel. They sat in silence for a good ten minutes. It might have been a comfortable silence for Kobi, but Lisa was feeling miserable.

"Lisa," Kobi finally spoke, his voice nervous, "I need to find an apartment in Phoenix and, well, I think it'd make a lot of sense for us to look for an apartment together."

"You want me to help you pick out a place to live?"

"A place for us to live."

"What?" Lisa blushed.

Kobi laughed nervously. "I want us to get married."

Lisa's eyes filled with tears of relief and she was unable to reply. Kobi correctly interpreted her silence as an acceptance.

After lunch the next day, the two of them decided to skip napping, brave the desert sun, and go for another walk.

"Be careful not to do any real planning," Rena cautioned Lisa before she left. "General plans are okay, but specifics are a no-no on Shabbos."

Their hostess was almost as excited about the engagement as Kobi and Lisa were. She'd married right after her seminary year, and at twenty-three, she was half the age of the other women in the community. The women were warm and friendly, and several treated her as their equal, but none of them could relate to her after she'd been up all night with her son's ear infection or when she was feeling green from morning sickness. She missed having women her own age to talk to.

Rena knew her husband felt good about his teaching. They were having a positive influence on his students with their Shabbos hospitality, and the salary the school paid was above average. However, it wasn't until after Rabbi Levi, the principal and community rabbi, had informed Yechiel that he was bringing in another young couple with a baby that the Frankels signed the contract for the coming year. Now Rena was not only looking forward to Brachie Fisch moving in, she also had Lisa and Lisa's cousin coming. The average age of the women in the women's section at shul, at least on the holidays, was getting lower.

Although Rabbi Frankel was just as pleased as his wife, he didn't let Kobi announce the engagement in shul that morning. "I know you're bursting with your news, but think how your folks would feel if they knew that Chaim Yankel from Phoenix knew their son was getting married before they did. And," Rabbi Frankel stroked his red beard, "you should ask Lisa's parents for permission."

Kobi told Lisa the rabbi's instructions as soon as they were settled on the bench. "My father will like that," Lisa said, beaming. "We can call them tonight, and then your parents, and then the world! I can't wait to tell Sondra!"

"I'm looking forward to telling Danny myself. When do you want to get married?"

"As soon as possible, but I think I should wait till I finish summer school."

"I wonder how many of my aunts and uncles will come."

"Do you think that they'll like me even though I'm American?"

Instead of reassuring her, Kobi jumped up with a cry of surprise. It took Lisa just a second to understand why. Someone had turned on the sprinkler system and Kobi's pants and shoes were getting soaking wet. A second later, she was splashed in the face.

Lisa was stifling giggles as they ran to the sidewalk, but Kobi didn't find the situation funny.

"If they don't want us sitting there, they should have a sign posted," Kobi sputtered.

"Oh, Kobi." Lisa stopped laughing. "I don't think anyone did it on purpose. The sprinklers are probably on a timer."

"No one waters during the heat of the day. It burns the grass."

Lisa shrugged. "Maybe you're right, but it feels good to be wet in this heat."

Kobi had to agree with her. "Let's walk over to the Weins. We can sit by the pool and talk there."

Bayla and Harold Wein had come to Phoenix five years earlier, when their family doctor in Oak Park instructed them to move to a warm climate that would be good for Harold's debilitating arthritis. Despite the fact that she was old enough to be her mother, Lisa found Bayla to be a real friend.

"You know," she remarked to Kobi on their walk over, "it couldn't have been easy for the Weins to leave all their family behind in Detroit."

"They never complain, though," Kobi pointed out.

"And they do so much for the community! Bayla told me they bought such a big house, even though it's just the two of them, because they love having guests."

"I must say their guest rooms are as comfortable as a hotel."

"I'm sure it beats sharing the Frankel boys' room," Lisa said wryly.

"Next Shabbat, why don't you stay with them and I'll sleep at the Frankels?" Kobi grinned.

"Great idea!" Lisa was pleased with his gallantry. They opened the gate to the Weins' backyard.

"Would you like something to drink?" Kobi inquired as Lisa seated herself on one of the lounge chairs next to the swimming pool.

"Sure."

On the patio was an old refrigerator full of cold juice and summer fruit. Kobi helped himself to a peach and, taking a cup from the stack on the picnic table, poured a glass of lemonade for Lisa.

It wasn't long before Harold and Bayla woke up from their naps. Harold tapped on the arcadia door and opened it a crack. "Do you want to be alone or could you stand some company?"

"If the company is yours, we'd love some." Kobi gave his most charming smile.

Harold came outside wearing the clothes he'd worn in shul that morning, minus his tie and jacket. Bayla, on the other hand, had exchanged her wig for a scarf and was wearing a brightly colored housedress. She grinned knowingly at the couple.

"Do you have any news to tell us?"

"Bayla!" Harold remonstrated.

"I don't know who else ate at the Frankels," Bayla answered him innocently.

Kobi couldn't help himself. "As a matter of fact, we're engaged!"

"I knew it!" Bayla exclaimed. "I could tell by looking at your faces."

"We weren't going to tell anybody until after we talk to our folks," Lisa said with a small, worried frown. She was confident that her parents would be thrilled at the news. Kobi's parents, on the other hand, were a whole different story, and Lisa wasn't at all sure how they'd react. She pushed that thought away, though, refusing to allow it to mar her joy.

"Don't worry. I won't tell a soul."

Harold winked at them. "You better tell your parents fast, before Bayla tells the whole world."

Bayla glared at her husband and then burst out laughing. In spite of herself, Lisa joined in. "It'll be hard," Bayla admitted. "I'll just stay inside my house and not speak to anybody until...when are you talking to your parents?"

"After Shabbos."

"Okay. I can stay quiet that long. Now, remember, we want to make you *Sheva Brachos*."

Lisa basked in the Weins' warmth. It was so easy to picture herself living in the community as their neighbors.

Kobi leaned back in his chair, watching their easy rapport. He appreciated Bayla's enthusiasm as much as Lisa did, but in the back of his mind, there was the nagging worry about how his parents would react to the news. Would they be able to look past the fact that Lisa was an American and an Ashkenazi, and realize they were getting a lovely daughter-in-law who understood him better than anyone he'd ever known?

CHAPTER
Eleven

"*O*ma, Abba, I have wonderful news!"

Lisa sat across from Kobi in Rabbi Frankel's study, chewing her cuticle while Kobi told his parents their news. Through the receiver, she could hear cries of mazal tov and smiled with relief. The Chazons had taken the news just as well as her parents had. Her relief was short-lived, though, as Kobi handed her the phone.

"They want to speak to you."

Blushing, Lisa managed a shalom and struggled to sound friendly in her broken Hebrew.

"Welcome to..." she heard Shula, Kobi's mother, say and then there was some crackling.

"*Todah*." Lisa hoped it was appropriate to say thank-you.

There was more crackling and then Lisa thought she heard Tzachi, Kobi's father, ask when the wedding would be. Giving up, she surrendered the phone to Kobi, who said they hoped it would be the first Sunday in September.

"I'll make reservations," Tzachi answered over the static.

Seated on the ornate couch in his Beit She'an apartment, he hung up the phone and faced his wife. Her normal complacent smile was missing. Instead, she glared at him.

"What's wrong?" he asked innocently.

"You know I don't want to fly in an airplane," she declared. A big-boned woman who'd moved to Israel in her teens, she appeared as if nothing would frighten her, but that was an illusion. She was a woman who didn't appreciate modern inventions.

"It'll be fine," Tzachi tried soothing her.

"No!" Shula crossed her arms over her chest, her mouth set in a firm line.

"Come on, Shula," her husband coaxed. "Don't you want to go to your only son's wedding?"

"My only surviving son," Shula reminded him tersely.

"Exactly!" Tzachi smoothed down his thick moustache, confident he'd made his point.

He had. The next day he made reservations for five with El Al. Shula took her mother and mother-in-law shopping for dresses. Their daughter, Riki, arranged a work vacation, and Tzachi talked to his brother-in-law about running the store while he was away. Shula was just beginning to relax about the idea of flying when an Air France plane en route to Israel was hijacked to Entebbe.

Like most Israelis, Shula spent the following week glued to the radio. She rejoiced with the rest of the country after Israel's spectacular rescue operation, but nothing anyone could say after that made her feel that it was safe to fly.

"I can't take care of our mothers without you," Tzachi appealed to her sense of responsibility.

Shula remained uncharacteristically obstinate.

Tzachi wasn't going to tell Kobi about his mother's fears. Instead, during the next phone call, he made a diplomatic suggestion. "Why don't you and Lisa come to Israel after the wedding? That way she can meet all the family and it will be much cheaper for me." Tzachi forced a laugh. "Almost a third of the price."

"Oh, Abba, what happened?"

"It's not going to work out," Tzachi said vaguely. He was a man who liked to be in charge and didn't want his son to sense his irritation.

"I can't get that much time off a brand-new job." Kobi tried to hide his disappointment.

Tzachi swallowed his frustration. As much as he wanted to be at his son's wedding, he wasn't willing to upset his wife. Riki, loyal little sister that she was, ignored her mother's worries and continued with plans to travel by herself.

❋ ❋ ❋

Kobi and Lisa found an apartment in the same complex as Danny and Sondra had, several blocks from the synagogue. That helped make Sondra feel a little more positive about living in Phoenix, though she still viewed Lisa as her younger cousin, someone to influence and teach, and not a real equal. Lisa had made great strides in becoming observant but, as she'd informed Sondra several months earlier, she wasn't going to be a fanatic about Judaism. Keeping Shabbos was great and she'd gotten used to not eating out. She learned the laws of family purity and she intended to keep them. Kobi didn't expect her to keep her head covered, though, and she had no intention of isolating herself from the rest of the world. Sondra couldn't confide in her cousin how hard she found it to dress modestly in the Phoenix heat.

She couldn't confide in Rena Frankel either. Rena, who was a good twenty pounds overweight and felt the heat far more than Sondra did, never complained about wearing long sleeves in the summer. Of course, Sondra had never heard Rena grumble about anything. Recently, while she was visiting the Frankels' home, Yechiel called to tell his wife that he'd invited a family of six who were passing through town and needed a kosher meal. They'd be coming in an hour. Rena didn't blink an eye at the news. She instructed her boys to play with Zvi Chaim and invited Sondra into the kitchen.

"It's so hot I thought I'd just serve cottage cheese and fruit tonight." She paused thoughtfully. "I think I'd better add a tuna casserole and salad, though. And maybe a cake. Do you mind cutting the salad?"

"Not at all." Sondra asked for the cutting board. "Does this happen often?"

"About once a month." Rena smiled. "But I don't mind. It's fun to meet all the people passing through."

"Wow!" Sondra exclaimed.

She admired Rena for her good nature and flexibility, and she thought the rabbi's wife made a good role model, but she couldn't picture her as a real friend.

It was in Brachie Fisch, who'd also just moved to town, that Sondra found a kindred spirit. A diminutive blonde, she was a bundle of energy. Instead of just bemoaning that there were no women's lectures to attend, she organized a class on the weekly Torah portion in her home. And it was Brachie's idea that she and Sondra go out for lunch to Farrel's, the old-fashioned ice cream parlor in the mall that carried ice cream from the kosher dairy.

"Our banana splits are just as healthy as peanut butter and jelly sandwiches," Brachie declared, once the noise of the banging drums that accompanied one patron's large order died down.

"You think so?" Sondra looked at her new friend skeptically.

"Sure! There's protein from the nuts, calcium from the ice cream, and potassium from the bananas. It's probably even healthier than peanut butter and jelly."

Sondra grinned, thankful for finding a good friend in Phoenix.

"How about sharing a sitter once we start teaching?" Brachie suggested.

"That would be great!" Sondra jumped at the idea. "Zvi Chaim is becoming sociable and I didn't want to put him in a day care center, but your Ariela would be a great playmate for him. As long as we're making plans, maybe we should talk about carpooling together to school."

"My husband would like that," Brachie said. "Maybe my first graders and your second graders could do some projects together."

"Great idea!"

✱　✱　✱

By the time Labor Day weekend arrived, Sondra felt she'd put down some roots in the desert town. With a feeling of pride, she showed off some of the sights to her parents and the other relatives who came for Lisa's wedding. Sitting in the elegant hall at the Camelback Inn on Sunday afternoon, Sondra answered all of her mother's questions.

"Why isn't Lisa getting married outside like you did?"

"It's an Ashkenazic custom and Kobi is Sephardic. Anyway, you should be glad," Sondra added. "We would roast if it was outside. This is the hottest part of the day."

"The air-conditioning is nice," Helga concurred.

"Why aren't you the bridesmaid?" Helga whispered as first Danny and then Riki came down the aisle.

"Lisa appreciated so much that someone from Kobi's family came that she wanted to give his sister that honor," Sondra explained.

Her mother nodded. "Tell me again, who's the couple taking Kobi to the chuppah?"

Just as Sondra finished explaining who the Weins were, Rabbi Frankel began the ceremony. Sondra watched the ritual through a haze of tears. At her own wedding, almost half of the guests had been strangers to her. Here, she knew almost everyone. Holding the chuppah were her father, her uncle, and two friends from Los Angeles. She knew each of the men who recited the wedding blessings and why they'd been chosen. And of course, she couldn't forget how far Lisa had once been from having this kind of wedding.

Most of Lisa's relatives had seen the separate dancing at Sondra's wedding, but her friends from ASU had not. For weeks afterwards they talked about how those religious Jews and Kobi's Israeli friends picked up the bride and groom and danced with them. Carol was most impressed with Danny dancing on top of a huge serving tray that some others had held up over their heads.

Before the conclusion of the meal, Lisa's father rose to make a speech. He couldn't toast his daughter and new son-in-law without remembering his son Howie. At the same time, he mentioned Kobi's brother, Uri. Sondra wasn't the only one to blink back tears as she opened her *bentcher*.

Then it was all over. Kobi and Lisa took off for the Grand Canyon. They would be returning the following night and there would be *Sheva Brachos*. There would also be work for Kobi and school for Lisa. She planned to graduate in three years instead of four and she was going to be busy.

CHAPTER
Twelve

As she heard her infant cry, Sondra glanced at the digital clock. A little after twelve in the morning. Quickly, she padded into the children's room and settled down in the rocking chair with little Batsheva. A year had passed since she, Danny, and Zvi Chaim had moved to Phoenix. Now their three-bedroom apartment felt like home. Fortunately, Zvi Chaim was a deep sleeper and never seemed to hear his sister, who woke up a few times each night.

At three months, Batsheva ate swiftly. It wasn't even twelve-thirty when Sondra settled her baby daughter back down in her crib. Instead of crawling back into bed herself, she entered the living room. She pulled back the curtain over the picture window just a crack and gazed out onto the courtyard below. All was quiet in the apartment complex. Sondra chewed her lip, full of indecision, and then she heard the sound of voices. Again she pulled back the curtain, and this time she was rewarded with the sight of her husband, her cousin, and Kobi. Tying a scarf over her head and a robe around her, she slipped out of the apartment.

"Lisa," she cried, grabbing her cousin in a hug. "How was it?"

"Really good." Lisa smiled.

She and Kobi had taken his father up on the offer to fly them to Israel, albeit a year after the offer had been made. Kobi had earned himself a two-week vacation and Lisa had graduated.

"You must be exhausted."

"That's not the word for it." Lisa pulled her wheeled suitcase behind her. "The flight from Israel was fine, but I had a crying baby next to me all the way from New York."

"I offered you my earplugs," Kobi reminded her as he unlocked their door.

"It would have helped like a Band-Aid for a corpse," Lisa retorted.

No one laughed at her joke, though. As soon as they entered the apartment, they felt like they were in a sauna.

"Did you turn the air conditioner off before you left?" Danny asked.

"I turned it up," Kobi replied. "I didn't want to waste the electricity, but it was set at seventy-eight."

"Maybe the electricity is off." Lisa flicked the light switch and the room lit up, proving her wrong.

"I'll adjust the thermostat." Kobi set down the two bags and went to the hall. He turned the dial down to seventy, but the unit did not click on.

"The air conditioner must be broken," Sondra said matter-of-factly.

"Oh," Lisa moaned, collapsing onto the couch. "All I want to do is shower and fall into bed. I can't sleep in this heat."

"No, you can't." Danny opened the living room window. "It's probably 130 degrees in here. Let's open all the windows and get some air into the apartment."

"Like 104 degrees outside is going to cool things off," Sondra said, but she headed toward the kitchen to take her husband's advice.

"This is ridiculous," Kobi announced, his exhaustion getting the best of him. "I'm calling the manager right now!"

"Kobi, you can't do that," Lisa cautioned him. "He's sleeping."

"And I want to sleep too!"

"Lisa's right," Danny said. "They won't be able to fix it till the morning. Come sleep at our place."

"By the time you take your showers, the guest room will be ready," Sondra added.

Kobi agreed. Leaving their suitcases in their living room, he and Lisa walked across the courtyard with their overnight bags. The Kleins' apartment was a comfortable 72 degrees, and Kobi and Lisa were able to fall asleep as soon as their heads hit the pillows.

It was after eleven o'clock when Lisa finally came out of the guest room the next morning. With her blonde hair tied in a ponytail and no makeup, she looked almost as young as she had in junior high school. Sondra smiled warmly at her cousin and offered her some coffee.

"That sounds good." Lisa gave Zvi Chaim a kiss. The toddler was sitting at the table in the sunny kitchen, busily scribbling with a blue crayon all over a pile of scrap paper. His mother sat across from him, peeling vegetables. Lisa poured herself a cup of coffee and settled down between the two of them.

"I was so jet-lagged, I didn't hear a thing this morning. Where's Kobi?"

"He's over at the apartment with the repairman."

"Oh good." Lisa took a sip of coffee.

"So tell me all about it." Sondra put down the peeler and waited expectantly.

Lisa stretched. "I like Kobi's mother. Riki, of course, was wonderful to me. That was such good advice you gave me about asking Kobi's sister to be the bridesmaid. I couldn't communicate with his grandmothers. They only speak French and Arabic, but my Hebrew has improved enough to have conversations with his mom. We get along."

"Good. Zvi Chaim, don't color on the table, sweetie. And what about Kobi's father?"

"He thinks if it wasn't for me, Kobi would have returned to Israel already."

"That's not true!"

"I know that. You know that. Kobi knows that. But no one can convince his father of that. He talked to me more than once about giving up all my American luxuries and moving there. Yes, Zvi Chaim, that's really a pretty picture."

"Do you think you ever will?" Sondra asked with just a touch of envy.

"Oh, definitely," Lisa answered matter-of-factly. "Although we decided on the way home that Kobi should get American citizenship. It'll be good for him to have until we do move to Israel."

"Can you really see yourself living there?"

"I can," Lisa said enthusiastically. "The only thing is I think we'll become vegetarians. I couldn't deal with all the live chickens on their way to the *shochet* in the buses, and I certainly don't see myself plucking all those pin feathers. Of course, that would really clinch things for me with my father-in-law if he would hear me make such a statement. But," Lisa hastened to add, "he was good to me the whole time we were there."

"And the rest of the family?"

"I met them all at once and can't keep any of them straight except for Kobi's Aunt Tirza. She and his grandmother are the only ones who are truly observant. The others range from traditional to secular. Aunt Tirza speaks Hebrew and she's thrilled that Kobi became religious in America, so she spent a lot of time talking to me."

"That's neat."

"Uh huh." Lisa took a sip of coffee. "I have greetings for you from Tamar and Eliezer."

"So you did get a chance to see them."

"Juice, pease," Zvi Chaim piped up.

"Sure, sweetie." Sondra opened up the refrigerator. "How about some breakfast, Lisa?"

"A bowl of cornflakes would be great. We spent a Shabbos with them."

"Really?"

"Yeah. One Shabbos in Beit She'an and one in Jerusalem. The one in Beit She'an was hot and long, but I almost forgot to tell you. Mom's cousin Leah lives on a kibbutz ten minutes away, and we went there Saturday night. She said you spent a couple of Shabboses with them."

"I did." Sondra nodded. "The summer I was touring and another the year I was learning in Jerusalem. They were lovely to me."

"I told Kobi that next time we should spend Shabbos on the kibbutz."

"That would probably be better than at Kobi's parents." Sondra rolled her eyes. "I assume the Shabbos with the Glinkers was more spiritual."

"It sure was! We walked to the Kotel Friday night. The walk was long, but it was worth it."

"I bet!" Sondra's face shone with Jerusalem memories. "How are they doing?"

"Great. They're really happy they left Los Angeles and made *aliyah*. And, of course, they wanted to know all about you and send their love."

"I must write her. Oh…" Sondra stood up again and opened a drawer. "Here's your mail."

Lisa leafed through the stack. "Bill, bill, advertisement, another bill, oh, an invitation. I bet it's from Carol." Lisa quickly opened the formal, cream-colored envelope from her former roommate and smiled.

"So she and Bill are getting married?"

"Bill gave her an ultimatum several months ago. Either she takes him to meet her parents so he can ask for her hand in marriage — those were his exact words — or he breaks it off."

"So she took him to Florence?"

Before Lisa could answer, Batsheva began crying. Sondra brought the baby into the kitchen and began feeding her.

"She's so beautiful," Lisa sighed.

Sondra smiled. She had very tender feelings for her little girl, who had given her such an easy pregnancy.

"So what happened with Carol's folks?"

"It was fine. Bill charmed them. They only demanded one thing — that they be married in the church, and he agreed. The wedding's three weeks from Sunday in Florence."

"Are you going?"

"To the reception. Carol's cool with that. She understands that it's a problem for a Jew to go into a church."

"Too bad she didn't understand that problem a few years ago," Sondra said dryly. As much as Lisa and Carol were good friends, Sondra was still uncomfortable with the person who'd suggested that Lisa convert.

Lisa blushed at her cousin's comment. Sometimes she wished she knew of Sondra's errors from her high school days, before she became religious, as well as her cousin knew about her own. "You know," she said with dignity, "it's forbidden to remind a *ba'alas teshuvah* of her mistakes from the past."

"I'm sorry." Sondra was instantly contrite. "You're right. It sounds like you did some learning when you were in Israel."

"As a matter of fact, I did. Tamar has this neat book in English about *lashon hara* that I began reading Shabbos afternoon when we were there. I want to order it and maybe we can learn a page or two every time we have our learning group. I need to speak to Brachie about it."

"That's a great idea." Sondra was visibly impressed. "It will really add to our learning. I'm meeting her and some of the others at the Weins' pool this afternoon. Want to come too?"

Lisa thought for a moment. Her cousin's wholehearted compliment had taken the sting out of her earlier words, and she nodded her head decidedly. "Next week I start work and there won't be any time to spend a relaxing afternoon with my friends. It'll be great to do it today."

CHAPTER
Thirteen

"Will that be cash or charge?" Lisa cheerfully asked her elderly customer.

"Let's see." The woman searched her purse and finally pulled out her billfold.

As she counted her money and weighed her decision, Lisa struggled to remain patient. It was ten minutes to five. Now that the holidays were over, candle lighting was getting earlier. She was supposed to be off at five, but filling in for a sick salesclerk looked like it was going to keep her longer than she wanted. Last week, a problem with a display case had resulted in her having to go into Shabbos without her usual shower. This week she was better prepared. She'd showered in the morning, the table was set from last night, and all the food was waiting to be put on the hot plate. All she'd have to do was set the lights and take the phone off the hook.

It was just a few minutes after five when she took the elevator to the second floor and walked back to the offices to collect her belongings and say a few goodbyes. She smiled with satisfaction. Kramer's was one of the most exclusive department stores in Phoenix, on the same level as

Goldwater's and Saks Fifth Avenue. And she had landed a job there as floor supervisor straight out of college at the tender age of twenty-two. If all went well, she was scheduled to move into the promotions division in six months. That would mean going on buying trips, planning the fashion shows, and organizing shopping nights for the preferred customers. After that, well, she had pinned her hopes on becoming an assistant to the fashion director. She smiled at her dreams as she pushed the button for the elevator.

"Lisa," her supervisor called to her. "Before you go, let me give you the new schedule for next month."

"Sure." Lisa took the paper as the elevator doors opened. Stuffing it into her bag, she took off without a glance behind her.

She could feel Shabbos as soon as she came in the front door. Kobi had already moved the food to the hot plate and cut up the salad. He'd added a bouquet of flowers in a Lenox vase to the set table as well. Her candles were waiting for her on the end table next to the couch.

Since they were planning to move to Israel eventually, the Chazons had opted to rent a furnished apartment. Although all the furnishings were in nondescript earth tones, they matched perfectly. Their apartment had the same picture window, the same large dining room/living room combination, and the same airy kitchen as the Kleins' apartment. Yet it felt completely different. One of the differences, of course, was the lack of children's toys and messes. Another was Lisa's artistic talent. With pictures, flowers, and bursts of color here and there, she'd managed to make their apartment feel like a unique home and not a carbon copy of the other twenty-two furnished apartments in the complex.

Lisa studied the table carefully and decided to move the vase to the windowsill. She wasn't sure how well the Hirsch children would behave at the table and she didn't want her wedding present from the Weins broken.

Mordechai Hirsch had been transferred to Phoenix from Monsey three months earlier. An easygoing man, he had made the adjustment well. His three children, aged eight, seven, and four, had made new friends. Only Shaindy, his pretty wife, was having a hard time and she never missed an opportunity to complain about Phoenix. The summer was too hot and there was no autumn. There was no *eruv* and the divider in the shul was too low. The classes at the day school were mixed and didn't have enough religious study hours.

Lisa, who was used to her other friends' enthusiasm to improve the community, didn't know how to react to Shaindy's constant litany of Phoenix's faults. Last Shabbos, at the *Kiddush*, Shaindy had cornered Lisa and compared the meager spread to what had been served at the ones in her Monsey shul.

"You should taste the white fish we had there. Pure heaven." Shaindy sighed and took a bite of her cracker topped with herring.

"I never thought the food was the main thing about a *Kiddush*," Lisa offered. "I thought it was important to bring the congregation together."

"It's hard to bring everyone together if most of the women can't come," Shaindy retorted.

"Um, I think my husband's calling me," Lisa mumbled and made her escape.

Later that afternoon, she talked it over with Sondra.

"Not that I want to talk *lashon hara*," she prefaced her conversation, "but I don't know what to do. She drives me crazy!"

"She's really unhappy."

"You don't like Phoenix that much either, but you make the best of it."

Sondra settled Batsheva down on the blanket by her feet and handed her a push toy. She thought over her cousin's statement carefully.

"I'd love to be in a stronger community," she admitted. "Thankfully, there's some good role models here for making the best of things. And it wasn't like I thought Los Angeles was the end-all of places to live. Shaindy was very happy in Monsey and she feels bad to have left it all behind. I think she's really lonely here."

"Of course she is!" Lisa exclaimed. "Who wants to listen to her complain all the time?"

"I know." Sondra nodded. "I guess we should make more of an effort."

Sondra called Shaindy that week and talked her into coming to the weekly learning group. Not to be outdone, Lisa had gritted her teeth and invited the Hirsches for the Friday night meal. Shaindy had sounded thrilled with the invitation, and Lisa hoped that once the Shabbos dinner was over, she'd still feel the warm glow she'd felt after the phone call.

"So, how'd it go?" Sondra asked after the Shabbos morning meal. Lisa was in the kitchen helping her dish up the pareve ice cream for dessert. Kobi and Lisa were often Shabbos guests at the Kleins.

"Okay." Lisa hesitated. "Mordechai said a nice *d'var Torah* and there was a lot of singing."

"But?" Sondra prodded.

"I don't know. When they left, Shaindy really thanked me and I said we'd have to have them again soon. She liked the idea, but she didn't say a thing about having us over. I mean, that would have been the polite thing to do. It's not like you. You can't come to us until Batsheva starts walking."

Sondra rolled her eyes. "I can't wait." She handed Lisa two bowls. "As for Shaindy, I guess we just have to keep trying harder."

Kobi was rinsing the last pot from the Shabbos meals when he heard what sounded like yelling. He turned off the water and, sure enough, there were screams coming from the bedroom.

"Lisa?" He dried his hands on his pants as he went rushing to his wife.

"No, no, no." Lisa was sitting on her bed, practically in tears.

"What's the matter?"

"Look!" Lisa thrust the paper that her supervisor had given her in Kobi's face.

Her husband scanned it. "They changed your hours?"

Lisa nodded glumly. "Noon till eight every weekday, including Fridays."

"Didn't you tell them about Shabbos?"

"Of course I did," Lisa moaned. "I said I'd be happy to work on Sundays. They even said that they respected me for holding onto my principles."

"Okay," Kobi soothed. "So someone flubbed up. You can speak to the supervisor tomorrow and straighten it out."

"She's not the one who arranges the schedules." Lisa rose and began pacing. "It's Miss Kramer. She never comes in on Sundays."

"So you'll talk to her Monday. It'll work out," Kobi reassured her.

"I hope you're right," Lisa said worriedly.

Miss Kramer set up a meeting with her on Monday during Lisa's lunch break. By eleven o'clock, Lisa was sure that if anyone had checked her blood pressure, she'd have been sent straight to the hospital. At eleven-thirty, she wiped the palms of her hands with a tissue, straightened her suit jacket, and timidly knocked on Miss Kramer's door.

Miss Kramer's father had first founded the Kramer Department Store in Flagstaff. With the advent of air-conditioning, he opened a second, higher-class store in Phoenix. It was a big success, and it wasn't long before he sold the Flagstaff store. Now there was a branch in Las Vegas and another in Beverly Hills run by his two sons. His daughter was in charge of the Phoenix store.

Lisa couldn't help comparing Miss Kramer to Cousin Berta. Widowed at a young age, Berta ran Apple's children's department in Lincoln, and the store never had a more loyal employee. The family joked that Berta was married to Apple's. It seemed as if Miss Kramer was married to her store too. Already in her late fifties, she was still single.

She motioned for Lisa to sit down and looked at her over her moon-shaped glasses. "How can I help you?"

Lisa quickly explained her problem with the new schedule.

"I see." Miss Kramer folded her hands in front of her. "I think I recall you telling us you could work any day but Saturday."

"I said I couldn't work on the Jewish Sabbath."

"Mrs. Chazon, I'm Jewish too." Lisa's boss spoke briskly. "As long as you can make it to synagogue in the morning, I don't understand the problem."

"Shabbos begins Friday night, eighteen minutes before sundown. After that, I don't drive, touch money, all sorts of things..." Lisa faltered, seeing the annoyed expression on Miss Kramer's face.

"Mrs. Chazon, I can't believe an intelligent, college-educated woman like you would follow such medieval practices. Now —" she banged her desk with the palm of her hand, "— if you cannot make your job your priority, I don't think there's room for you here at Kramer's."

"Isn't that religious discrimination?" Lisa gasped.

"I just told you, I'm Jewish too." Miss Kramer picked up her pen and scribbled something on her memo pad. "Fine," she said. "You can stick with your old schedule, but don't expect to make any career advances here."

"I see." Lisa rose. "Thank you for your time." Lisa left Miss Kramer's office with a heavy heart.

She called Kobi right away, but he was only able to talk for a minute.

"I think it sounds positive," he comforted his wife. "You get to keep your old schedule. You weren't going to be put up for promotion so soon, anyway. In another six months, they'll be so impressed with you they'll forget all about this."

"You don't understand..." Lisa began, but Kobi was called away and that was the end of the conversation.

Frustrated and too upset to eat her sandwich, Lisa returned to the display case she was working on. That kept her mind off her problems, but once in her car and on her way home, she began facing her worries again.

It was no use talking to Sondra. Her cousin had decided to make a full commitment to Yiddishkeit and began to keep Shabbos during the week of shivah for Howie. She'd told Uncle Simon, their great-uncle and the founder of Apple's, that she had a non-Jewish friend who'd work in her place on Saturdays and Uncle Simon had exploded. He'd given her a choice to change her mind or be fired. Without thinking twice, Sondra had let herself be fired. But then, she'd only worked in Apple's to help out and have some spending money.

Lisa, on the other hand, loved everything about the department store. She felt an adrenaline rush every time she made a sale. She enjoyed meeting with the salesmen and helping to decide which merchandise to carry. Probably her favorite part of the job was picking out the outfits and accessories for the mannequins.

She knew she could do the same at Apple's and Cousin Oscar would let her work the hours she wanted, but Lincoln was not a place for her now and certainly not a place for Kobi. Without giving it much thought, she found herself turning right instead of left, onto Rose Lane, and pulling up in front of the Frankels' house. Rena was her mentor, as well as her confidante.

It wasn't the best time for a visit. Rena was in the kitchen trying to organize supper. The boys were fighting over a truck at her feet and the baby was screaming in the swing. Still, Rena greeted her warmly.

"Do you mind changing the baby's diaper while I separate these two?" Rena had grabbed the hands of both boys.

"No problem."

Suri was clean and calm by the time her mother returned to the kitchen with the truck under her arm.

"Moishy's looking at books, and Zevie's doing puzzles, and we'll see how long that lasts." Rena grinned good-naturedly. "What's on your mind?"

Lisa picked at her nail polish as she explained everything, and Rena listened with all her attention.

"I must say, I agree with Kobi."

"You don't understand either." Lisa sighed. "In another couple of weeks, I won't even be able to work until five on Friday. I'll have to ask to get off early."

"Oh." Rena looked thoughtful. "I guess this isn't the time to tell you about my grandfather, who got fired every Monday morning during his first year in America until he finally opened his own business."

"I've heard those stories." Lisa grimaced. "And the truth is, we could probably get by on Kobi's salary if we need to. But this is a dream job!"

"You're going through a big test."

"Maybe I could continue working till five. Candle lighting is never any earlier than that, and I could just walk home. It's only about three miles. And we're only talking about a few weeks."

"That's a thought," Rena answered carefully. "You have a few snags to work out, though."

"Like what?"

Rena took a deep breath. "Where would you leave your purse? What if they needed you overtime? Is it safe to walk home by yourself when it's getting dark? Would you just skip lighting candles?"

"You don't think it'll work?"

"I didn't say that. I'm just saying that you have to give it a lot of thought. And it wouldn't hurt to talk to a rabbi."

* * *

Lisa expressed her worries to Kobi over supper that evening.

"This job really means that much to you?" he asked.

"It really does," Lisa admitted.

"I see." Kobi took a sip of juice. "Does Shabbat means a lot to you too?"

"Of course." Lisa didn't raise her eyes from her plate.

"You know, lots of people start Shabbat when it's convenient for them."

"Kobi!" Lisa's head snapped up and she looked at her husband with an expression of shock.

"Don't worry, I'm just playing devil's advocate." Kobi grinned, proud that he was able to use an English idiom so well.

Lisa played with the hamburger casserole on her plate, but didn't take a bite. "The truth is, I thought about it. I thought about bringing in Shabbos half an hour late and ending it half an hour late. But I think that's more or less what happened with my family when they came to America. You just pull out one little thread, and eventually the whole garment unravels. I don't want to go back to my old lifestyle."

"I'm glad to hear it." Kobi nodded his approval. "What *do* you want to do?"

Lisa shook her head. "I don't know. I think I'll take Rena's advice and talk to her husband."

* * *

Sitting at the Frankels' dining room table an hour later, she related her plan again.

"According to Halachah, your ideas aren't so bad." Rabbi Frankel wrinkled his forehead in concentration. "You could arrange with a co-worker whom you trust to take care of your personal items and then reclaim them Saturday night or even Sunday morning. The three-mile walk is perfectly permissible inside town, and if you stick to busy streets, I don't think it's dangerous at that time of the evening. As far as candle lighting, Kobi can light for you."

"So my idea is okay?"

"As I said," Rabbi Frankel stroked his beard, "according to Halachah, there's no problem. The question is how it'll affect your Shabbos. Will you be able to enter it with peace of mind and a full heart?"

"I guess I'll only know if I try."

"Well," Rena entered the discussion, "you'll come to us for lunch the first week you try it. At least you won't have making that meal on your head."

The first week it took Lisa a little over an hour to walk home. Kobi wasn't home from shul yet, so she removed the key from under the doormat and let herself in. She took off her suit, splashed herself with cold water, picked out a Shabbos dress, smoothed down her hair, and was ready to go as soon as Kobi returned. Sondra had invited them for the Friday night meal and Lisa was grateful for the help.

The second week, Lisa and Kobi ate at home without any guests. It was a pleasant but fast meal, not the kind of *seudah* they were used to having, but acceptable for once in a while. In the morning, Lisa decided that, just once, she'd skip going to shul and sleep in.

The weather was nasty the third week, and when Kobi came home from shul on Friday morning, he gave Lisa a worried look.

"I don't think you should walk home in this weather."

"What do you want me to do?" Lisa made no attempt to hide the irritation in her voice.

"Take the day off."

"I already took seven sick days with the holidays and I still have Pesach and Shavuos. What if I really get sick?" She didn't mention that she already had a scratchy throat.

"You probably will if you walk home in this." Kobi poured himself a cup of coffee and glared at his wife.

She glared back. "Maybe it'll clear up by the afternoon."

"You're determined to do this?"

Lisa nodded stubbornly.

"Well, take your coat and hat."

Shabbos morning, Kobi came into the bedroom and stood at the side of her bed.

"Lisa," he whispered, "do you want to get up for shul?"

"I don't want to go anywhere," she moaned. She opened her eyes and looked at her husband. "Don't say 'I told you so,' but I feel horrible."

"You look like you have fever."

"My throat hurts and my bones ache."

"I'll get you some tea and Tylenol."

"Okay."

Kobi sat with her while she drank the tea. "I'm going to put a pitcher of juice and a glass on the nightstand. Drink as much as you can while I'm gone. I'll refill it after shul."

"We're supposed to go to the Weins for lunch," Lisa groaned.

"You're not going anywhere. And I don't want to go without you."

"There's nothing to eat here."

"We have chicken left from last night, and there's a roll from yesterday, and I can make a salad. I can make a nice Shabbos lunch for just the two of us."

"I don't want to eat anything," Lisa said. "I just want to sleep. You go by yourself and have a nice Shabbos. I've done my best to ruin this one."

"Oh, Lisa, don't flog yourself."

"Please go to the Weins."

"Well, maybe," Kobi said. "I'll stop by after shul to see if you're feeling better."

She wasn't. Kobi gave her another Tylenol and was fairly sure she had a strep infection. Sunday morning the doctor confirmed Kobi's diagnosis. Lisa called in sick. Monday, after she had been on antibiotics for twenty-four hours, she came to the miserable conclusion that she'd better start working on her résumé. By the time Pesach was over, she'd probably be fired.

CHAPTER
Fourteen

Batsheva was sleeping and Zvi Chaim was playing at the Fisches. Instead of working on lesson plans, Sondra was using the quiet time to schedule her Pesach cleaning, plan menus, and make the Pesach shopping list. She'd learned that the only way she could cope with the holiday was to start getting organized immediately after Purim. As she scribbled away, the phone rang.

"Sondra, guess what!" Her mother-in-law was clearly excited. "I just had a call from Dorothy, and she and Stan are taking their vacation in April. They're going to Las Vegas by way of us, and they'll be here for the Seder!"

"That's nice," Sondra answered politely.

Last year, Danny had asked his *rav* from Los Angeles about letting his parents drive to them for Seder. He was instructed that they should arrive before candle lighting and it should be clear that there was a room ready for them to stay in. If they chose not to stay there, that was their business. This year, Sondra reasoned, she could make up the hide-a-bed in the living room for Dorothy and Stan, as well as the beds in the guest room, and make sure all the guests knew they were welcome to sleep over. It'd be a waste of time, but it'd be for *shalom bayis*. And she had to admit, it would be good to see Danny's sister and brother-in-law.

"Listen, Sondra," Shirley continued. "Doc and I want you to get some cleaning help, our treat."

"Thank you," Sondra said, "but I'm managing okay."

"I just don't want you overdoing things in your condition..."

"What condition?"

"Well, uh," Shirley faltered, "I thought you were expecting again."

"How could you know?" Sondra asked icily. "I'm not even two months along."

"I just sensed it," Shirley replied with a forced laugh.

"Did you sense it or did Dr. Taylor tell Doc?" Sondra blinked back angry tears.

"Oh, Sondra, calm down," Shirley replied nervously. "I guess I put my foot in it. No, Ed didn't say anything. I was filling in for the receptionist last week and I saw your name in the appointment book with a *p* next to it, so I came to the obvious conclusion. I'm not trying to interfere. I just want what's best for you."

"I know," Sondra kept her voice even. "Thank you."

"So do you want to use my cleaning lady or find your own?"

"I'll have to think about it. I'll let you know, okay?"

"That's fine."

"Oh, Shirley, Batsheva's crying," Sondra lied. "I'll have to get back to you."

Two hours later, Sondra still hadn't calmed down. When Lisa poked her nose in on her way home from work, the apartment was no longer quiet. Batsheva was awake and playing with a noisy shape sorter in the playpen. Zvi Chaim had set up his toy farm next to the couch and was making the appropriate animal sounds to go along with it. Sondra had the food processor running in the kitchen and barely heard her cousin's knock. She opened the door and gave Lisa a weak smile.

"What's the matter?" Lisa asked as they settled down at the kitchen table.

"Nothing, I've been making Pesach plans."

"So why are you twisting the ends of your scarf and playing with your wedding band? I can tell you're upset about something."

"You know me too well!" Sondra laughed in spite of herself.

"Only all my life." Lisa smiled.

As she listened to Sondra rehash her conversation with her mother-in-law, Lisa's smile faded.

"So you're going to have another baby?"

"If all's well; it's still early and we didn't want to tell anyone yet. I guess I should consider looking for a new doctor, although I was really comfortable with Dr. Taylor. Do you like your gynecologist?"

"He's okay," Lisa answered flatly.

Something in her cousin's face made Sondra change the subject.

"How's it going at work?"

Lisa took a deep breath. "Today Miss Kramer complimented my window displays. I don't know. Maybe she won't go ballistic when I take off for Pesach."

"Do you think you'll get the promotion?"

"Your guess is as good as mine." Lisa shrugged.

"And if you don't?"

Lisa took a sip of her tea. "I'm really trying not to worry about it. Everything's for the best, and if I lose this job, I'll find something better."

"Good for you!" Sondra exclaimed.

Lisa smiled at her cousin's approval. "And things will work out with your mother-in-law too."

Later that evening, as Danny ate his warmed-up dinner, Sondra repeated the conversation with Shirley. Even though he was exhausted, her husband listened patiently.

"Sondra, we've got a little over a year left here. This is the first time my mother has committed an indiscretion. There's no point in changing doctors for such a short time."

"I guess you're right," Sondra conceded. "What about a cleaning lady? Should I accept your mom's offer?"

"Of course!" Danny exclaimed. "And keep her coming after Pesach, as long as my mom's willing to pay for it."

Sondra raised her eyebrows.

"I'm not proud." Danny stabbed his baked potato. "My folks want to help and you can use the help, can't you?"

Sondra hesitated and began twisting the ends of her headscarf.

"Tell me." Danny grinned. "What's bothering you?"

Sondra took a deep breath. "Cleaning help or not, I'm not sure how I'm going to manage next year. When this baby's born, if all's well, Zvi Chaim will barely be three and Batsheva not even sixteen months. You'll be at the hospital more than at home. I'm kind of scared."

"I know." Danny raised his hands up. "We just have to get through next year and we'll be okay."

"Yeah," Sondra made her tone upbeat. "Do you want some applesauce?"

"Sure."

"Sondra?" Danny spoke seriously as his wife handed him his dessert bowl. "Maybe you should stay home next year and we should take out a loan to get through. Half your salary will be going to the sitter anyway. What do you think?"

"I don't know," Sondra answered honestly. "I like teaching, but I'm really not sure how I'll manage."

"When do you have to let Rabbi Levi know if you want to teach next year?"

"Probably by the end of the school year."

"So let's table this till after Pesach."

"Okay." Sondra smiled gratefully at her husband. Suddenly, she decided she wanted a bowl of applesauce too.

CHAPTER
Fifteen

Pesach had been over for a week when Lisa met Rena Frankel at Farrell's Ice Cream Parlor on her way home from work. Surprisingly, the outing had been Rena's idea. Even more surprising was that Rena was waiting for Lisa all by herself.

"Where're the kids?" Lisa asked as she slipped into the booth.

"Yechiel's home. I wanted some time to talk to you without being interrupted fifteen million times."

"What's up?"

"Well…" Rena's eyes seemed to be darting everywhere except Lisa's face. "Don't you want to order?"

"Sure." Lisa motioned for the waitress.

While they waited for their order, Rena told Lisa a funny story about their return flight from her husband's parents. Once their sundaes were in front of them, she played with her whipped cream.

"Rena, your ice cream's melting. What's the matter?"

Rena put down her spoon. "This is hard," she said.

"What's wrong?" Lisa asked again with concern.

Rena sighed. "We didn't go back east for Pesach just to be with

Yechiel's family. Yechiel had a job interview in Far Rockaway and he got it. He gave Rabbi Levi his resignation this morning, and I didn't want you to hear from anyone else."

Now it was Lisa's turn to play with her ice cream.

"I guess this is a good move for you," she said softly, staring at her bowl.

"It is." Rena leaned forward. "Moishy's going to be in first grade come September, and even though the secular program here is good, he needs a stronger religious one. Yechiel will be doing some administrative work, so his salary will be higher, and I'll be living in a stronger community." She smiled sadly. "I'm really going to miss you."

Lisa lifted her face and Rena saw tears in her eyes.

"You've not only been my teacher; you've been my friend."

"And you've been mine." Rena reached across the table and took Lisa's hand in her own.

"I always envisioned your husband being the *mohel* when we had a son," Lisa said ruefully.

"Are you telling me something?"

"Just hoping."

"It'll happen." Rena patted Lisa's hand.

Lisa bit her lip. "I guess we better eat before we end up with cold soup."

Rena picked up her spoon. "You know, every time you fly to Israel, I expect you to make a stopover to see us."

"It would be good to break the trip up a bit. So when are you moving?"

"Not until the middle of the summer."

"What's the matter?" Lisa quipped. "You can't bear to leave the heat?"

Rena chuckled — more than the joke was worth — but she was relieved that Lisa was taking the news so well.

"Yechiel has a commitment to tie up a lot of loose ends here. Then we'll go."

"Do you think, maybe, before you go..." Lisa hesitated.

"Yes?"

"Maybe you could go with me to buy a wig?"

Rena gave her a searching look.

"I'd like to have one to wear to shul and for the Kassels' bar mitzvah party coming up."

"That would be fun." Rena's eyes lit up. "Thursday evening sound good?"

"Great!" Lisa smiled sadly. "I'm going to miss you."

It hadn't been a good day, Lisa decided as she drove home. Her feet hurt; and for all her brave talk, she was worried about her job; and that morning she'd learned that another month had come and she still wasn't expecting. Now Rena was leaving. As she entered her apartment, the phone was ringing. Certain it was Kobi, who was working late, she grabbed it on the third ring.

"Hello, Lisa."

The voice on the line was not Kobi's, but one she'd once waited so many months to hear. It felt strange. Her pulse wasn't racing. Her breathing was normal. Hearing Tim affected her as much as a call from a vacuum cleaner salesman would.

"Hello," she said.

"This is Tim, uh, Billings."

"How are you?" Lisa responded with little enthusiasm.

"I'm fine." *Did Tim actually sound nervous?* "I'm back in Lincoln and I saw your uncle. He told me you were married. Um…" Tim faltered.

"Yes," Lisa smiled, "almost two years."

"You know, I have to be in Phoenix next week for business. It'd be nice to get together and catch up on each other's lives."

Lisa caught her breath. What she would have given for such a suggestion once. Now it had no place in her life.

"Tim, I don't think that's a good idea. I know it would make me feel uncomfortable if my husband went to meet one of his old girlfriends."

"I only meant meeting for a cup of coffee. You wouldn't have to tell your husband about something so harmless."

"Yes, I would," Lisa said firmly and began putting dishes away. "That's the kind of marriage we have. I'd never go sneaking behind his back."

"Okay," Tim answered quickly. "Forget I said anything. Obviously I made a mistake."

"Yes," Lisa agreed softly.

As she replaced the receiver she felt as if she would burst from excitement. She couldn't wait for Kobi to come home and tell him how she'd stood up to the test of Tim's romantic aura. Not only that, but she had no regrets about the life she'd left behind. Although certain things could be better, she was happily committed to the Torah and her husband, and no one — not Tim or anyone else — was going to make her change her mind.

As she hugged herself in delight, there was a knock on the door. Sondra was standing on the porch, sympathy all over her face.

"Danny was at shul and they're all talking about the Frankels. How're you doing?"

Lisa was more than touched that Sondra had taken time away from one of Danny's few evenings at home to come comfort her. She didn't speak about the Frankels' move, though, but rather about the euphoria she felt about her reaction to Tim's call.

"This calls for celebrating," Lisa announced impulsively. "How about going with us to Payson for the day this Sunday?"

Sondra looked interested. She knew that Kobi and Lisa loved to go up to the nature reserve near Payson, a little mountain town ninety miles north of Phoenix.

"Don't you and Kobi want to be alone?" she asked.

"As if we never get time for just the two of us," Lisa said deprecatingly.

"It sounds nice." Sondra hesitated. "I don't know if Danny can get away, though."

"So come without him if he can't," Lisa insisted. "I'll help you with the kids."

"Okay," Sondra agreed, smiling.

She practically danced her way back to her apartment. Not only was Lisa handling her disappointment about the Frankels' moving well, Lisa had also stood up to the Tim mystique. For the first time, Sondra felt totally certain that Lisa had not chosen a Torah-true life simply because of Kobi.

CHAPTER
Sixteen

Sondra was feeding Naomi when the phone rang. She grabbed it on the first ring, hoping it wouldn't wake Batsheva, who was taking her afternoon nap.

"Sondra?"

"Hi, Danny!" She smiled, happy for a chance to talk to her busy husband. "Guess what Zvi Chaim brought home…"

"Sondra," Danny interrupted, "I'm in the emergency room with Kobi. Everything's going to be fine, but Lisa's really upset. Try and find someone to watch the kids and get over here."

"Uh, I'll try," Sondra faltered. "What's the matter?"

"Strangulated hernia. He's being prepped for emergency surgery."

Sondra gasped. "I hope Stacy can babysit. If not, I'm calling your mother."

"Go ahead. She'll be happy to help. Lisa needs you."

Stacy wasn't home. Sondra hesitated for a minute and then slowly dialed her in-laws' phone number. It had been more than ten months since she'd last asked Shirley for a favor.

"Sondra, it's so nice to hear from you," her mother-in-law responded to her nervous hello.

Sondra winced. Their conversations had been sporadic and stilted ever since Shirley had indiscreetly told Sondra that she was aware she was expecting. Naomi was already two months old, and Sondra longed for their cold war to end. How would Shirley react to her request?

"I'm really sorry to bother you like this, but I need a babysitter."

"When, dear?"

"Now," Sondra said nervously.

"Oh!" There was a slight pause. "Is everything okay?"

"With us, yes, but I need to help out someone else..." Sondra's voice trailed off.

"I guess that someone else is none of my business."

"Well, uh..."

"It's okay," Shirley said quickly. "I understand the importance of confidentiality. Do you want to bring the kids here or should I come there?"

"If you can come here, it would be great," Sondra said with relief. "Batsheva's sleeping. I'll take Naomi with me."

"I'll be there in a quarter of an hour."

Poor Lisa, Sondra thought as she threw supplies into the diaper bag. What a rough summer Lisa'd had. Kramer's had terminated her job, the Frankels had left, and then Shaindy, of all people, had found a new job for her. A former neighbor of the Hirsches from Monsey had moved to Scottsdale and opened a select gift shop. She was looking for a manager. Lisa fit the job description and was hired on the spot. Before long, though, Lisa realized that the job was really just to be a glorified salesclerk. Although she didn't complain, Sondra knew her cousin well enough to understand that she wasn't happy with the job.

After her mother-in-law came, it was a ten-minute ride to the hospital. The surgical waiting room was bright and sunny, yet had a tense quiet about it. Next to the entrance sat two women, a mother and daughter. Under the windows was a Spanish-speaking family. Lisa was on the far side of the room, standing next to the water fountain and running her fingers nervously through her honey-blonde hair. The wig she'd bought with Rena was reserved for Shabbos and special occasions. During the week, her hair hung shoulder length and was stylishly done.

Now it was a mess, but Sondra refrained from saying so. Instead she gave Lisa a hug.

To Sondra's consternation, Lisa burst into tears.

"Lisa, I know it's scary, but it's really not a serious operation."

"I know." Lisa drew a tissue from her pocket and wiped her eyes, obviously embarrassed.

Sondra guided her cousin to sit down.

"I grabbed some fruit on the way out. Do you want some?"

"I guess so," Lisa said listlessly.

Sondra poked around Naomi's diaper bag and produced an apple. "How long's Kobi been in surgery?"

"About ten minutes."

"Where's Danny?"

"He's back on the floor. I have his beeper number if I need him." Lisa gave a half smile. "He's been really supportive."

"Good."

Lisa ate her apple in silence. "I *was* hungry," she admitted ruefully.

"Did you have lunch?"

"I forgot it at the store."

"Oh, no. I'm going to look for something for you."

Sondra wheeled Naomi out into the hall and found a bank of snack-food machines. The first machine was full of sandwiches, none of which were kosher, but the second one had a bag of Fritos. Maybe those would bring a smile to Lisa's face.

They did. Lisa eagerly tore open the bag and then politely offered some chips to her cousin.

Sondra just shook her head. "I still have at least six pounds to take off." She patted her stomach. "It gets harder with each baby."

To her dismay, Lisa started crying again.

"Lisa, don't you remember Cousin Oscar had a hernia operation last year? He was up and around in just a couple of weeks."

"You're right." Lisa blew her nose and gave a halfhearted smile. "What's with Zvi Chaim and Batsheva?"

"Shirley's watching them."

Lisa raised her eyebrows.

"Yeah," Sondra responded to the unasked question. "It was hard for me to ask her, but she was happy to do it. I mean, really happy. She loves her grandchildren and, the truth is, I think she loves me too, but we're just so different." Sondra was rattling on, eager to have Lisa's mind diverted from Kobi's surgery. "At least we have the kids in common. That gives us something to talk about. If it wasn't for..."

A tear trickled down Lisa's face as she listened to her cousin. Sondra noticed it and stopped short. She stood up, took Lisa's hands in hers, and looked down into her cousin's eyes.

"What is it?"

Lisa took a deep breath and exhaled.

"I've been taking my temperature for the last four months," she whispered. "Today was the first time in four months it was right, but I guess Hashem doesn't want me to have a baby."

"Oh, Lisa." Sondra bent down and put her arms around her cousin, whose face was wet with tears again. "You haven't been married *that* long."

"More than two years! I was patient the first year."

"Have you been to a specialist?"

"Kobi doesn't want to go. I went by myself. Believe me, it's not fun. I did all sorts of blood tests to check out my hormone levels. They seem to be okay, so I started taking my temperature, and now look what happened."

Sondra settled down in the seat next to her cousin, keeping Lisa's hands in hers. "Lisa, I remember learning that one of the reasons Sarah, Rivkah, and Rochel had such a hard time having children was to teach us not to give up hope. I...I had a miscarriage before Zvi Chaim, and knowing that really helped me."

Lisa's head snapped up. "I never knew you had a miscarriage."

"I never told anyone except Doc, and that was by accident."

"But Zvi Chaim was born after you'd been married just over a year."

"True, but at the time, I didn't know if I'd ever be able to carry a baby to term. I was really scared."

"And now you have three," Lisa said wistfully.

"Maybe you will too, one of these days."

"Maybe."

Lisa didn't sound all that optimistic, but the tears had stopped.

"Lisa," Sondra stroked her cousin's hand. "Did Kobi say why he doesn't want to go to the specialist?"

"Oh, Sondra, he's not like Danny, with a father and a grandfather in the medical profession. Half of Kobi's family would rather go to the graves of rabbis before going to a doctor. It's a different culture."

As Sondra absorbed Lisa's explanation the doors to the operating rooms opened and Lisa sat forward eagerly, but the nurse who came out went to the two women by the door.

"You know," Sondra offered tentatively, "the year I was in Israel, I saw women saying psalms all the time. It wouldn't hurt for us to say a couple of chapters now, but I don't have a *Tehillim* with me. Do you?"

"No, but when I was in third grade, we had to learn the twenty-third psalm by heart. For some program, I don't remember what. I remember it to this day, but, boy, does it feel different when Kobi sings it in Hebrew. The English seems so stilted. 'Yea, though I walk through the valley of the shadow of death, I will fear no evil...'"

Sondra smiled at Lisa's pompous tone. "We learned that chapter of *Tehillim* when I was in seminary. I remember being amazed that King David could really write 'only goodness and kindness pursue me.' I mean, *come on*, I don't want to sound disrespectful, but he had a lot pursuing him besides goodness and kindness. Yet his faith in Hashem was so strong that he believed even what we see as bad is good."

"I guess putting it in that perspective," Lisa mumbled, "I shouldn't complain about not having a baby."

"Oh Lisa!" Sondra cried out. "I didn't mean it that way. Of course you have a right to feel bad."

"But I have to remember all the good Hashem has done for me and be thankful for that."

"Wow, Lisa."

"What?"

"Sometimes you really impress me."

Lisa blushed and changed the subject. "Do you miss teaching this year?"

"Sometimes," Sondra admitted. "But I still have the two nights at Hebrew High."

Rabbi Levi had accepted her resignation gracefully and suggested she teach a class on the role of Jewish women to teenagers at the Jewish Community Center. That was where Danny had first been exposed to Yiddishkeit, and Sondra hoped she could have a positive influence on her students.

"It's nice not to have to get everyone dressed and out first thing in the morning," Sondra continued. "I figure I have another forty years until retirement. I'll go back to teaching second grade eventually."

"You know...," Lisa examined her nails as she spoke, "I'm thinking about teaching high school."

"Really?"

"They're beginning something new, Market Education — sort of a pre-business course. I'm qualified from my degree and experience. If I get teaching certification, my salary will go up."

Sondra was clearly amazed. "You always seemed to thrive on being in a department store."

"Well, yes, but this is related. And I won't have to worry about Shabbos."

Sondra nodded her head in understanding. Before she could comment, the nurse came out of the double doors once more and made her way to Lisa.

"Your husband's out of surgery and has been moved to the recovery room," she said. "We'll be calling you in shortly."

Lisa breathed a sigh of relief and Sondra smiled sympathetically.

"Take a few minutes now to go to the bathroom and wash your face and brush your hair," she instructed.

"I must look awful!"

"Not awful," Sondra was diplomatic, "but not as good as you usually look. You want Kobi to recognize you when he wakes up."

❀ ❀ ❀

Lisa never made it back to the store that day. Kobi was groggy, yet wanted her company. Although it was rather boring to watch him doze, she nevertheless sat patiently by his bedside. It was almost dinnertime when her friend Bayla swept into the room with a grocery bag that gave off delicious smells.

"I know Kobi can't eat yet," she grinned. "But you must be famished, Lisa."

She pulled two pieces of chicken, a salad, and a baked potato out of the bag and arranged them on a paper plate with plastic silverware.

"Eat," she instructed. "Sondra told me you had an apple and a bag of chips for lunch."

Lisa glanced anxiously at her husband.

"Don't worry about me," he smiled. "I'm getting plenty to eat." He motioned to the IV bag. "Besides, don't waste your time trying to say no to Bayla."

"He's right." Bayla pulled a vacant chair over from the other side of the room and settled herself in for a visit. "You should know, Lisa, that we have Shabbos all planned for you. I'm making challah and Sondra's doing the soup..."

Bayla rattled off the rest of the menu. Lisa noticed that Shaindy Hirsch's name was missing from the list, but made no comment. Perhaps Shaindy thought she'd done her fair share by finding a job for Lisa.

Putting that thought aside, Lisa impulsively grabbed her friend's hand. "I really thank you for all your organizing and help, Bayla, but Kobi's the one who's sick, not me."

"Yes," Bayla retorted, "and we all know that Kobi helps in the kitchen a lot. Besides, I'm sure he'll be an ornery patient, like most men, and run you ragged." Bayla gave Kobi a mischievous grin, but he was sleeping again, oblivious to what she had said. "Also, Lisa," Bayla continued more seriously, "you help everyone out when they need it. It's your turn to get a little spoiling."

Lisa swallowed the lump in her throat. It was true. Any time someone in the community gave birth, they could count on her to make a meal and a cake. Now there was finally a reason for others to reciprocate. Only it wasn't the reason Lisa wanted.

If Bayla noticed Lisa's discomfort, she gave no indication. She stayed for a quarter of an hour and chatted about all sorts of amusing things going on in the community. At the end of the visit, Lisa walked her to the elevator and returned to the room refreshed and ready to deal with her "ornery patient."

❋ ❋ ❋

Kobi really wasn't that ornery. He was released the following afternoon and Lisa picked him up on her way home from the store. On Friday night, as they ate Brachie's pareve ice cream, she brought up the subject of her temperature.

"I didn't want to tell you," Lisa confessed. "I didn't want you to feel bad, but it's been eating at me and I thought you should know."

"I'm glad you feel comfortable talking to me," Kobi said, smiling at her.

Lisa smiled back. "So," she raised her hands in question, "do you want to try going back to the specialist with me?"

"No," Kobi replied shortly.

"No?"

"No," Kobi repeated. His eyes were hard and stubborn. "Lisa, suppose we go through all the tests and we find out that you can't have a baby? I'm not going to divorce you and get a new wife. What are you going to do if you find out *I* can't have kids? Divorce me?"

Lisa shook her head silently. Already she regretted mentioning going to the specialist again.

"So what are we going to accomplish by doing the tests? I'm going to get my stitches out next week and I hope I don't have to go to a doctor again for a very long time. I've had my share, thank you."

"But..." Lisa played with her ice cream.

"But what?" Kobi frowned.

"What if they find a problem that can be solved?"

"You obviously have a lot more faith in doctors than I do. Can we say *Birkat HaMazon* already? I'm tired from sitting up."

He rose from his chair with a grimace of pain, took a deep breath, and walked slowly toward their room. After four steps, he paused, turned, and eyed his wife compassionately.

"Next time we go to Israel, we can pray at Kever Rochel if you'd like."

Lisa nodded and that was the end of the conversation. Shabbos morning Kobi didn't go to shul, of course, but a number of visitors popped in during the afternoon. When Danny came for their learning session, Lisa slipped out to Bayla's. Sometimes it was worth the longer walk to sit and visit with her friend who didn't have little children constantly interrupting.

As Lisa walked back to her apartment, she contemplated how different her life would be if she ever did have a baby. Maybe Kobi was right and she should be more patient.

That evening, after she had put away the last of the Shabbos china, she pulled the thermometer out of her nightstand drawer and slipped it back into the medicine cabinet where it belonged. For the time being, at least, she would leave matters up to Hashem.

CHAPTER
Seventeen

Sondra had her head in the empty refrigerator and a bucket of soapy water by her side. Methodically, she dipped her rag into the bucket, squeezed out the excess water, and rubbed down the walls of the fridge. When she'd finally finished, she sat back on her heels to survey her work. The inside of the refrigerator was sparkling. Now she just had the shelves waiting for her in the bathtub. She pushed the hair that had escaped her scarf away from her brow and checked her watch. It was only three-fifteen. She was doing fine.

The plan had been for Shirley's cleaning lady to wash out the refrigerator, but Carmen had called earlier that morning to say she was feeling sick and wouldn't be coming in that day; maybe tomorrow she'd feel better. With Pesach a week away, Sondra wasn't willing to depend on any maybes. She was feeling quite discouraged when her mother-in-law called just a half an hour after Carmen.

"I heard Carmen has the flu," Shirley said, getting straight to the point.

"Yeah," Sondra sighed. "I was going to have her do the fridge today. I guess I'll attack it tonight after the kids are in bed."

"I have a better idea."

"What?"

"I'll pick up Zvi Chaim from nursery school and take him and the girls for a fun afternoon, and you can do the refrigerator then."

"Really?" Sondra felt as if Shirley had just offered her a million dollars.

"Sure, and we'll come get you at six and go out to the deli for supper. How does that sound?"

"It sounds like heaven." Sondra wasn't exaggerating. The kitchen was practically empty except for food for Shabbos and a frozen chicken and rice casserole that she was saving for tomorrow when Danny came home. She hoped that by Saturday night he'd have enough energy to kasher the oven and then they could switch the kitchen over to Pesach dishes. With the holiday beginning Wednesday night and then going into Shabbos, she needed at least four days to get the cooking done. What a lousy time for Carmen to be sick and Danny to be away.

She had no complaints about Danny's trip to visit medical practices, though. She'd been waiting ever since they came to Phoenix for him to do these interviews. Together they'd chosen three cities for him to check out: Denver, St. Louis, and Chicago. Tomorrow he'd be home and then they'd weigh his findings and make a decision. Whatever the decision, Sondra knew they'd be moving to a stronger Jewish community. And they promised each other that after several years, maybe they could begin thinking about moving to Israel.

The next day, Stacy babysat when Sondra drove to the airport. Although he was worn out from visiting three cities in just as many days, Danny fully reported his views of the communities and the pediatric practices he'd seen. By the time they entered their apartment, it was clear that his first choice was St. Louis. He didn't need to give the doctors an answer for another two weeks, but Danny and Sondra made their decision that night. With their choice made, they were able to go forward with Pesach preparations.

❁　❁　❁

The first night Seder was a relatively small crowd for Sondra and Danny, with only Shirley, Doc, Lisa, and Kobi as guests. Danny kept things moving along for his parents' sake, and Zvi Chaim was able to stay up until after the meal.

Thursday night was a different story. They had a crowd and there were lively discussions. No one seemed to mind that they finished the Seder at almost two in the morning.

Sondra was thankful that they'd been invited out for lunch the second day. What a treat it was to wheel the baby stroller to shul on the holidays. How she wished that Phoenix had an *eruv* so she could do it every Shabbos.

She and Danny hosted more guests Friday night and Shabbos lunch. By the time they cleared the table Saturday afternoon, they both felt like they were falling off their feet. Miraculously, all three children fell asleep, and Danny and Sondra were able to nap at the same time.

Sondra took a book to bed with her, but didn't even remember opening it. Her head hit the pillow and she was out cold. She'd been sleeping all of forty-five minutes when loud banging awakened her. Totally disoriented, she saw that Danny was already up.

"I'll get it," he mumbled.

"Get what?" she asked groggily.

"The door."

So that's what the banging was. Curious, Sondra pulled herself out of bed, grabbed a snood, fastened a robe around herself, and followed Danny. She was surprised to see Doc's non-Jewish partner, Dr. Taylor. She was even more surprised — and dismayed — to hear what their visitor was saying.

"I know you don't drive on your Sabbath, but I'm going right back to the hospital and I think I should take you with me. Your father's asking for you."

When Danny turned to his wife, his face was drawn. "Dad had a heart attack and it doesn't look good. I'll go with Dr. Taylor."

"On Shabbos?" Sondra gasped.

"It's a matter of life and death." Her husband raised his fist to his mouth and visibly composed himself.

Sondra nodded her understanding. "Doctor, let me give you a bag for Danny."

It took her just a minute to throw in some food and a book of Psalms for her husband. Dr. Taylor would carry, open the car door, and drive for him.

Sondra had never spent such a long Shabbos afternoon. Once the children woke from their naps, it seemed as if they asked nonstop where their father was. Sondra alternated her time between saying *Tehillim*, reading nursery rhymes, playing memory games, and trying not to worry.

What a relief it was to make Havdalah. She knew she should start bathing the children or begin cleaning up, but somehow she felt paralyzed, waiting for the phone to ring.

It did, thirteen minutes after Shabbos ended. Danny was serious and guardedly told her that his father was in intensive care, but stable.

"It looks like he might pull through."

"*Baruch Hashem*." Sondra blinked back tears of relief. "Zvi Chaim and Batsheva, Grandpa is doing a little better."

Zvi Chaim gave a whoop. Batsheva smiled, more or less oblivious to the seriousness of the situation.

"How's your mother doing?" Sondra returned her attention to her husband.

"Dorothy's here. She got a flight as soon as she heard. She's keeping Mom calm. I think Mom'll sleep up here. Dorothy will probably go to the condominium."

"And you?"

"I'll come home about midnight. I have to be on the floor at seven."

"Okay." Sondra felt energized. "I'll clean up here and get a sitter and come be with you and your mother."

"I'm looking forward to seeing you," Danny said softly.

"Me too."

CHAPTER
Eighteen

Sondra sat on a boulder staring at the clear, blue sky. Here she could believe she was as far from the city as she was when she wandered in her father's pasture in Lincoln. Facing south was the panorama of Phoenix and its suburbs spread in front of her. Facing any other direction, though, she saw saguaro cacti, juniper trees, and desert wildlife.

Before leaving the hospital, she'd used Doc's bedside phone to call home. Stacy, the babysitter, was giving the kids their supper and everything was under control. So before going to the apartment, she made a detour to Squaw Peak Park, the nature reserve inside the city, just a ten-minute ride from their home.

Doc had been out of the ICU already four days, and with the danger behind him, Dorothy had returned to Chicago. He was getting stronger and there was talk of him being released soon. But he would be released with a lot of restrictions, including substantially cutting back on his work hours. That wasn't going to be easy for him. He and Ed Taylor had built up their practice from a simple partnership to a large family clinic. They'd offered the opening for a third pediatrician to Danny back in January, but he'd declined, determined to take his family to a stronger religious environment. Doc had accepted his decision gracefully then. Now he was no longer doing so. He complained daily to Sondra that he wouldn't be able to give his all to the practice and how he'd anticipated Danny coming in and making sure everything was going as Doc wanted.

Sondra never knew how to respond. If her father-in-law's dream of taking Danny into the practice came true, her dream of living in a stronger community was doomed. Whose dream was more important?

It wasn't just for herself that Sondra wanted to move, but for her children. She'd known what it was like to grow up different from everyone else. Just yesterday, she and Brachie Fisch had been discussing the challenge. One of the boys in the nursery school was having a birthday party at his home on Sunday and all the children were invited. The only problem was that Robert's house wasn't kosher. Brachie had spoken to the mother and suggested all sorts of kosher refreshments that could be bought and served, but the mother was adamant that Robert wanted a cake baked by her.

"So," Brachie had decided, "I told her that Ariela wouldn't be able to come. I'm going to take her to the zoo instead. Do you want to come with us?"

Sondra had shaken her head. The Phoenix Zoo was lovely in the winter, but a sauna the rest of the year. Besides, Robert was Zvi Chaim's best friend and he was determined to go to the party. So Sondra had baked a batch of cupcakes and put one on the side for her son to take with him.

"It's just that I don't know how to explain to him *why* Robert doesn't keep kosher," she had fretted to Brachie.

"You told me you always felt special growing up and not eating pork like everyone else did."

"Yes," Sondra had retorted. "I felt special because I was different from the non-Jews. What's my explanation for Zvi Chaim being different than Robert? If I make excuses for them not keeping kosher, it's like *kashrus* isn't that important. And if I tell Zvi Chaim that they're wrong, it's like I'm condemning them."

"Just tell him that no one explained the beauty of mitzvos to Robert's parents." Brachie, having grown up in an observant home, was far more relaxed than Sondra was. "Zvi Chaim can understand that."

"Yeah," Sondra had quipped, "he can set the world's record for the youngest outreach worker."

That quip had nagged at her all day, though. Outreach work was important and she was doing some with the Hebrew High. Both of the girls who'd been with them for Seder were interested in coming back for Shabbos. Another student had discussed with her the idea of learning in an Israeli seminary the following year. Would she be able to have that kind of influence in St. Louis?

Still, she wasn't willing to make Phoenix her permanent home. She saw how the Levis and some of the other families sent their teenagers to Denver for high school. They came home three times a year: Sukkos, Chanukah, and Pesach. There was no way that in ten years' time she was going to send Zvi Chaim away like that!

Suppose, though, that they agreed to give Phoenix three more years, just like they planned to give St. Louis, and then they would think about moving to Israel. There, he'd have his pick of friends from kosher homes. In the meantime, he and Batsheva had each other, as well as Ariela and the new teacher's four-year-old twins. But how much longer would those teachers stay in Phoenix? Brachie always joked that the day school movement was so called because of all the moving the teachers did from one city to another. Sondra didn't think the joke was very funny.

How would she manage for another three years in Phoenix if Brachie moved? She'd still have Lisa until Kobi decided it was time to move back to Israel. Bayla was a dear, but she was old enough to be Sondra's mother. Shaindy wasn't going anywhere, but Sondra couldn't really call Shaindy, with all her complaining, a friend. Of course, there was Danny.

As Sondra brooded, the sun began setting, casting magnificent shadows on the rocks. There would be no sunsets like this in St. Louis. It wasn't an easy decision, but by the time she'd hiked down to the parking lot, her mind was made up. She was willing, if Danny wanted, to give another three years to her father-in-law.

※　※　※

Rabbi Levi received the news of the Kleins' change of plans warmly. He'd been satisfied with Sondra as a teacher and was pleased that she was interested in returning to the staff in addition to staying on in Phoenix.

"I have to tell you, though, that I promised the second-grade class to the wife of the new teacher. However," Rabbi Levi drummed his fingers on his desk thoughtfully, "the sixth grade class happens to be only girls. Perhaps instead of having one of the rabbis teaching them religious studies, it would be better to have a woman. Would you be interested in doing that under my constant supervision?"

Sondra didn't answer immediately. Sixth grade would be more challenging than second, but the challenge interested her.

"Would it be the same hours?" she asked cautiously.

"Yes, and I'll let you in on a secret. We're making plans to open a high school and a day care center here on the campus."

Sondra's eyes opened wide at the news.

"Rabbi Levi, sixth grade sounds really interesting. Let me discuss it with Danny and get back to you."

"Okay," Rabbi Levi agreed. "Sondra, I want you to know you and Danny add a lot to the community. We're glad you've decided to stay."

Lisa was just as enthusiastic as Rabbi Levi was. She'd been accepted to teach at the local high school the coming fall and was getting ready to work on her teaching certification. Instead of making the forty-five minute commute to ASU, she'd found a Christian college close by where she could take her courses. In the beginning, Sondra had been horrified at the idea, but Lisa had laughed at her cousin's reaction.

"Don't worry," she said. "They're not going to convert me. I'll sit in the back and not socialize. Besides, it's more comfortable there than at ASU. At least the Christian students dress more reasonably."

Sondra refrained from reminding Lisa how she used to dress. Gone were her shorts and tank tops. Now Lisa had two wigs, one for everyday and one for Shabbos.

Helga, too, had been thrilled with her daughter and son-in-law's decision, which surprised Sondra.

"I thought you'd want us in St. Louis. It's closer."

"Not really," Helga had explained during their weekly long-distance phone call. "A ten-hour drive is much farther than an hour-and-a-half flight, even if we have to drive an hour to the airport. Besides," she added, "Phoenix is a lovely place to visit."

Sondra felt a warm glow after that phone call. Her father had found someone to help out with the cows, and now, twice a year, her parents took four days off to come for a visit.

The most enthusiastic about Sondra's decision was Shirley. Not an hour after Danny informed his father of his acceptance of the position in the practice, Sondra's phone rang. She quickly wiped the Play-Doh off her hands and wasn't surprised to hear her mother-in-law on the line.

"Sondra, is it okay if I stop by for a bit?"

"Of course," Sondra answered graciously. She had to give her mother-in-law credit for never dropping by unannounced.

When Shirley arrived, she had a houseplant of sunflowers in her hands, as well as gifts for the children. Sondra couldn't help but laugh at the present her mother-in-law had picked out for her. Although sunflowers were the Kansas state flower, Sondra had never liked them, but she wouldn't tell Shirley that now. Just one more proof of how little the older woman understood her. At least, Sondra reminded herself, Shirley was trying. Her mother-in-law was lavish with her appreciation.

"You won't believe the difference in Doc since Danny spoke to him," Shirley declared. "His color is better. He can sit up straighter. I know it's going to speed up his recuperation." Shirley took a deep breath. "It wasn't an easy decision for Danny and he wouldn't have made it without your support. Thank you, Sondra." She took a tissue from her purse and wiped her eyes.

"Why you crying, Grandma?" Batsheva placed her chubby hands on Shirley's cheeks and peered at her grandmother's face with concern.

Shirley laughed self-consciously. "They're happy tears. I'm happy because Grandpa's getting better."

"I miss Grandpa."

"Would you like to visit him in the hospital?" Shirley suggested.

Batsheva nodded seriously.

"Me too!" Zvi Chaim exclaimed.

Shirley exchanged glances with her daughter-in-law.

"Do you think Doc's up to an invasion?" Sondra asked.

"Yes, I do," Shirley spoke decisively.

She helped Sondra get the children ready for the outing. It was only in the car, halfway to the hospital, that Sondra realized she'd never acknowledged her mother-in-law's appreciation. It was just as well. There were no words for all her conflicting emotions.

CHAPTER
Nineteen

Although they were among the first to deplane, Lisa and Kobi were the very last from their flight to go through Customs. It was all because of the battered, gray suitcase that had inside it, among other items, the new, powder-blue suit that Lisa had bought for the wedding. They'd seen the ticket agent tag that suitcase the same as their three other bags, but all the luggage had been taken off their flight and the gray suitcase was nowhere to be found.

Lisa let Kobi deal with the El Al agent. Her Hebrew had made great strides in the three years she'd been married, but when she was tired or upset, she could only manage well in English. Now she was both. The trip had been exhausting and she wanted that powder-blue suit. It'd caught her eye before Pesach, but was absurdly expensive. She watched as it was marked down, first 10 percent, then 15. The day after it hit 25 percent off, Kobi's sister, Riki, called with the news that she was engaged.

There was no question about going to the wedding. The next day, Kobi requested a two-week vacation in August. Lisa notified Shaindy's friend that she'd be quitting in the middle of July, instead of a month later. On the way home from work, she bought the suit.

"We'll put a tracer on the bag," the El Al agent informed Kobi after he finished filling out the various forms. "Hopefully, you'll be hearing from us in a day or two."

Lisa groaned. The wedding was in two days.

"Don't worry," Kobi assured her as they walked through customs. "Even if you have to wear your Shabbat dress, you'll look lovely."

The compliment warmed Lisa, and she was smiling when they exited the airport and were greeted by the hot Mediterranean sun and swarms of Israelis waiting for their loved ones. Toward the back of the crowd, she was able to spot her father-in-law. As they drew closer, she saw her mother-in-law standing next to him.

"Kobi, Lisa," Shula called shrilly.

Tzachi elbowed his way through the crowd, grabbed his son, and kissed him warmly on both cheeks. He turned to Lisa and did the same. His dark moustache tickled and, although Lisa hadn't minded this kind of greeting when she first met Kobi's father, it now bothered her. Her smile was a little forced when Shula gave her the same greeting.

"Lisa, what's happened to your long, beautiful hair?" Shula cried.

"It's still there," Kobi hastily explained. "Lisa covers her hair now."

"Very nice," Shula said politely.

"Now that you're so religious, maybe you can give me a grandson," Tzachi interjected jovially.

Lisa cringed, but no one noticed. Kobi was preoccupied with making sure none of the suitcases fell off the luggage cart. Tzachi was searching for the car and Shula was chattering away about wedding plans.

Lately it seemed to Lisa that everyone was reminding her of her barrenness. Last month, her old roommate Carol, of all people, had called to tell her she was expecting. She and Bill were so involved with their family counseling center in Tucson that Lisa hadn't dreamed they would be starting a family of their own. Excited, Carol was totally oblivious to the envy her announcement stirred in Lisa.

The next day, Sondra had stopped by and announced ecstatically, "I'm an aunt! Danny's sister had twin girls!" Lisa had smiled bravely and wished her mazal tov.

On the plane, when they first settled into their places, the woman sitting next to Lisa had made friendly conversation. She was from Detroit, a bank teller, and this was her first visit to Israel. Lisa had answered her overtures courteously, but had frozen when the woman asked how many children she had. Replying shortly that she had none, she turned to Kobi before she could see the pity in the woman's eyes.

The worst, though, had been the Hirsches' bris the same day as their flight. Lisa had endured Shaindy's complaints all through the pregnancy. While others listened and ignored her, Lisa felt like it was all she could do to keep from screaming at the woman.

Finally, she broke down and spoke to Sondra at the library. Zvi Chaim and Batsheva were with the librarian for story hour and the two cousins were able to visit quietly in the reading room. It wasn't *lashon hara*, Lisa justified herself; if she didn't talk to someone, she would probably strangle Shaindy.

"I would give my eyeteeth to be pregnant and hot and nauseous and have swollen feet, whatever. She's so insensitive to complain to *me* nonstop."

"Um-hum," Sondra had agreed softly.

"She's always complaining, not just about the pregnancy, but about everything. Have you *ever* heard her say something good about anything in Phoenix?"

"Not that I remember."

"I've invited her at least half a dozen times for a Shabbos meal and she's never once invited us. Has she invited you?"

"No, but I've only invited her twice."

"There has to be a reason for this," Lisa insisted.

"We should give her the benefit of the doubt," Sondra said. "Can you come up with a story to explain this?"

Lisa took a deep breath. "They didn't move here because her husband's job was transferred, but because Shaindy has some rare disease; she can't cook or she'll transfer the disease to us."

Sondra rolled her eyes. "That's a good one, but how can she cook for her family and be pregnant?"

"So you do better."

Sondra was lost in silence for a good five minutes while Lisa read the first few pages of the novel she'd picked out.

"How about this? Back in Monsey they were very rich and had a full-time cook, but Shaindy's husband witnessed a Mafia murder and went into the Federal Witness Protection Program, so they had to leave it all behind, and she doesn't know how to cook, so she just serves frozen food all the time."

"That's good," Lisa chuckled. "Hard to swallow, but good."

Before Sondra could respond, the story hour ended.

"I guess the bottom line," Sondra whispered as she rose to greet her children, "is that she needs our support."

"I'll try and stay patient." Lisa sighed.

Apparently she was successful because Shaindy called two days after she came home from the hospital.

"You're not supposed to invite people to a bris," she explained, "but I'm not sure how many people in this G-d-forsaken town understand that. Whatever," Shaindy continued. "We really hope you will be at the bris on Sunday?"

"Of course," Lisa dutifully answered. "Is there anything I can do to help?"

"No, the meal is catered at our house, at noon. The *mohel* is flying in that morning."

Instead of a baby outfit, Lisa picked out a family game as a present. She and Kobi arrived right on time and discovered that the two of them were supposed to be the godparents, the ones to bring the baby to the *mohel* at the beginning of the ceremony. Lisa knew it was an honor often given to a childless couple and wanted to decline. Kobi wouldn't let her.

"Who knows," he whispered. "It might work."

Certain that all the eyes focusing on her were feeling sorry for her, Lisa took the infant from his mother and handed him to Kobi. As soon as they could leave the meal politely, though, they said their goodbyes. Thank goodness their flight was leaving that evening.

* * *

"These are the new apartments they've finished building. We wanted to buy Riki an apartment here."

Busy with her musings, Lisa had fallen asleep, and now they were already in Beit She'an. Disoriented, she awoke as Tzachi parked the car in his special space under the building which held the Chazons' apartment. As Lisa trudged up the two and a half flights of stairs, she was struck, as always, by the contrast between the stark cement entranceway and the ornate furnishings of the apartment where Kobi had grown up. Tzachi's grocery had done well and he'd furnished his home accordingly.

When she entered the front room, Lisa's eyes were drawn to the wall behind the sofa. There hung a series of pictures, a shrine to Uri, Kobi's older brother. If he were still alive, he'd be twenty-nine. In her parents' home, the pictures of her brother, Howie, stayed in a special box in the living room cabinet. This was Lisa's third visit to Israel, and yet she was still drawn to the pictures. While she studied them, she tried, unsuccessfully, to stifle a yawn.

Shula, with her ever-discerning eyes, noticed.

"Why don't you go into your room and put your feet up," she suggested. "Riki will be here in about an hour and we'll wake you then."

"That sounds wonderful," Lisa answered gratefully.

It was Riki who woke her up. Ever since Sondra had suggested that Kobi's sister be her bridesmaid, there'd been a good rapport between the two young women. Now Riki couldn't wait to show Lisa her engagement ring.

"It's beautiful," Lisa exclaimed over the modest diamond in a silver setting.

"I think so!" Riki concurred. "Abba thinks it's too small and Efraim is being cheap."

"No!"

Riki nodded complacently. "Abba likes to show off, and Efraim and I intend to live within our means."

As she readjusted her wig, Lisa studied her sister-in-law. Riki was no longer ten pounds overweight and her clothing didn't strain against her skin as it had during their previous visits. Her hair was loose from the ponytail she'd always worn and now hung smoothly to her shoulders. Most importantly, her eyes were shining and she appeared to be truly happy.

Riki, in turn, observed Lisa carefully. She made no comment about the head covering, but then, she'd always been rather apathetic about her brother's religious observances.

"Hurry up." She pushed Lisa toward the door. "I want you to meet Efraim."

Efraim was a classic redhead, with blue eyes and freckles, obviously Ashkenazi. Lisa had the distinct feeling as they entered the living room that he and Kobi had been in the middle of a heated discussion. Tzachi was glowering and Shula looked worried, but Riki appeared totally unconcerned. She settled herself on the sofa next to Efraim, who smiled warmly at her.

"What are you two arguing about?" she asked.

"We're not arguing," Kobi answered defensively.

"I was just telling your brother how I grew up on a religious kibbutz, and he was surprised that I stopped wearing my *kippah*."

"Which kibbutz?" Lisa interjected quickly.

"Sde Moshe, not far from here."

"It's just down the road from the kibbutz where your mother's cousin Leah lives," Kobi added.

"The wedding's going to be at Sde Moshe," Shula said.

"Like I can't afford a wedding in a nice hall!" Tzachi exclaimed.

"Where is there a nice hall in Beit She'an?" Riki asked scornfully.

"We could have made a fine wedding in Tiberias."

"And make everyone drive that far just to show off?" Riki shook her head from side to side.

"Who's showing off? I want everyone to know how much I love my daughter and how much I'm willing to spend on her."

"So spend the money on an apartment for us." Riki's eyes were no longer shining with happiness. They were dark with anger.

"If you'd live in the new apartments here, I'd be happy to."

"Ramat Gan is not the end of the earth," Riki shot back. "And it's a lot closer than America!"

Tzachi's face was flushed and wet with perspiration. Before he could answer, Shula put a protective arm on his shoulder and whispered softly in his ear. With considerable effort, he seemed to get himself under control.

"Kobi, Lisa, I'm so sorry. Come, let's sit down at the table. Ima has made us a feast."

It was a feast, but the underlying atmosphere was tense.

"How did you two meet?" Lisa made an effort to lighten the mood.

Efraim grinned. "In the army. It's crazy. We grew up fifteen kilometers from each other, but had to go almost all the way to Eilat to meet!"

Lisa and Shula laughed with appreciation. The others managed smiles.

"The truth is," Efraim continued, "I used to stop in Tzachi's grocery to buy treats we never had on the kibbutz. I never dreamed that the owner would become my father-in-law."

Even Tzachi laughed at that comment.

"So now you can have all the ice cream bars you want for free," Riki announced. "Right, Abba?"

"I guess I don't have a choice," Tzachi grumbled with a half smile.

The wedding was pleasant, although nothing like Lisa and Kobi's at the Camelback Inn. Lisa's suitcase was found in time, but, as Kobi had said, she would have been fine in her Shabbos dress. Many of the kibbutz members, all of whom were invited, came in their work clothes. It was easy to tell who was there from the bride's side and who from the groom's. There was little, if any, mixing between the two groups.

On the evening following the wedding, Lisa found her in-laws' apartment stifling — and not just from the lack of air-conditioning. She suggested to Kobi that they take a walk in the nearby park that was built around some Roman ruins, and he readily agreed. He felt he couldn't listen to one more complaint about Efraim being Ashkenazi and how the cultural differences between him and Riki would doom the marriage.

"Is that the way your father felt about me?" Lisa asked her husband warily as they circled the Roman columns.

"I don't think so," Kobi answered carefully. "I wasn't here, of course, but from what Riki said, I think he was relieved just that I had found someone Jewish. His sole complaint about you is that he thinks you're the one keeping us in America."

"*You* know that's not true," Lisa tried not to sound defensive.

"I know," Kobi reassured her hastily. "I'm the one dragging my feet. I just want to make sure I have enough experience to land a good job here when we move back."

"*When* or *if?*" Lisa questioned her husband gently. "Maybe you should do some job hunting and investigating while we're here."

"Maybe." Kobi wasn't willing to commit himself.

"Only..." Lisa hesitated.

"What? "

Lisa felt the smoothness of one of the Roman stones and avoided looking at Kobi. "I don't think I could handle living in Beit She'an so close to your parents."

"You don't think you could handle it!" Kobi burst out laughing. "I know I can't!"

Lisa breathed a sigh of relief and her laughter blended with his.

CHAPTER

Twenty

"Eliezer said that if we take the bus to Ashkelon, he'll pick us up," Kobi told Lisa later that week. "They're a half-hour drive from there."

"That means we won't be in Jerusalem for Shabbos."

"He said we'd have a really meaningful Shabbat, even without the *Kotel*. Do you want to go?"

"What do you think we should do?" Lisa chewed her bottom lip.

"I think it might be interesting. Besides, we don't have anyone in Jerusalem inviting us for Shabbat."

"That's true," Lisa admitted.

Little did she realize that their decision for that Shabbos would completely change their lives. Six months earlier, the Glinkers, their friends from Los Angeles, had moved out of their nice, convenient apartment in Jerusalem and relocated to a tiny mobile home in the middle of the Gaza Strip.

When the Chazons met Eliezer at the Ashkelon bus station, they saw that their friend hadn't just changed his address. Although he was still tall and bearded, his pale face was suntanned and weather-beaten, and his arms were muscular. Instead of a suit, he was dressed in jeans and a work shirt. Most surprising was the M16 thrown casually over his shoulder.

With little effort, he took Kobi's bag from him. Finding room for it in the back of the crowded Peugeot station wagon was a different story.

"Whenever I come to town, Tamar gives me a shopping list a mile long," he explained sheepishly.

"Don't you have a grocery store?" Kobi stared at the bags full of staples and fresh produce, as well as a cooler obviously full of perishables.

Eliezer shook his head and snapped down the back door. "The Shekem truck comes twice a week, but sometimes it's out of things."

"What's a Shekem truck?"

Eliezer started the engine. "Shekem's a department store for army personnel and they send out trucks full of merchandise to the outlying areas."

"What kind of place do you live in?" Alone in the backseat, Lisa was looking for her seat belt. She didn't find it and gave up.

"You're not going to believe it when you see it," her host chuckled. "We've joined a new moshav."

"You're a farmer!" Kobi exclaimed. "What about your degree from UCLA?"

"There's not a lot I can do with a history degree besides teach, and I really don't enjoy teaching. I learn in the mornings, and in the afternoons, I grow flowers."

"There's an income in that?" Kobi asked, still in astonishment.

"There will be," Eliezer answered confidently.

"Is Tamar also growing flowers?" Lisa sat forward with her head between the two men.

"Tamar works two long days in a dental clinic in Sderot. Honestly, it's her income that's keeping us going until the flower business gets on its feet."

As they left Ashkelon, the Mediterranean seemed to get bluer. Lisa decided it was because they were far away from all of the Tel Aviv pollution. Fifteen minutes later, Eliezer pulled off the highway, drove through an Arab village, and turned down a narrow blacktop road. To the right there was a plantation of date palms.

"What's the weather like here?" Kobi asked.

"It's like Los Angeles. My neighbor is growing dates too."

For the next five minutes, Kobi and Lisa marveled at the scenery. Suddenly there was a sign welcoming them to Mizpeh Itzhak. Eliezer waved to the guard in the shack at the entrance.

"That's my neighbor, Moshe," he remarked. "He's spending Shabbat in Ashdod with his in-laws, so you'll be staying in his place."

He continued driving on what seemed like a dirt path. Except for the hothouses, there wasn't one permanent structure in sight; rather, sixteen mobile homes — caravans, Eliezer called them — were arranged in a large circle on a bed of white sand. In the middle of the circle was a double caravan that served as the synagogue. Next to it was a shiny, new children's playground. Eliezer drove up to the caravan with American lawn chairs in front of it and Tamar came running out.

Eliezer was right about his assessment of Shabbat. Lisa marveled at the easy, two-minute stroll to the synagogue. After morning services, the rabbi talked to both of them about joining the moshav. Only several years older than they, he spoke eloquently about rebuilding the Land of Israel. Still, it wasn't until the last meal of the afternoon that Lisa could imagine herself doing such a thing.

There was a good half an hour before sundown when Kobi helped Eliezer move their dining table outside near the synagogue. The same activity was going on in all of the caravans. Once the tables were outside, the women brought tablecloths and food, and the men brought the chairs. In a few minutes, everyone was seated outside, enjoying a communal meal. There was a baby stroller next to almost every table and a handful of preschoolers took over the playground. While they were eating, the rabbi stood up to say a *d'var Torah*, and then the singing began.

It was at that moment Lisa decided she would love to live in a place like Mizpeh Itzhak. Her eyes locked with her husband's, and she saw he was just as enchanted as she was.

After Havdalah, they talked about practicalities with the Glinkers.

"I just can't see myself farming." Kobi shrugged. "I have a profession that I can use in Israel."

"Then you might want to check out some of the community villages in Yehudah or the Shomron," Tamar suggested.

"How far away are they from the center of the country?" Lisa asked.

"We have friends who joined a group that is planning to break ground about thirty-five kilometers east of Kfar Saba."

"That wouldn't be far from the electronic industry," Kobi said thoughtfully. "It wouldn't hurt for us to talk to your friends."

"It would be better to speak to the head of the group," Eliezer suggested.

He took Kobi to the moshav office to use the only telephone. Avi Ben David would meet with them Sunday morning in Kfar Saba.

The next day, they caught the seven-fifteen bus from Ashkelon and arrived at their appointment right on time. Avi welcomed them with glasses of juice as they sat down in his cluttered office. He explained that the new settlement would be situated on a mountaintop that had a breathtaking view, and among the industries they wanted to develop was tourism.

"Of course, with only eight families, there are a lot of other things to get started first." Avi laughed heartily. A big man, his belly shook as he laughed, something he did often.

"Would I have to work in the settlement?" Kobi asked warily.

"No." Avi laughed again. "You can do whatever you want — within reason, of course."

"What sorts of things couldn't we do?"

"Kfar Yonatan is going to be a religious village. We'll expect our members to act accordingly."

"Observe Shabbat," Kobi offered.

"Of course, and modest dress, and a kosher kitchen. Not just that, though. We want people who understand that following the Torah and settling the land is the most important thing they can do with their lives." Avi laughed a little self-consciously. "So do you want to sign up?"

"Maybe," Kobi said. "There's one thing that bothers me, though."

"Yes?" Avi asked.

"When Israel signed the peace treaty with Egypt, they agreed to give away Yamit and some moshavim. Couldn't that happen here too?"

"It could happen anywhere," Avi answered seriously. "For all I know, the government could sign a peace treaty with Jordan and give away Jerusalem." He tossed his hands in the air impatiently. "I really don't understand some of the politicians' Land-for-Peace philosophy. Why can't we have peace for peace? When all's said and done, we just have to trust Hashem."

"I see." Kobi stroked his chin. "I guess there are no guarantees."

"No." Avi shook his head and then turned to Lisa, who had been listening silently. "What do you think?"

"It sounds exciting, but I'd like to meet some of the women in the group."

"Of course," Avi exclaimed with a laugh. "There are two families from Ra'anana, one couple from Petach Tikva, three from Netanya, and another from Jerusalem. I'll give you their numbers and you can set up meetings with whomever you want."

"I can't commit to anything yet," Kobi hesitated, "but I like you and I like what you have to say."

"I like you too," Avi responded impulsively and laughed. "I'll give you the forms and you can think it over. Call me before you go back to America and tell me where you're holding."

●　●　●

They did meet the three families in Netanya, and Lisa was relieved to discover that two of the women and one of the men in the founding group were native English speakers.

"I don't think I could go to a totally Israeli place right from the start," she explained to Kobi as their flight took off.

"I understand," Kobi said, and he did. After spending seven years in America, he wasn't sure how ready he was either.

"When do you think you'll hear from Israel Aircraft?"

"I don't know. The interview went well. If they don't hire me, someone else will."

"But you didn't say anything to your parents yet, right?"

"Right! No point getting them excited if it doesn't work out. But they'll sure be happy when we move back."

Lisa nodded. She wished her parents would be as happy. Thinking about telling them their plans gave her butterflies in her stomach. As a matter of fact, she felt queasy and nauseous. An hour into the flight, she decided it wasn't just nerves about her father. She shouldn't have eaten that baklava Shula had made yesterday. What a relief it would be to finally land in Phoenix and get off the plane.

CHAPTER

Twenty-one

*L*isa listlessly pushed the food around her dinner plate.

"You're still suffering from jet lag." Kobi made it a statement, not a question.

"I was awake four hours last night. I've got to get over this before school starts."

"Why aren't you eating?"

"Still queasy, and it's already been ten days since I got off the plane. I can't believe I have to get on another one next week."

"Maybe we should cancel the trip?" Kobi suggested.

"No, the sooner we tell my parents our plans and have it off my head, the happier I'll be."

"Okay, if you're up to it." Kobi studied her face with concern and then changed the subject. "This casserole's delicious, Lisa. Try some."

She shook her head.

"Do you think," he cleared his throat nervously, "that you might be expecting?"

His wife studied her hands. "I don't want to get my hopes up," she whispered.

"You know, I can go to Walgreen's and pick up an early pregnancy test tonight."

Lisa's eyes lit up at the suggestion and Kobi took off as soon as he finished clearing the table.

Before going to sleep, Lisa got the kit set up in the bathroom, ready for first thing the following morning. Jet lag kept her tossing and turning until the wee hours though, and again she didn't wake up until almost noon. Once up, she immediately went to the kit, but it'd be an hour before she'd see the results. She couldn't believe how long that hour was. It seemed as if her watch had stopped, but when she looked at the clock in the kitchen, she saw it was the right time. Finally, finally sixty-three minutes passed. Slowly, as if the results were of no consequence, Lisa made her way to the bathroom. She glanced expectantly at the kit and her face crumpled.

Lisa fell on her bed and burst into sobs. She cried long and hard, ignoring the phone that rang several times. At last she got hold of herself and dried her eyes. Going into the bathroom, she saw that her face was a mess. She washed it, reapplied her makeup, and vowed she wouldn't leave the apartment until her eyes looked less swollen. At that moment, the doorbell rang. For some reason, she found it more difficult to ignore a ringing doorbell than a ringing phone.

"Who is it?" she called out.

"Sondra."

Reluctantly, Lisa opened the door to face her cousin, who had Naomi resting on her hip. Sondra's eyes widened in alarm when she saw Lisa's eyes.

"What's the matter?"

Without waiting for an answer, Sondra entered the apartment. With her free hand, she put an arm around Lisa and led her to the couch.

"Kobi called me. He tried calling and you didn't answer; he was worried. I thought you'd just gone out, but he didn't think so and asked me to come check on you."

"I'm sorry I made you come out in the heat," Lisa whispered.

"Don't be silly." Sondra tried to keep the irritation out of her voice, but she was worried. "What's the matter?" she repeated.

"I, um..." Tears welled up in Lisa's eyes. She swallowed hard. "Go look in the bathroom on the counter."

With a few deep breaths, Lisa pulled herself together once more.

"Lisa." Sondra's face was full of sympathy as she sat back down next to her cousin. "How far along did you think you might be?"

Naomi squirmed in her mother's arms and Sondra set her on the floor. Then she jangled her key ring and handed it to her, hoping it would keep her toddler entertained.

Lisa studied her hands. "Maybe a month." She blushed. "Maybe less. I feel so nauseous."

"I don't want to give you false hope, but those home tests aren't that accurate the first few weeks."

Lisa's head shot up. "How do you know?"

"Doc and Danny were talking about it a couple of weeks ago. The margin of error is really high in the beginning. Blood tests are the most accurate."

"Really?" Lisa gave a tentative half smile.

"Do you want to go to your doctor?"

"I don't know." Lisa rubbed at her polished nails nervously. "If I'm not expecting, then everyone in the office will know."

"So what?"

"I don't want everyone feeling sorry for me!"

"Oh, Lisa," Sondra said wearily, "don't be so self-centered!"

Lisa stared at her in shock.

"I'm sorry," Sondra apologized hastily. "I'm really sorry. It's just that everyone has a lot on their minds. They're thinking about a hundred different things. Whether you're expecting or not may be a major issue for you, but it's not for them. They've got their own things they're thinking about."

Lisa smiled weakly. "Do you think I can get an appointment today?"

"With your doctor, I don't know; but if not, I can get you an appointment with Doc or his partner."

"You know, I think I'd like a new start. What's their office number?"

* * *

"Don't you agree, Sondra?"

"Huh?" Sondra stammered. "Uh, I'm sorry, I didn't hear."

She didn't hear because she hadn't been listening. Although she was sitting on her in-laws' patio, participating in their Labor Day picnic, her mind was at Sky Harbor Airport, picturing Lisa and Kobi debarking from their flight. Sondra had wanted to be there to meet them, but Bayla and Harold had offered first. Now she would have to wait good-naturedly until after the barbecue to find out how their trip had gone. Resolutely, she turned her attention to her mother-in-law.

"I was just saying," Shirley repeated patiently, "that you've outgrown your apartment and should begin looking to buy a house. Don't you agree?"

"We're managing," Sondra answered shortly. "Batsheva, let me help you with the ketchup."

While she squeezed the ketchup on her daughter's hamburger, she struggled to keep her resentment in check. Hadn't Danny told them that he was giving the practice three years and then they were moving on?

"Even if you really leave at the end of three years," Shirley continued as if she had read Sondra's mind, "It makes sense to buy a house and have something to show for it instead of just throwing away money on rent."

"I guess so," Sondra admitted reluctantly. She glanced at her husband for his reaction.

"We're managing because you're so organized, but it would be nice for the children to have a place to play besides the living room." Danny offered some French fries to Zvi Chaim. "And once Naomi is out of the crib, it will be way too crowded in their room."

Doc cleared his throat and they turned their attention to him. "Your mother and I have decided that we would like to loan you ten thousand dollars for a down payment." He raised his hand to forestall any interruptions. "It would be a no-interest loan, payable over ten years. We did that for your sister and Stan, and we want to do the same for you."

"Wow, Dad, thanks!" Danny reached over to shake his father's hand.

"Thank you," Sondra echoed, her dimple deepening as she pictured her children playing in the backyard of their future home.

"I have a friend who's in real estate," Shirley announced, "and I thought we could go out with her tomorrow after you finish teaching. How does that work for you, Sondra?"

"Well..." Sondra groped to pull her thoughts together. How could she feel such appreciation one minute and such resentment the next? Fortunately, Danny came to her rescue.

"Mom, maybe it's best if Sondra and I look together. Give us your friend's number and we'll call her."

"I just thought I'd save you some legwork, Danny."

Shirley was obviously a little hurt by her son's response, but tried to hide it. Sondra was relieved that she wasn't the one who'd upset Shirley this time.

Sondra waited until all three children were bathed and in bed before she slipped out of the apartment. Tomorrow would be a big day for all of them, with school and day care starting. Lisa was also having a new beginning. Sondra found her lounging on her couch, already in her nightgown and robe. Classical music was playing on the stereo. Lisa pulled her feet up and made room for her cousin to settle down.

"What can I get you to drink?" Kobi offered.

"Nothing, thanks." Sondra grinned. "I came to talk, not drink."

"Then I'll leave you two alone." He grinned back.

"So," Sondra asked, "how's Oma doing?"

Lisa made a face. "She hates the old age home. She's driving our mothers crazy, while our fathers ignore her. Your mom offered her to come live with them, but she refused. She wants to go back to her house."

"I thought they sold it."

"They did."

Sondra sighed. "It's so hard to grow old." She made a visible effort to push her negative thoughts away. "How's everyone else?"

"Good. Bernice was there for the weekend and she sends her love."

Sondra's eyes lit up at the mention of her older cousin. They'd once been very close. "How's she doing?"

"Okay." Lisa shrugged. "She's got a boyfriend."

"Really!"

"He's not Jewish."

Sondra's face fell. "I really should write her."

"You think you can save her like you saved me?"

"I didn't save you," Sondra answered firmly. "You saved yourself. Tell me," she changed the subject, "how did you survive the flight, and what did you tell your parents, and how did they react?"

"The flight wasn't nearly as bad as the one back from Israel. I had the saltine crackers Dr. Taylor suggested that I keep on hand and they helped a lot. I don't think I'm going to go *anywhere* without them."

Sondra laughed. "That's great if they work."

"Thank goodness. On the flight to Wichita, Kobi suggested that we should wait until the summer to leave America."

"Really?"

"Yeah." Lisa shrugged her shoulders. "He thinks I should have the baby here with a doctor I feel comfortable with and a medical system that I understand. I think he's right."

"What about his job?"

"He didn't sign a contract, and if Israel Aircraft doesn't want him when we get there, he'll be able to find work somewhere else in his field." Lisa picked up her cup of tea and took a long sip. "Waiting is much better for me for so many reasons."

"Like?"

"Well, I won't have to quit teaching in the middle of the year, and my parents will have ten months to get used to the idea."

"Did you tell them you're moving?"

"We did it together."

"And?" Sondra prompted.

Lisa stirred her tea slowly. "I really thought Dad would hit the roof, but he was calm. He said we'd been telling them we were going to move to Israel ever since we got engaged. It was Mom who surprised me."

"Was she very upset?" Sondra asked gently.

"You know, Mom almost never cries, but she was blinking back tears when we told them."

"I can imagine."

Lisa spoke in a rush. "I know it's far away, and if I was a good daughter I'd move closer, especially since I'm the only child they have left, but Kobi really belongs in Israel and I belong with him and I really think living in Israel will be good for me. So I asked Mom which she'd prefer: me happily married to a Jewish man and living far away in Israel or me close by in Lincoln with Tim as a husband and a Xmas tree in the living room."

"Wow!" Sondra exclaimed. "You actually asked her that? What'd she answer?"

"All she said was, 'But you're not married to Tim.' She got the message, though. She didn't say anything else, and when all the relatives came by, she calmly told them our plans."

"Does she know you're expecting?"

"No. Kobi thinks you're right and we should wait till I'm three months along to tell anyone. I really want to tell her in person, though. I think I managed to talk her into coming for a visit after the holidays."

"You'll tell her then?"

"I hope so. She said if she can't talk Dad into coming, she'll get your mother to take a long weekend and come with her. I suggested that the four of them should come together for Thanksgiving."

"That would be so neat!" Sondra's eyes shone at the idea. Seeing Lisa yawn, she realized it was time to leave. "I guess I should get home and finish up the sandwiches for tomorrow. Are you excited about your first day of school?"

Lisa smiled. "Yes. Kobi wanted me to tell them I wouldn't be teaching, but the doctor said there was no reason for that and I can't see myself just hanging out for nine months."

"I can't either." Sondra grinned at the idea.

"But Kobi did talk me into dropping the teaching courses."

"Yeah?"

Lisa shrugged her shoulders. "I have no deep desire to be a teacher. I was just looking for something to do that wouldn't require me to work on Shabbos. I think, once we're in Israel, I'll be able to find plenty of stores that are closed on Shabbos."

"You're right!" Sondra patted her cousin's feet and rose to go. "Good luck tomorrow."

CHAPTER
Twenty-two

"Nothing like having in-laws come visit to make a person finish unpacking his moving boxes," Danny declared as he slipped his last Gemara into its place in the bookcase.

"It *is* an incentive," Sondra agreed, laughing happily as she carried one more box of toys into the den.

"This place will look great by the time your parents land tomorrow evening."

"It sure will." She stacked the blocks on one of the lower shelves. "You know, I'm glad the other house didn't work out."

"But you really wanted to live next to Brachie," Danny reminded her, sorting through the children's games.

"I did. I had dreams of making an *eruv* between our houses, and taking turns going to shul and watching each other's babies on Shabbos. But Naomi will be taking her first steps soon and in no time we'll be walking the half block to shul."

"True." Danny smiled. "I appreciate that we're close enough for me to walk to minyan every day. And I love all our orange trees."

"I love the bay windows!" Sondra exclaimed. "This room's finished. Let's take a break."

● ● ●

Lisa had decided that the best time to tell her parents about her pregnancy was Thursday morning, while they were eating a relaxed breakfast. However, once she sat down to her omelet, she discovered she was too tense to eat. How would her parents react to the news that they were becoming grandparents to a baby who would be moving halfway around the world? A desperate glance at Kobi caused him to clear his throat.

"We have an announcement to make," he said confidently. "If all goes well, with G-d's help, you'll be having a grandchild born in the spring."

There was a sharp intake of breath from Irene, and then she managed a wide smile. "Are you feeling okay, dear?"

"I wasn't in the beginning, but I'm fine now." Lisa blushed.

"You have good medical care?" Herbert asked.

"We have maternity insurance from my work," Kobi said, smiling proudly. "Lisa will be able to stay in a private room when she gives birth."

"Very good," Herbert responded. "It should come with *mazal* and *brachah*."

"Amen," Irene nodded and took a bite of her omelet. "Kobi, these eggs are delicious."

Lisa picked at her hash browns and smiled wanly. She was thankful there'd been no tears or recriminations, but couldn't her parents have shown a little more excitement? Kobi caught her eye and gave her a wink. She smiled back, but found she was able to eat very little of the breakfast he'd prepared.

Later, as they washed the dishes, Irene asked if they could tell Helga and Julius the news during the Thanksgiving dinner. Lisa thought that was a great idea. The less people she had to make the announcement to, the better.

Aunt Helga's reaction was all Lisa could have wished for. She hugged her and exclaimed how it was only yesterday that Lisa had been a baby herself. Uncle Julius shook Kobi's hand excitedly and, like his brother, wished them *mazal* and *brachah*.

"Let's go tomorrow and buy some maternity clothes for Lisa," Helga suggested.

Irene liked the idea and it was decided that Julius and Herbert would take the children to the zoo. At first, Sondra was hesitant to join in, but the others convinced her that they would help her with the Shabbos cooking, and in the end, she happily came along.

So it was a brand new maternity dress that Lisa wore to shul on Shabbos. No one made a comment, but she was greeted with a lot of smiles and questions about how she was feeling. Monday morning, when she arrived at school, she was wearing one of Sondra's maternity jumpers. This time there were comments in the teachers' room.

"Lisa, do my eyes deceive me or are you in the family way?"

That was from the drama teacher, who always tended to dramatize things. Lisa blushed and inclined her head.

"Really?" Kay, one of the home economic teachers, asked sympathetically. "How are you feeling?"

"Better than I was before." Lisa smiled.

"And when are you due?" The coach joined the inquisition.

Lisa mumbled her due date and Kay shook her head.

"The principal isn't going to be happy," she said ominously. Lisa chose to ignore the comment.

Two weeks later, though, she met the principal in the hall, just as she was leaving school.

"Mrs. Chazon, may I have a word with you?"

"Sure." Lisa followed the balding, middle-aged man into his paneled office. Mr. Groves had been in education for thirty-three years. He'd been a principal for the past ten. Sincere concern for the students made him a respected administrator.

"I won't beat around the bush." He motioned for Lisa to sit down. "Rumor has reached my ears that you are expecting in April."

Lisa blushingly replied in the affirmative.

"What are your plans when the baby is born?"

"I understand that I'm entitled to a six-week maternity leave. With the few weeks of school remaining after that, I plan to get a sitter to come into my home."

"I see." Mr. Groves nodded. "Tell me, Mrs. Chazon, did you consider how disruptive it would be for your students to have you leave so close to the end of the year?"

Lisa knew she should feel intimidated, but she only felt resentment. She spoke without thinking.

"Mr. Groves, I have been married for over three years and wanted to start a family from the very beginning. This baby was not conceived when it was convenient for my students or anyone else."

"I'm happy for you, Mrs. Chazon." The principal's tone stayed even. "But, frankly, I am concerned about your students, and," he paused and gave Lisa a long look, "they are my first priority."

"I understand," Lisa responded. "I intend to leave very clear and concise lesson plans for my substitute."

"Of course," Mr. Groves continued cryptically, "I may not be able to find a substitute for such a short period of time. You may want to start your maternity leave before the baby is born."

"I see." Lisa searched for the right words. "Are you giving me notice?"

"Oh, no," Mr. Groves reassured her. "I'm just giving you some options to consider."

"I see," Lisa repeated. The meeting was over. She thanked Mr. Groves for his time and made her way to her car.

Updates on the Shah's fall in Iran were blasting on the four o'clock news, but Lisa paid no attention. She was a bundle of emotions. Truth be told, she wasn't a born teacher and didn't really enjoy teaching. Taking an early maternity leave, Mr. Grove's euphemism for resigning, didn't sound half bad. Still, there was the part of Lisa that wanted to succeed in what she'd begun. She'd left Kramer's Department Store as a failure because of her commitment to Shabbos. Would she have to leave teaching for her desire to build a Jewish family?

CHAPTER
Twenty-three

"I still can't believe you gave up that dream job at the department store," Rachel Katzner remarked.

It was Shabbos afternoon and Kobi was in shul. Lisa had been looking forward to having the time alone with her cousin, but now she was beginning to wonder why.

Once she and Rachel had been so close. She remembered how eagerly she used to wait for the Katzners' monthly trip to Lincoln to visit Oma and Opa and the rest of the family. How excited she'd been when they became pen pals in second grade. Their first letters had been written on lined tablet paper, but as they matured, their stationery grew more sophisticated, as did the content of the letters. For very special occasions, their parents would even let the girls call each other long distance. Herbert would always stand outside the kitchen giving Lisa her privacy, but making sure she spoke no longer than her privileged three minutes.

Every summer Lisa got to spend a week in Kansas City with her cousin, and later Rachel had her week in Lincoln. It was the highlight of the girls' summers. When they got their driver's licenses, those visits back and forth increased until their senior year of high school. Looking back, Lisa had to admit that she'd been so obsessed with Tim that she'd neglected the relationship. Was that the reason they were so distant now? Or was it because she had become religious like Sondra? When Rachel called a week earlier and asked if she could spend the weekend, Lisa had fond hopes that once Rachel had experienced a real Shabbos, she'd understand why that job at Kramer's was no longer so important.

Rachel didn't experience a real Shabbos, though. She was in Phoenix to cover the Pima Indian Convention and was staying with Lisa to save the money she would have spent on a hotel. In fact, this was the first chance they'd had to have the semblance of a real conversation. Lisa chose her words carefully.

"You have no idea how beautiful Shabbos is — a real Shabbos, not like the watered-down Shabbos you had in Kansas City. If you'd been here with us today, I think you'd have been able to understand my decision."

Rachel looked at her skeptically, clearly unconvinced.

"Well, are you happy with the teaching?"

Lisa blushed. "I gave it up." Briefly she explained why.

"I don't believe it!" Rachel exclaimed. "That's discrimination! You have grounds for a good lawsuit."

"Maybe," Lisa conceded, "but there's no time for that. I want to move to Israel soon."

"So what're you doing with yourself besides being pregnant?"

"Well, I do sleep a lot." Lisa smiled calmly. "I'm doing most of the groundwork for the move. And I'm helping the youth group organize their Purim celebration. And I'm in charge of the goods and service auction to raise money for the *mikveh*."

"The *mikveh*? People still use a *mikveh*? Isn't that archaic?"

"Not at all." Lisa's serene face masked the tension she felt.

"Do you use the *mikveh*?"

"Of course. Would you like to see it?"

"What for?" Rachel made a face.

"Maybe it would make an interesting article for your paper."

Rachel wrinkled her nose. "No one would be interested in that."

"I don't know why not. They're interested in Pima Indians."

"That's different." Rachel folded her arms across her chest.

"Do they know you're Jewish at the paper?"

"Why should they? It has very little to do with who I am."

"I see." Lisa nodded slowly. How different she and Rachel were now. Unlike her cousin, being Jewish was the most central part of her being. Lisa knew Rachel would probably not let anything conflict with her job at the paper. In another couple of years, she'd most likely move up the ranks and become an editor. Meanwhile, Lisa had no career, but somehow she had the feeling that her life was far more meaningful than Rachel's was.

CHAPTER

Twenty-four

"Say bye-bye to your mommy." The nurse settled Batsheva on the gurney.

"Bye, Ima." The three-year-old waved confidently as she was rolled through the double doors to the operating room.

Sondra smiled weakly at her daughter.

The ear infections had started seven months earlier, at the very end of the summer. Sondra had returned from a morning swim with the children at the Weins' pool and Batsheva refused to come to the table for lunch. Instead, she settled herself listlessly on the floor near the front door. After an hour, Sondra called Danny.

"Something's wrong with Batsheva," she fretted to her husband and described how their daughter didn't want to eat or drink or go to sleep.

"Does she have a fever?"

"No, but something's not right."

"Trust your motherly instincts," Danny said. "Hold on, let me check the appointment book."

While waiting, Sondra mentally juggled her to-do list and wondered what she'd have to sacrifice to go to the doctor. Probably the laundry.

"Okay." Danny was back on the line. "Dr. Kraeger can see her in half an hour. Okay?"

Sondra groaned. "I just love loading everyone in the car in this heat. Isn't there anything later?"

"Sorry. Do you want to wait until tomorrow morning?"

"No," Sondra said resignedly. "We'll be there soon."

Dr. Kraeger examined little Batsheva carefully and, after looking in her ears, announced that she had an ear infection. He prescribed antibiotics for ten days. Two days later, Batsheva was her normal happy self and excited to start nursery school. All was well until two days after she'd finished the medicine and came home from nursery school pulling at her ear.

Once again she was back on antibiotics and once again they helped. But two weeks later, she woke up in the middle of the night screaming and pulling at her ear.

"How am I supposed to teach with a sick child and no sleep?" Sondra complained to Danny in the morning.

"I'm sorry." He was sympathetic. "You know, my mother said she's willing to babysit."

"Yeah, but what if Batsheva gets an infection during Rosh Hashanah?"

"I'll make sure to have Moxypen powder at home," Danny reassured her. They didn't need the medicine then, but they did on Simchas Torah.

"My middle son had ear infections, one after the other, but he grew out of them by the time he was six," Bayla told her.

Shaindy, with her constant pessimism, was far less supportive. "I can't believe you've given Batsheva so much medication. There's got to be some side effects. You should try a dairy-free diet."

Sondra refrained from asking why she was giving medical advice to a doctor's wife and instead asked Danny what he thought of the idea.

"It can't hurt," he said.

"That means no pizza for any of us."

"We can sneak some when Batsheva's sleeping," Danny joked.

For three months, the family refrained from cheese sandwiches, lasagna, and ice cream, but there was no let-up in the ear infections. Vivian,

Rabbi Levi's wife, recommended olive oil in the ear and old Mrs. Cohen swore by garlic. Dr. Kraeger sent Batsheva to the ear specialist, who put her on antihistamines, but nothing seemed to help.

Then, in February, Danny noticed that Batsheva was reading his lips. He had Batsheva back at the ear specialist first thing the next morning for a hearing test. There'd been a considerable loss in the child's hearing.

"You can wait to see if her ears dry out in the summer or we can put in tubes. I recommend tubes."

Danny agreed and explained to Sondra that it was a very simple operation. Batsheva would be asleep for no more than half an hour and, with the tubes in place, the fluids would be able to drain out of her ears, the infections should stop, and Batsheva would be able to hear clearly again.

It sounded good to Sondra. Still, it hadn't been easy to see her daughter wheeled away from her.

"Here." Danny handed his wife a granola bar. "Eat!"

"Thanks." Sondra tore open the wrapper. "I'm starved!"

"Of course you are." Danny smiled at her. Besides the obstetrician, they were the only ones who knew that Sondra was six weeks pregnant.

"I really should be saying some *Tehillim*," Sondra declared after her second bite.

"You eat, I'll recite."

He'd had time to say only two chapters when the same nurse informed them that Batsheva was in the wake-up room and one parent could come in.

"Go ahead." Danny waved his hand at her.

Batsheva had the same smile she'd had on her face when she was wheeled away.

"How was it, sweetie?" Sondra kissed her daughter's cheek.

"Fun!"

"Fun?" Sondra gave the nurse a questioning glance.

"She must have had a nice dream."

After Batsheva was able to sit up and drink, Danny walked in. Batsheva was thrilled to see her father, but Sondra was surprised.

"I thought they only let one parent in."

"That's right, but I'm here as a doctor. Don't worry," he reassured his wife. "We'll go by the rules. Give me a few minutes with Batsheva."

With mixed feelings, Sondra left the wake-up room. As she entered the waiting room, she was shocked to see Kobi standing at the entrance.

"Kobi, what are you doing here?"

"Looking for you." Kobi smiled broadly. "I wanted to tell you that I'm the father of a beautiful baby boy."

Sondra let out a squeal of excitement. "Is everything okay? Isn't it early?"

"Just a week." Kobi was beaming. "We didn't tell Lisa's real due date because we didn't want everyone driving us crazy the last month."

"When can I see Lisa and the baby?"

"Right now. Go to room 506. I'll wait here and come get you as soon as Batsheva and Danny come out."

CHAPTER
Twenty-five

Sondra caught her breath as she walked into Lisa's room and then, to her consternation, burst into tears.

"I'm sorry." She hugged her cousin. "I'm so happy for you, but, oh, I'm going to miss you so much."

She looked at the little boy who was dark like his father, but reminded her somehow of Howie, Lisa's brother.

"Did you talk to Aunt Irene and Uncle Herbert yet?"

"Yes!" Lisa was euphoric. "They're planning to come for the bris." Her face clouded for a second. "I wish Oma could come too," she sighed.

"We'll take a lot of pictures to show her," Sondra comforted her cousin.

To Lisa's delight, Rabbi Frankel agreed to be the *mohel*. It was just a little more expensive to fly him in from Far Rockaway, where he and Rena had moved, than to bring in the *mohel* from Denver, and Rabbi Frankel made it clear that he wouldn't accept any payment.

Bayla Wein took charge of organizing the cakes for the *shalom zachar* and the meals to be sent in the first week. Finally, the women of the community were able to return all the help Lisa had given them. Her mother was suitably impressed with the religious community of Phoenix.

"Are you sure you want to leave?" Irene asked after accepting a chicken dinner from Vivian Levi. "Everyone is so good to you."

"They are, Mom," Lisa answered. "But Israel is Kobi's home and I'm ready to make it mine too."

"I know," her mother said understandingly.

"I'm sorry." Lisa wiped her eyes.

"Don't be," Irene spoke resolutely. "You have a good husband and a beautiful baby. You're going to build a wonderful life in Israel. There's nothing to be sorry about."

Lisa nodded, wondering which one of them her mother was trying to convince. It was true, she'd been the one to encourage Kobi to make the move, but now, snuggling her newborn, she wondered where she would find the strength to leave all that was familiar and dear to her.

Sondra had been sure the baby would be named for one of his uncles and was caught off guard when Danny, who'd been given the honor to name the boy, pronounced him as Yehoshua ben Yaakov.

Later, when Lisa was in a side room feeding Shuki, as they would be calling him, she explained the choice to her cousin.

"I first thought we'd name him after Uri, since you'd already named Zvi Chaim after Howie, but Kobi didn't want to use the name of someone who had died so young. We decided on Yehoshua after Yehoshua bin Nun, since our baby is the one taking us into the Land of Israel."

Once again Sondra was impressed with Lisa's grasp of *Tanach*, yet she felt a pang of sorrow at the thought of their upcoming separation.

"You must be so excited about moving," she said in an upbeat voice.

Lisa's quivering chin was the only response.

Sondra took her cousin's hand in hers. "Are you having second thoughts?"

Lisa took a deep breath. "My whole life has changed drastically, and before I'll have a chance to get used to being a mother, I'm going to move halfway around the world and everything is going to be different. Everything! The food. The language. The lifestyle. Everything!"

"Not everything." Sondra patted Lisa's hand. "Kobi will be the same."

"That's true." Lisa managed a weak smile.

"And Shabbos will still be Shabbos, even though you'll be calling it Shabbat."

Lisa nodded her head in agreement.

Encouraged, Sondra continued. "*Parshas hashavua* is still *parshas hashavua*."

"You're right." There was a little more enthusiasm in Lisa's voice.

"If you'd gone before Shuki was born, you'd probably be all adjusted to Israel and would just have to adjust to motherhood, but it meant so much to your parents to have him born here."

"I know," Lisa whispered. "And I feel so guilty taking their only grandchild so far away from them."

"It's hard." Sondra squeezed Lisa's hand. "But you know this is the best thing for you and Kobi. And your parents are happy for you."

Lisa nodded again, biting her lip.

"And if you go while Shuki is still a newborn, he'll never have to adjust to living in Israel."

"That's what we've been saying all along." Lisa managed a smile. "Sondra, do you think you'll ever leave Phoenix?"

"I hope so!" Sondra threw her hands up impatiently.

Lisa gave her a long look.

"Brachie told me at the *seudah* that they're moving this summer."

"Oh, Sondra, I'm sorry. Where to?"

"Los Angeles."

"That's not so far."

"I'll get to see her from time to time." Sondra frowned. "But I want a friend here. She's leaving. You're leaving."

"Rabbi Levi will be bringing someone to replace the Fisches."

"Yeah, and there are the teachers at the high school, but why should I become friends with them if they're just going to leave in another year or two?"

Now it was Lisa who squeezed Sondra's hand with sympathy and Sondra managed a smile. As happy as she was about the bris, she wasn't in a particularly good mood. Right after Brachie had shared her news, Shaindy had cornered her and begun asking about Batsheva's operation.

"I would never have done what you did," she had rebuked Sondra. "The scar tissue in the ears can cause more problems than it can solve."

Sondra clenched her teeth and decided to ignore her, but Shaindy wouldn't let up.

"I had a friend in Monsey whose son had tubes put in when he was three, and he still got infections, and now he's seven and in a special school for children with serious hearing problems. And there..."

"Shaindy," Sondra had cut her off angrily. "The operation's over and your doom-and-gloom stories are not constructive. I'm going to go check on Lisa." She had flounced away before Shaindy could say another word.

Still, Sondra reminded herself, she'd come to make sure Lisa was okay, not to share her problems with her cousin.

"What's so nice about you moving to Israel," Sondra said, "is that if you don't like Kfar Yonatan, there are dozens of other communities you can move to. And I bet you won't have any trouble finding a store that stays closed on Shabbos to hire you."

"You're right." Lisa had her optimism back. "But you know what? I'm not in such a hurry to find a job. I want to be home with Shuki for now."

CHAPTER
Twenty-six

*H*erbert flew back home right after the bris and Irene followed him five days later. She left feeling confident that Lisa would manage fine without her. Lisa wasn't so sure. What would she do if someone came to the door when she was feeding Shuki? That was exactly what happened barely two hours after her mother had left for the airport. Picking up Shuki carefully so she wouldn't disturb him, she gingerly made her way to the door.

"Who's there?"

"Vivian Levi."

"One minute."

With one hand, Lisa balanced Shuki. With the other, she slowly turned the doorknob. At the same time, she positioned herself behind the door so the *rebbetzin* entered what seemed like an empty room.

"Lisa?" she asked softly.

Lisa nudged the door closed with her foot and Vivian turned around to face her.

"Oh, I'm so sorry I disturbed you."

"It's okay." Lisa smiled. "I had to figure how to open the door while I'm feeding Shuki sooner or later."

"Good for you," Vivian said laughing. She refused the offer of a cold drink. "I wanted to check on you. Can I get *you* something to drink?"

"Well, uh..."

"Something hot or cold?"

"There's some orange juice in the fridge."

"It's important for you to drink a lot," Vivian called from the kitchen, "especially since the hot weather's started."

She handed Lisa the glass and settled down next to her on the couch.

"The women from shul were talking about making you a goodbye party, but then we thought it would be much more practical to make Shuki's *pidyon haben*, even though it will be a good month before you leave. What do you think?"

Lisa laughed in astonishment. "The *pidyon haben* is just a couple of days after Pesach ends!"

"That's a lot easier than a couple of days before it begins," Vivian retorted good humoredly.

"It sure is," Lisa had to agree. "It sounds wonderful, but let me check with Kobi."

Kobi was pleased to have one less arrangement to make and the plans went forward. Lisa made up a guest list. Besides the members of the shul and out-of-town relatives, there were Kobi's co-workers, Danny's parents, and Carol and Bill.

"Won't Carol and Bill feel strange being in a synagogue and the only non-Jews there?" Sondra asked when she went over the list with Lisa.

Lisa's reply was in the negative. Despite the differences in their lifestyles, the two former roommates had remained fast friends. And it turned out that Carol and Bill weren't the only non-Jews present. To Lisa's surprise, her cousin Rachel warmly accepted the invitation she'd half-heartedly extended.

"I hope you don't mind if I bring a friend with me." Rachel hadn't really given Lisa any chance to refuse.

"Who are you bringing?" She was happy that Rachel wouldn't be driving by herself.

"Jeffrey Marks. He's a photographer on the paper."

"Great." Lisa was thrilled that Rachel was seeing someone Jewish.

The atmosphere of the *pidyon haben* was full of love and warmth, but it was hectic. Lisa didn't have a chance to speak for more than a few minutes to each of the guests, so she didn't know what Sondra discovered. Although Jeffrey had a Jewish-sounding name, he was no more Jewish than Carol or Bill. Raised a Methodist, he was now an amiable agnostic.

Sondra didn't share her information with Lisa. Whatever influence Lisa might have had on Rachel would be over when she left America in just another month. She herself had learned years ago that she didn't have any influence on her Kansas City cousin. They'd never been close, and yet it made her sad to think another cousin might marry out.

Resolutely, she pushed that depressing thought away and fingered the blue envelope resting in her pocket. Addressed to her in a familiar, curly script, the back of the envelope bore the return address of Debbie Friedman in Lakewood. Debbie Friedman — née Debbie Greenbaum — had been Sondra's first *shomer Shabbos* friend. It was Debbie, the cantor's daughter, who'd invited her to join the Kansas City youth group, and it was at Debbie's home where she had spent many Shabboses. With Debbie at her side, she'd made the big move to Stern College in New York. The two were together for their year in Israel and Debbie had been with her that fateful Shabbos when she first met Danny. She'd been Sondra's bridesmaid, and a year later Sondra had flown to New York for Debbie's wedding to a native New Yorker who was learning in the Lakewood Yeshiva.

Dearest Sondra, the letter read. *Sit down to read this because you're going to be shocked by my news. Shraga and I have decided the time has come for him to leave yeshiva and begin teaching full-time. He made a number of inquiries and had several offers — all from out-of-town schools. Yesterday, we made a decision and he accepted the offer in Phoenix!!! Can you believe we'll be together again??? I can't wait to see you!!!*

Sondra had read the rest of the letter, her heart beating with excitement. Debbie's oldest, Sima, was the same age as Batsheva, and her other daughter was just a few months younger than Naomi. Hopefully, the girls would get along. As she was pulling out her stationery to write her own letter, Sondra was already daydreaming about learning with Debbie again.

It's true, she thought, *Hashem never sends the sickness without first sending the cure.*

Twenty-seven

"Hello, Sondra. This is Carol, Lisa's friend."

"Hello." Sondra spoke into the phone politely, but her stomach muscles tightened. She still hadn't been able to forget that Carol was the one to suggest that Lisa convert.

"I was wondering, have you heard anything from Lisa?"

"Not directly." Sondra balanced the receiver on her shoulder, pulled the long cord over to the sink, and began the dinner dishes. "She's spoken to her mother several times, and Aunt Irene reported the conversations to my mother, and she reported them to me." Sondra was resigned to the fact that Lisa probably wasn't going to tell her parents the things that Sondra was most interested in hearing about.

"I wrote her twice, but I haven't heard…" Carol's voice trailed off.

"The mail's really slow," Sondra reassured her. "And they just moved into Kfar Yonatan this week."

"Just this week?"

"Yeah." Sondra scrubbed at the spaghetti pot. "They spent a week in Lincoln, a few days by friends in New York, and then two weeks by Kobi's parents until their lift came."

"I'd really like to call her."

"So would I," Sondra agreed fervently, "but it'll be months before they get a phone."

Carol whistled. "I never thought Lisa had it in her to move to the middle of nowhere without even a phone."

Sondra had to laugh. "She's changed a lot since you first met her."

Carol hesitated. "Will you keep me informed on how she's doing?"

Sondra heard the hesitation and felt uncomfortable. Obviously, Carol had sensed her disapproval. A lot of time had passed since Lisa had broken up with Tim. It was time to let go.

"I'll try and let you know anything worth knowing," Sondra committed herself.

While Sondra and Carol were on the phone Thursday evening in Arizona, it was already Friday morning in Israel. Lisa had just finished giving Shuki his first feeding of the day and now she was trying to talk herself into climbing out of bed.

When they'd first arrived in Israel, Kobi's father had surprised them with the present of an ornate bedroom set. Fortunately, it hadn't fit into the tiny prefab they now called home and this gave them a good excuse to tell Tzachi why they'd returned it. With the credit, they'd been able to buy a simpler set made of teakwood plus a dinette set that could seat as many as eight.

They were the twenty-sixth family to settle in Kfar Yonatan. Their new home was as large as the apartment they'd had in Phoenix, with two bedrooms, a big living area, a tiny kitchen, and a bathroom that could hold a washing machine. Of course, the laundry had to be done according to a schedule since no one was hooked up to their own electricity yet and the generator couldn't handle too much of a demand at once. Elisheva, Avi Ben David's pretty wife, explained to Lisa that she could run her machine for two hours on Sunday mornings and again on Wednesday afternoons. Lisa liked Elisheva, which was good since Kobi's friendship with Avi that had begun back in the office in Kfar Saba had blossomed upon their arrival in Kfar Yonatan two weeks earlier.

They'd arrived with their lift, and in the midst of all the bedlam, Miriam Gruenberg, from the pre-fab next door, had appeared with a plate of muffins in her hands and a toddler at her side.

"Avi said you're originally from Kansas." The dark-haired woman smiled warmly. "I'm from Denver."

"Practically neighbors!" Lisa laughed, charmed by Miriam's friendliness.

"Well, we're really neighbors now. We want you to come for dinner tonight."

"Really?"

"Really." Miriam grinned.

"That's so nice!"

"You're going to get invitations every day this week."

"Really?" Lisa repeated.

"Well, it'll take a while to get unpacked and organized, and it's not like you can go out for pizza or Chinese."

"I couldn't do that in Phoenix, either."

"Good, one less thing for you to adjust to here. Tell me, how's your Hebrew?"

"Passable, but I speak to my husband in English. How's yours?"

"I went to day school, so my Hebrew was already good when I first got here — good enough for me to marry an Israeli, communicate with Yehezkel's family, and be able to run a translating business out of my house."

"Wow!"

"Still, it's always fun to have someone around who knows what Trix cereal and Keds sneakers are."

Lisa chuckled with delight. "Do you remember the Trix commercials?"

"Not really. We didn't have a TV, but I was a bookworm so I didn't miss it."

"I brought some cartons of books, if you want to borrow any after I get unpacked."

"I sure would!" Miriam exclaimed. "My mother sends me books with anyone coming to Israel, so you're welcome to check out what I have."

In the following two weeks, Lisa learned that it wasn't just Israeli husbands and a love of English books the two of them had in common. Miriam had also had a long wait for her first child to be born. Lisa discovered that Yehezkel was Rav Yehezkel, the rabbi of Kfar Yonatan, and that he and Miriam had moved to the village just three months ago.

Lisa felt so comfortable with her new friend that she'd invited the Gruenbergs to be their first Shabbat guests. Remembering they were coming, Lisa resolutely climbed out of bed, ready to get to work.

It wasn't true, she reflected as she washed her hands, that Shabbos was still Shabbos in Israel. In Eretz Yisrael, Shabbat was far better than it had ever been in Phoenix. For the two weeks they'd been in Kfar Yonatan, she'd found herself pushing Shuki's stroller along the flowered walkway to the synagogue to join in the *Kabbalat Shabbat* prayers, something she'd never done in Phoenix. Already, the tune of *Lechah Dodi* was replacing the rock music that still ran through her mind from her high school days. On Shabbat mornings, she'd taken Shuki with her to listen to the Torah reading. And in the afternoons, he'd accompanied her and Kobi on their long strolls as they explored different corners of Kfar Yonatan.

The village, nestled on a hilltop, was on the site of a former Jordanian army post. The abandoned barracks were used for various community needs like the *beit knesset*, the library, the day care center, and a social hall. The old caravans, vacated as couples moved into the new prefabs, were taken over by the yeshiva. Pine trees with a fragrance that reminded Lisa of the Grand Canyon sprinkled the grounds. She reflected how they used to go to Payson to get fresh air and quiet. Now they were living in the mountains and had fresh air and quiet all the time. Lisa found the change thrilling.

She'd also been thrilled to discover that she could buy chicken that was cleaned and quartered. Apparently, her mother-in-law bought live chickens because Tzachi refused anything but ice cream from the freezer. Lisa had just put her chicken on to simmer when Kobi walked in with a full basket of groceries and a bouquet of red and purple anemones, her favorite flower.

"I called my parents before I went shopping," he said, avoiding his wife's eyes, "and my father wants us to come soon."

"Oh, Kobi," Lisa groaned. "Even with the new car, it will take us two hours to get there and two hours back." She thought quickly as she arranged the flowers in a vase. "I guess I could prepare for next Shabbat on Thursday and we could go next Friday."

"He asked us to come for a Shabbat."

"No," Lisa said sharply.

"I know, I know." Kobi tiptoed into the bedroom to peek at his sleeping son.

Every Friday, Kobi drove to Maalei Tikvah, an older, more established settlement twenty minutes away. Besides buying the *challot* and other last-minute items for Shabbat, he called his parents from the pay phone there. It seemed to Lisa that his father always had some request that was difficult for them.

She waited until he returned to the living room. "Kobi, you know we promised each other we wouldn't spend another Shabbat by your parents."

He nodded his head dolefully.

"Trying to ignore the Jordanian TV shows and watching your sister chain-smoke is not my idea of an uplifting Shabbat."

"Riki's not going to be there," Kobi protested half-heartedly.

Lisa threw her arms up in exasperation.

"You're right, you're right," he appeased her. "I'll call them from work Sunday and tell them we can't come."

Lisa was mollified. "I've got a better idea," she responded. "Invite them here for Shabbat."

"It won't be too much for you?"

"I can handle them coming here far better than us going there."

CHAPTER
Twenty-eight

*L*ate Shabbat afternoon, Lisa congratulated herself on her plan's success. Tzachi had complimented Lisa's cooking. Shula had managed to be a help in the small kitchen without getting in the way. Both grandparents enjoyed Shuki, who was beginning to play peek-a-boo.

Everything was fine until just before *seudah shlishit*. It was almost six o'clock when Tzachi came out of the bathroom and reported to Kobi that the toilet wouldn't flush and there was no water coming out of the faucet.

"Oh," Lisa exclaimed, overhearing his remark. "The water tank must be empty!" She ran outside and grabbed a couple of used wine bottles from under the porch. They were filled with clean water. "Here, Kobi."

Kobi poured enough water into the toilet tank to flush down its contents and handed his father the other bottle.

"Abba, you can use this to wash your hands, but don't waste it."

Tzachi took the bottle and did as he was told. As Lisa stashed the empty bottle in the kitchen, though, he confronted Kobi.

"You act as if this is a normal occurrence."

"Well...," Kobi hesitated, "the water truck comes every day except Shabbat and fills up the village's tank. Usually we manage fine. Once in a while it runs out. I guess there were more guests than usual this week."

"How are you going to bathe Shuki?" Tzachi's face was beginning to flush.

"We'll have water by tomorrow morning at the latest," Kobi said calmly.

"How can you live like this?" Tzachi sputtered. "Is this some crazy idea of your American wife?"

Standing in the kitchen, hearing every word, Lisa felt trapped. The only way out was through the living room and she didn't want to face her father-in-law.

"Abba," Kobi placated him, "you didn't have such good living conditions when you first started out, either."

"That was thirty years ago! What's the matter with you? Why can't you settle in Beit She'an and live like human beings?"

"Riki doesn't live in Beit She'an, either," Kobi quietly reminded him.

Lisa knew from her husband's tone that he was doing his best to control his anger.

"At least Riki lives in a normal apartment with running water."

"Tzachi." Lisa heard her mother-in-law's soft voice, but couldn't make out her words. A minute later, she heard the front door close and peeked out from the kitchen. Kobi was alone in the living room, sitting on the couch with his fists clenched.

"My parents went for a walk. They'll be back in time to eat."

"I'll put the food on the table."

"I'll help." Kobi stood up.

"I can manage just fine on my own, thanks," Lisa replied coldly.

Kobi didn't sit back down, but followed his wife into the kitchen.

"Lisa, I'm sorry about what my father said, but you know I have no control over it."

Angrily, Lisa turned around to face her husband. "I know that, but you never, ever say anything to defend me to your father. Living here wasn't my idea, it was *our* idea. And staying in America for so long was because of *you*, and you always let your father think it was because of *me*. He blames me for everything he doesn't like and I'm sick of it!"

Lisa slammed the stack of plates she was holding down on the counter and flounced out of the room. Kobi followed her into their bedroom, but as soon as he entered, Shuki began stirring.

"I want to calm down before I feed him." Lisa glared at her husband. "Please leave me alone."

"Lisa..."

"*Please*." She raised her voice and Shuki began to cry.

Kobi gently took the baby out of his crib. "Should I walk him for a bit?"

Lisa just shook her head and held out her arms for the infant. Kobi sighed and left the room. Taking a few deep breaths, Lisa settled herself on her bed and addressed the needs of her son.

For years, Lisa had watched other women take care of their children and had done her best to stifle her feelings of envy. That she was now able to feed her own child was nothing short of a miracle to her. She couldn't take the simple act for granted, and as she held Shuki, her anger dissipated.

Not sure what the situation would be between Kobi and his parents after they returned from their walk, she gingerly left the bedroom twenty minutes later. To her relief, she saw the table ready for the meal.

"Shall we wash and sit down?" she asked her husband.

"How are we going to wash?" Tzachi demanded before Kobi could answer.

"We have more water bottles," Kobi replied quickly. Before another comment could be made, he hurried outside to get one.

The meal was decidedly tense. Kobi tried singing, but Tzachi wasn't in the mood, and only Shula joined in. It was Shuki, gurgling happily, who kept the Shabbat from ending on a totally sour note.

The following morning there was water again and Lisa washed up from Shabbat, bathed Shuki, and did a load of laundry. In the evening, Kobi came home with the latest Mary Stewart mystery, sheepishly holding out the Steimatzky's bookstore bag as a peace offering. Lisa was happy to have something new to read in English and appreciated Kobi's thoughtfulness. Still, it rankled that they hadn't thrashed out their disagreement about his father.

She wished that Sondra was there to talk to. She knew that her cousin found her mother-in-law overbearing, and talking to her wouldn't be *lashon hara*, but would help her to cope. Unfortunately, Sondra wasn't a simple phone call away. Lisa knew she could write her, but it would take about a month before she would hear back. A month was better than never, though. Somehow, Lisa had the feeling the problem wasn't going to disappear by then.

CHAPTER
Twenty-nine

"Rachel." Cradling the phone, Sondra glanced at her watch as she heard her journalist cousin croak a groggy hello. It was only nine-thirty on a Monday evening in LA, where she was calling. "Did I wake you?"

"No, well, I guess I dozed off while I was working on an article."

"I'm so sorry."

"It's okay," Rachel reassured her. "I have to finish this, but if it bores me, I wonder what it will do to the readers."

Sondra had to chuckle at that. "What's it about?"

"Tax proposals."

"Oh." Sondra smiled. "It does sound boring. Listen, Rachel, I have some good news. We had a baby boy Saturday night."

"Mazal tov," Rachel responded dutifully.

"Thank you." Sondra ignored her cousin's lack of enthusiasm. "G-d willing, if all's well, the bris is going to be Sunday, and my parents are planning on coming, and Oscar and Rose, and maybe even Aunt Irene and Uncle Herbert. I thought maybe you'd want to join us."

"It's nice of you to think of me." Rachel sounded genuinely pleased. "Can I bring a friend?"

Sondra had prepared herself for that exact question when her close friend Debbie had visited her in the hospital Sunday afternoon.

After oohing and ahhing over the baby, Debbie became practical. "Have you thought about the bris?"

"Danny already talked to the shul about using the social hall." Sondra grinned. "Zvi Chaim's bris was on Shabbos, and since there wasn't an *eruv*, we had it in our teeny-tiny apartment. Only the family and close friends nearby enough to walk came."

"You'll have a crowd with a Sunday bris," Debbie pointed out. "Most people won't have to work."

"Yeah." Sondra wiggled happily in her hospital bed. "We can invite Shirley and Doc's friends and everyone from the office."

"When are your parents coming?" Debbie asked.

"My mother's on her way right now and Daddy's coming Thursday evening. I wonder...," Sondra hesitated, "if I should invite Rachel."

"Why not?" Having grown up in the same neighborhood, Debbie still remembered Sondra's younger cousin from Kansas City.

"She might ask to bring her boyfriend with her." Sondra pulled at her headscarf nervously.

"That's not your problem."

"I don't want her to think I approve of her dating a non-Jew," Sondra said worriedly.

Debbie waved her hand dismissively. "Don't get so involved. Just tell her you're glad she won't be driving by herself."

"I wish she'd just fly in for the day," Sondra said ruefully. "I don't want her driving on Shabbos on my account."

"If she drives on Shabbos, it won't be because of you," Debbie reassured her friend. "There's plenty of time to get here Saturday night after Shabbos is out, and if she does come Saturday night, her boyfriend can stay with us."

Sondra marveled at Debbie's easygoing attitude and wondered if her children, growing up in an observant home like Debbie had, would be able to be less rigid than she was.

With that conversation in mind, Sondra answered her cousin's question without missing a beat. "I guess you don't want to drive by yourself."

"Right," Rachel agreed.

"And you'd like to bring Jeffrey?"

"Jeffrey?" Rachel echoed. "Oh, Jeffrey, no. We broke up several months ago. Karen, one of the reporters, will probably come with me. I helped her drive to Portland to visit her relatives for Thanksgiving."

Sondra breathed a sigh of relief as she hung up the phone. Glancing around her hospital room, she was overcome with a longing to speak to Lisa. For the past four months, dozens of pale blue aerograms had been exchanged between the two cousins, but there was nothing like a real conversation. In Israel, it was almost eight in the morning, Sondra realized. She had her credit card and she could afford an overseas call.

The only problem was that the Chazons still didn't have a phone. It would be coming soon, Lisa had written. Already fifteen families had been hooked up. The phone company had promised that they'd be back soon to add additional lines.

In the meantime, Lisa went to her neighbor's every Sunday evening to wait for the prearranged call from her parents. Surely they'd told her yesterday about the baby's birth. But Sondra wanted to talk to Lisa herself. She wanted to describe the baby's dark eyes and his head full of hair. She wanted to explain how it hadn't been easy to dial the rotary phone using her little finger on Shabbos afternoon in order to call a taxi to take them to the hospital. And she wanted to let her cousin know how much she would miss not having her at the bris.

She could call Lisa's neighbor, Sondra thought, and ask her to bring Lisa to the phone. But what if it was raining? Or Shuki was asleep? Or the neighbor was too busy? Or not home?

With a sigh, Sondra opened the night table drawer and pulled out an aerogram. With another sigh, she took out a pen. Lisa's letters read as if she was talking. Sondra's were far more stilted. She remembered how much trouble she'd had answering that aerogram back in August. It had taken three tries written on scratch paper before she'd got it right.

In some ways you have it a lot easier than me, she'd written. *You began your marriage with your father-in-law far away. Even now, how often do you see him? How much can he really interfere? On the other hand, I have to say that Danny has always defended me to his mother. But he — actually, none of us — were raised with that intense parental respect that Kobi was raised with. Honoring one's parents is a really important mitzvah, so maybe it would be best if you let Kobi keep the charade going.*

To Sondra's relief, Lisa had written back that she liked the advice. She was willing to ignore Tzachi's implied criticism as long as Kobi never actually blamed her. So far, from what Lisa had written, it was working okay.

With a derisive smile, Sondra wondered what Lisa would have thought about the conversation they'd had with her mother-in-law earlier that morning. Glowing, Shirley had breezed into the hospital room with sunflowers for Sondra.

"Doc is supposed to meet me here as soon as he finishes his rounds," she declared. "Let me see that baby."

Danny lifted the infant from the bassinet and handed him to his mother.

"He's beautiful," she declared. "I think he looks like Doc."

Danny and Sondra had exchanged amused glances. They'd just decided he was remarkably similar to the pictures of Sondra's grandfather and had decided to name the baby Yosef after him.

"Now I don't want the two of you to worry about a thing for the bris," Shirley declared. "It can be at our clubhouse and I'll take care of the caterer."

This time the looks Danny and Sondra exchanged were not amused.

Danny cleared his throat. "Um, Mom, we want the bris to be at the shul."

"Okay." Shirley faltered for just a second. "I'm sure the caterer can work there."

"Mom," Danny spoke patiently, "we need to use a caterer that has experience with the shul's kitchen. Sondra is going to take care of it tomorrow."

"I guess you don't need me then." Shirley smiled, hiding her hurt feelings.

"Of course we need you," Sondra spoke up from the hospital bed. "Who's going to get all the children ready for the bris?"

Shirley's face lit up. "Maybe I'll take them shopping for new outfits before you come home."

"That'd be great," Sondra had agreed, and it had all ended well. Thank goodness Danny had been visiting her then.

Using her tiniest handwriting so she could fit in as much as possible, Sondra described the baby, the scene, and her conversation with Rachel. It wasn't a phone call, but at least she and Lisa were keeping in touch.

If Sondra had placed that call to Lisa, she would have been disappointed to learn that no one was home at the Chazons' house. By eight o'clock, Lisa had already dropped Shuki at the sitter and was on her way to Kfar Saba. She had meetings with Tnuva and Angel's to arrange for daily dairy and bread deliveries to Kfar Yonatan. Gone was Lisa's aspiration to get a job with an Israeli department store that would be closed on Shabbat. Instead, she was planning on opening a *shomer Shabbat* grocery store. It might not be as glamorous as working at Kramer's, but it would certainly fill a need. And it would be her very own store.

When they first moved to Kfar Yonatan, Elisheva, Ari Ben David's pretty wife, explained that there were two ways of shopping for food.

"You can schlep to the city or Maalei Tikvah and stock up, or you can make a list and send it with Boaz Freed."

"Who's he?"

"He's the single man, the blonde living in the caravan next to the yeshiva. He's the driver for Kfar Yonatan and takes the three-year-olds to nursery school in Maalei Tikvah. While there, he's happy to fill anyone's food order. You just need to give him your list the night before."

"Oh." Lisa was impressed. "Do we pay him?"

"No, it's covered in his salary, but..." Elisheva hesitated. "He's very nice and pleasant and very easygoing. So sometimes he replaces skim milk with whole milk or chicken legs with wings or sliced bread with pitas. Also, we don't get the food until he brings the kids back after nursery school. You have to be willing to go with the flow."

"I see." Lisa resolved to do her own shopping as much as possible.

When Sukkot ended, Lisa faced an almost empty refrigerator and there were no eggs to be borrowed.

"Schools are off tomorrow," she complained to Kobi, "so Boaz won't be going shopping. What am I supposed to do?"

"I'll hitchhike to work and you can have the car to go shopping."

"Thanks, Kobi." Lisa smiled.

"It's in my best interest," he grinned. "I want a good dinner when I come home."

Elisheva joined her on the shopping excursion, and it was on the way there that Lisa got her inspiration.

"It would be so nice to have a store in Kfar Yonatan."

"Sure would!" Elisheva agreed.

"Do you think forty families could keep one going?"

"When Maalei Tikvah's began, there were only thirty families."

"Maybe," Lisa kept her eyes on the road, "I should start a grocery store."

"As head of the village, I know Avi would do anything he could to help you," Elisheva said encouragingly.

That evening, over their good dinner, Lisa presented her idea to Kobi.

"There's a need, and you know all about retail." He was just as enthusiastic as Elisheva. "My father can help by introducing you to all his distributors. Only be careful. He'll overwhelm you with advice."

"I'll preempt him and ask him for suggestions."

She did, and there were numerous phone calls to her father-in-law. Right before she opened a week after Purim, he gave her guidance on extending credit.

"First of all," he expanded with pride, "you have to set a limit on credit, both on the time and the amount. No one should be allowed to sit down to their Shabbat meal owing you money, and no account should go over three hundred shekels."

"Okay."

"And," Tzachi continued, "everyone should sign when they take something on credit, so there is none of that, 'I never bought this much.'"

Lisa nodded in agreement.

"Once the kids there are big enough to come to the store on their own, make sure you have the parents' permission to let them charge things. Otherwise, you're setting yourself up for problems."

"Okay," Lisa repeated, this time with a huge smile. Her father-in-law's last statement seemed to imply that he envisioned them staying in Kfar Yonatan for a long time. For the first time since meeting him, Lisa felt relaxed with Tzachi. Perhaps he would be a valuable source of help for her.

"**N**atan told me he forgot to sign out on the bread he took this morning." Lisa's neighbor was clearly embarrassed. "I'm sorry."

"No problem." Lisa recorded the purchase along with Myra's eggs, cheese, chicken, and a candy bar.

"Does anyone ever take bread or milk without letting you know?"

"So far, no." Lisa smiled. The dairy and bakery deliveries were placed in front of the store every morning at around six, and Kobi's job was to bring the orders inside before he left for work. It was understood that in the hour and a half they stood outside, anyone could help themselves as long as they made a note of their shopping on the sign hanging on the door.

"I'm so happy to have a store here." Myra bagged her items in the plastic shopping bag she'd brought with her.

"I'm glad," Lisa answered sincerely. Her vision had been a reality for four months already. Housed in one of the caravans the yeshiva wasn't using, the store, she felt, had full community support.

"Is this what you did in America?"

"No." Lisa grinned. "But I did work in a big, uh…" She struggled for the word for *department store* in Hebrew. "Um, a big store like HaMashbir, only bigger."

Israeli-born Myra gave her a skeptical look.

"Really," Lisa insisted. "You should have seen how I got dressed to go to work. Suits and high heels, not like here." She smoothed down her jean skirt and glanced at her sandals.

"You look fine," Myra assured her. "I've got to go. They're supposed to be coming soon to finally connect another ten telephones."

"Myra," Lisa asked uneasily, "were you upset when I got connected before you?"

"Absolutely not! You needed a line to make food orders so I can go shopping. No one minded. But now we're relieved to be able to finally rejoin the outside world."

Lisa laughed as Myra left the store, and then she turned her attention to Shuki. The fifteen-month-old was happily stacking blocks in the playpen next to the cash register.

"Would you like some juice, sweetie?"

He nodded vigorously and handed his mother a red cube in exchange for his cup.

Lisa used the lull in business to finally pull the blue aerogram from Sondra out of her pocket.

You'll never guess who called and asked if she could come for Shabbos, Sondra wrote. *Rachel! She's coming by herself and she's flying in Friday afternoon. I'm so excited!*

The letter continued with news from the community. Lisa finished the letter and glanced at her watch.

"Are you ready to go home?" she asked Shuki.

"Home." He raised his chubby fists to his mother.

She hugged him tight before settling him inside the umbrella stroller. Although he was a good walker, he was easily distracted when he walked. An interesting bug crossing his path could mean a ten-minute stop. Lisa was in a hurry to get home and bake a cake for the Gruenbergs' brit tomorrow. The grocery store would be closed in honor of the occasion.

❈   ❈   ❈

Sondra balanced little Yossi on her hip as she unlocked the front door. "Come on, Naomi." Batsheva pulled her little sister into the house.

"Zvi Chaim, don't drop the swimming bag by the door," Sondra directed.

"In the laundry room?" her oldest asked.

"Right. Batsheva, put the inner tube with the bag, and I'll get everyone something to drink. Zvi Chaim, you're in charge while I put Yossi down for a nap."

"You both have to listen to me," she heard him say. "I'll tell you a story."

Pleased, Sondra knew she'd have a few quiet minutes to check and maybe even read the mail. Among the bills and advertisements were three letters. One was addressed to Zvi Chaim and looked like an early birthday card. The second was a blue aerogram from Lisa, and the third was a legal-sized envelope with Rachel's return address. Curious, she opened Rachel's first and pulled out a full-page newspaper article. The headline blared, "Orthodox Jews: A Modern Look at an Ancient Society." *Thanks for your help* was scrawled across the top.

Intrigued, Sondra began reading. The piece was a fair description of the lifestyle of observant Jews. Sondra found it troubling, though. The writer, her cousin, wrote with complete emotional detachment. Halfway through the article, she realized that Rachel's Shabbos visit and questions hadn't been motivated by an interest in her roots, just research for an article.

Lisa's newsy aerogram was a salve to her disappointment and made Sondra long to really speak to her cousin. It was still the middle of the night in Israel. Once the kids were in bed, she resolved she'd call Lisa.

Although she was duly sympathetic to Sondra's frustration with Rachel, Sondra sensed that Lisa was preoccupied.

"Is everyone okay?" she queried

"Everyone's fine," Lisa responded.

"You sound worried."

"Well…," Lisa hesitated, annoyed with herself for not hiding her feelings better. "Kobi got hit with a rock yesterday, and —"

Sondra gasped. "I thought you said everyone's okay!"

"No one's hurt," Lisa reassured her. "The car was hit, not him, but the front windshield was shattered, and one of us has to go to the police and file a complaint and get the verification to get the window fixed at no cost." Lisa took a deep breath. "Kobi's talking to someone at shul to see if he can sub for me in the grocery store. If not, he'll have to take a sick day."

"Does it happen often?"

"Boaz worked in my place when Shuki was sick with —"

"Not the subbing," Sondra interrupted impatiently, "the rocks."

"Oh, well, not that often, but more than we'd like. But let's not waste your money on talking about this. How is everything there?"

"Good, school's —"

"One moment, Sondra. I'm really sorry, but I have to grab Shuki."

Sondra glanced at Rachel's article again while waiting for Lisa. In half a minute her cousin was back on the line.

"Sorry," Lisa repeated. "How are the kids? Is Yossi sleeping through the night?"

"He is, thank goodness. I'll be putting him in day care at the school and Zvi Chaim will be in first grade."

"I can't believe it! He'll do great. Is Naomi talking yet?"

Sondra sighed. "A few words here and there. We've finally decided to take her to a specialist. She has an appointment next week. Tell me about Shuki."

Lisa felt her face flush. Her toddler's vocabulary was far bigger than his three-year-old cousin's, but she didn't want to make Sondra envious. She searched for something innocuous to say.

"Next week he's going to start going to a playgroup."

"You have a free morning to do that?"

"No." Lisa laughed. "This is a playgroup you pay for. My neighbor, Myra, watches four two-year-olds in the mornings. Shuki's too big to count on him napping in the playpen at the store. I'll expand my morning hours and only open two afternoons a week."

"Good. I hope it works out."

"Me too. What grade are you teaching this year?"

"I'm back in..."

Before Sondra could finish the sentence, there was a shriek from the girls' room that Lisa could hear loud and clear.

"Is everything okay there?"

"Sometimes Naomi gets nightmares," Sondra answered. "I better go to her."

"Give her a kiss for me," Lisa instructed. "I'm glad you called. Let me know about the appointment."

"Write me about the playgroup."

"Love you."

"Me too."

"Oh, Sondra..."

"Yeah?"

"I don't want my parents to know about the rock."

An hour later, Lisa was in her car and on her way. Elisheva had offered to watch Shuki since Lisa didn't want him in a car with a shattered windshield. She wasn't alone, though. On her way out, she'd picked up Myra's niece and a new neighbor, Gavriel, who were at the bus stop waiting for a ride. The teenager had scrambled into the back and promptly fallen asleep, but Gavriel was happy to converse.

"Where'd Kobi get hit?" he asked.

"From what I understand, right after the gas station."

Gavriel shook his head. "It looks so pastoral here, but in just a second that can all change."

Lisa nodded and tightened her grasp on the steering wheel. Gavriel and his wife were the latest newcomers to Kfar Yonatan.

"You know," she commented, "in America, I would have never let someone I hardly know into my car, especially if he had a gun. Here, I'm thrilled to have you and your weapon."

Gavriel chuckled and then turned serious. "I have a friend from Ariel who was surrounded by a mob of rioting teenagers last year. He really thought his life was in danger, so he shot into the air. It took a couple of shots before the gang dispersed. Later, one of the teenagers was reported dead and he was arrested for premeditated murder. He spent eight months in prison before he was finally brought to trial and acquitted."

"Are you serious?" Lisa exclaimed.

"I am."

There was a strained silence that Lisa finally broke.

"Are you and Yaffa happy in Kfar Yonatan?"

"So far, yes. What about you?"

"Oh, I think it's home! We want to build."

"You mean a permanent house?" Gavriel asked.

"Uh-huh, I'm really looking forward to the town meeting with the architects tomorrow."

"I understand the mortgages the government's giving out for building are really good. You get even better as a new immigrant, right?"

"Right."

That was something she could write to her parents, Lisa thought. She was relieved Sondra hadn't reminded her how she'd taken Sondra to task for not telling her parents about her burns years earlier. This rock-throwing incident was different, though. No one had been hurt. Her parents had seen everything when they visited in the spring. Lisa hoped they would make another visit soon and she prayed that when they did, everything would stay calm.

CHAPTER
Thirty-one

*D*anny and Sondra sat nervously in the children's neurologist's office, watching her work with Naomi. Their three-year-old cooperated nicely, and at the end of the session was rewarded with a bag of potato chips and a packet of crayons.

"I want you to draw a nice picture while I talk to your parents," the specialist instructed.

"There are no neurological reasons for her delayed speech," she explained to Danny and Sondra once Naomi was occupied. "I suspect that she's getting everything she wants without talking."

Sondra nodded thoughtfully. "My four-year-old does do an inordinate amount of talking for her. Do you think being in nursery school will help?"

"It should, but to be on the safe side, I suggest taking her for speech therapy."

"So," Sondra told Debbie that evening, "I'm going to be taking Naomi for speech therapy every Monday afternoon."

"It can't hurt."

"Right." Sondra cradled the phone while scraping at a stubborn glob of Play-Doh. "How'd your appointment go today?"

"Fine, except he told me to cut back on salt."

"I did that when I was expecting Naomi. There's a salt substitute that's not bad."

"Want to go food shopping together tomorrow?"

"Sure — no, wait. Zvi Chaim's teacher wants us to take him to be evaluated by an occupational therapist. There's got to be a reason that such a bright boy has such atrocious handwriting. That appointment's tomorrow."

"Do you want me to watch the girls?"

"Debbie, thanks, that's so nice of you."

"Isn't that what friends are for," Debbie quipped. "You'll be there for me when I go into labor, right?"

"For sure! But, Debbie, I'm glad you've got a few months to go. Yesterday, I had Batsheva at the doctor for another ear infection. Ever since the tubes fell out, we're back to the same old routine. This was the fourth visit to the pediatrician in three weeks. And Yossi's teething, and last night I was up with him shrieking twice. I feel like I'm falling off my feet and I still have lesson plans for tomorrow and there's Rosh Hashanah in two weeks and I don't have that much in the freezer."

"You'll pull it off. You always do."

"How do you manage? You teach more hours than I do!"

Debbie chuckled. "I only have two kids and, *baruch Hashem*, they rarely have me schlepping to doctors. By the way, I'm counting on you coming to us for first day lunch."

"It won't be too much?" Sondra asked, worried.

"Not at all!"

Even with Debbie's invitation, there were still plenty of meals to prepare, so Sondra didn't stop cleaning chickens when her mother called the following Sunday evening.

"Aunt Lotte just called us with some nice news." Sondra could hear the smile in Helga's voice.

"Yes?"

"Rachel's engaged."

"How nice. To whom?"

"That nice man she brought to the *piydon haben*."

"Mom!" Sondra abandoned her chickens. "How can you call that nice news? He's not Jewish!"

"Are you sure?"

"Of course I'm sure." Sondra began pacing the kitchen, trying not to wrap herself in the long phone cord. "What did Aunt Lotte say?"

"They're getting married Thanksgiving weekend in Los Angeles. Daddy's already looking for someone to take care of the cows."

"You're going to go to the wedding?!"

"I think so," Helga faltered. "Why not?"

"Because it's a mixed marriage," Sondra sputtered.

"Well, I didn't know. I guess I'll have to discuss it with your father, but I know Lotte wants us there. Tell me, how are the children?"

Sondra gave her mother a brief rundown on the kids, said a quick hello to her father, and cut the conversation short. Danny finished tucking Naomi and Batsheva into bed just as Sondra replaced the receiver. Her husband listened sympathetically as she moaned about intermarriage, but there wasn't much he could say to comfort her.

Wednesday afternoon the phone was ringing when they returned from occupational therapy. Yossi had already fallen asleep in the car and Sondra was trying to get him into his crib without waking him. Zvi Chaim grabbed the phone on the sixth ring.

"It's Rachel," he yelled to his mother.

"Shhh," she whispered, but it was too late. Yossi opened both eyes and was beginning to whimper. "I'll take it in my bedroom," she told her son. Bracing herself for an unpleasant conversation at best, she settled down on her bed and picked up the bedside phone.

"Hello," she said, hoping she didn't sound as uncomfortable as she felt.

"Sondra, guess what!"

"What?" Sondra's voice brightened. Perhaps Rachel was calling to say she'd broken her engagement. But no, Rachel's intention was to tell her the news, and she didn't understand why her cousin wouldn't be happy about it.

"I thought you two had broken up."

"We did for a while, but we were both miserable without each other, and we began seeing each other again in the summer. Are you coming to the wedding?"

"I don't think so," Sondra answered uncomfortably and was immediately sorry that she hadn't answered with an outright no.

"Please come," Rachel begged. "We're getting married by a judge. The wedding will be totally nondenominational. And I'll make sure to have kosher food for you."

"It's so important to you that I be there?"

"Yes." There was a pleading note in Rachel's voice. "You were a big part of my childhood. And I want at least one of my cousins at my wedding. Lisa's in Israel, Howie's dead, and you're only an hour's flight away."

"I'll think about it." Sondra didn't know what else to say.

When her parents called Sunday, Helga broached the subject of the wedding.

"I understand Rachel really wants you there."

"I don't understand," Sondra answered impatiently, "why you and Daddy are planning to go. You boycotted Brenda's wedding."

"That was different," her mother answered tolerantly. "Brenda's just a second cousin and she was married in a church."

"But even before you knew where the wedding was going to be held, all the family was upset she was marrying out."

"Times were different then," Helga replied and changed the subject.

"I think you should talk to a *rav* about the whole thing," Danny told Sondra after she repeated the conversation with her mother.

All their children were asleep and the two sat quietly in the den. It was Sondra's favorite room in the house. Three walls were full of shelves, with the lower ones holding toys and the upper ones full of favorite books and texts. The fourth wall had a full bay window that looked out on their tree-filled backyard. During the day, the floor was usually cluttered with playthings and was clearly a children's room. In the evening, it became a good spot for Sondra and Danny to mull over their day together. Sondra usually knitted as they spoke and Danny would invariably have a cup of tea.

"I wish I could call Rabbi Feingold," Sondra said wistfully. He'd been the head of the seminary where she'd learned in Jerusalem.

Danny glanced at the clock. "Why don't you? In another hour it will be after eight in the morning."

"Okay," Sondra said. "I'll get a paper and pencil and you can help me get my thoughts together."

CHAPTER

Thirty-two

"Are you Boaz's sister?"

Surprised, Lisa turned to face a wrinkled, heavyset woman wearing a navy blue dress and a matching headscarf.

"I'm his neighbor."

"Oh, you're dressed so fancy, I thought you were part of the family."

Lisa shook her head. "You must be one of the bride's relatives."

The woman nodded happily. "I'm her great-aunt."

"You're getting yourself a wonderful great-nephew," Lisa said warmly. "And I'm looking forward to having a new neighbor. I hope Chava will enjoy living in Kfar Yonatan."

"Are all the women as fancy as you?"

Before Lisa could answer, a young teenager grabbed the older woman by the hand. "Come, Aunt Shira, they want to take a family picture now."

Lisa laughed to herself as she watched the woman walk away. The blue suit she'd bought almost three years earlier still looked like new. Combined with her wig, instead of a scarf, she did indeed look elegant enough to attend a wedding at the Camelback Inn.

Of course, the simple wedding hall in Petach Tikva was a far cry from the exclusive Camelback Inn, but Lisa was enjoying the relaxed atmosphere. The only problem was that the invitation called the chuppah for seven-thirty and now it was almost eight. Lisa looked at her watch impatiently.

"Is this the first Israeli wedding you've been to?" Elisheva asked her, noticing.

"Except for my sister-in-law's. Why?"

"Israeli weddings never start on time."

"How come?"

Lisa's Israeli-born friend waved her hand dismissively. "People come when they finish work. Some get off later than others. When there're enough people, they have the chuppah."

The look Lisa gave Elisheva was incredulous. "It seems like a lot of people end up wasting a lot of time."

"It's an opportunity to relax and see people you haven't seen in a while. Put your things down at that table where I'm sitting and get some juice."

As she followed Elisheva's advice, Lisa remembered how hard she'd worked on the seating arrangements for her wedding. Here, the tables were filling up and she wondered where the latecomers were going to sit. It wasn't her problem, though. The chuppah finally began forty-five minutes late, and afterwards, Lisa sat down between Miriam and Myra. She ate a roll spread with hummus and enjoyed visiting with her neighbors while waiting for the new couple to emerge from the *cheder yichud*. It was after nine when they finally did, and following the first round of dancing, Kobi appeared at her side.

"I'm ready to go," he announced.

"Let me have a piece of chicken first," Lisa protested. "I'm hungry."

"Okay," Kobi acquiesced. "I guess I'll have some schnitzel. And then we'll go?"

"Fine. By the way, the Bergers aren't going back with us."

"Great." Kobi grinned. "If no one else asks for a ride, we can have almost an hour of uninterrupted time together."

No one did ask and there wasn't anyone at the hitchhiking station when they drove by.

"So what did you think of the wedding?" Kobi cast a fond look at his wife, then returned his eyes to the road.

"Very nice, but I wish it had started on time."

"I should have warned you," Kobi apologized.

Lisa shrugged and smiled.

"You know, Lisa," Kobi spoke seriously. "I sat next to Amnon. He said they're moving down to Yamit next month."

"What about his work?"

"He has a number of sick days and vacation days coming to him. Plus, he's worked there long enough to take a leave of absence."

"Is his wife taking a leave of absence too?"

"No, she only teaches twice a week. She'll commute."

Lisa stared at Kobi. "That's a long commute."

"Only two hours. There're all sorts of empty apartments in Yamit. They'll have one for the taking. Also, the Gellers are probably going down."

"Is he taking a leave of absence or commuting?"

"Neither. He'll go into the office every few weeks and then take his work down there. Some of the others are talking about going down when it gets closer to Pesach."

Lisa caught her breath as Kobi carefully passed an army jeep.

As part of the peace agreement between Israel and Egypt that was brokered by President Jimmy Carter, the evacuation of Yamit and several of the nearby moshavim in the Sinai Peninsula was slated for the spring. Some of the residents had taken their compensation money and left. Others were staying, hoping that the decree would be annulled and they'd be able to remain in the pioneering town the government had encouraged them to settle. Rav Zvi Yehuda had called on the public to join the remaining pioneers and a number had responded, although Amnon and his family would be the first from Kfar Yonatan to do so.

"Does Amnon really think he'll be able to change Prime Minister Begin's mind?" Lisa asked carefully.

"He thinks that Begin doesn't want to evacuate the Sinai at all," Kobi explained. "He gave in to American pressure. If enough of us go down there, he can tell Carter that the public's against it and call off the evacuation."

"And you think enough people will go to Yamit?" Lisa was clearly skeptical. "You heard what your sister said on the subject. It's a chance for peace."

"Riki always liked fairy tales!" Kobi said impatiently. "Tell me about another country that was attacked, won the war defending itself, and gave away the territory it gained. We need that land! We need the oil! My brother fought in that war! He died in that war!"

"I see," Lisa responded softly.

Kobi took a deep breath and concentrated on the road. He drove in silence for a quarter of an hour. Just before the turnoff to Kfar Yonatan, Lisa spoke.

"Kobi, I don't feel I can leave the store. Too many people depend on me. But if it's so important to you to go to Yamit, I'll give you my blessings to take a leave of absence from work and go. On condition," Lisa gave a shaky laugh, "that you come home for Shabbat."

Kobi turned his eyes from the road. "Maybe I will." He smiled at his wife. "I'll think about it."

CHAPTER
Thirty-three

"Brachie," Sondra asked her friend anxiously, "does my *sheitel* look okay?"

"Just fine." Her friend smiled encouragingly.

"What about this bracelet? Is it too much?"

"No," Brachie reassured her. "You look great."

"Sondra," Danny entered the living room with Yossi in his arms. "You're beautiful. The dress is perfect for you, but even if you go in your bathrobe, your family will still think you look wonderful."

"I'm not sure about all of them," Sondra muttered, but her husband's compliment calmed her down somewhat.

Rabbi Feingold had been warm and patient when she'd called him two months earlier. After hearing Sondra's description of the situation, he asked one important question.

"If your cousin has any children, they'll be Jewish. Will you be able to persuade her to give them a Jewish education?"

"I — I don't know," Sondra had admitted honestly. She described how she'd thought Rachel was interested in exploring Yiddishkeit, only to learn it had been part of research for an article. On the other hand, she'd certainly been an influence on Lisa.

"You say your cousin wants you at the wedding?"

"Yes."

"Then I think you should go, but by yourself. If your husband goes also, it will seem too much like you are condoning intermarriage. You by yourself will send a strong message of caring for your cousin, but not approval of what she's doing."

Originally Sondra had thought that she'd just fly to Los Angeles for the day. That was before Danny told her he was getting Thanksgiving weekend off.

"We can make it a mini-vacation," he suggested. "We'll take the kids to Disneyland, go to the Jewish stores on Fairfax, buy all the kosher food we want, and spend Shabbos with the Fisches. How does that sound?"

"Amazing!" Sondra exclaimed. "Especially the Shabbos with Brachie."

The Shabbos *was* amazing. Danny had almost forgotten what it was like to go to a minyan where no one parked his car around the corner and pretended to walk to services. While the men were in shul, Brachie and Sondra were able to talk their hearts out and the children played happily together.

It had been a delightful three days, but now that Rachel's noon wedding was an hour away, Sondra was feeling decidedly nervous. No doubt she would be the only one there wearing a wig and one of the few to wear a dress with a hem below the knees.

"Sondra," Brachie called out, "your parents are here."

"Where are my grandkids?" her father exclaimed.

They came running, and both Julius and Helga were overwhelmed with hugs.

"What about me?" Uncle Herbert boomed. He and Irene both got their share of kisses.

"Are you ready?" Helga asked her daughter.

Sondra took a deep breath and nodded. She settled in the back seat of the rental car and tried to enjoy the ride down the coast to the Coronado Resort, where the wedding would be held.

No matter what her feelings about the marriage, Sondra had to admit that the beach was a beautiful site for a wedding. The ceremony, officiated by a justice of the peace, was totally secular and was over quickly. Afterwards, the guests, who were eager to party, were ushered into a private room adjacent to a lavish smorgasbord featuring almost every breakfast food imaginable — including ham and bacon.

Before Sondra sat down, the headwaiter discreetly approached her. "I need you to break the seal so we can heat up your kosher meal."

Surprised, Sondra glanced at the aluminum tray holding a kosher meal just like the ones she received on an airplane. She wrinkled her nose in distaste. With all the kosher food in Los Angeles, this was the best Rachel could do? Along with the kosher certification was stamped "roast beef and potatoes." Sondra made a quick decision.

"I'll pass on the meal, but thank you anyway."

She found a bank of pay phones, made a quick call to Danny, and headed to the smorgasbord to pile cold fruit and sliced vegetables on her plate. With that in hand, she was surprised to learn that her parents hadn't saved her a place.

"Joey and Ruthie have a seat for you at their table."

"Really?" Sondra smiled, pleased to think her younger cousins wanted her to sit with them. It had been years since she'd seen either of Rachel's siblings. Somehow, the quick stops she'd made in Kansas City never coincided with their visits home.

"It's so good to see both of you!" Sondra exclaimed.

"It's been a long time," Joey agreed.

"Where's your husband?" Ruthie moved slightly so Sondra could pull her chair in.

"He's babysitting." Sondra knew she could have left it at that, but that wouldn't have been true to Rabbi Feingold's guidelines. "We probably could have left the kids with our friends for a few hours, but he wasn't willing to come to a mixed wedding."

"How come you came?" Ruthie demanded, turning her head to stare at Sondra.

"Rachel really wanted me here, and since it wasn't a church wedding, I came."

"So if I get married in a church, you won't come?"

"Are you engaged?" Sondra asked with a sinking feeling in her stomach.

"No, she's not," Joey interjected. "Ruthie just loves to play devil's advocate. It's one of her favorite pastimes and drives the rest of us crazy."

Sondra smiled politely. She'd almost forgotten what a stubborn, argumentative child Ruthie had been. Aunt Lotte had almost torn her hair out over her youngest. More than once, Sondra had heard her mother soothe her aunt by telling her Ruthie would grow out of it. Ruthie was a college senior now, and it didn't appear that she had.

"Do you have plans for after graduation?" Sondra changed the subject, quietly made a blessing, and bit into a carrot stick.

"I'm joining the Peace Corps," her cousin answered brightly.

"Really? Where are you going to be stationed?"

"Wherever they send me."

"That's unusual."

"Not typical for a Jewish American Princess, is it? You'd never do it."

"I really don't think of myself as a J.A.P.," Sondra said honestly. She thought about her childhood on a farm, her struggle as a teenager to learn more about Judaism, her commitment as an adult to the Torah.

"Maybe not a princess, but you are such a typical Jewish woman — married to a doctor. I bet you spend your days shopping and playing mah-jongg or bridge." There was a challenging note in Ruthie's voice.

Sondra stared at her cousin. "You don't know anything about me," she said tightly.

Ruthie didn't answer. Instead, she stood up with her plate in hand. "I'm getting some more bacon," she announced to the table. "Can I get anything for anyone?"

"Don't pay any attention to her," Joey spoke softly as his sister left the table. "She had a bad experience with the youth group when she was in high school, and since then has resented anything to do with Judaism. She puts me down all the time for wanting to be a cantor."

"How's that going?"

"It's good. Are you still teaching?"

"Yes, I have a really good class this year and I'm enjoying it."

Joey was affable and kind, just like he had been as a young boy. Still, Sondra found herself searching for something to talk about.

"How often do you get back to Kansas City?"

"I'll be there for winter break. For Passover, though, I'll be in Israel."

"That's so nice."

"I always thought you'd end up living there," Joey said.

Sondra nodded in agreement. Ruthie returned to the table with a full plate and a glass of juice in hand.

"I thought you'd like something to drink." She set the glass down in front of Sondra. Touched, Sondra smiled a genuine thank-you. As Ruthie handed out the food, the conversation around the table turned to the latest movie releases. Sondra surreptitiously checked her watch and realized Danny would be coming for her in less than half an hour. It was time to begin saying goodbye.

Her parents escorted her to the hotel entrance. "That wasn't so bad, was it?" her mother soothed as they waited for Danny to drive up. "There was nothing at all religious about the wedding."

Sondra inclined her head but didn't really answer. The whole situation made her sad, but this wasn't the time to talk about it.

"Give Oscar and Rose and everyone else my love," she said as she hugged her parents goodbye.

They walked her to the car in order to give one more kiss to each of their grandchildren. Sondra climbed in and they all waved until none of them could see each other.

"So, how'd it go?" Danny asked. He handed his wife the pizza slices she'd requested.

Sondra twisted her hands thoughtfully. "I don't know how Jeff's family felt about him marrying a Jew, but my family is fine with Rachel marrying out as long as they had a nonreligious wedding. I mean, it's like no one feels bad that there was no chuppah, no broken wine cup, no remembering Jerusalem, no mazal tov."

"Mazal tov," Naomi echoed from her car seat.

Sondra couldn't help but laugh. Two new words for her daughter! She put the conversation about the wedding aside and initiated a game of I Spy. Later, after they passed Indio, and the children were sleeping, Danny reopened the discussion.

"Sondra, I was thinking about this wedding all day. It's just so unbelievable. Every year you and I see mixed marriage as more and more of a tragedy, and at the same time, our families become more and more accepting."

"And it's like we're the ones who are wrong because we're so intolerant." Sondra sighed, gazing at the scenery flashing by out the window.

"Sometimes I feel we need to make a bigger break than just moving to St. Louis."

Sondra caught her breath. "What are you saying, Danny?"

"I think we should go to Israel this summer with the kids for a few weeks and take a serious look. Maybe the time's come for us to make the move."

"Oh, Danny!" Sondra's eyes shone at his suggestion. "I can't wait to write Lisa!"

Danny grinned at his wife's enthusiasm, but his voice was cautious. "Don't tell anyone we're thinking of *aliyah*. We're just going to have a special vacation and we'll see what comes out of it."

CHAPTER
Thirty-four

Lisa glanced at her watch as she locked up the grocery store. Already a quarter to two! She'd probably be the last mother to arrive at Myra's. She hated for Shuki to be the only one left to go home, but Tzachi had warned her against throwing out a late customer.

"Post your hours clearly on the door," her father-in-law had instructed her, "and make sure, if necessary, your sitter is willing to do overtime. You can hint that you're in a hurry, but only with a smile."

Lisa had felt her smile plastered on her face while her late customer took his time picking out what was obviously going to be his lunch. The man wasn't from Kfar Yonatan. Lisa surmised he was one of the builders, and, if satisfied, he'd become a long-term customer. The construction of permanent houses had finally begun.

As she slipped the key into her pocket, Lisa broke into a run. She arrived at Myra's panting, and her neighbor laughed at her.

"He's in the middle of a puzzle and Sarale's helping him. Don't worry."

Lisa smiled sheepishly and bent down to greet her son.

"Are you ready to go home?" She made a point to always speak to him in English.

"Soon," he answered, also in English.

"You see," Myra said. Although she only spoke Hebrew to Lisa, she understood English as well as Shuki did.

He put the last piece in the puzzle and Myra's three-year-old dumped it out again.

"Okay, Shuki," Lisa said. "This time it's Sarale's turn. Let's go home and have lunch."

The weather was beautiful and Lisa made a spontaneous decision to take a detour home, past the construction site. Four acres of land located on a plateau overlooking the caravans of the yeshiva had been cleared for twenty homes. Fifteen of those houses would be two stories high with an unfinished basement. The Chazons' house and four others would have only one floor, which was certainly big enough for them. If their family grew, they could either add the second story or finish the basement.

For a two-year-old, there's nothing more fascinating than noisy trucks and machinery. Shuki sat in his stroller and watched, mesmerized. Lisa was also captivated, but by dreams rather than the building equipment. In her eyes, her house was already built, complete with a flowering garden and swing set. She envisioned herself strolling next door to Miriam for a quick visit or to borrow the newest book sent from America. She pictured Kobi cutting though the backyard to the house behind them so he could sit and learn with Avi.

Kobi! Thinking of her husband brought her back to reality. If only he could share her enthusiasm about the building. Nothing got Kobi excited anymore. Ever since the evacuation of Yamit a month earlier, he'd slumped into a depression.

"Ima, I'm hungry," Shuki's voice broke into her thoughts.

"Me too. Let's go home and eat."

All through lunch, she was preoccupied and couldn't stop brooding about Kobi. After Shuki's nap, Lisa strapped him into his stroller as she did every afternoon. Instead of heading to the playground, though, she turned right and went to the Kfar Yonatan office. She'd decided she needed to talk to Kobi's best friend. Avi was on the phone when she entered the building, but he motioned for her to sit and wait. Thankfully, she didn't wait long. Once he hung up, Avi gave her his full attention.

"I'm here because of my husband," Lisa said without preamble. "I'm really concerned about him."

Avi just gave her a questioning look.

"You know, back in the winter, Kobi asked his boss for a leave of absence to go down to Yamit."

"He told me his boss wasn't very sympathetic," Avi replied.

"Yeah, well, I remember how you said we should have peace for peace, not land for peace, but his boss saw giving up Yamit and Sinai as a great opportunity to have true peace." Lisa tried to keep the scorn out of her voice. "To be fair, though, he was willing to give Kobi his two-week vacation then, even though he was going to have to report for Army Reserve duty soon after."

"I remember that. Kobi thought it wouldn't be a vacation if you and Shuki weren't going to be with him."

"I probably should have just closed the store for two weeks and gone with him. Or encouraged him to go by himself. It's like —"

"Ima," Shuki interrupted her. "Juice! Please!"

"It's like," Lisa repeated as she handed her son his cup, "he thinks he could have prevented the destruction if only he'd gone to Yamit. He's so angry about it!"

"Well, it was upsetting."

"It was," Lisa agreed. "You know, when the army shipped you all back here from Yamit, Amnon was really angry too, and he said that if the IDF was going to be used to destroy Jewish settlements, then he was done with the IDF. But he's going to work normal hours and takes his kids to the playground after supper, and gives his *daf yomi* class every evening. You were upset when you said that it was a dangerous precedent to give away land, but you're back in the office working as hard as ever and still laughing a lot."

"Kobi's not working his full hours." It was a statement, not a question.

"He's late for work a lot." Lisa didn't mention the mornings that he didn't bother to get up for services. She also avoided her suspicions that on those mornings he didn't even put on tefillin.

"I've been concerned too," Avi admitted, twiddling his thumbs as his hands rested on his belly. "Kobi keeps pushing off our learning sessions, and when he does come to shul, he's the first one out the door, never waiting around even to say hello. I thought he might be mad at me."

"He's mad at the world!" Lisa exclaimed.

"He never asked me about what happened in Yamit. Does he talk to you about the evacuation?"

"Not really. Except to say that he doesn't understand why his brother had to die in the Six Day War if the government was going to return all the land we gained then."

"I didn't know he had a brother." Avi stopped twiddling his thumbs and sat forward in his chair.

"Uri would be in his thirties if he'd lived."

"Does Kobi talk about his brother with you?"

Shuki dropped his cup and Lisa bent down to retrieve it.

"We'll go to the park soon," she soothed her son. Turning back to Avi, she said, "No one in Kobi's family talks about Uri, even though there's a wall full of his pictures at my in-laws' house."

"Ima," Shuki whined as he dropped his cup again.

"Soon, Shuki," Lisa answered. She looked at her husband's friend and shrugged, her palms turned upward. "Maybe he should go for counseling."

Avi drummed his fingertips thoughtfully on his desk.

"Ima!" Shuki repeated and began kicking his feet.

"I'd better get going." Lisa stood up. "I'm open to any advice or suggestions."

Avi nodded pensively. "Let me think about it."

Chatting with neighbors while watching her son play on the jungle gym was calming for Lisa. She was in an optimistic mood when Kobi came home from work and kept a cheerful chatter going throughout suppertime. One of her remarks even got a smile from her husband, but he wasn't smiling when he came home from shul later that evening.

"Were you and Avi talking about me today?" he demanded furiously.

Lisa took a deep breath and nodded. Now she knew why Kobi was late coming home. She'd been hoping he'd stayed for the fifteen-minute Halachah class.

"I can't believe my wife and best friend would be talking about me behind my back!"

"We weren't talking behind your back." Lisa blinked back tears of frustration as she sank down on the sofa.

"I wasn't there, was I?" Kobi demanded, his hands clenched.

Lisa shook her head and impatiently wiped a tear off her cheek.

"You weren't there," she answered wearily. "But we weren't talking against you. I went to Avi because I want my husband back."

"I'm right here."

Lisa stared at the floor.

"You're not acting like yourself," she whispered softly.

"That's absurd!" Kobi began pacing the room.

"Abba," Shuki called from his bed.

"Go to sleep!" Kobi called back.

"Abba!"

Kobi strode angrily to the bedroom door. "What?"

"Kiss."

Kobi bent over and kissed his son.

"I want a story!" Shuki demanded.

"Not now."

"Please."

"I said not now!" Kobi snapped.

He stomped back into the living room, ignoring his son's tears, and was chagrined to find his wife weeping softly.

"Why are you crying?" He tried to sound patient as he sat next to her on the couch.

Lisa struggled to gain control.

"You always loved telling Shuki stories," she finally said.

"Well, I was in the middle of a discussion with you and I didn't like being interrupted."

"When was the last time you told Shuki a bedtime story?"

"I'm tired when I get home from work."

"When was the last time you brought me flowers for Shabbat?"

"What, you think I don't care about you?" Kobi crossed his arms in indignation.

Lisa grabbed a tissue and wiped her face. "Kobi, I think something's bothering you so much that you can't be nice to anyone, even yourself."

"That's ridiculous!"

"None of this is ridiculous." Lisa was sobbing.

Kobi stood and began pacing again. "What do you want from me?"

"Go for counseling, find a way to get rid of all your anger, be yourself."

Kobi groaned. "I hate counselors."

Lisa hid her face in her hands. Kobi stared at her for a good five minutes and finally sat down next to her.

"Lisa, I'm sorry. I — I guess I have been hard to get along with lately. I'll try harder. Please, I don't want to upset you. Please stop crying."

Lisa lifted her head and grabbed for some more tissues. She stared at her husband intently, weighing his words, trying to decide if they were sincere.

"I really do care about you," Kobi spoke softly.

Lisa looked at him searchingly.

"If I go tell Shuki a story now, will you stop crying?"

Lisa managed a little smile. As Kobi went to their son, she said a silent prayer, begging Hashem to indeed bring her husband back to himself.

CHAPTER
Thirty-five

"My first time seeing Eretz Yisrael!" Zvi Chaim exclaimed, breathless with excitement, his face pressed flat against the plastic window. Sondra smiled indulgently and blinked back sentimental tears as the plane landed. Cuddling Yossi, sleeping on her lap, she reflected that it'd been eight years since she'd been in Israel. Eight years since she'd been a young bride coming with Danny to finish his summer session in yeshiva. Now she was the mother of four. She wondered if the country had changed as much as she had.

Across the aisle, Danny was trying to reassure Naomi, who'd been awakened by the landing plane and clapping passengers. Adorable with her curly pigtails and red cheeks, she kept repeating, "Go home, go home." A casual observer would think that the three-year-old was making two-word statements because she was tired. Naomi, however, was just beginning to string together three-word sentences.

Danny poured some apple juice for his groggy daughter and then beamed at his wife. "Welcome to Israel!"

"Welcome to Israel." Sondra smiled back.

The doors to the plane opened and passengers began filling the aisles. "Let's go!" Zvi Chaim begged.

"Patience, dear," Sondra told him. "Your father wants to wait until most of the people have cleared out and we can gather up all our things without bothering anyone."

"Lisa and Kobi are waiting for us!"

"I know, I know." Sondra felt she was speaking to herself as much as her son. "But we won't be able to see them until we get our suitcases, and that's going to take a long time, so we might as well be patient here."

"Okay," her seven-year-old said resignedly.

Outside the airport, Lisa was waiting as impatiently as her young cousin.

"Is that them?" Shuki called out as each new family emerged from the sliding glass doors. He was perched on his father's shoulders with a bag of treats, happy as could be.

"Not yet," Kobi answered calmly. Since his talk with Lisa, he'd made an enormous effort to overcome his inner anger.

"I'm so glad they didn't cancel their trip because of the Lebanon War," Lisa told Kobi for probably the fifteenth time.

"They thought about it, though."

"But they saw that the fighting's localized in the north."

"Well," Kobi said cynically, "if you give away land for peace on one border, you shouldn't be surprised to get war on another."

Before Lisa could answer him, Shuki called out again, "Is that them?"

It was. As the Klein family finally emerged from the terminal, Lisa shrieked with delight.

"Sondra! Sondra!"

In just a minute they were all gathered together, hugging, talking, and exclaiming how each other looked. Zvi Chaim was the only one of the children who truly remembered Lisa and Kobi, but the others had been primed with pictures and stories, so only Yossi was bashful.

"You must be exhausted." Lisa took the stroller from Sondra.

"It's been a long day," Sondra laughed, "but I'm so happy to be here."

"I have a yummy supper waiting for us when we get home, and the beds are all made at Myra and Natan's house."

"She's your friend who takes care of Shuki?"

Lisa nodded as the men began loading the luggage into the van Kobi had borrowed from Avi. "Her husband volunteered for a special Army Reserve unit of soldiers from the area, so she packed up the kids and went to her mother in Petach Tikva. Worked out great for us!"

There was lots of laughter and giggles over supper, but once it was over, reality hit with the children whining and crying from exhaustion.

"I think you all should go straight to sleep," Lisa suggested as she escorted them to Myra's house.

"I'm dying for a shower," Sondra groaned.

"Take one," Danny offered generously. "We'll bathe the kids in the morning. I'll get them in PJs while you shower."

"Okay." Despite her fatigue, she smiled gratefully. "I'll give Batsheva her medicine."

"She flew with an ear infection?" Lisa asked.

"*Baruch Hashem*, no," Sondra answered. "Didn't I write you that she has asthma?"

"No!"

"Yeah, she was diagnosed two months ago and she's on preventative medication for the time being. Danny brought his otoscope with him. And there are the flashcards for Naomi's vocabulary and worksheets for Zvi Chaim's occupational therapy. There's no such thing as a 100 percent vacation for mothers," Sondra concluded and sighed.

"Things will look better after a good night's sleep," Lisa soothed as she unlocked Myra's door and handed Sondra the key.

Even though the kids fell asleep right away, their jet lag kept everyone from getting a good night's sleep. A few minutes after one, Sondra woke to the sound of balls bouncing in the children's room.

"What do you think you're doing?" she yelled in a whispery voice. "It's the middle of the night. Get into your beds immediately!" She tiptoed back into her room and heard a mumbled thanks from her husband.

Forty-five minutes later, there was giggling coming from the room. Sondra got up again and saw they hadn't disobeyed her. All three children were sitting up in their beds, with the girls listening intently to Zvi Chaim's story.

"We're not going to have a nice day tomorrow if you don't sleep now," Sondra threatened.

Her children dutifully lay down, but after another hour, both she and Danny were awakened by their voices. This time Danny got up.

"If anyone makes any more noise before the sun comes up, they're going to get a good spanking. Is that understood?"

It was, and it was midmorning before they got out of bed. It wasn't just any morning, but Friday morning. Preparations for Shabbat were being made in every corner of Kfar Yonatan.

Sondra had always felt that she could almost touch Shabbat when she was in Israel. This Shabbat was no exception. The glow of the sunset, the peace in the village, the smell of Shabbat food from every house, the laughter of children, and the sounds of prayer coming from the synagogue made her feel that this would be a most special Shabbat.

Friday night, Zvi Chaim made friends with Moshe, an eight-year-old whose family had made *aliyah* the previous summer. Batsheva and Naomi also found playmates and were able to communicate with their body language. To her parents' surprise, Naomi picked up several Hebrew words in the course of the day.

After Havdalah, Zvi Chaim declared he didn't want to go to Jerusalem the following day.

"Zvi Chaim," Danny tweaked his son's cheek playfully, "we already paid for your bed at the hotel."

"You can take the money out of my allowance." Zvi Chaim crossed his arms stubbornly. "I want to stay in Kfar Yonatan."

"But Zvi Chaim," Sondra pleaded, "we have so many special things to do in Jerusalem."

"I want to play with Moshe."

"Oh, Zvi Chaim," Lisa entered the discussion, "it's so great you found a friend here, but Moshe still has school for another two weeks. He won't be available to play."

"Okay," Zvi Chaim graciously conceded defeat. "I'll go."

"Thank you." Sondra smiled at her cousin later as they sat over their cups of tea. "You know, in Phoenix, Zvi Chaim doesn't have another boy in his class who wears his *kippah* outside of school. It's really special for him being here and not feeling different from everyone else."

"I hope you're doing a lot of child-friendly things during your sightseeing," Lisa said anxiously.

"I think we have a good balance of activities."

The Kleins had a magical time visiting old friends, whose children were more than willing to share their toys. Their touring included the Biblical Zoo, playgrounds, and plenty of ice cream stops. Whenever they boarded a crowded bus, friendly hands reached out to grab the children, and the youngsters found themselves sitting on the laps of kind strangers. When they rented a car, they made a point of stopping for hitchhiking soldiers, who piled in the back with the children.

Once, they themselves even hitchhiked. Somehow, they'd gotten the bus schedule wrong on their way back from Kever Rochel. They stood patiently at the bus stop in Bethlehem, but after twenty minutes, the children had finished the water in their canteens. It was hot and Yossi was getting sunburned. The children began whining. Sondra looked anxiously at her watch. Then a gray van stopped. The driver, a smiling man with a large *kippah* and red beard, leaned over and rolled down the window.

"Are you going to Jerusalem?" he asked in American-accented Hebrew.

"We're waiting for the bus," Danny explained in English.

"Get in!" the man commanded.

"Do you live here?" he asked them once they were all in.

"We're here on vacation," Danny answered.

"Oh, you've got to make *aliyah*!" the friendly driver exclaimed.

"Maybe," Danny concurred.

"No maybes. You owe it to your beautiful children. And don't worry. Life might seem hard here, but it's one miracle after the other."

❋ ❋ ❋

After ten days of touring, the Kleins returned to Kfar Yonatan for the pilot trip phase of their visit. Lisa found a teenage girl who'd already finished her school year to watch the children. Sondra and Danny rented a car and explored several communities that had sounded good in theory. One in particular appealed to them. The following day, Lisa had Boaz mind the store so she and Sondra could take the children on an outing while Danny visited with several doctors.

His long face when he returned that evening told Sondra better than any words could that she wouldn't be moving to Israel in the near future.

"That bad?" she asked.

"No better than Yerushalayim," Danny answered dejectedly.

Sondra raised her eyebrows at that comment. Her husband had taken an afternoon when they were in Jerusalem to check out the medical situation there and hadn't been impressed. He'd thought that Ra'anana, with its large Anglo-Saxon community, might be better. He was wrong.

"Barry's a good doctor," Danny sighed as he sat down at the kitchen table in Myra's house, "but I can't believe how he runs his practice. He has no secretary. So in the middle of weighing a newborn, the phone rings and he tells the mother to watch the baby. The mother is standing next to the naked baby; thank goodness it's summertime. Barry's talking on the phone. He calls the caller by name and discusses her kid's bedwetting problems. So much for privacy. He finishes the phone call, apologizes to the baby's mother, and finishes the weighing.

"The mother dresses the baby and takes the extra diaper she had off the scale. Barry doesn't have those disposable sheets we have in the office at home. He has the mothers put down a diaper or a receiving blanket. So much for accurate weights." Danny fiddled with his *kippah* and sighed again.

"Did you ask Barry about it?"

Danny nodded woefully. "Socialized medicine."

Sondra gave him a questioning look as she poured him a cup of tea.

"He makes a pittance working for the health fund system and he's too idealistic to go private, so he does the best he can by cutting corners."

"What do you think?" Sondra joined her husband at the table.

"Sondra, I can't practice sloppy medicine and I must support our family."

His wife let his words sink in and then spoke softly. "Everyone tells us that you live on miracles here."

"In theory that sounds great, but in practice..." Danny took a swallow of his tea. "I'm not moving my family to Israel unless I know I'll have the wherewithal to pay for what we need." He held his hand up to stem Sondra's rebuttal. "You know I'm not talking about fancy clothes and birthday parties and toys. I'm talking about speech therapy, occupational therapy, ear specialists. Those things aren't cheap at home, and they're only more expensive here. I'm sorry."

Danny rested his forehead on his hands, the picture of dejection.

His wife twisted her hands and searched for something to say that would comfort both of them.

"Are the kids sleeping?" Danny raised his head, having noticed the quiet.

"Naomi and Yossi, yes. Batsheva's playing with her friend, Tzippie, and Zvi Chaim's running around with Moshe."

Danny met Sondra's eyes and sighed once more. It was such a positive atmosphere for the children in Israel. In a few days, they would be back in Phoenix. There would be no running outside to join friends in the neighborhood. Sondra would be driving the kids to prearranged playdates.

"I guess I should have been thinking about an alternative to Israel in case it didn't work out here. As soon as we get back," Danny spoke resolutely, "I'll contact that practice in St. Louis and see if there's still an opening."

"Danny, we'd be crazy to move an asthmatic child to St. Louis. You know that."

"I'm sorry, Sondra."

She forced a smile. "Phoenix has grown a lot the last three years. It won't be so bad."

"You really mean that?"

"No." Sondra smiled, showing her left dimple. "But I'm going to talk myself into believing it!"

"Oh, Sondra, you're wonderful."

✽ ✽ ✽

To Lisa, Sondra openly expressed her disappointment. They were at the playground Shabbat afternoon and the sun was high in the sky, but there was a nice breeze. When the children complained about being hot, Sondra handed them their water canteens. A nice camaraderie had grown between Naomi, Shuki, and Yossi in the short time they'd been together, and the three of them played harmoniously in the sandbox.

"I'm sure there are plenty of asthmatics living in St. Louis," Lisa said as she took a sip of water.

"I'm sure there are too," Sondra agreed. "But that's not the point. It's one thing to be living there and have asthma. It's another thing to move there from an environment that's good for asthmatics."

"Why is it so good?"

"It's warm and dry."

"What about moving back to Los Angeles?"

"Too much smog."

"I see." Lisa put her fingers to her lips thoughtfully. "Oh, Shuki!" Her son's foot had just knocked over Naomi's sand sculpture. Preempting any cries, she pulled out a bag of Bamba and poured a few of the puffed peanut snacks into each of the eager little hands. She also poured a good handful for herself, but Sondra declined the offer.

"This would be the perfect place. Clean air, mild climate." Sondra shook her head ruefully.

"You know," Lisa said, half joking, "the Gemara says if one spouse wants to move to Israel and the other doesn't, it's grounds for a divorce."

Sondra gave a shocked laugh. "I don't want to divorce Danny!"

"I'm glad to hear it," Lisa answered. "But maybe if you brought the subject up, it might push him to change his mind."

Sondra narrowed her eyes at her cousin. "Is that the way you and Kobi work?"

Lisa blushed. "Sorry."

"There are a lot of good things about Phoenix." Sondra spoke more to herself than to Lisa and they sat in silence for a while. She enjoyed feeling the breeze cool her cheeks, hearing the birds calling to one another, smelling the fragrance of the honeysuckle, and watching the children play so nicely. Batsheva and Tzippie passed by, pushing a doll stroller. Sondra waved, but the two little girls were so engrossed with each other, they didn't notice.

"Lisa," Sondra finally broke the stillness, "do you ever think about coming to America for a visit?"

Lisa shrugged. "As long as my parents keep visiting me, probably not."

"Do you miss it?"

"I miss you and the Frankels and Bayla." Lisa wrinkled her nose as she thought. "When we first came, I missed all kinds of food, but I've even gotten used to Israeli peanut butter. You know," she said earnestly, "Miriam took her whole family to Denver for her sister's wedding. Her parents paid for it and she said it was wonderful. But I don't have any sister that'll be getting married. Howie's dead. And somehow I don't picture myself wanting to come for any of my cousins' weddings. Maybe for Zvi Chaim's bar mitzvah."

That made Sondra smile. "It's only six years away."

Where would they be in six years?

"I never told you about Rachel's wedding, did I?"

Lisa made a face. "I never asked."

"You know Rav Feingold said to go to keep the line of communication open with Rachel — that if she has children, they'll be Jewish and perhaps I can have some influence." Sondra paused to take a deep breath. "In theory it sounded good, but I'm sorry I went."

"Oh?"

"With due respect to Rav Feingold, I think he's been away from America so long that he can't even begin to fathom the degree of assimilation there is now. I'm afraid it was a *chillul Hashem.*"

"Why?"

"One of Uncle Ludwig's relatives saw me taking food from the smorgasbord and assumed I had been overcome by the desire to eat *treyfe.* She didn't say anything to me, but she did to my mom and Mom repeated it to me."

"Sounds like *rechilut* to me," Lisa said with disdain. "What did you eat?"

"Raw vegetables and cold fruit!" Sondra took a deep breath. "I thought by moving here, I'd leave all the family complications behind me."

"Hi, Ima," a voice yelled. The two women saw Zvi Chaim and Moshe running by. "We're going to the yeshiva and then I'm eating at Moshe's. His mother invited me. Okay?"

"Okay," Sondra called to the back of the running streak.

"Sondra," Lisa spoke seriously, "next summer send Zvi Chaim to me for a month."

Sondra stared at her cousin in amazement at the generosity of the suggestion. "Maybe we will. That just might make things work out okay."

CHAPTER

Thirty-six

Sondra and the kids were still blurry eyed with jet lag when they met Debbie and her children at Bayla's pool two days after their return from Israel. That didn't stop Sondra from pouring out her heart to her friend as they sat on the steps playing lifeguard.

"I know I should be telling you I'm sorry Israel isn't going to work out for you," Debbie began, smiling sheepishly, "but I'm really glad you're not moving. Shraga and I are pretty happy here, but the best part is having you and Danny nearby."

"Debbie, your living here is one of the reasons I can make the best of it. Except I don't just want to make the best of it. On the way back from Israel, I decided that I'm going to try to make sure that Phoenix becomes the kind of community I'll be happy to live in for the rest of my life."

"Good for you." Debbie gave her a thumbs-up. "You know, there's been a lot of growth here."

"Yeah." Sondra sighed. "Bayla told me that the cow pasture near the shul was sold for condominiums."

"Well, it's not just religious Jews who've gotten fed up with the hard winters back east."

"I guess I can go to Squaw Peak whenever I start feeling claustrophobic."

"There are a lot of new young couples now — the Chabad rabbi, the rabbi for the high school, and the rabbi for the new shul that just started. They all have young wives and kids. Plus Vivian said that one of the new teachers her husband is bringing in has a son going into second grade and so does the shul rabbi."

"Oh, I hope they'll be friends for Zvi Chaim," Sondra exclaimed. "With these new families, maybe it's time to remodel the *mikveh*."

"That's a good idea. I'd love to get rid of all the mold in the bathroom."

"Uh-huh. Do you want to take on the project with me?"

"Maybe." Debbie hesitated. "I've got fifth grade this year. Let me see how the class goes first."

"If we get some of the new women involved, it won't be that much work for any of us."

"You're right. And it's a good way to make them feel part of the community."

"Should I make an appointment with Rabbi Levi to talk about it?"

"Yes, if Shraga agrees to do the babysitting, I'll go with you."

Shraga did agree and Rabbi Levi was enthusiastic. They decided that fundraising could be combined with education. The first event was held on a Saturday night in the middle of November at Shirley and Doc's clubhouse. Along with the refreshments, discreet cards were passed out announcing a women's class on Jewish marriage laws to be taught by Shoshie, the new rabbi's wife. Bayla had graciously offered her house for the learning sessions and Sondra came early to help her set up.

"Do you think we'll get a good turnout?" Sondra worried as she folded the napkins.

"You're here, Vivian Levi's coming, and Debbie and I think Shaindy's planning on showing up too."

"So are Chani and Tova and Goldie, but I want some women not already using the *mikveh* to come."

Sixteen women attended the class that evening. Although several felt they could use a refresher course, most came to give moral support to Shoshie. There were two women, though, both of them with children in Sondra's third grade class, who came because they wanted to learn more about Judaism. Sondra was elated when she went home that evening.

Zvi Chaim now had three boys from religious homes in his class — Shoshie's son Benny, the new teacher's son, Eli, and Ari, an Israeli boy whose father had come to work at Intel. They soon became an inseparable foursome, much to Sondra's delight. So her feelings about Phoenix were positive when Mark Rossner, chairman of the board for the day school, called.

"We're making changes with the board," he informed her, "and want to expand to have both a parent representative and one from the staff. We'd like you to be the staff representative."

Flattered, Sondra agreed and attended the first meeting in December. She found the pros and cons of beginning bussing rather boring and sat concentrating on the sweater she'd begun knitting for Batsheva. When it was announced that the quality of the Hebrew studies program for the coming year would be the topic of the January meeting, her ears pricked up. That was the reason she'd joined the board.

Monday morning, two days before the meeting, just as Sondra was tying Yossi's shoes and urging Batsheva to get her sandwich in her lunch bag, the phone rang.

"Sondra," her mother's voice sounded like she'd been crying and Sondra felt a stab of fear. "Your Oma passed away in her sleep. The rest home just called."

"Oh, Mommy! *Baruch Dayan HaEmes*," Sondra said quietly. "I'm so sorry."

"Yes, well," her mother blew her nose, "I thought you should know."

"Is Daddy there?"

"No," Helga sniffled. "He and Herbert have gone to the home to make the arrangements."

"Ima," Zvi Chaim came in the front door, "are you walking with us? We're going to be late."

Sondra nodded at him and he herded his younger siblings outside. She returned her attention to the phone.

"Mom, the kids and I have to get to school. Do you know when the funeral is?"

"Not yet."

"I'll call you as soon as I get home. I love you."

Sondra scurried outside to her waiting children and plunked Naomi into the double stroller with Yossi. "Come on, Batsheva, Zvi Chaim, let's walk double-time."

She taught her class on automatic pilot that morning, and when they were in the middle of their Torah test, she let her mind wander. Her grandmother had lived long enough to have five great-grandchildren, but the last two had made almost no impression on her. For three years, she'd been bedridden in the old age home. Sometimes she recognized her daily visitors and sometimes she didn't.

Sondra remembered all her Oma's fascinating stories from when she'd been a child growing up in Lincoln. Her grandmother had shared her best recipes with her and taught her to do fancy handwork. Sondra's knitting wasn't bad, but it couldn't compare to her grandmother's. As she blinked back tears, she resolved that she would go to Lincoln for the funeral.

It was a nice resolution, but not an easy one. Although she'd worn only a sweater on her way to school that morning, it was snowing in Lincoln. Taking any of the children with her would be foolish. Rabbi Levi would have to let her take some time off. And who knew if she would be able to get a ticket.

Apparently Hashem wanted her to be at the funeral. Shirley came through and offered to take care of her grandchildren. Rabbi Levi was gracious about finding a substitute. And the travel agent got her reservations to Wichita early the following morning.

She had her forehead pressed to the window as the plane made its descent. There was not a patch of ground to be seen; only white snow and blacktop surfaces where the snowplows had been. *How was her mother going to be able to pick her up?*

She wasn't. When Sondra entered the waiting lounge, she searched for Helga, but didn't see her.

"Hello, Sondra."

She turned in the direction of the hoarse voice and saw Mac, Uncle Herbert's hired man.

"Hello, Mac," Sondra answered, puzzled.

"I got my four-wheel drive. We'll make it home in that. Let's go get your bags."

That was the most Mac spoke for the next hour. As soon as they entered the pickup, he turned on the radio, unwrapped a plug of tobacco, and popped it into his mouth. He drove slowly, concentrating on the highway. Sondra spotted several cars that had skidded off to the side. She was thankful when they finally pulled up to her parents' farmhouse.

"I'm right sorry about your grandmother," Mac said formally as Sondra thanked him for the ride. Before she could answer, Helga was already opening the passenger door.

"Sondra," she said and burst into tears. She led her daughter into the kitchen, where Lotte was already seated.

"Sondra!" Her aunt rose and hugged her. She, Oma's daughter, was far more composed than Helga, Oma's daughter-in-law. Of course, Sondra remembered, her mother had always had a hard time whenever there was a death in her father's family. Perhaps it was because Helga never had a chance to properly mourn her own mother, father, and sister, who'd been murdered in the Holocaust.

"I'm glad you made it, dear," Lotte said. "Joey got in last night, but Rachel couldn't get off work, and Ruthie and Lisa are too far away."

"How's Ruthie doing in the Peace Corps?" Sondra asked as she accepted a cup of hot tea from her mother and sat down across from her aunt.

"She thinks it's fascinating and she's really enjoying the hot African weather."

"That sounds good to me." Helga sighed. She stood at the window staring out at the snow. "I really don't know how they're going to dig a grave in this."

"Mother's not the first person to be buried in the dead of winter," Lotte answered.

Helga turned from the window. "I don't understand how you can be so calm, Lotte, when it's your mother who's dead."

"Oh, Helga." Lotte's eyes filled with tears. "We all knew this was coming. I began mourning my mother when she first stopped recognizing me." Several tears rolled down her cheeks.

Sondra watched the two women, concerned for her mother. Just then, Joey entered the kitchen.

"Hey, Sondra, how're you doing?"

"Considering the circumstances, okay." Sondra smiled at him warmly.

He turned to his mother. "When are we leaving for the chapel?"

"Mac's coming back for us in about another half an hour," Lotte answered. "Sondra, you made it just under the wire."

The little university chapel wasn't even half full. A few friends and a couple of Jewish students joined the family to make a minyan. Joey spoke, and then he and the other men dropped the women back at the farmhouse. They stayed at the freezing cemetery just long enough to say Kaddish.

"It's good you're here for your mother." Aunt Lotte gazed approvingly at Sondra while they ate the mourners' meal.

"It's good for me too," Sondra replied. She surveyed her relatives lovingly and smiled warmly at her aunt. "There's something so cozy about being inside here with so much of my family when it's so cold outside."

Thirty-seven

*J*ust as Helga was calling Sondra on the morning of her mother-in-law's death, Irene was placing an overseas call to Lisa. It was late afternoon in Israel. Irene matter-of-factly shared the same news and then asked to speak to Shuki.

"Oma," the three-year-old cried in delight, "I miss you!"

"I miss you too, Shuki," Irene said. "Did you go to Myra today?"

"Yes," Shuki said enthusiastically. He was far past the stage of nodding and shaking his head and thinking his grandmother could see him over the line. "There's a new truck. A big truck."

"Do you like trucks?"

"Yes!"

"Would you like us to bring you a truck when we come again?"

"Yes! A big red truck."

"A fire truck?"

"Yes! When you coming?"

"I'll talk to Opa about it. Soon, I hope. I love you, Shuki."

"I love you!" He blew a kiss into the phone and Lisa felt a stab of sorrow. How well could her son know her parents with only yearly visits and weekly phone calls? She took the phone from him and said a loving goodbye to her mother.

Then she sat silently, lost in thought. How does one mourn a grandmother who died halfway around the world? She knew she wouldn't be going to the funeral. If she was honest with herself, she had to admit that she didn't feel much sorrow. Her feelings were very similar to those of her Aunt Lotte. Lisa couldn't forget her last visit to Lincoln before she made *aliyah*. She'd entered Oma's room proudly with Shuki in her arms and had sat next to her grandmother's bed. Oma had been having a good day and she recognized Lisa. With pride, she handed her the blue blanket she'd crocheted for her newest great-grandchild. She and Lisa visited quietly for a bit, and then Oma looked at her granddaughter strangely.

"That's such a sweet baby," she said. "Who does he belong to?"

"He's mine, Oma," Lisa had answered calmly.

But later, outside her grandmother's room, the tears had come. There were no tears now, just a dazed feeling. Lisa knew a part of her childhood was gone forever.

The ringing phone broke her reverie. It was Myra.

"Hi, Lisa. How are you?"

"Okay…"

Myra didn't seem to notice the subdued note in her voice. "I called to ask if I can go with you when you go to pick out your floor tiles and wall ceramics."

"Kobi and I haven't decided when to go yet," Lisa replied. "As soon as we do, I'll let you know."

"Great. Have you spoken to anyone who went already?"

"Just Elisheva. She told me there're three different patterns to choose from. If we want anything else, we have to pay extra. She fell in love with large, dark floor tiles, but Avi talked her out of them. He told her as head of the village he needs to set a good example." Lisa chuckled. "What a line to feed your wife!"

"I'm going to have to stick to the basics, that's for sure," Myra sighed. "We're already over budget."

"I don't know if Kobi wants to go with me because he's finally enthusiastic about the house or because he wants to make sure I don't make any expensive decisions."

Myra laughed. "You know, I'm so thankful it's going smoothly. There were some horror stories when they built in Maalei Tikvah."

"Really?"

"Uh-huh. The contractor for the building project went bankrupt. It took months to settle all the finances, since the families had been building together and all the payments were in one account. Once the accounts were settled, each family had to figure out on their own how they were going to finish their house. Some hired a contractor to finish the job right away. Others are still waiting because they don't have the money."

"Do you think that could happen here?"

"Probably not. We're really close to the end. I know the Gellers and the Schwartzes plan to move in before Pesach."

"Where are you holding?"

"Ours is going slower. Natan doesn't have much time to help with any of the decisions, and between the playgroup and the housework, I'm not all that free either."

Lisa murmured her understanding. "I'll let you know what Kobi and I decide."

She hung up the phone feeling sorry for Myra. While her husband, Natan, had served in his special Army Reserve unit, her friend had spent most of the summer in her parents' crowded city apartment, coming back only after her younger brother was injured on the Lebanese border. Natan had finally come home for good after Rosh Hashanah, but he seemed to be perpetually busy, either making up work time or catching up on his learning, or helping to shuttle his brother-in-law to rehab, so everything fell on Myra. Lisa couldn't help but wonder why some women had it so hard.

Dinner was ready to be served when Kobi came home. Lisa was aware that most of her friends either fed their children early or had chaos at the dinner table. She was grateful for the long and leisurely conversations the three of them were able to have around their table, but some evenings she longed for just a little bedlam. Tonight, especially, she couldn't help but wistfully think how nice it would be to have a baby girl to name after her Oma. With a sigh, she pushed that disheartening thought away.

"Kobi," she took a deep breath, "my mother called a little while ago. My Oma died."

"Oh, Lisa." Kobi set his fork down and gazed at his wife. "I'm so sorry."

Lisa smiled bravely at his sympathy.

"Oma?" Shuki asked.

"Not your Oma," Lisa answered patiently. "Mine."

"Okay." Shuki nodded as if he understood.

"Do you want to go to the funeral?" Kobi suggested.

Lisa gave her husband a look of disbelief. "I'd never make it in time. Besides, they're in the middle of a snowstorm there. And besides that, how could I leave the store? And even if all that could be worked out, how could we afford it?"

"We'd find the money," Kobi said resolutely, but he seemed relieved that Lisa found his suggestion impractical.

She concentrated on her pasta and he cut Shuki's squash for him.

"Sometimes it's hard to be so far away," Lisa spoke softly.

"I remember how I felt when I was in America." Kobi looked sympathetic. "Are you sorry we came here?"

Lisa shook her head. "Shuki, aren't you glad we live in Kfar Yonatan?" she asked as she poured some juice into his cup.

"I go to Myra." He grinned happily.

"That reminds me..." Lisa told Kobi about Myra's request.

Kobi's face clouded over. "I don't think we need to feel obligated to Myra for anything."

"Obligated?" Lisa was puzzled.

"If anybody owes anyone anything around here, it's her."

"I don't understand." Why was Kobi sounding so irritated?

"Don't you remember how she left you in the lurch last year?"

"Left me in the lurch?"

"When she closed down the playgroup and took off for her mother's." Kobi's voice had an edge to it and Shuki looked worried.

"Kobi," Lisa narrowed her eyes and replied, "that was ages ago. And I found one of the high school girls to babysit right away. And she let Sondra and Danny use her apartment. She didn't want to be here by herself without her husband during the war. I understood."

"Well, I didn't," Kobi snapped. "Who asked Natan to volunteer anyway?"

Lisa stared at her husband, shocked. "Myra is my friend. Let's watch what we say about her." She raised her eyebrows and motioned to their son, who sat taking in every word.

"She's your friend." Kobi made a visible effort to calm down. "And she's Shuki's friend too, right?"

"Right." Shuki nodded his head vigorously.

"It's just," Kobi smiled sheepishly, "I wanted to get a sitter and take you out for a romantic dinner when we go to Kfar Saba. Maybe, though, it's not appropriate, since your grandmother just died."

"No, Kobi." Lisa was touched. "I'd love to go out for dinner with you. Don't worry. I'll explain to Myra."

As she cleaned up from dinner, Kobi bathed their son and got him into bed with a story. All that was left, he said as he went out the door for evening services, was for her to give Shuki a kiss.

Shuki was almost asleep when Lisa entered his bedroom. She brushed his brown hair back from his forehead and planted a kiss there. As she turned to leave, her eyes rested on the blue baby blanket he still sometimes clutched in his chubby fist when he was sleeping. Lisa knew that baby blanket was one of the last pieces of handwork her grandmother had made. Seeing it was what finally brought the tears for her Oma.

Thirty-eight

Shirley was waiting for Sondra at Sky Harbor Airport when her plane arrived from Kansas Thursday afternoon.

"I know you'd prefer to see Danny," she pecked her daughter-in-law's cheek, "but he couldn't rearrange his appointments."

"I'm glad to see you," Sondra answered graciously. "Were the kids okay?"

"They were fantastic! We had a great time, but," Shirley chuckled, "I'm exhausted!"

"I'm sorry." Sondra flushed.

"Don't be, I'll rest up tomorrow. Meanwhile, you'll have about an hour to unpack and relax before your crew comes home. They're looking forward to seeing you."

"I'm looking forward to seeing them! Thank you so much."

Sondra had just said goodbye to her mother-in-law when the phone rang. It was Mark Rossner from the school board.

"So," he asked without preamble, "what do you think of Rabbi Levi's bombshell?"

"Huh?" Sondra heaved her suitcase onto her bed.

"Didn't you talk to Danny?"

"Not since yesterday. What's going on?" She began unpacking with one hand.

"Last night Rabbi Levi handed in his resignation, to take effect at the end of the school year."

"Are you serious?"

"He and Vivian are moving to Israel."

"Wow!" Sondra dropped her cosmetic bag and sat down in shock. "That's great!"

"For them," Mark spoke shortly. "We talked him into staying on for several months next year to help the new principal get started. But we have to find a new principal. What do you think? Any ideas?"

"Mark," Sondra was polite, but firm, "I just walked in from my grandmother's funeral. Let me call you back after Shabbos."

"Okay, but we're going to need an emergency board meeting."

Sondra quickly finished her unpacking and had enough time to grab an apple before dashing out to get the children. As soon as she walked back into the house, the phone rang again. This time it was Shaindy.

"I was sorry to hear about your grandmother."

"Thank you," Sondra answered and braced herself to hear a litany of complaints. Instead Shaindy just asked a question.

"What do you think about Rabbi Levi's resignation?"

"I just found out about it," Sondra answered, trying to be patient. "And the kids just got home, and I need to spend some time with them."

After saying goodbye, she took the phone off the hook and turned to her children.

Naomi was begging for apple juice "from Ima" and Yossi wanted a story. Zvi Chaim had a good math test to show her and Batsheva wanted to tell her about Mindy's birthday party. After an hour, Zvi Chaim went to play with Eli, and the others began playing nicely in the den. Sondra sheepishly returned the receiver to its place and groaned as the phone immediately began ringing again. This time, though, it was Debbie.

"Hi, welcome home! I have a casserole for your dinner."

"Really! I haven't had a chance to even think about food."

"Good. I'll come by in about ten minutes?"

"Perfect!" Sondra hung up the phone with a pleased smile.

Debbie's three girls went straight to the den when they arrived, while she and Sondra settled at the kitchen table.

"I remember your grandmother." Debbie took the coffee cup Sondra handed her. "She was such a classic grandmother, with her hair in a bun and constantly busy with her handwork."

"I cherish everything she made for me, and now I don't know if I should use the things or save them so my girls will have something from her when they get married."

"Don't hide them in the drawer." Debbie shook her head emphatically. "My mother-in-law did that with some of her things from her grandmother, and when she took them out for me, they were stained from age and mildew."

"Whoa." Sondra made a face. "That would be terrible!"

"Yeah, use them carefully, and hopefully you'll be able to pass them down. How's everyone in Lincoln?"

Sondra gave a brief rundown of the family. It was so comfortable to talk to her friend who knew her so well. How, she wondered, would Rabbi Levi's resignation affect Debbie and Shraga's jobs? Would the new principal decide he wanted a new staff? As if she read Sondra's thoughts, Debbie asked her what she thought of the resignation.

"You too?" Sondra sighed.

"What?"

"I just got home, and everyone's asking me what I think about it, and I don't know any of the details. Can't I have a day to recuperate?"

"No," Debbie answered firmly. "I think it's important that you know what's going on. There's a controversy coming."

Sondra looked at her friend quizzically.

"I heard from one of the parents that there's a push to merge with the Reform school and have one community school."

"But...but," Sondra stuttered, "the charter calls for an Orthodox school."

"The charter can be changed," Debbie answered ominously.

"That would be terrible." Sondra stood and began pacing the length of the kitchen. "And I think the religious studies program is weak enough as it is."

"Sondra, listen, that's just part of the story," Debbie said in a placating tone. "Another parent already spoke to Shraga about taking over as principal."

"Really?" Sondra's eyes lit up as she sat back down.

Debbie laughed at her friend's sudden change of mood, but shook her head.

"There's no way he can take over Rabbi Levi's position. He does have the background and experience to be a principal, but not to run the city's kosher supervision and the community board."

Frustrated, Sondra set her elbow on the table and rested her head on her fist. "How many parents want this merger?"

"I'm not sure, but it really doesn't matter. It's a board decision."

"And I'm on the board," Sondra added ruefully. "Well, I guess it's a good thing I agreed to be on it."

The emergency board meeting was held the following Sunday evening. It turned out that one of the biggest proponents for the merger was Mark Rossner, and his reasons were all financial. Ever since the big Reform temple had opened a school, the Jewish Federation had been consistently lowering its allocation to the day school. Before Mark could get anywhere with the proposal, though, he was shouted down by one of the school's founding board members, and most of the others sided with him. Two even committed themselves to making up the deficit left by the Federation.

"Okay." Mark was pleased with that order of business. "Now who can we get to replace Rabbi Levi?"

"What about Rabbi Shraga?" the parent representative suggested.

Sondra didn't have a chance to comment as another board member spoke up. "He's a good teacher, but his three years of experience isn't enough to make a good principal. I suggest bringing Yechiel Frankel back."

"That's a great idea!" someone exclaimed.

"Yeah, he's been doing some administrative work in Far Rockaway."

"Everyone loved him!"

"And his wife!"

"Would he want to come back? He left here because he wanted a larger community and stronger religious program for his kids."

"But it would be a great opportunity for him, and a raise in salary."

"As principal, he can make the program stronger."

"So," Mark interrupted the discussion, "do I have a motion to contact him?"

The motion passed unanimously and the next day Mark called to tell Sondra that Rabbi Frankel would be flying out the following Sunday for an interview. Would she be willing to host him? With a surge of excitement, Sondra agreed. It'd be good to have Rena back in the community. Although she and Debbie had never met, Sondra was certain they'd take to each other.

The interview went well, although there were all sorts of details to work out before a contract could be signed. Sondra turned her attention to Purim, which was coming up in two weeks. She called Debbie to make arrangements for the *seudah*.

"I don't think we'll be doing it together this year." Debbie seemed rather breathless, as if she'd run for the phone. "Someone else invited us and Shraga didn't want to say no."

"But, but..." Sondra felt her face flush. "We've had the Purim *seudah* together every year since you moved here."

"I'm sorry," Debbie repeated. "Listen, the baby just woke up. I'll call you back."

But she didn't. And suddenly Sondra realized that Debbie hadn't called at all since the day Sondra came back from the funeral. Debbie had begged off going to the library or shopping or anything else together. Something was bothering her, but Sondra didn't have a clue what it was. She did know that Shraga was learning with Harold Wein at Harold's house that evening. She also knew that Debbie always had her girls in bed by seven. So at eight-thirty, with her heart beating wildly, Sondra stood in front of her friend's house and knocked on the door.

"What're you doing here?" Debbie was puzzled.

"I came to find out what's wrong."

"Everything's fine."

"No, it's not," Sondra pressed. "You're avoiding me and I deserve to know why. Can I come in?"

With her eyes lowered, Debbie opened the door wider. Sondra followed her friend to the couch and they sat down next to each other.

"*Nu*," Sondra prompted.

"I'm just kind of upset about something and I need some time to get over it."

"Over what? What did I do?"

"Nothing." Debbie's green eyes flashed. "Absolutely nothing!"

"Let's try this another way." Sondra struggled to stay calm. "What was I supposed to do?"

"Help your best friend's husband get a promotion."

Sondra felt as if she had been slapped by Debbie's angry tone.

"Debbie," Sondra began, taking a deep breath first, "you told me Shraga couldn't do the job."

"Well, you didn't have to accept my opinion."

Sondra just stared at her friend.

"Not all of us are married to a rich doctor. Some of us have to worry constantly about making ends meet, and the promotion would have made a big difference. Maybe I could've stayed home next year with the new baby instead of breaking my head teaching."

"So you're expecting?" Sondra queried softly.

"Don't think the pregnancy is the reason I'm upset."

"Debbie, I don't think you're being very fair. You clearly said that Shraga couldn't take Rabbi Levi's place."

"No, he can't, but he could've become principal and the community responsibilities could have been delegated to the new shul's rabbi."

"Why didn't you suggest that to me?"

"Why didn't you think of that on your own?"

"I'd just come home from my grandmother's funeral!"

"You're always making excuses," Debbie cried. "Why can't you just tell me you're sorry that we're having a hard time?"

Stung, Sondra was ready to stand up and flounce out of the house. Instead, she forced herself to breathe deeply and calm down. "I didn't realize you were having a hard time," she whispered. "Of course I'm sorry. Would it help if I promise that if it falls through with Rabbi Frankel, I'll push for your idea?"

Debbie nodded, but didn't raise her eyes to meet Sondra's gaze.

"Debbie," Sondra continued, "we've been friends since high school. Please don't let this ruin our friendship."

Debbie sighed and wiped at her cheeks. "I don't want it to," she answered slowly. "I've been telling myself that you're just an agent of Hashem, and if He wants Shraga to have the job, He'll make it all work out."

"I never thought about your financial situation." Sondra was embarrassed. "All I thought about is how glad I am that you're here in Phoenix and I hope you'll want to stay on."

"We'll see."

The two women sat side by side in silence for a while. Debbie was the first to speak. "Do you still want to do the Purim *seudah* together?"

"What about the other family?"

"I made that up," Debbie said shamefacedly.

Sondra just looked at her.

"Well, what was I going to say? That I was too mad at you to plan the *seudah* together?"

"And you're not mad at me anymore?"

"No, I'm, uh... I really appreciate that you came over to talk to me. I'm sorry I was such a jerk."

Sondra smiled. "I'm sorry I was insensitive."

"Okay." Debbie rolled her eyes. "That's enough talk about our feelings. Let's talk about the *seudah*."

CHAPTER

Thirty-nine

"Hi, Lisa. Are you busy?"

"I guess not." Lisa hesitated. She'd already asked Riki several times not to call her at the store, but obviously her sister-in-law didn't get the message. "What's up?"

"I called to tell you what to bring to the barbecue Monday."

Why don't you ask me what I want to bring? Lisa thought, but didn't say. Instead, she listened patiently as Riki instructed her to bring enough meat for her family and a big salad.

"We're meeting at Mount Gilboa at one o'clock. Don't be late," Riki instructed. "See you then."

"Bye," Lisa answered halfheartedly.

She and Kobi had already had a long talk about the barbecue just the night before.

"You know," Lisa had suggested after Shuki fell asleep, "this year, instead of going to your family for Yom HaAtzmaut, why don't we stay home and join in the hike that Elisheva's planning? Afterwards everyone's getting together for a barbecue here."

"Don't you like being with my family?" Kobi teased.

"You know I do." Lisa blushed. "They're warm and loving to me. It's just that I could do without the long drive."

"I'll be doing the driving. You can nap," Kobi coaxed.

"Yeah, but it's going to be so hot and crowded there."

"Lisa," Kobi spoke softly, "I don't want to put you out, but it would mean a lot to me if we went. It's a chance to get together with all my aunts and uncles and cousins, and I'm looking forward to it. But if you really feel strongly about it, we won't go."

"Okay." Lisa smiled at Kobi's charm. "We'll go."

His brown eyes sparkled with appreciation.

She'd felt good about her decision then, but now she wasn't so sure. Maybe, she admitted to herself, she was just having a bad morning. Kobi had forgotten to turn on the washing machine, so she was behind with the laundry. Shuki had wanted a peanut butter sandwich for playgroup instead of the cheese one she'd already prepared, and he'd put up a fuss. Even though Pesach had ended a few weeks ago, she still felt bloated and uncomfortable from all the matzah, so she had skipped breakfast. Now hunger pains were beginning to catch up with her. She grabbed a candy bar and took Sondra's aerogram out of her pocket to reread.

> *Dear Lisa,*
>
> *I want to wish you a wonderful Pesach, even though I know you won't be receiving this until afterwards. I tried calling you, but I guess the lines were overloaded, so I'm taking a few minutes to wish you a good yom tov. I hope all's well there and you didn't work too hard getting ready for the chag.*
>
> *I have wonderful news that I can finally share with you. The Frankels are coming back to Phoenix! Yechiel is taking Rabbi Levi's place! Shraga, Debbie's husband, is becoming the vice principal, so that means they'll be staying on at least another year.*
>
> *Phoenix isn't Eretz Yisrael, but it seems to be working out a lot better here than I thought it would when we spoke that last Shabbos in Kfar Yonatan.*

Give Shuki a kiss for me and send my regards to Kobi.

I miss you.

Love,

Sondra

Lisa sighed as she finished reading. For the first time since moving to Kfar Yonatan, she felt a stab of homesickness. How nice it would be to be back in Phoenix and have Rena Frankel there, Sondra nearby, and her parents a short flight away. Before she could get too carried away with her negative thoughts, though, the door opened and Miriam entered the store. "So what did you guys decide to do next Monday?"

"We're going to Mount Gilboa, with Kobi's family."

"That's nice."

"Yeah," Lisa answered without much enthusiasm. "I'm glad we're not going to be meeting in Beit She'an. It's even hotter there. What are you doing?"

"Yehezkel has to give some classes in Ramat Gan in the morning, and he's going to his parents in the afternoon, and I'm staying here with the kids." Miriam disregarded Lisa's concerned glance. "We'll join in the barbecue."

"Oh." Lisa decided her plans weren't so bad after all. As she rang up her friend's purchases, she resolved to make the best of the day.

In the end it was lovely, but the way home was a different story. Shuki was overtired and crabby. Lisa had eaten too much and had a stomachache. There was a suspicious object in the middle of the road in Shechem and they'd sat in the car for over an hour waiting for the army sappers to show up and detonate it. Fortunately, it had been a false alarm, but they arrived home only minutes before afternoon services were supposed to start.

"Lisa," Kobi said as they drove into Kfar Yonatan, "I had a wonderful day. Thank you so much for agreeing to go."

"Oh, Kobi." Lisa was touched. "I had a good time too."

"I'm glad. You just worry about Shuki." He smiled at his wife. "I'll run to services and come right back and unload the car."

Lisa smiled her appreciation and led Shuki to the bathtub. He was already in pajamas and tucked into bed, though, and Kobi still wasn't home. Irritated, Lisa began unloading the car. When she finished unpacking, Kobi still hadn't returned and she began to feel a burning resentment. With angry strides, she made her way to the washing machine and put in a load of laundry. Just as she'd decided to go ahead and take a shower, the front door opened.

One look at her husband made her annoyance evaporate. His face was ashen and he sank down into the easy chair, face in his hands.

"Kobi, what's wrong?"

There was no answer.

"Kobi!" Lisa spoke sharply as she sat across from him. "You're scaring me."

Slowly, in a monotone, her husband spoke through his hands.

"A group of Arabs from Al-Duba attacked our hikers today. Boaz was in the rear and they managed to take away his gun." Kobi ignored Lisa's gasp. "He has a concussion and is in the hospital overnight for observation. Chava needed stitches next to her eye. She's home. Kaylie was shot in the leg." Lisa moaned and again Kobi ignored her. "Moshe Geller was shot in the shoulder. And," Kobi groaned, "Avi is dead."

Lisa brought her two fists to her mouth as if to stifle a scream, but she didn't make a sound.

"Who, who, who's with Elisheva?" she finally asked.

Kobi shook his head, his face still in his hands. "It's a madhouse over there. She doesn't need anyone else."

"But, but... I need to see her," Lisa stated simply. "Can you take care of things here so I can go now?"

Kobi barely nodded. "Be happy you have a friend to go see," he said miserably.

The Ben Davids' house was packed with people. Rav Yehezkel was standing in the kitchen talking to someone from the *chevrah kaddisha*.

Dudu, who was in charge of the village's security, had two reporters questioning him in the hallway. Myra was cleaning up the kitchen with one of the National Service girls, trying to stay out of the men's way. The other National Service girl had just come out of the children's bedroom. A group of eight women sat gathered around Elisheva, with her sister and Miriam on either side of her. Miriam made room for Lisa to come close to Elisheva. She bent down to hug her friend, and to her embarrassment, began crying.

"I'm so sorry," she whispered, and then, to her mortification, realized she'd spoken in English. She simply wasn't able to find the words for that simple sentence in Hebrew. Understanding her distress, Miriam rose, took her hand, and led her out to the little laundry porch.

"It's okay to cry," Miriam said kindly.

"I'm not the one who lost my husband." Lisa swiped at her cheeks.

"No," Miriam's voice caught, "your friend did. And it hurts us all."

Lisa nodded silently as the tears dripped down her face.

"What's going to happen?"

"The funeral's tomorrow afternoon..."

"No," Lisa interrupted sharply. "What's going to happen to Elisheva, the kids, us? How can we go on?"

"How did your family go on after your brother died?"

"No one murdered him!"

"Lisa," Miriam continued, reaching out to take her friend's hands, "remember what we say at the Seder every year. 'In every generation they rise up against us to destroy us and *HaKadosh Baruch Hu* delivers us from their hands.' The safe childhood free from anti-Semitism that we knew in Colorado and Kansas was an oasis of time. This is the reality and we have to be strong. For ourselves, for our children, and for Elisheva."

Lisa understood. In the days to come, she found reservoirs of strength she didn't know she had. First thing the next morning, she had to face her son and explain why she was so sad. Kobi wasn't there to help her. He'd left early for work and told her he'd meet her at the funeral.

Then there were the phone calls from America. Her parents, Sondra,

Rena, and loyal Carol had all heard about a murder of someone from Kfar Yonatan on the evening news and stayed up late, waiting for morning in Israel, so they could make sure that the Chazons were all well. Lisa struggled to keep her voice even and assure them that they were fine, at least physically.

"Did we meet that man?" her mother probed.

"Yes, he's, or he was, Kobi's best friend."

"Oh, that big man with the big laugh. What a shame. So how's Shuki?"

"He's fine." Lisa ended the conversation feeling distant from her parents.

At the funeral, she caught a glimpse of Avi's tallit-wrapped body and remembered her mother's description. That strong, vibrant man seemed so tiny now that he was being returned to his Maker.

She spent a good part of the shivah week sending in food from the store, taking Elisheva's three little boys and Shuki to the playground in the afternoons, and stopping in at the shivah house as much as possible. So much so that Kobi complained she was neglecting her own family. Lisa didn't take his complaints to heart. She knew they came from the pain he was feeling over the loss of his friend. *If only*, she thought, *Kobi would do something constructive with his grief.* She feared he would become even angrier than he'd been after the destruction of Yamit.

That first evening after she came back from Elisheva, Natan came to the door to tell Kobi there was a meeting for the men at the *beit knesset*, but Kobi had refused to go.

"I don't want to hear all the platitudes," he'd said, dismissing the idea. "Avi's murder is not for the best and if it's part of Hashem's plan, I don't understand Him."

The next morning there were reports that some of the fields of Al-Duba had been burned. The news labeled it an act of retaliation. Kobi reacted with bitterness. "Where's the retaliation? A field is equal to a man?"

Throughout the week of shivah there was talk of beginning a new settlement at the site of the murder. Kobi's response was derision. "No one's going to make it happen."

But he was wrong. On Erev Shavuot, a cornerstone was laid at the site of the murder, six caravans were erected, and six young couples moved in.

After Shavuot was over and all the dishes were washed, the house in order for the following day and Shuki sound asleep, Lisa nervously insisted her husband sit down with her, even though it was late.

"Kobi..." Lisa sat very still with her hands folded in her lap, her heart beating wildly in her chest. "I know it's been very hard for you, losing Avi, but I have some good news for you."

Kobi just raised his eyebrows. He'd been so apathetic lately that Lisa knew he didn't have an inkling of what she was about to tell him.

"I was at the doctor Monday. I'm two months pregnant."

Kobi smiled at her, but it wasn't his old smile and his eyes held no sparkle.

"Kobi, be happy," Lisa pleaded. "If it's a boy, we'll name him after Avi."

"I told you when Shuki was born, I don't want to name after anyone who died young."

Kobi's tone was icy and, despite her good intentions, tears began coursing down Lisa's face.

"Lisa." Kobi was contrite. "Don't cry. I'm sorry. It is good news. It's wonderful news. It's funny how life works," he mused. "I wasn't sure we'd ever have another baby, and now, right after I lost my best friend, we're bringing another child into the world." He looked baffled. "How're you feeling? I should've asked you right away."

"I'll be fine," Lisa smiled weakly, "if you can be happy about the pregnancy."

"I'll try."

With that reassurance, Lisa allowed herself to hope, just a bit, that Kobi's anger was behind them.

CHAPTER
Forty

"How was it being back at school?" Danny asked his wife.

"I held up okay," Sondra answered ruefully.

The two of them were settled in the den, but instead of sitting side by side in the easy chairs, Sondra lay prone on the couch with her left foot elevated.

"But your ankle hurts, right?"

"Are you asking as a doctor or as a husband?"

"A husband!"

Sondra nodded sheepishly.

"You're as horrible a patient now as you were when you got burned."

"Sorry," Sondra said in a small voice. "I stayed off it for a week, though. Even with Carmen and your mother helping, that wasn't easy."

"I understand." Danny tried to sound patient. Sondra had somehow tripped walking out of shul on the second day of Shavuos. He'd been almost certain that she hadn't broken anything and an X-ray at the emergency room later that night showed she only had a bad sprain. "But just because the orthopedist OK'd you going back to using it normally doesn't mean you have to do everything all at once."

"I know, but I felt bad leaving my students for so long."

"You weren't pleased with Tova as a substitute?"

"Actually, I was." Tova was Ari's mother, whose husband had come to work at Intel. Sondra grimaced as she changed her position. "She did a great job and I know she'd love to be a regular teacher next year. I'm thinking, if, um, Rabbi Levi thinks it's a good idea and it's okay with Rabbi Frankel, I'd like to take a year off. What do you think?"

Danny sat forward, looking intently at his wife. "We don't need your salary."

"I know."

"But you really enjoy teaching."

"I do."

"So what's bringing this on?"

"Two things." Sondra counted off on her fingers. "I feel like I'm getting a little stale. And I think we're expecting."

"Have you been to the doctor?" Danny asked.

"No, it's too early." She smiled. "It's just a feeling I have."

"What a great feeling!" Danny exclaimed.

Sondra laughed happily. "We'll see."

"Well," Danny said, "if you are, it's good that you'll have the summer behind you before the last trimester. They're already predicting 100 degrees for tomorrow."

"Thank goodness we have air-conditioning," Sondra said in the resigned voice she used every May when the intense heat began. "The kids wanted to go swimming today. If it's 100 degrees tomorrow, I'll have to take the girls."

"Do you really think you're up to it?"

"I can think of nothing better than soaking my foot in the water. Goldie's willing to watch Zvi Chaim in the afternoon and you can take him to the pool after dinner. Okay?"

"Sounds good," Danny agreed.

✳   ✳   ✳

Debbie and Tova were already at Bayla's pool with their children when Sondra arrived. They were more than willing to give Sondra a hand with her children and beach bag.

"I have the catalogue from Parks and Recreation," Debbie announced as she smoothed sunscreen on her youngest daughter's back.

"Anything good?" Sondra asked.

"There's a dance and rhythm class that would be good for the girls."

"Where?"

"Not too far from here. At the Colonnade Mall."

"I bet Batsheva and Naomi would like that." Sondra paused in blowing up the beach ball. "Is there anything good for Zvi Chaim?"

Debbie handed over the catalogue. Sondra exclaimed over an ice skating class at Thomas Mall, but Tova wasn't interested.

"I'm taking the kids to my mother for the summer," she announced. "Yaacov will meet us for the last two weeks."

"You're going back to Israel and leaving your husband alone all summer?" Debbie exclaimed.

"Listen," Tova explained while she took off her robe and entered the pool with her daughter in her arms. "Yaacov neglected to tell me how hot it gets here in the summer. This place makes Beersheva seem like the Alps. I can't take it."

Sondra and Debbie smiled in sympathy.

"Don't worry about Yaacov," Tova continued as she floated on her back with her toddler on top of her. "I'm leaving him a freezer full of food. His office is air-conditioned. Utilities in our apartment are included in the rent, so he can run the air conditioner as low as he wants. He'll be fine."

"He can always come to us for Shabbos meals." Sondra had taken off her shoes and was dangling her feet in the water. Yossi settled on the steps next to her, playing with the toy dishes she'd brought.

"I know." Tova smiled gratefully and made her way to the steps. She sat down next to Sondra and spoke softly.

"Doesn't it bother you to put Zvi Chaim in a class with a bunch of non-Jews?"

Sondra flushed and tried not to sound too defensive. "If he goes with Benny or Eli, they'll have each other; and I'd rather have him in a program with non-Jews for an hour or two a week than enrolled in the JCC day camp. Then he'd be all day with kids eating *treyfe* as well as ones who aren't even Jewish."

"Maybe next summer we can get the day school to have a camp."

"Maybe," Sondra wasn't all that optimistic.

"Well, if you still want to send Zvi Chaim to your cousin for the summer, I'll be happy to have him travel with us."

"Wow! What an offer!" Sondra's girls, both good swimmers, were playing pool tag. Their shrieks and laughter mixed with those of the other children, and Sondra knew she could probably discuss the idea without any little ears overhearing. Still, she told Tova she'd think about it.

For the next few hours, that was all she thought about. She made a couple of quick phone calls. Goldie, Eli's mother, told her they'd be going back east to her in-laws for the second half of the summer, and Shoshie, the rabbi's wife, said they would only be gone for two weeks in August. After the children were in bed, she broached the subject with Danny.

"I know that Lisa's offer was one hundred percent sincere." Sondra took a long sip of iced tea. "But a lot's happened since then."

"I don't know how safe it is to be in Kfar Yonatan now," Danny said slowly.

"That doesn't worry me," Sondra said. "You know there can be shootings anywhere."

Danny nodded somberly. Three months earlier, one of his friends from high school, a lawyer and a member of the Jewish community at large, had been gunned down and seriously injured by a mentally disturbed client. It was the type of thing one saw in action movies, not in real life. The lawyer's ongoing struggle in rehabilitation was real enough, though.

"What concerns me," Sondra continued, "is that two months is a mighty long time for someone not quite eight years old to be away from his family."

"Agreed," Danny said emphatically. "Why don't I take a week's vaca-tion in August, when none of Zvi Chaim's friends will be here, and the other week you can take the kids to Kansas. What do you think?"

"That's a good plan. Between Bayla's pool and the library and some Parks and Recreation activities, we'll manage to have a good summer." Sondra resolutely took a deep breath. "Especially if there's a trip to look forward to at the end."

Somewhere in the back of her mind, Lisa remembered making an offer to take Zvi Chaim over the summer vacation, but she was relieved when Sondra wrote a letter describing her summer plans for the chil-dren. Kobi continued to have bouts of anger off and on, but he seemed optimistic about the new baby.

"Lisa," he had said the day following her announcement, "I want you to go to a special obstetrician."

Lisa looked at him quizzically.

"Someone at work told me about a practice that just opened in Kfar Saba. Four American doctors made *aliyah* several ago and they weren't happy with the status quo in the Israeli medical system, so they grouped together and opened an American-style practice, complete with a secre-tary, nurse, lab, and long hours."

"It must cost a fortune," Lisa objected.

"No." Kobi shook his head. "It's under the health system and you pay a reasonable monthly fee that more than equals the service they give. You're worth it, Lisa."

Her first appointment was the following week. She left Shuki at Myra's and stuck a "closed" sign on the grocery's door, adding a message that it would be opened for two hours in the afternoon. A few days later when Elisheva was the only one there shopping, Lisa experienced a severe bout of nausea.

"I couldn't imagine what could make you close the store last week," Elisheva said sympathetically.

"Boaz still has too many dizzy spells to replace me." Lisa wiped her face with a damp cloth.

"Why didn't you ask me?"

"You?" Lisa exclaimed. "Do you think you're up to it?"

Just a week earlier, Elisheva had confided to Lisa that it was a struggle for her to get out of bed every morning. Only by concentrating on the blessing "Who gives strength to the weary" was she able to put her feet on the floor and stand up. Then it was only by focusing on the needs of her boys that she was able to remain standing and not return to her bed and hide under her covers.

"My boys lost their father." Elisheva squared her shoulders. "I'm not going to let them lose their mother too. I have to get on with my life."

Lisa looked closely at her pretty, petite friend. It seemed as if a strong wind could knock her over, but Lisa knew differently. Elisheva hadn't had a paying job since she'd married. Her vocation, she'd felt, was to run the house so Avi could devote himself to the management of Kfar Yonatan. Now the village had a new manager.

"Elisheva, I can't think of anyone I could trust more."

CHAPTER
Forty-one

With Yossi napping and the older children all at friends, Sondra took advantage of the quiet to look over brochures from San Diego. The ringing phone interrupted her vacation planning though, and as soon as she heard her mother's voice, her heart began racing. The last time Helga had called during the most expensive time of day had been to tell her that Oma had died.

"How are you, dear?"

Was it Sondra's imagination or did her mother's accent seem more pronounced?

"I'm fine, but why are you calling? Is something wrong?"

"Actually," Helga sighed, "there is. I am sorry to be the bearer of bad news, but I feel you should know. You know, ever since the time you got burned so badly, you promised you would not keep secrets from me, and I do not want —"

"Mom," Sondra made a tremendous effort not to yell, "just tell me what's wrong."

Helga sighed again. "Your Uncle Herbert is in surgery right now. He was gored by a bull and there is some internal damage."

"Oh my gosh," Sondra gasped.

"Well, it is serious," Helga began rambling again. "I thought maybe you should be praying for him. I am on my way to the hospital right now. Aunt Irene is beside herself, as you can imagine. Oh, by the way, if you call Lisa, do not mention a thing. Irene does not want her to know yet."

Sondra sank down onto one of the kitchen chairs.

"Aunt Irene's the one who called me on the carpet for not telling you about my burns. I can't believe she's going to keep this from Lisa."

"I know, I know. She says Lisa has enough on her head right now. She does not want her flying when she is pregnant and she knows Lisa will want to come to be with her. Maybe you should not speak to Lisa at all until we know more, okay?"

"Okay," Sondra conceded reluctantly.

Ever since Avi's murder, Sondra had been calling her cousin weekly. She'd been thrilled to learn that Lisa was expecting two months before her. She sensed, though, that things weren't going so smoothly in the Chazon household as Kobi continued to struggle with the loss of his friend. Aunt Irene was probably right. It'd be far better to wait and see how the surgery went. Sondra made a quick phone call to Danny and then took out her *Tehillim*.

It was late that evening when her father finally called. "Your uncle's out of surgery," he said simply without preamble.

"*Baruch Hashem*," Sondra breathed.

"Yes," Julius agreed, "thank G-d. He's in the ICU and his prognosis is good if he stays calm and there's no internal bleeding."

"How's Aunt Irene?"

"You know your aunt. Now that Herbert's out of surgery, she's back to her unruffled self. She's sleeping at the hospital, though."

"Please send my love."

"Keep praying." Her father ended the conversation.

"Guess what!" her mother said two days later. "Herbert is out of the ICU."

"That's wonderful!" Sondra exclaimed.

"Yes!" Helga spoke happily. "All those years of hard work as a rancher kept him in good shape."

"Does Lisa know?"

"Irene just called her."

When Sondra called before Shabbos, her parents informed her there was a good chance Herbert would be released on Monday. After the first call from her mother, Sondra had stuffed the San Diego brochures into a drawer. Now she promised herself she would finish up the vacation plans on Sunday.

On the Sundays Danny was on call, he always went to the early morning services, came home for a quick breakfast, and left for his rounds at the hospital. This Sunday, Sondra woke up to find her husband sitting at the kitchen table, not eating and staring into space.

When she looked back at that week, she remembered how Shirley always said bad things come in threes. Following two negative incidents, her mother-in-law would always break an egg so that it would be the third "bad thing." She was sorry she hadn't broken a dozen eggs right then and there.

"What's wrong?" she asked with concern.

Danny's eyes moved to his wife's face and he shook his head slowly. "Mordechai Hirsch was killed in a car accident last night."

"Oh, how terrible!" Sondra's hand flew to her face. "How'd it happen?"

"A drunk driver ran a stop light."

Sondra gasped.

"Vivian Levi was there with Shaindy all night." Danny rearranged his *kippah*. "Bayla's there now. The funeral will be later this afternoon, after his sister gets here."

"I can't believe it." Sondra's voice was hollow as the implications sank in. "Shaindy's a widow. How will she ever manage?"

"I hope Mordechai had life insurance."

He and Sondra exchanged a long look. It'd have to be a very good policy to cover the tuition for two children in day school, one in yeshiva, and one in preschool. Neither of them could imagine Shaindy, with her negative outlook on life, getting a job with an income high enough for all of her family's expenses.

Switching into autopilot, Sondra brought a bowl of cereal to the table. "You've got to eat." She poured two glasses of orange juice and sat down with her husband.

Danny took a swallow of the juice and left the food untouched. Sondra watched him leave and continued to sit at the table, lost in her thoughts, until Yossi came toddling into the kitchen, demanding juice. The others followed soon after and kept her busy until she put on an Uncle Moishy record. She used the break to call Debbie.

Shraga volunteered for the *chevrah kaddisha*, so he knew that the funeral was scheduled for five o'clock. He'd told Debbie that Shaindy was totally distraught, repeating over and over that she never should've sent Mordechai out for ice cream. Vivian was organizing food to be sent in and Bayla was in charge of the volunteer shifts.

"It's not like when Shraga sat shivah for his father," Debbie explained. "My sisters-in-law and I were there and took care of all the cooking and serving and cleaning up. Here, everyone's a mourner."

"Isn't any of Shaindy's family coming?"

There was a silence on the other end of the phone.

"Debbie?" Sondra prodded.

"You know, I've never heard her mention any family."

Sondra searched her memory and came to the same conclusion. She said goodbye to her friend and dialed Shaindy's house.

Bayla answered the phone, sounding decidedly strained.

"Shaindy's resting, although I don't have much hope of her sleeping."

"I feel so bad for her," Sondra said, "but it's really you I wanted to talk to. Can you sign me up on the volunteer list for Tuesday evening?"

Bayla hesitated. "Sondra, I'm going to be frank with you. I've a line out the door of women willing to come in the evenings. The mornings aren't too bad when some of the children are in day camp, but the afternoons are empty. I know you young girls don't want to leave your kids in the afternoon, but Vivian and I can't do it all."

"I see," Sondra said. "Let me call my mother-in-law and see if she can help me out."

Shirley's sympathy brought tears to Sondra's eyes. She was more than willing to entertain her grandchildren Wednesday afternoon so Sondra could be on duty at the shivah house.

Goldie was cleaning up the kitchen when Sondra entered Shaindy's house later that week. "They've had lunch," she informed Sondra. "The girls and Faygie, Mordechai's sister, are in the living room with Shaindy. Her older son's in his room and Reuvie's at Shoshie's. I've got to get my kids. Call me if you have any questions." She hurried away and Sondra nervously entered the living room.

Shaindy looked far less agitated than she had been when Sondra had paid her a shivah call two nights earlier. Her eyes were no longer swollen and she'd managed to put on a *sheitel* instead of a snood. She kept her hands folded calmly in her lap as she listened to words of comfort from the Chabad rabbi, who was preparing to leave. Sondra quickly realized that although there were crowds of comforters in the evenings, in the afternoons, visitors were almost as sparse as volunteers.

"Mommy, let's look at these." Shaindy's younger daughter pulled out a box of old photographs.

Shaindy managed to look interested and held up a black-and-white photo. "Here's your father's first grade picture."

"Is this you?" Her daughter held up a snapshot of a teenage girl with a sixties hairstyle, flanked by a middle-aged couple.

Shaindy just nodded.

"Who's with you?"

"My parents." Shaindy bit at her cuticle.

"They look different than I remember."

"They were a lot younger."

Next were a handful of pictures from her older son's bris, taken in the synagogue in Monsey. Shaindy's father was obviously the *sandek*.

"Look, Shaindy, here's your house in Monsey," Faygie said. "You loved that house."

"I loved Monsey," Shaindy whispered.

"I guess you'll move back now," her sister-in-law said.

The color drained from Shaindy's face and she shook her head.

"Why not?" Faygie seemed totally unaware of Shaindy's discomfort.

"I'll never move back there." Shaindy clenched her fists.

"Why ever not? What's keeping you here?"

"Faygie Becker, just leave me alone and mind your own business," Shaindy snapped and began crying.

Shamefaced, her sister-in-law stood up and took her nieces' hands. "Let's go into my room and rest for a while. I'll tell you some stories about your Abba and me when we were little."

The girls followed their aunt uncertainly, leaving Sondra alone with their mother.

"Can I get you a cup of tea?" Sondra asked uncomfortably.

"That would be nice." Shaindy sniffled.

"Do you want to be alone?" Sondra asked when she returned with the tea.

Shaindy shook her head, so Sondra sat down beside her, putting a hand on her arm. Shaindy slowly sipped the tea. Once she finished, she turned to Sondra.

"I've had a lot of time to think." She paused. "I owe you and the others an explanation." She took a deep breath.

"It's okay, Shaindy." Although she and Lisa had always wondered about Shaindy's standoffishness, Sondra felt uneasy about what was about to come.

"Just listen, Sondra," Shaindy spoke sharply. "I was always spoiled," she began. "I'm the only child of Holocaust survivors, and they gave me whatever I wanted. My father had a successful business and they could afford the prettiest clothes, the best piano teacher, the most exclusive camp. You get the picture?"

Sondra nodded.

"When I married, they agreed to support us for two years so Mordechai could learn in *kollel*. I was the only wife in our *kollel* with full-time help. At the end of two years, my father took Mordechai into the business. He — Mordechai," Shaindy's eyes filled but she wiped away the tears before they could fall, "had a good aptitude for business, but my father was a gambler. Not," she hastened to explain, "on horses or slot machines or cards. Just on business deals.

"Six years ago, he went bankrupt and he tried to blame Mordechai. We had words, horrible words — my father and I — and we haven't spoken since. Mordechai found a good job here, but not with the salary he was earning in Monsey. I never gave Phoenix a chance, even though you were all so nice to me. I'm sorry."

"Oh, Shaindy." Sondra took her hand.

"Now everyone's putting themselves out for me, and I never put myself out for any of you."

"It's okay." Sondra swallowed the lump in her throat. "We're happy to help you; we're just sorry it's for such a sad reason."

Shaindy let her fresh tears fall unchecked.

Sondra handed her a tissue, opened her mouth to say something, and then closed it again.

"What?" Shaindy asked.

"Um..." Sondra hesitated, "don't you think someone should tell your parents what happened?"

"Maybe." Shaindy covered her mouth with the fingertips of one hand thoughtfully. "Maybe I'll ask Rabbi Levi to call them."

Sondra was pensive as she left the shivah house. Mordechai hadn't been that much older than Danny. If anything ever happened to her husband, well, Sondra didn't want to continue that train of thought. She wondered if she and the others would be able to give Shaindy the support she needed.

If only Lisa was still here, Sondra thought. Of all the women in the community, Lisa was the one who'd had the most patience with Shaindy Hirsch. Certainly she'd want to make a phone call and offer her comfort long distance.

Sondra glanced at her watch. It was still the middle of the night in Israel, but in a few hours Lisa would be awake. She was always in the grocery store well before eight in the morning. If she waited until ten o'clock at night, Phoenix time, to call, the morning rush in the store would be over and Lisa would have time for a leisurely conversation.

With her children all asleep, Danny still out learning, and the house peacefully quiet, Sondra settled herself in the den, picked up the phone, and dialed the number of the grocery store. The phone rang and rang, but no one picked up. Perhaps it was out of order.

Sondra decided to call her cousin's house. After six rings, a strange voice answered.

"Is this the Chazon family?" Sondra asked uncertainly in Hebrew.

"Yes."

"May I speak to Lisa?"

"Who's calling?"

"Her cousin, Sondra. I'm calling from America."

"Just a minute."

It was more like five.

"Hello?" Lisa's voice was thick, as if she'd just woken up.

"Lisa, are you okay?"

"Yeah, I'm fine." She didn't sound fine.

"Listen, I have some bad news from here." Sondra cleared her throat nervously. "I think you should know."

"Yeah?"

"Shaindy's husband was killed in a car accident Saturday night."

There was a brief silence and then Lisa mumbled half to herself, "Well, at least she knows where he is."

Horrified by her cousin's inappropriate response, Sondra cried out, "Why would you say such a thing?!" But as she spoke, she realized the line was dead.

CHAPTER

Forty-two

$\mathcal{I}$n the space of three days, Lisa's life had turned totally upside down. It began Sunday morning when Kobi announced he wouldn't be coming home that evening.

"I'm racing against the clock on the project that's due. So I'll probably pull an all-nighter."

"You've got to be kidding." Lisa stopped making Shuki's sandwich and turned to face her husband, hands on her hips. "How productive will you be tonight if you don't sleep?"

"Lisa," Kobi said as he closed his briefcase, "I know what I'm doing. If I need to sack out for a bit, there are couches in the lounge."

Lisa made a face. "If you don't want to drive all the way home, why don't you go sleep at Riki's in a real bed?"

"Get off my case," Kobi snapped at her. "I told you I'm working against the clock. Do you want me to get fired?"

"No, Kobi," Lisa answered wearily. "I don't want you to get fired. I just want you to take care of yourself."

"I appreciate your concern," Kobi muttered sarcastically, "but I know how to take care of myself."

"Okay." Lisa swallowed a retort. "Call me tonight when you take a break."

"Sure thing." Kobi kissed Shuki goodbye, grabbed his overnight bag, and was out the door.

But he didn't call that evening, and when Lisa finally tried to call him, the switchboard was closed.

She slept poorly that night and woke up late. It was hectic trying to get Shuki ready and out to Myra's, and rushing to get the store open on time. Then there was a steady stream of customers until after ten o'clock. Lisa finally sat down, caught her breath, and picked up the phone to call Kobi.

"Hi, Ilana. It's Lisa. May I speak to Kobi?"

"Uh, he's not in."

"Oh, did he say when he'd be back?"

"Uh, not really."

Ilana was an experienced, middle-aged secretary. Lisa wondered why she sounded like a nervous teenager on her first day of work.

"Please give him a message to call me as soon as he comes in."

"Lisa, I, uh..." the secretary faltered.

"What, Ilana?"

"I don't know if it's my place to tell you this, uh, but, uh, Kobi, uh, stopped working here at the end of last month."

The end of last month! Lisa almost screamed, but clamped her jaws tightly together. She felt her face flush and it seemed as if her heart was beating so loudly that Ilana could hear it.

"Lisa, are you okay?" She heard Ilana's question, but it sounded so far away, like from the inside of a long, long tunnel. She was not okay. She was confused and frightened, but she didn't want Ilana feeling sorry for her.

"I'm fine," she managed to utter. "I'm sorry, I got confused and called the wrong number."

She wondered if Ilana believed her. *What kind of wife doesn't know her husband quit his job two weeks ago? What kind of husband does that without telling his wife?* How could Kobi have kept it a secret from her? She'd always been able to read him like a book. He used to complain he could never make a surprise party for her. What had happened to their marriage? Surely he had some reasonable explanation for everything. But where was he?

Lisa sat staring at the phone, wishing she knew who to call to answer her questions. Shula would be the obvious choice, but what daughter-in-law wants to admit to her mother-in-law that she doesn't know where her husband is? Maybe she should call Riki. Not to ask about Kobi, of course. She'd have to think up some inane reason, and once they began talking, maybe Riki would let some information slip about her brother, if she knew anything. It was certainly worth a try.

What could she call about though?

The door to the grocery opened and Lisa forced a smile on her face to greet Shifra Lev. Shifra and her family were Americans who'd just moved to Kfar Yonatan after six months in an absorption center. They were the fifty-fifth family to settle in the village and they'd made their home in the Gruenbergs' old prefab. Miriam and the *rav*, as well as fourteen other families, had finally moved into their permanent homes.

"Did you tell me your sister-in-law's a travel agent?" Shifra asked after she came up to the check-out counter and pulled her items out of her basket.

"Yes," Lisa answered eagerly. Was this going to be her inane reason to call Riki?

"My brother just got engaged and we want to check out if it would be cheaper to buy the airline tickets here or in America. I want to start with someone I can trust."

"I'll be happy to give you Riki's number." Lisa smiled. "I'll call her first and tell her to be especially nice to you."

Riki was in a good mood when Lisa called. Pleased to have been recommended, she chatted with her sister-in-law until one of Lisa's customers walked in. Kobi wasn't mentioned until the end of the conversation, and that was just Riki telling her to give him her love.

Lisa stayed preoccupied the rest of the morning, trying to think of someone else to call. Just as she was locking up the store, a name came to her. Noam Berger! He'd been in school with Kobi years ago. They'd lost contact with each other, and then last year Kobi had been pleased when Noam began working at the company. He would surely know why Kobi had quit! Of course, Lisa reasoned as she headed home, Kobi would probably be home in time for dinner and then he would explain everything himself. If not, she'd call Noam once Shuki was in bed.

But Kobi did not come home for dinner. Shuki whined for his father the whole meal and wasn't impressed by Lisa's explanations. Lisa wasn't impressed either, and, against her will, began to imagine horrible scenarios that were keeping Kobi from calling or coming home. It wasn't easy getting her three-year-old to bed. Finally, after listening to his mother read four books, Shuki gave in to sleep. Lisa hurried to the drawer where Kobi kept his personal phone book.

It wasn't there. And, as she rummaged through the drawers, Lisa realized his passports were also missing. Fighting her rising panic, she turned to their closet. Perhaps Kobi had moved the items there, but she couldn't find them. Her bottom lip wouldn't stop trembling as she ran into the living room and began emptying out the wall unit. Two hours later, after rummaging around in every room of the house except Shuki's, she came up empty-handed. There was no sign of Kobi's passports or phone book, but almost all of his clothes seemed to be in place. Most of his toiletries were in their normal spots in the bathroom too. And his tallit and tefillin were waiting for him in the cabinet by the front door. *Had he forgotten them? What had he done that morning?*

She sank dejectedly onto the couch, trying to decide what to do. Outside a west wind was howling and the neighbor's loose shingle was banging, grating on Lisa's nerves. Inside, though, the house was far too quiet. Suddenly the phone rang, breaking the silence. Lisa pounced on it, certain Kobi was on the line. He was not.

"Hi, Lisa," Miriam's friendly voice came through the receiver. "I'm in dire need of a good book. Can I come take a look?" There was a pause as Miriam waited for an answer. "Lisa, are you there?" All Miriam heard was the sound of soft weeping. "Lisa, I'm coming over."

Lisa had dried her face by the time Miriam knocked on the door, but there was nothing she could do about the worry etched on her face. In a dull monotone, she recited everything that had transpired that day.

"I don't know what to think," she concluded. "Did Kobi quit his job and not tell me because he found a better one and wants to wait until he's settled in? Has he run off and left us? Was he the victim of a terrorist kidnapping? Did he leave his tallit and tefillin and electric shaver here because he's coming back or because he doesn't need them where he is? What's going on?"

Lisa refused to let the word *suicide* take over her thoughts, but her friend knew that Kobi had been depressed off and on since Avi's murder.

"Lisa," she spoke decisively, "give me Kobi's parents' number."

Lisa shrugged her shoulders and shrank into herself.

"Don't worry," Miriam reassured her. "I won't tell them that you don't know where he is."

Reluctantly, Lisa mumbled her in-laws' number. She would have liked to hide in her bedroom while Miriam made the call. Instead, she sat still as a stone and listened to the one-sided conversation.

"Hi, this is Miriam Gruenberg from Kfar Yonatan... Fine, how are you? Kobi's working late and we need to get a hold of him about something. No, everything's great with Lisa and Shuki. It's for the *beit knesset*... She's not answering the phone. I think she's sleeping... Sure, I'll hold on... Yes, I have a pen... Okay, thank you."

Hanging up the phone, Miriam showed the number to her friend. "Lisa, is this Kobi's old work number?"

Lisa glanced at the scribbled number Miriam held in her hand and nodded dejectedly.

"I think we should call the police."

Again Lisa nodded. Should she have called already in the morning? But in the morning, she hadn't thought he was missing. Lost in her thoughts, she paid no attention to what her friend was now saying. Miriam finally hung up the phone and turned to Lisa.

"You need to go into Kfar Saba to file a report. I'll stay here and babysit. You get ready while I find someone to drive you."

"I can drive myself," Lisa hesitated, "if I can borrow a car. I don't want anyone to know about this."

"I think you're too stressed to drive safely," Miriam said firmly. "And I think you should have a man with you. The police will take you more seriously that way than if you come in alone. Don't worry, I'll find someone discreet."

She found Natan, Myra's husband. Not only was he discreet, but as Miriam told Lisa, if she didn't hear from Kobi by morning, she'd have to explain everything to Myra so she could be sensitive to Shuki's needs in the morning playgroup.

The little boy was a heavy sleeper and didn't hear his mother leave or return in the wee hours of the morning. Miriam was sleeping on the couch, but she became instantly awake as soon as she heard the front door open.

"*Nu?*" She immediately stood up and made her way into the kitchen to prepare two cups of tea. Lisa followed her and shrugged.

"There've been no reports of unidentified bodies. That's good. But they won't start looking for him until after he's been missing for forty-eight hours."

"Why not?!"

"Policy for missing adults." Lisa chewed on her fingernail. "They were going to wait until Wednesday night since we just filed the report, but Natan argued that he's been missing since yesterday, so they agreed to start tomorrow. If I don't hear from them before, I'll go back Wednesday afternoon. Unless," Lisa brightened, "I hear from Kobi first."

"I pray you do," Miriam said warmly. "Do you think you'll be able to sleep okay tonight?"

"I'm going to try."

But she didn't succeed. She tossed and turned, trying to imagine where Kobi could be, and it was almost dawn when she finally fell asleep. Tuesday morning was a repeat of the Monday morning rush, only worse, and this time Shuki kept asking for his father. The west wind had brought in a heat wave. Lisa was short-tempered at the store and several customers left insulted. When she picked up Shuki, Myra was sympathetic, but told her emphatically that she had to give some sort of explanation to her son.

"What am I supposed to say?" Lisa demanded irritably.

"The truth."

"And what's that?"

"That Kobi had to go away for a while."

Lisa gave her friend an impatient look as she left with Shuki's hand in hers. At lunch, though, after Shuki had asked about his father for the fourth time, she tried telling him what Myra had suggested. The answer seemed to satisfy him and he stopped asking.

The neighbors, too impatient to wait for the police, began their own detective work. Miriam took it upon herself to call all of the nearby hospitals. Natan made a detour to Ben Gurion Airport after work, and with a picture of Kobi in hand, made the rounds of the airport personnel. No one came up with any information. Rav Yehezkel went to the company where Kobi had worked and spoke to his boss and the employees there. He learned that Kobi had given his two weeks' notice almost a month earlier and no one had been in contact with him since he'd left. Lisa wondered what in the world he had been doing every day when she thought he was at work.

Wednesday came and was just as hot as Tuesday. Lisa was even more exhausted. She made arrangements for Shuki to stay at Myra's all day, and as soon as she closed the store, Rav Yehezkel took her to Kfar Saba. The police station was stuffy and smelled like dirty socks. Fortunately, as soon as she walked in, one of the policemen recognized her.

"We were just about to call you," he said.

"Yes?" Lisa whispered. Her heart was beating wildly and her palms were so wet she could barely hold onto her purse.

"Come, sit down." He motioned her to the seat across from his desk.

Slowly, Lisa sat down. Rav Yehezkel stood at her side, radiating support.

"It looks as if your husband's okay."

Lisa smiled and gave a sigh of relief. "Where is he?"

The policeman cleared his throat and smiled apologetically. "He left the country Sunday morning on a Tower flight to New York."

The room seemed to spin and Lisa put her head down before she could faint. The *rav* sprinted to the cooler and handed her a plastic cup of water as soon as she raised her head.

"What do I do now?" she asked.

"Let's get you home," Rav Yehezkel answered.

Once in the car, though, he turned to her. "Maybe we should stop at the bank and check on your account."

Lisa sucked in her breath and limply nodded her agreement.

The bank was packed and Lisa waited in line for over an hour to find out that Kobi had emptied half of their account. *It could've been worse,* she told herself. *He could've taken it all.*

Miriam was waiting for her at her house. Her husband had called her from the bank so Lisa didn't have to tell her anything.

"Let's get you something to eat," she fussed over her friend. Lisa let herself be led, like a child, into the kitchen and listlessly ate the bowl of soup that Miriam handed her.

"I need to go get Shuki," she declared once the bowl was empty.

Miriam looked at her intently. "Myra's more than willing to keep him tonight. Don't you think you need some time for yourself?"

"What for?" Lisa shrugged.

"To come to grips with what's happened."

Lisa closed her eyes and moaned. "How am I supposed to come to grips with the fact that my husband has left me pregnant with his child, abandoned Shuki, and run off to America without a word or a goodbye? I don't want to even think about it!"

She slammed her fist down on the table as the tears rolled down her face and then the sobs began. Miriam let her cry herself out and afterwards put an arm around her.

"I can't believe how much I've cried this week," Lisa said with embarrassment.

"Crying can be good," Miriam sympathized. "The Sages teach that the gates of prayer were closed when the *Beit HaMikdash* was destroyed, but the gates of tears remain open. Our prayers should move us to tears. Right now your tears can be your prayers, but make sure they're tears of hope and faith that Hashem will help. Don't cry out of depression or despair."

"I'll try," Lisa whispered.

"We're here to help you."

"I know. Thank you," Lisa spoke woodenly. "Maybe you're right about Shuki staying at Myra's. I could use some time alone just to shower and get into bed. Maybe I'll be able to face him tomorrow."

"I do want to send in one of the National Service girls to sleep here, if that's okay. She can take care of the phone and be here to help you if you need anything."

"Okay," Lisa agreed wearily. "Just tell her not to bother me unless I call her."

Lisa stood up and slowly left the kitchen. She took a shower, turned on the fan in her bedroom, unplugged her bedside phone, and closed the door to the world.

CHAPTER

Forty-three

"Lisa, are you okay?"

Lisa swallowed hard. She'd lain awake for several hours the night before. With ironic timing, it was then that she had first felt the baby move. Did Kobi even care about his unborn child or Shuki or her?

She began replaying in her mind the weak goodbye he'd given her. Again the tears started and she'd sobbed herself to sleep. It was a deep sleep of exhaustion and she'd woken only minutes before Sondra's call. She was ashamed of the way she'd responded to Sondra and appreciated that her cousin had made a second try. Yet she had no idea how to answer her question.

"Sondra," she tried to keep her voice steady, "Kobi has disappeared."

She heard Sondra gasp. "What happened?" The simple question made her eyes well up again. "Lisa?"

"I'm here." Lisa struggled for control. "Sunday morning he went to work and never came home. Yesterday the police told me that he'd flown to America. They said he landed at JFK, but that's all we know."

"Oh my gosh!" There was a moment of silence on the other end of the line. "Oh my gosh!" Sondra repeated. "Do your parents know?"

"I just found out yesterday." Lisa didn't even bother to stop the tears this time. "There's a lot to sort out. I haven't even told Shuki."

"Did he leave a note?"

"Nothing."

"Oh, Lisa, I wish I could help you. Is there something I can do from here?"

"Find Kobi!" She knew the demand was ridiculous, but she was here in Israel and Sondra, at least, was on the same side of the ocean as Kobi.

"I wish I could." She heard Sondra's sympathy through the phone line. "I can't believe he walked out on you!"

"He's been depressed ever since Avi was murdered."

"Yes, that was awful, but that's no excuse."

"You're — just a minute…" The National Service girl was at her bedroom door, apologetically informing Lisa that Elisheva had arrived. "Sondra, Elisheva's at the door. I totally forgot about the store. I need to hang up."

"Okay," Sondra said, sounding very far away, "but I'm calling in the morning, my time."

Kobi had disappeared! Although the word hadn't been uttered, Sondra knew that if Kobi didn't reappear, Lisa was technically an *agunah*. She remembered hearing stories from the Gemara about merchants who didn't return from their travels, leaving their wives to be grass widows. She knew that, after the Holocaust, there were many women who didn't know for sure whether their husbands had survived or not and were *agunot*. She'd also heard of cases of spiteful husbands leaving their wives, but refusing to divorce them. According to Jewish law, a woman couldn't remarry without a proper Jewish divorce or positive proof that she was a widow.

Sondra put the brakes on her negative thoughts. Surely Kobi would call before Lisa had a chance to consider herself an *agunah*. She waited impatiently for Danny to come home so she could tell him what had happened.

He found the news hard to absorb. "I'm sure Kobi will be in contact with Lisa before you call tomorrow." He narrowed his eyes and tried to sound optimistic. "He'll have a reasonable explanation for everything."

"I sure hope you're right," Sondra muttered.

Meanwhile, after Lisa hung up the phone from Sondra and left her room to face Elisheva, she had only one thought. *Maybe Kobi will call today.* Elisheva came to her and put her arms around her.

"I'm so sorry," she whispered.

"I know," Lisa acknowledged the sympathy. She couldn't help remembering how she'd put her arms around Elisheva and given her condolences barely three months earlier.

"I'm sure you don't have an appetite," Elisheva led her into the kitchen as Miriam had the day before, "but you must eat something. What can I give you?"

"Some cornflakes, I guess."

Elisheva prepared her a bowl and looked around to offer some to Rivka, but the National Service girl had disappeared into Shuki's room to pray.

"I went to the store this morning and saw it was closed with no note on the door, and then I ran into Miriam and she told me everything. So I came here to let you know I'm with you. I'm here for you and I can open the store if you want me to."

Lisa looked at her friend in amazement. "Where do you find your strength?" she finally asked.

"I'm not that strong." Elisheva flushed. "There are countless times I'm paralyzed by the memories of the murder. Sometimes it's a struggle to put one foot in front of the other. But we're taught that Hashem doesn't give us a test without giving us the tools to pass it if we want. I want to pass the test."

Lisa nodded.

Unbidden memories flooded her consciousness and she saw in her mind her eighteen-year-old self hiding in her dorm room, crying her eyes out and barely eating as she bemoaned Tim's rejection. She didn't have the luxury to do that now. She was an adult with responsibilities, and the first was to her son and to the baby inside her. There was a lot to do and she had friends who were there to help her, but first she had to turn to *HaKadosh Baruch Hu*.

"Elisheva, if you could open the store that would be great. I want to pray and pull myself together a bit and get ready to pick up Shuki."

After she finished with her prayers, she turned to Rivka. "You can go on to the nursery school," she said, anxious for some privacy. "I can manage now."

"Hadas thinks they'll be okay without me and that I should stay and help you with the house."

Lisa's first impulse was to refuse the offer. Then she looked at Rivka's kind, freckled face and willing smile. She admitted to herself that the house was a disaster. She hadn't done a thing to clean up since Sunday evening. Tomorrow was Shabbat and she was so tired.

"Thank you." She swallowed her pride.

"If someone calls and you want privacy," Rivka said, "just talk in English. I won't understand a thing."

In spite of everything, Lisa smiled at the girl's good humor. She sorted laundry while Naomi attacked a sink full of dishes. Once a load was in the washer, though, she collapsed on the couch with her feet up and her hands resting protectively over her pregnant stomach. The phone rang several times, and each time Lisa felt a surge of hope. Would it be Kobi? Each time she was disappointed.

"I don't want to talk," Lisa instructed Rivka to tell the neighbors who were calling to offer sympathy and support. "Just write down their names and I'll get back to them sometime."

Rivka had just finished filling a bucket of water to wash the floors when the phone rang again. This time it was Miriam, and Lisa took the receiver.

"Yehezkel and I want to come over. Is that okay?"

"I guess so." Lisa hoped she didn't sound rude.

They arrived a few minutes later with a pad of paper and pencils. "We want to get organized," Miriam declared.

"Kobi will surely be coming back any day," Lisa insisted. "He'll have a good explanation for all of this."

"In the meantime," the *rav* spoke gently, "the community wants to help take care of you and Shuki, and there's no reason to duplicate jobs."

"Chava's in contact with the social worker to find out what benefits you have. Myra's going to keep her eyes open for any warning signs of stressful behavior from Shuki and arrange babysitters for whenever needed. Shifra's already organized a meal to come in this evening and will continue to do so. Rivka's willing to come in several afternoons a week to help with the housework." Miriam smiled. "We all love you and want to help."

Lisa listened in silence. She couldn't help but be touched by the caring. Still, she didn't know who would prepare the Shabbat candles for her the next day. Who would give Shuki his blessing at night before *Kiddush*? Who would bring her anemones for the Shabbat table and smile into her eyes as he handed them to her? Before she could spend too much time dwelling on these questions, Rav Yehezkel brought up a second topic.

"Someone needs to be in contact with all of Kobi's relatives, since he might have called one of them."

Lisa bit her bottom lip and groaned.

"I suppose I should call my in-laws to tell them what's happening and ask them to be in contact with the others."

Miriam cleared her throat nervously. "Yehezkel, I did speak to Kobi's mother Monday night." As she told him about the phone call, Lisa listened in stunned silence. She didn't remember that conversation at all. Where had she been?

"Okay," the *rav* continued. "I'll call and explain everything, and say we didn't want to worry them by telling them Kobi was missing until we knew for sure."

"And now we know for sure," Miriam stated. "I hope your in-laws will be supportive of you and Shuki."

Shuki! Lisa looked at the clock. It was almost one o'clock and time to face her little boy.

He ran to his mother eagerly as soon as she arrived at Myra's.

"Is Abba back?"

"No, Shuki," Lisa said gently. "We'll talk about it on the way home." Shuki held tightly to his mother's hand as they walked down the path. "Your Abba has been very, very sad ever since Avi died." Lisa spoke slowly, praying for the right words. "It's like he has a big boo-boo on his heart. Abba has gone away for a while until his heart gets better."

"When will it be better?"

"I don't know, Shuki." Lisa squeezed her son's hand. "It may be a couple of days or it may be a long, long time. We have to be patient and ask Hashem to make him better."

"Okay," he agreed solemnly.

Lisa was relieved at how well he took the news. Later, though, after picking at the macaroni and cheese that Shifra had sent in, he threw a temper tantrum, saying that he wanted his father to give him his bath. And he threw another one, crying for his Abba to read him a story. Lisa felt like a wrung-out dishrag when she finally left his room. Maybe she should have let Rivka stay and help her. Exhausted, she collapsed on the couch, too drained to move.

She probably would have fallen asleep if not for the ringing phone. Again she dared to hope and again she was disappointed.

"Lisa," Riki's voice was clearly irritated, "why didn't you call yourself and tell my parents what's going on? They had to hear about Kobi leaving the country from some rabbi? That's no way to treat them!"

Lisa slammed down the receiver.

The phone rang again immediately and Lisa looked at it with indecision. If it was Riki, she didn't want to answer it, but if it was Kobi... On the fourth ring, she picked it up.

"Don't hang up, Lisa," Riki's voice was contrite.

"Are you calling to attack me or to give me some support?" Lisa's voice was brittle.

"I'm sorry. It's just that my mother was so upset. She feels like you don't trust her enough to tell her what happened."

"If it was Efraim who'd abandoned you, would you have called his mother?" Lisa spoke coldly.

"That's not fair. You know Efraim's mother is a real witch to me. My mother loves you."

"I'm glad to hear she does," Lisa's tone softened. "My mother's far away, and Shuki and I are going to need a lot of emotional support until your brother decides to come back."

"Are you going to call my mother?"

"Not tonight."

"Tomorrow?"

"I guess so, if I have the strength. She can call me too, you know."

"Lisa, call her." Riki paused. "Please."

Her bossy tone grated on Lisa. More than anything she wanted to slam the phone down again. Instead she counted to ten, twice.

"Riki, I need sympathy, not orders. If you can't be understanding, then it's probably best if we don't speak."

"I'm sorry," Riki said for the second time. "This is difficult for all of us. Listen, we want to be supportive, but we want to feel that you want it from us and aren't angry with us because we're Kobi's family."

"Of course, I want the support. But I need your sympathy and understanding more."

"We'll try."

Somehow Lisa found the energy to drag herself off the couch and get ready for bed. She'd just turned off the light on the nightstand when the phone rang yet again. Lisa didn't want to talk to Shula now. There really wasn't anyone she wanted to speak to except, of course, Kobi.

"Lisa, how did the day go?"

"Oh, Sondra, I didn't expect to hear from you."

"I said I was going to call as soon as I got up." Sondra's concern carried across the overseas line.

"You did?" Lisa wondered what else she'd forgotten. "Well, I didn't hear from Kobi."

"No?" Sondra didn't mask her disappointment. "How's Shuki?"

Lisa told her cousin everything and Sondra listened patiently.

"What about your parents?" she finally asked.

"I'll tell them when they call Sunday if I haven't heard from Kobi by then."

"Okay." Sondra didn't object. "I won't say anything to my folks and I'll pray that by the time you talk to yours, this will all be over."

CHAPTER

Forty-four

Sondra's parents called earlier than usual that Sunday, and from the moment the conversation began, it was clear that they'd already heard about Kobi.

"Sondra, dear," her mother was obviously upset, "do you know what is going on with Lisa?"

"Um…" Sondra was noncommittal, but she knew Helga would assume the cousins had been speaking to each other.

"It is just terrible!" she continued. "Aunt Irene is beside herself. And Uncle Herbert, well…" Helga's voice trailed off.

"How's he doing?"

"How do you expect him to be doing?" Julius interjected.

"Irene was having a hard enough time with him being bedridden before," Helga said. "Now he wants to jump up and go on a wild goose chase to find Kobi. Thank goodness he knows he cannot, but he is talking about hiring a private detective."

Sondra didn't think that was a bad idea, but refrained from saying so. Instead, she asked her mother if Irene was planning on going to visit Lisa.

"There is no way she can leave Herbert now," Helga said. "He would be back at work the minute the plane took off. Oh, I feel so bad for Lisa. And I thought that Kobi was such a nice young man. I never thought a religious man would treat his wife this way."

"Maybe there's more going on than we realize," Sondra said half-heartedly, feeling defensive. She wondered if her parents were thinking of how Kobi and Lisa had met.

"Well, if you find out what it is, tell us." Her father, usually so even-tempered, was clearly angry. "How're the kids?" he asked, changing the subject.

"They're looking forward to our vacation next week," Sondra said, relieved to talk about happier matters.

As she spoke, though, she wondered how she'd manage to enjoy herself at Sea World and the San Diego Zoo when she was so worried about Lisa. Their phone conversation Saturday night hadn't been very encouraging. Lisa told her that she and Shuki had been invited out for all the Shabbat meals.

"Everyone feels sorry for us now, just like they do with Elisheva," she'd said ruefully. Sondra had asked about Elisheva and found out that she was going into the grocery every morning in Lisa's place.

"But I'll go in Monday afternoon to check the stock." Lisa's voice sounded almost belligerent, but Sondra heard the forlornness underneath.

She didn't know whether to ask about Kobi's family or not. Right before they hung up, Lisa mentioned that Tzachi had called and asked her to let him know if they needed any financial help.

Sondra couldn't stop worrying about Lisa all Sunday. When she called again later that evening, though, Lisa sounded a bit stronger. "I was back at the police station yesterday and spoke to a team of detectives," she reported.

"How'd you get there?" Sondra asked, as she dragged her long phone cord back and forth across the kitchen.

"Natan, Myra's husband, took me. And tomorrow Boaz is supposed to take me to the bank to close out the joint checking account, just in case."

"I hope that goes well. Lisa, I made a list of people here who might have had contact with Kobi. Is it okay to call them?"

"Sure!" There was a drop of enthusiasm in Lisa's voice. "Let me give you the numbers of some of our friends from Intel," she suggested. "Oh, and Sondra, can you tell Carol what's going on?"

"No problem." Sondra added Lisa's old roommate to her list. Just as she hung up, Danny returned from a shul meeting. "Any news about Kobi?" he asked eagerly.

Sondra shook her head and he studied her closely.

"I don't know how you're going to enjoy the vacation next week."

She smiled sheepishly, but avoided his gaze.

"Maybe you should take the week to fly to Lisa."

Sondra stared at her husband in amazement. "Has the heat gotten to you?"

"I'm trying to do something nice and you insult me?" Danny frowned at her.

Sondra was about to make a flippant reply, but realized her husband was in earnest. "I'm sorry." She felt contrite. "I just don't think it would be very easy for you to manage four children by yourself."

"You mean I'm not capable of doing what you do every day?"

"No, that's not what I mean," Sondra retorted. "Don't twist my words."

"You said I can't handle four kids by myself." He faced her with his shoulders squared.

"On vacation. Here, in their normal routine, I know you'd be fine."

"So you expect us to cancel the trip?"

"Who said anything about canceling the trip?" Sondra snapped. She jumped up, ready to stomp out of the room and get ready for bed. Instead, though, she took a deep breath and let it out slowly. "Danny, why are we fighting?"

"I don't know. I guess we're both stressed out about Lisa and Kobi. And," Danny continued, running his hand through his hair, "I'm afraid you blame me for bringing Kobi into our lives."

Sondra opened her mouth to deny his statement, closed it, and pressed her lips together thoughtfully.

"He seemed too good to be true in the beginning," she said carefully, thinking back to Kobi's early courtship of her cousin. "But then he won me over, and when Aunt Irene said she thought he and Lisa were going to get married, I was ecstatic. Things seemed so good between them."

"They were good! There's got to be a logical explanation for all of this."

"Like what?"

Danny held his palms up, unable to come up with any ideas. "I'm worried about my friend," he said at last. "I pray we don't find a corpse."

"Someone who contemplates suicide doesn't clean out half a bank account."

Sondra wasn't sure if her words were a comfort or not, but Danny lowered his head in acknowledgment of their truth.

"I feel terrible for Lisa. That's why I suggested you go to her."

"I'd love to be there to help her," Sondra said, her thoughts returning to the despondent voice on the other end of the phone just a few minutes earlier. She looked around the den and remembered the children asleep in their bedroom. "And I appreciate your offer with all my heart, but I think it would be too difficult to take a vacation with the kids by yourself, and I don't want to disappoint them."

Danny spoke thoughtfully, "Maybe I could ask my mother to go along."

CHAPTER

Forty-five

So that was how Sondra found herself landing at Ben Gurion Airport a week later, her gratitude to her husband for his generosity eclipsed only by her concern for her cousin. Her eyes filled when she spotted Lisa in the crowd waiting outside the terminal. She was smiling and waving wildly, but once Sondra hugged her, the smile faded and the sobs began.

Sondra fished in her handbag for tissues, and after they had both dried their faces, Sondra saw that her cousin's eyes were tired and full of worry. Lisa made no reference to her tears. Instead, she took charge of the luggage cart and pushed it in the direction of the parking lot.

"We don't have to take the bus," she said over the commotion of people shouting and cars honking. "They found the car abandoned on a little side street in Jerusalem. After a few days of red tape, I was able to claim it." She smiled. "You can't believe what a difference having a car again can make. I'm so thankful."

Inside the car, Sondra studied her cousin closely. Lisa's hands were steady on the wheel and her voice seemed to have more energy than it had during their many phone calls. Her face was gaunt, though, and her body seemed too thin for her pregnant belly.

"Are you still having morning sickness?" Sondra asked.

"Not really." Lisa navigated the turn out of the airport. "I just don't have much of an appetite." She didn't mention that half the food that was sent in seemed strange and unappealing. Lisa glanced at her cousin. "You look like you've put on some weight. It looks good on you."

Sondra took a deep breath and wondered how Lisa would react to her news. "I'm at the start of my fourth month."

"Wow!" Lisa whooped. "We'll have babies two months apart! I hope we both have girls."

Sondra laughed. "Zvi Chaim wants another brother. I'll be happy with a healthy baby."

"Me too," Lisa agreed seriously. "I really am trying to eat, but it's hard."

"How about if I make your mom's cheese pancakes for supper this evening?"

Lisa sucked her breath in. "I haven't made those since before Pesach. You know, just thinking about them makes my mouth water."

"They were always among your favorites. And how about Oma's broiled chicken?"

"You make it the way she did?"

"She told me her secret recipe a couple of years ago, when she was having a good day. I'll make it tomorrow."

"Yes!" Lisa exclaimed with a laugh. "Sondra, it's so good to have you here!"

Sondra was glad to be supportive as Lisa entered her third week without Kobi. It was a week with almost daily crises.

Elisheva called first thing Tuesday morning with the news that the store was totally out of cheese, there were only three packages of frozen chickens left, and the produce distributor had called and asked if they wanted their standard order.

"I thought you've been checking the stock," Sondra said after giving Lisa the message.

"I couldn't find the energy to deal with the store." Lisa hung her head in embarrassment. "But just because my husband left me doesn't mean my neighbors have to starve," she continued.

"Let me take care of Shuki this morning and you can go in," Sondra suggested. "Or would you rather ask Myra to watch him and I'll come with you to help?"

"No," Lisa replied. "This is Myra's two-week vacation and she watched Shuki when I picked you up yesterday. I don't want to bother her again today." She rubbed her forehead. "Even the simplest things seem so difficult." Then she bit her fingernail and stood up resolutely. "It probably won't take me more than an hour or so at the store. I'll ask Shuki if he'd like to stay with you."

The little boy happily consented to go to the playground with his mother's cousin, with the promise of a treat afterwards. It was early enough that the playground was pleasant, especially in the shade, and Sondra was warmly welcomed by the other mothers there.

"It's so nice you came in for Lisa!"

"How's your family managing without you?"

"We have such nice memories of your children from last summer."

Everything was fine until one of the little boys, impatient to go down the slide, gave Shuki a push. He lost his balance, caught himself, and wasn't hurt. Still, he began crying and screaming Abba over and over again.

"It's okay, Shuki." Sondra grabbed him in a hug and returned to the bench to cuddle him on her lap. Hearing him cry only fueled her anger at Kobi, but she managed to control it and focus on the little boy.

The mother of the impatient boy brought him over to apologize. Another mother pulled a cookie out of her bag. A third handed Shuki a balloon, and once Sondra blew it up, he left her lap happily and returned to the slide.

Wednesday evening the phone rang just after Lisa had finally finished tucking Shuki into bed. Sondra answered it for her and mouthed, "Riki." Lisa's face fell, but she came to the phone.

"Anything new?" Riki began the conversation.

"No." Lisa tried to keep the irritation out of her voice. "You know I'd let you know if I had any information."

"Uh-huh. I wish I was calling you with some news. But I'm not. Listen, Lisa," Riki's voice was apologetic, "could you please call my mother? She says she's been calling you and you never call her and she's still worried that you're mad at her."

Lisa closed her eyes and counted to ten. "Okay."

"Thanks," Riki said. She kept Lisa on the phone until Shuki cried out that he wanted a drink.

Sondra had already gone to the kitchen for a cup, but Lisa was glad to have an excuse to hang up.

"What am I supposed to call her about?" she grumbled to Sondra.

"Call her tomorrow after your doctor's appointment and tell her what's happening with the pregnancy."

Sondra accompanied her and Shuki to the checkup. Lisa was proud to show off the American-style medical center, and Sondra was quite impressed.

"I'll have to tell Danny about this," she declared.

She was also impressed with Lisa's obstetrician, who greeted Shuki in a friendly manner. Not only did he explain what he was doing, but he also took the time to check the little boy's blood pressure and weight. The doctor wasn't pleased with Lisa's low weight gain, though. Calmly but firmly, he made up a suggested menu for her.

Sondra didn't give Lisa a chance to fret as they left the office. Instead, she declared that they were going out for lunch — her treat — and they would have ice cream for dessert.

"Do you want me to talk to Shifra about the meals?" she asked as they waited for their order.

Lisa looked at her quizzically, and pulled paper and crayons out of her purse for Shuki.

"They're sending you food because they want to help. It's not helpful if you don't like the food. And it's a waste if you're throwing out a perfectly good meal because you don't like the spices."

"I like *your* food," Lisa said. "I think I should tell Shifra to stop sending in the meals and I'll start cooking again."

"No way!" Sondra banged her palm on the table for emphasis. "When you start going into the store regularly and that goes okay, then you can start thinking of telling Shifra to stop."

"Do you think I'm slacking off too much?" Lisa asked in a small voice.

"No, I think you were hit with a tidal wave and you have to recover. You do need to go back to the store and you need to start cooking again — all in its proper time. In the meantime, your neighbors know how to cook meals, but they don't know how to run the store. How about if I talk to Shifra and tell her what the doctor said, and that you don't like eggplant or lentils or cumin?"

With a sigh, Lisa agreed.

That evening, Shimon Pingle, who had taken over Avi's job, stopped by. While everyone in Kfar Yonatan had been bending over backwards to help Lisa, Shimon was the exception.

"I'm sorry to bother you," he apologized, taking in how the two women were already in their bathrobes and slippers. He declined Lisa's offer of coffee or juice and went straight to business. "We have to take care of the house matter."

"The house?"

Shimon looked at Lisa as if she were a simpleton. "I spoke to Kobi over a month ago. All that's left is to open an account with the electric and water companies. Once you're connected, there's the cleanup and you have to give approval, pay the final check, sign the final papers, and you're free to move in." As if anticipating hesitation, he added, "We have a waiting list of families who want to move here, and we need the house you're presently occupying."

The color drained from Lisa's face and she nodded.

"When will you be taking care of this?" Shimon asked as Lisa walked him to the door.

"As soon as I can," she answered dully.

"If money's a problem, I suggest reopening the grocery in the afternoons. Not everyone can shop in the morning and some people are going elsewhere for their food."

Lisa closed the door behind him, sank down on the couch, and put her face in her hands. Sondra sat down beside her.

"Is there enough money left to finish up?"

"I think so." Lisa's voice faltered. "But I'm not going to be able to pay Elisheva unless the social worker arranges the benefits for us. I guess I can take money out of my American account," she said halfheartedly. "My grandparents opened it for me when I was born. I planned to use it for Shuki's education or emergencies...but I hope this is as big an emergency as I'll ever have."

"How about I give you a loan?" Sondra put an arm around her cousin. She knew Lisa could turn to her father or father-in-law for money, but she also knew that was the last thing Lisa wanted to do. She hadn't told either of them that Kobi had pulled money out of their bank account.

"Thank you, Sondra, but you've done enough for me already."

"Lisa," Sondra spoke sternly, "I have money to give. You need it. We'll make it a free loan, and once you're able to pay it back, you can take it and pass it on to someone else who needs the help."

"Thank you." Lisa swallowed. "I still don't know how I'll manage the move. I can't do any lifting."

Both women understood that she wouldn't have to worry about finding movers and lifters among her neighbors. That wasn't her real concern. It was her way of expressing her anxiety about how she would cope with her dreams being dashed. She'd looked forward to moving into her new home with her husband at her side for such a long time!

Sondra had no answers for that, so she decided to change the subject. "Didn't you tell Riki that you'd call Shula?"

"I guess I should." Lisa groaned. "What should I tell her? That I'm not gaining enough weight?"

Sondra made a face and shook her head. "Tell her that the house should be ready by Rosh Hashanah. Maybe she'll offer to help."

"That's a good idea, but I'm too tired now. Will you remind me to call tomorrow?"

Before Shabbat, Lisa suggested that Sondra spend it with friends in Jerusalem. She and Shuki were taken care of, eating every Friday night at Myra's and Shabbat lunch with Miriam and the *rav*. But since Sondra had made the trip to Israel to be there for Lisa, she declined the suggestion. Still, she toyed with the idea of maybe taking the morning bus to Jerusalem and praying at the Kotel if everything was under control on Sunday. However, she didn't say anything to Lisa about her idea. So when Elisheva called Saturday night to say that her son had fallen and broken his tooth, and she needed to take him to the dentist first thing in the morning, Lisa didn't hesitate to turn to Sondra.

"I guess Hashem's telling me it's time to go back to the store. Would you mind watching Shuki for the whole morning?"

Sondra agreed immediately. And so, when she boarded her plane late that evening, she left Israel without having been to one holy site. She had no regrets, though. She felt certain that the support and help she'd given her cousin were just as important as any prayer she could have said at the Kotel, Kever Rochel, or Hebron.

CHAPTER
Forty-six

"Are you sure you don't want to push off the trip to Lincoln until you recover from jet lag?" Danny asked Sondra during the call she made from the Ben Gurion Airport.

"The kids will be already going back to school by then."

"You can go by yourself," he suggested.

"The whole idea was to give them an end-of-the-summer treat," Sondra objected.

"They had a great time in San Diego."

"I'm glad." Sondra felt a renewed flash of gratitude to her husband and his mother. "We could probably have a nice week in Phoenix, but I think I need to sit down with Aunt Irene and Uncle Herbert face-to-face and tell them everything about Lisa and Shuki as soon as possible."

"I hear you." Danny also heard the call to board over the loudspeaker and said a quick goodbye to his wife. "Have a safe flight!"

As her plane finally landed in Phoenix Monday afternoon, Sondra rubbed her eyes. She hoped the sleep she managed to catch on the flights would hold her until the evening. The "fasten seat belt" sign flashed off and Sondra jumped up. Without Danny to restrain her, she was among the first in the aisle and the fourth to leave the plane. She couldn't wait to greet her family. She almost broke into a run when she saw all of them standing at the end of the Jetway. To Sondra, each one was more beautiful than the next.

To be sure, she'd have preferred if Batsheva hadn't been wearing a flowered top with her plaid skirt. And she couldn't help noticing that Zvi Chaim's pants were too short for him. The important thing, though, was that they were all smiling and looked happy and well.

"I want you to see my shell collection."

"Did you bring me anything?"

"Does Shuki still speak English?"

"I lost a tooth."

Surrounded by her chattering children, Sondra exchanged smiles with her husband. She was looking forward to time with him that evening.

He'd just walked in from services and Sondra had poured two glasses of iced tea to take into the den when the phone rang. It was Shaindy with her impeccable timing.

"Sondra, good, you're still up. I waited to call you until I knew shul was over and Danny was home, just to make sure I wouldn't wake you. How's Lisa?"

"She's coping, but I was just sitting down with Danny for a few minutes before I collapse. Can I call you tomorrow?"

"Not really. The movers are coming."

"The movers?"

"Yeah," Shaindy's tone was matter-of-fact. "We're moving back to Monsey. My parents insisted."

"Oh!" Sondra's eyes opened wide. "I hope that works out well for you all."

"Me too! Rabbi Levi called them like you suggested. It was a good idea, and I wanted to thank you and say goodbye."

"Shaindy, wow," Sondra stammered. "This is so sudden. Let's stay in touch?"

"I'm not much of a letter writer, but I'll try," Shaindy said breezily. "I don't want to keep you any longer. Go enjoy talking to your husband."

Something in Shaindy's tone made Sondra wince, keenly aware that Shaindy no longer had a husband to talk to.

Shaindy wasn't the only friend to ask about Lisa. Over the course of the next two days, Sondra found herself fielding endless questions that she tried to answer in the vaguest way possible. The most complicated conversation, however, was the one she had with her aunt and uncle after arriving in Lincoln Wednesday evening.

Sondra couldn't help remembering how she'd sat in the same room with Aunt Irene six years earlier, discussing the likelihood of Lisa's engagement to Kobi. How excited she'd been then. Now the mood was somber as she related how Lisa and Shuki were managing.

Irene and Herbert heard her out patiently without interrupting once. Irene wiped away tears periodically. Herbert kept clenching his fists until his veins looked like they would explode. Then Irene would give him a look, and he would take a deep breath and open his hands.

After Sondra finished speaking, there was a long silence. Herbert was the first to speak.

"So, Miss Sondra, how do you feel about your fine friend now?"

"Herbert, that's not fair," Irene interjected softly, before Sondra could even frame a reply.

To Sondra's horror, her uncle lowered his head and began sobbing.

"How could he abandon my little girl like this?" he asked.

"Herbert, calm down," Irene soothed. "Calm down."

Sondra stared at the pattern on the carpet. Her face burned with discomfort. She'd cried her share of tears for her cousin, but to see her tough uncle weeping was shocking.

"Uncle Herbert," she finally found her voice, "you need to remember that you raised a very capable daughter. Lisa's going to get through this. She's getting a lot of help from the community, but even without it, she'll make it because she's a survivor."

"That may be true, but if I ever get my hands on her husband..."

"So far, the private detective's only found blind leads," Irene said. "But we're praying he'll be successful."

"So are we." Sondra sighed and lifted her eyes heavenward.

Kobi's name was mentioned daily in the prayers at the synagogue in Kfar Yonatan as Lisa finished her first month without her husband. Shuki began nursery school in September. Instead of spending the mornings in Myra's house with three other children, he was going to be with seventeen other three- and four-year-olds.

"I want Abba to take me to nursery school," he announced to Lisa on the first morning.

"I'm sure Abba would want to take you if he was here." Lisa was patient as she handed him his bowl of cornflakes. "I'm sorry, but you're going to have to settle for me."

"I want Abba." Shuki began kicking.

"I want Abba too." Lisa put her arms around her little boy, but he pushed them off.

"Why isn't his heart better?" he screamed, his dark brown eyes — so much like his father's — narrowed in indignation and his face reddened.

"Oh, Shuki." Lisa felt a burning anger toward her husband. "I know you're angry at Abba."

"Not Abba." Shuki kicked some more. "You!" he yelled. "Bring Abba back!"

"You bring Abba back!" Lisa snapped, blinking back furious tears.

"How?" Shuki's face clouded over.

"I don't know how." Her tears overflowed and Shuki began crying too. Now, though, he let his mother put her arms around him and they cried together.

"Shuki," Lisa said, once they were both cried out, "we're going to have to wait for Hashem to make Abba's heart better. Right now, we need to take you to nursery school and I need to open the store. Let's wash our faces and take our smiles out of our pockets."

The little boy pantomimed pulling something out of his pants pocket and then he slid his hand over his mouth. As it moved away, a smile appeared. Lisa mimicked him, pulling her smile out of the pocket in her maternity jumper. Their anger was put aside as they walked hand in hand to the nursery school. Waiting with Hadas, the teacher, was Rivka, back for another year of National Service. Seeing her, Shuki dropped his mother's hand and confidently ran to join the other children.

He was playing happily when Lisa came to pick him up and she allowed herself to be hopeful. Shuki had a schedule and she was back to working her regular hours at the store. The social worker had completed all the paperwork, and Lisa hoped that once her monthly government benefits started, she'd be able to stop accepting charity from the people of Kfar Yonatan. Perhaps she and Shuki would be able to make a normal life for themselves.

Several hours later, though, Shimon Pingle stopped by. Lisa left the door open after she invited him inside. As always, Shimon was in a hurry.

"Your house is all ready. All you have to do is sign the last check and papers."

Lisa tried not to compare Shimon to Avi, but she knew Avi would have handled her situation with more tact. Of course, if Avi hadn't been murdered, she wouldn't have been in her situation.

"I'll stop by the office tomorrow after I close the store to do the paperwork," she said.

"Great. And when can we have this house?"

Lisa closed her eyes and took a deep breath. "When do you need it?"

"There's a family that wanted to move in before Rosh Hashanah. Now they're agreeing to right after Simchat Torah. I'm sorry to pressure you, but everyone else who built has moved out already."

"I know. I'll try and be out before Sukkot."

Later that evening, after Shuki was asleep, she found the courage to dial her in-laws in Beit She'an, as Riki had been nagging her to do for weeks.

"Shula," she said, "I'm sorry to bother you, but I think I need some help."

"Of course, dear, whatever you need."

Lisa blinked back tears. Shula's reaction was as warm as it had been when Kobi was around. If only he was there. Briefly, Lisa explained to her mother-in-law about the upcoming move. In just a few minutes, it was settled that Tzachi would come up the following Tuesday afternoon with the truck from the store. That would give Lisa about five packing days and she would be moved in before Yom Kippur.

"Perhaps," Shula ended the conversation, "you'd like us to come for Yom Kippur and help with Shuki."

Lisa wasn't sure if she liked the idea, but she heard the plea in Shula's voice for Lisa not to be angry with her on her son's account. Knowing it would be good for Shuki to see his grandparents after all this time, she agreed.

CHAPTER

Forty-seven

Sondra had just finished taking clothes out of the dryer when the phone rang. She dashed from the laundry room off the carport into the kitchen and answered the phone on the fifth ring.

"Are you busy?" Danny asked.

"Not at all. I just finished polishing my toenails and was getting ready to twiddle my thumbs."

"Don't be so sarcastic."

Sondra laughed. "Sorry. What's doing?"

"I want to know if you can meet me for an early lunch."

"Let's see." Sondra made a mental review of what she had left to get done that morning. She'd planned to do some baking and refill the freezer now that the holidays were over, but that could be pushed off.

"Let me call Goldie and see if she can keep Yossi an extra hour. If she says yes, we'll meet at twelve?"

"That'd be great. I'll be with patients till then, so just leave a message at the desk."

Arriving at the kosher deli before her husband, Sondra grabbed a shopping cart. The deli not only offered sandwiches, but also had freezer cases filled with kosher pizza, knishes, and various cuts of chicken. There were shelves full of Tam Tov crackers, soup nuts from Israel, and packages of kasha. A full variety of fresh meat was also available. Sondra appreciated the fact that keeping kosher was far easier than it had ever been for her mother or grandmother.

Danny walked in just as Sondra noticed the new display full of Paskesz candy.

"Look at this!" she called to her husband. "Kosher candy necklaces! I'm getting some for the girls!"

"Nice," Danny replied, glancing over briefly before motioning her toward one of the deli's five tables. "I'm glad Goldie was able to watch Yossi."

"You know, the playgroup's working out great. I love having two mornings to myself. Yossi loves playing with Malkie and Berel. And I really needed the break from teaching."

"Um-hum," Danny mumbled.

"I'm not bored like Debbie predicted, and I think I have more energy for the allergy doctor and the speech therapist and the occupational therapy."

"I'm glad."

Sondra looked quizzically at her husband. He was obviously preoccupied.

"Let's wash and then we'll talk."

Sondra washed impatiently and then fidgeted in her seat as she waited for Danny to bite into his chopped liver sandwich.

"So?" she asked.

"I got a letter from Baruch Weinstock this morning," he said.

"Who?"

"Lisa's obstetrician," Danny answered somewhat impatiently.

Sondra put down her sandwich and opened her eyes wide. "I thought you weren't interested in hearing about him. Didn't you throw his card away?"

"I did not throw his card away. I filed it in my desk and more or less forgot about it. During the holidays, though, I did a lot of thinking. I looked around the shul and wondered what's going to be in another five years. Will we want to send Zvi Chaim to the high school here or have to send him away? Which of our friends will still be living here? How many of the kids' friends will have kosher homes? I didn't tell you because I didn't want you to get excited over nothing, but I wrote him."

"And?" Sondra prompted.

"He and his partners aren't interested in taking any more doctors into their practice, but," Danny smiled as Sondra's face fell, "he wrote that he has a good friend in Baltimore who's making *aliyah* this summer and putting together a similar practice."

"*Nu,*" Sondra said impatiently as Danny swallowed some Coke.

He grinned boyishly. "So I called Meir Rosen and it sounds really good. We were on the phone for about half an hour. He and another doctor from Silver Spring are opening a clinic with a doctor already in Jerusalem, and they'd like a fourth doctor to come on board. He wants me to fly to Baltimore to meet with him and Stan Schwartz, the doctor from Silver Spring, and see if we can make it work. What do you think?"

Sondra laughed, showing her left dimple. "What do I think?" she asked with shining eyes. "I think it sounds too good to be true."

"I know!" Danny raised his eyebrows. "But this time it may really happen." He finally took another bite and swallowed. "I'm not on call this Sunday and I can rearrange appointments for Friday and Monday morning. Do you think that Sharon can spend Shabbos with the kids, and my parents can take over on Sunday, and you can come with me?"

Sondra wiped her mouth with a napkin. "Do you think it's okay for me to fly?" she asked.

Danny nodded. "You haven't started your third trimester, but we can ask Ed to make sure."

She sipped her drink thoughtfully. Sharon had been a student in her Hebrew High class four years earlier, and as a result of Sondra's influence had spent two years in Stern College. Now, due to parental pressure, she was back at ASU and spending most Shabboses at the Kleins. She certainly knew the children and their routines. It'd probably work.

"If you're not comfortable with it," Danny continued, "I can take the night flight *Motzei Shabbos*. I just think it's a good idea for both of us to get to know these people."

Sondra appreciated her husband's emphasis on "both of us." "Danny," she said, "ask Dr. Taylor when you get back to the office, and if he says it's okay, I'll get on the phone with Sharon and start making arrangements."

* * *

A week later, lower back pains kept Sondra from sleeping and she was fed up with watching the digital clock change the time. At three twenty-eight, she finally gave up. Not wanting to wake Danny, she tiptoed out of the room and made her way into the den. Restless, her eyes fell on the phone. Without a second's thought, she dialed the number to Lisa's house.

"What're you doing up?" Lisa exclaimed upon hearing her cousin's hello.

"Back pains," Sondra replied shortly. "How're you handling the ninth month?"

"I'm feeling good," Lisa said. "I just sleep every chance I get."

"Did I wake you?"

"No, Shuki's going to be coming home soon, but I'm in bed with one pillow under my feet and another one under my back. But I'm reading, not sleeping."

"Anything good?"

"It's a Hebrew book. My first try."

"I'm impressed."

Lisa laughed self-consciously.

"Listen, I've wanted to call you ever since we got back Sunday night..."

"Back from where?"

"That's what I want to tell you about."

Quickly Sondra described the practice the other doctors wanted to put together.

"We spent Shabbos with the Rosens in Baltimore," she continued. "And it was lovely. We have so much in common. And then Saturday night, the Schwartzes came over. Danny felt as comfortable with Stan as he did with Meir. And Sunday, the three of them spent the day together talking about their approaches to their medical practices, and running an office, and finances. Lisa, we might really move to Israel this summer!"

"That would be wonderful!"

"Danny doesn't want me to say anything to anybody until they sign the contract, but I'm ready to pop, so he said I could tell you."

"In other words," Lisa said dryly, "I shouldn't say a word to anyone, especially my parents."

"You got it! I don't know how I'll tell my parents..." Sondra let her voice trail off.

"It won't be easy," Lisa stated matter-of-factly.

Sondra just sighed.

"I guess your mom and mine will have a lot to talk about," Lisa empathized.

"Thank goodness they have each other." Sondra closed her eyes, not wanting to think about saying goodbye to her parents.

"Yes," Lisa agreed. "Just a minute. Shuki just came in. Shuki, I'm in my room. Are you alone?" There was a pause. "There're carrot sticks on the table for the two of you. Yeah, Sondra, I'm back with you. Let me know what I can do to help from this end."

Sondra laughed. "I'll probably have tons of questions. I've already spoken to the *aliyah* office in LA and we've started the paperwork. I'm really excited!"

"I don't blame you."

"So, is Shuki okay with nursery school?"

"As long as Rivka, you know — the National Service girl who helped us so much — is there, he's fine. Last week she was sick and he balked, so he came to the store with me for those mornings."

"And in the afternoons?"

"He's got friends. He's doing okay."

"And you?" Sondra asked softly.

"I'm fine, but I'll be better after the baby's born."

Sondra could imagine Lisa's determined smile. "I miss you," she said.

"Well," Lisa answered, "if all goes well, we'll see each other this summer."

Lisa pulled herself out of bed to check on Shuki. He and his friend were happily munching carrots and playing with trucks. She poured herself a glass of juice and sat down at the kitchen table.

After seven weeks in the new house, it almost felt like home. Lisa wondered if any place would ever feel like home without Kobi. Impatiently she pushed that negative thought out of her mind. Elisheva was her role model, and she was as determined to pass the test that Hashem had given her as Elisheva was. She admired how her friend was always positive, at least to the outside world. No one knew what went on inside Elisheva's house once the front door was closed, though.

Lisa did know what went on inside her own home once her door was closed and her son was asleep. Then the fears and worries would begin. Would Kobi ever be found? How was she going to bear going to the hospital to give birth without even knowing where he was? Who would organize the brit if the baby was a boy?

Her mother was coming to Israel in the middle of Chanukah and staying for three weeks. Thank goodness her father was back at work, fully recovered except for a limp. He was planning on coming for a week after the baby arrived. Lisa didn't have enough fingers for counting the things she had to be thankful for, and she constantly thanked Hashem for them all. Still, there were many evenings when the house was so dark, quiet, and lonely that she cried herself to sleep.

CHAPTER
Forty-eight

"Chanukah, oh Chanukah, come light the menorah..."

The record was playing in the den while Yossi and Naomi took turns spinning the dreidel. Zvi Chaim and Batsheva were in the living room arranging the menorahs. As Sondra stood in the kitchen frying potato pancakes, she noted that her house would be perfect for a Norman Rockwell painting, if he wanted to paint a Jewish scene.

Thank goodness her back pains had let up and Sondra had the energy to make Chanukah special. The first night, Danny's parents had come for candle lighting and dinner. Now, the second night, Debbie and her family were joining them right after candle lighting. Every so often Sondra wondered what would've happened to their friendship if she hadn't gone over to speak to Debbie that evening last year. Would Debbie have gotten over her resentment on her own or would she have let their friendship die?

Whenever she began that train of thought, Sondra would remind herself of something she'd learned in seminary. A mind is like a radio station and she could control the channels. She'd concentrate instead on the bris that summer. After three girls, the Friedmans had had a baby boy. Most of the honors at the bris had been given to the family members who'd flown in for the occasion, but to Sondra's surprise, she and Danny were the ones chosen as godparents — the couple who carried the baby in for the ceremony. Sondra still got teary-eyed when she thought about it.

"Abba's here!" Batsheva cried, and Sondra's thoughts returned to the present. She flipped the last batch of pancakes, turned off the flame, and went to greet her husband as he came in from the carport. Suddenly, though, she left the surge of her children and headed to the back of the house.

"Sondra," Danny called once he'd kissed each of the kids, "is everything okay?"

There was no answer. Puzzled, he went to their room and found her lying on her bed, pale, with tears rolling down her face.

"What's the matter?!"

"My water broke," Sondra whispered.

"I'm calling Ed," Danny responded instantly. "Sondra, you're already in your seventh month," he reassured his wife as he dialed the bedside phone. "Are you having contractions?"

Sondra shook her head.

"Abba," Zvi Chaim came to the doorway with Yossi behind him, "it's time to light the candles."

"Soon."

"But you told me we need to light as soon as the stars come out."

"I said *soon*," Danny snapped.

"So can I light by myself?" Zvi Chaim whined.

"No!"

Yossi began whimpering. The girls, hearing their father's impatient voice, didn't know whether to stay by the menorahs or to come into the bedroom to see what was wrong.

So much for the pastoral Norman Rockwell scene, Sondra thought. "Zvi Chaim," her calm voice belied the turmoil she felt, "Abba has an important phone call to make and then he'll light."

By the time Dr. Taylor called back, the Chanukah lights were lit and the Friedmans had just arrived. Batsheva ushered the girls into the den, but left Debbie, Shraga, and the baby stranded in the entrance hall. Debbie and Shraga looked at each other uncertainly. Their hosts were nowhere in sight. Zvi Chaim was sulking. Yossi had been crying and Naomi had just slipped him a piece of candy. The Chanukah record was stuck and replaying the same line over and over. Something was obviously wrong.

"Should we leave?" Shraga whispered.

"No," Debbie replied. "I want to find out what's going on. Maybe they need some help."

"Well, let's sit down, at least."

Debbie settled herself gingerly on the living room couch with the baby. Shraga paced instead of heeding his own suggestion. They hadn't been waiting long when Danny entered the room.

"Um." He cleared his throat uncomfortably. "I need to take Sondra in to meet the doctor."

Debbie immediately jumped up from the couch. "Oh no! What's the matter? Can we help?"

"Her water broke." Danny rushed into the kitchen. "If you can give yourselves and our kids dinner, that would be great."

"No problem," Debbie answered, following him with Shraga behind her. "We're here as long as you need us."

"Thanks!" Danny turned his attention to his oldest son. "Zvi Chaim, I want to talk to you." The two went into the living room together, and when they came out, Zvi Chaim was no longer pouting. Danny spoke a few words to the other children while Debbie helped Sondra into the car.

"Don't worry about a thing," she comforted her friend. "But let us know what's happening."

"You'll probably be checked into the hospital," Danny said during their quick drive over. "Either you'll be having a baby or be put on bed rest. Ed's not going to let you out if your water broke. The chance of infection is too great."

Her husband was correct and once checked in, Sondra was taken for an ultrasound. With results in hand, Dr. Taylor and Danny had a conference in the hall. It was Danny who explained to Sondra what they thought.

"Your water didn't break, *baruch Hashem*, but you're leaking amniotic fluid. The baby's still a little small, so Ed thinks it's best for you to stay here and monitor you, the fluids, and the baby. Once the baby is a little larger or if, G-d forbid, is in danger, he'll either induce you or deliver you by C-section, depending on how much water you still have. Does that sound okay to you?"

"What does your father think?" Sondra asked.

"Do you want me to ask him?"

"Please." She was still pale, but no longer as frightened as she had originally been.

Doc agreed with his partner's assessment of the situation, and so Sondra resigned herself to being bedridden for the time being. Danny left to relieve the Friedmans, get a babysitter, call his in-laws, and pack a bag for Sondra. He returned an hour later with the news that her mother was making arrangements to fly in Monday to help.

"Oh," Sondra groaned, "this is the worst time of the year for her to get away."

She and Danny exchanged long looks, both remembering Sondra's hospitalization with her burns eight years earlier.

"If your mother thinks it's important to be here with you, Sondra, it's her decision."

"You're right. I'm glad I did most of the Shabbos cooking today. You'll have what to eat tomorrow."

"I'm going to be here with you," Danny stated matter-of-factly.

"What about the kids?"

"I already spoke to Sharon. Debbie's organizing meals and places for the kids to play next week so it won't be too much on our mothers."

"That's so nice." Sondra glanced at the phone on her nightstand. "I'll call her later and thank her. Danny...," she paused and pulled at the ends of her headscarf nervously.

"Yes?"

"How is this going to affect our plans?"

Danny steepled his fingers and took a deep breath. "I didn't sign the contract yet. The chances are good that the baby will be okay. We'll have to wait and see, though."

"How're you doing?" Debbie asked brightly on Sunday morning. It was Sondra's first phone call of the day.

"I'm trying not to complain."

"How's the food?"

"Like airline meals."

"Yuck!" Debbie exclaimed. "I'm bringing you some vegetable cutlets when I come up this evening."

"Thanks, but you're doing enough for me already," Sondra protested, shifting uncomfortably in the bed.

"Don't be silly! Do you need more books?"

"I'm almost done with the one you brought me Friday, but Bayla and Shoshie were here last night and brought me a pile. I think I'm using my siddur the most, though."

"I can imagine. So are you enjoying the bed rest?" Debbie asked mischievously.

"They keep me busy checking my temperature every few hours and putting me on the bedpan."

"It will be over soon," Debbie comforted her.

"You're right." Sondra didn't mention how much she worried what would be when it was over. Would her baby be all right?

"You know," she made an effort to sound upbeat, "they're treating me well here. I've got some *protexia* being one doctor's wife and another's daughter-in-law, and our insurance lets me have a private room. I shouldn't be complaining at all."

"Still, there's no place like home," Debbie declared.

"Spoken like a true Kansas girl." Sondra smiled. "Oh, here's Shirley with the kids. I'll call you later."

She was so grateful to her mother-in-law for bringing the children to visit. Zvi Chaim had made rounds with Danny many times and was happy to show off his knowledge of the hospital. Batsheva was full of concern for the other patients. Naomi and Yossi just wanted to know when Ima was coming home.

She stayed on the monitor for another nine days, with Danny also spending the second Shabbos with her. On Monday morning, Dr. Taylor decided to deliver the baby by C-section. Sondra gave birth to a tiny girl who was immediately whisked away to the neonatal unit, with Danny following after her. He was back at Sondra's bedside, though, by the time she woke up from surgery.

"Things are looking good," he told his wife with a radiant smile. "First of all, we have a daughter, and girls have a much higher chance of survival. Second of all, she weighs almost two pounds. Her reflexes are normal and I'm very optimistic."

Sondra smiled back weakly. "Did you speak to the children yet?"

"They're in school. I spoke to my father already and was waiting for you to wake up so you could call your mother."

"I am so glad the surgery is behind you." Helga's relief was heartfelt. "I will tell the children as soon as they come home, and we will be up to see you."

Although she was weak from the operation, Sondra was thrilled to be able to get out of bed again. She'd already been to the neonatal unit twice to see her tiny daughter in the incubator before Helga brought the other children. They came with smiles and drawings, and although they were eager to see their new sister, Helga was by far the most excited.

"Sondra," she kissed her daughter happily on the forehead. "Mazal tov to you and," her eyes sparkled, "mazal tov to Lisa."

"Lisa?"

"Yes," Helga nodded happily. "Aunt Irene called from Israel this morning. Lisa had a baby girl last night our time, Monday morning their time."

"Really?" Sondra squealed. "Is everything okay?"

Helga nodded again and handed her daughter a piece of paper. "Lisa wants you to call her at the nurses' station at this number."

Sondra slipped the paper into her nightstand drawer and turned her attention to the children. Now it was the middle of the night in Israel. She would call in the morning. Oh, was she looking forward to making that call!

CHAPTER

Forty-nine

It was four o'clock Monday morning and Lisa was loath to call Miriam. If Kobi was there, she'd have left two hours earlier for the hospital. Now her contractions were six minutes apart. She'd endured them silently, not wanting to wake her mother or Shuki, but she knew she was running out of time. Finally, she dialed her friend's number.

"Lisa?" Miriam answered on the third ring. "Do you want to go?"

"I'm sorry to wake you..."

"Not a problem," Miriam interrupted. "This is what we planned. I can be ready in five minutes. Is that good?"

"Thank you." Lisa wiped away tears as she hung up the phone. She grabbed her bag, left a note for Shuki and her mother, and went outside to wait by her friend's car.

Miriam was already out of her house and wide awake.

"This is so exciting," she exclaimed as she started the car. "How long were you in labor with Shuki?" she asked as she pulled away from the curb. Without waiting for an answer, she launched into a narrative of her own labors, pausing only to ask if Lisa was okay when she moaned.

"So then," she said as they neared the entrance to Kfar Saba, "the midwife broke my water and..." She stopped short as Lisa let out a shriek. "Are you okay?"

Lisa bit her lip. "How far are we from the hospital?"

"Five minutes."

"Hurry!"

Miriam ran a stop sign, pulled up to the emergency entrance, and yelled at the guard that she had a woman who needed to get to the delivery room fast. Once there, Lisa gave one good push and a healthy baby girl was born. A girl! There'd be no brit to plan. Miriam was with her in recovery and Lisa was euphoric.

"You'll tell my mother and Shuki as soon as you get home?"

"For sure." Miriam loved being the bearer of good news. "Anyone else?"

"Everyone in Kfar Yonatan! And I guess you should call Shula. Okay?"

"No problem. It will be good to give your mother-in-law some good news." Miriam stayed with her until they wheeled Lisa into her room. "Try to get some rest." She kissed her friend goodbye.

Lisa heeded Miriam's advice. She was rested and still euphoric when Irene and Shuki came to visit in the afternoon.

"What did Daddy say?" she asked eagerly.

"He's happy," Irene told her, "but we only spoke for a minute. He was in a hurry to get to the ranch. Don't worry, though, he plans to call the travel agent this evening and come next week. And he promised to call Uncle Julius and Aunt Lotte."

"I wish I could talk to Sondra," Lisa said wistfully. She willed herself not to think of how Kobi and her cousin had been at her side when Shuki was born. "Maybe," she hesitated, "you could call Sondra and tell her to call the nurses' station here."

"I think that's an excellent idea." Irene was enthusiastic. "Although, instead of calling Sondra at the hospital, I'll call the house and speak to Helga. She can give Sondra the number."

Lisa grinned at her mother, knowing Irene was thrilled to have any excuse to call her sister-in-law.

✳ ✳ ✳

Tzachi, Shula, Riki, and Efraim were all gathered in Lisa's room when the nurse entered and announced that Lisa had an overseas phone call. Shula held the baby, while the enormous rag doll they'd brought for her rested on Efraim's knee. Tzachi had several tiny, frilly dresses on his lap. As his daughter-in-law eagerly stood up to go to the phone, Tzachi cleared his throat.

"Visiting hours are over in five minutes. Don't you want to tell us goodbye first?"

"Tzachi," Shula remonstrated, "leave her alone and let her take the call. It's expensive to call from America."

"They can afford it," Tzachi snapped back.

"Abba, stop it." Riki wasn't as diplomatic as her mother. "Go on, Lisa," she instructed her sister-in-law kindly. "We'll take the baby back to the nursery and wait down in the lobby; you can come to us when you finish the call."

"Thank you," Lisa managed as she scurried out the door. Ever since she'd heard that Sondra had also given birth, she'd been waiting eagerly for this call. Now, instead of being excited, she was full of frustration. She unclenched her fists and took the phone the blonde nurse held out for her.

"Here, sit down," the nurse told her kindly.

Lisa smiled her appreciation, took a deep breath, and relaxed.

"Mazal tov!" she heard her cousin say.

"How's the baby?" Lisa asked.

"She's looking good," Sondra said. "She'll be in the hospital until she reaches four pounds, and then if her development is okay and she can suck properly, we'll be able to take her home. But tell me about your little girl. I want to hear all about her."

"She's very fair with huge eyes and a round face, just like Oma's."

"I'm glad you had a girl," Sondra said softly.

"Yes, they're going to have the same birthday, our girls."

"That's so neat!"

"Um, Sondra, I don't want them to have the same name, and I want to name my little girl after Oma. What about you?"

Sondra laughed. "Danny and I never think about names until the ninth month. We haven't had a chance to talk about it. Just tell me what name you want and we won't use it."

Lisa pushed away her envy over her cousin being able to choose a name with her husband. At least, she comforted herself, she could pick the name she wanted without asking anyone.

"Well, I don't want to use the name Frayda," she said, "but in Yiddish it means *happiness*, so I think I'll name her Gilit."

"That's lovely," Sondra's voice was warm with enthusiasm.

"You can't have it!"

"Don't worry." Sondra laughed again. "I miss you, Lisa."

"Yeah." Lisa wiped at her eyes with the back of her hand. "Do you think the baby will be ready to move in the summer?"

"I hope so." Sondra sighed. "Who's going to name your baby?"

"My father was going to, but he won't be here until after Shabbat and I don't want to wait, so Rav Yehezkel will do it."

"When do you think you'll be going home?"

"Tomorrow."

"Good. I'll call you there."

"Thanks, Sondra."

❋ ❋ ❋

A contrite Tzachi was waiting for Lisa in the lobby. Again, he cleared his throat uncomfortably.

"I didn't want to leave without giving you our present." He signaled to his wife.

Shula handed Lisa a tiny wrapped box. "Thank you for giving us a granddaughter."

"Open it," Riki demanded.

Lisa did as she was told and found a delicate necklace and earring set inlaid with diamonds. Her mouth fell open and she was left speechless.

"It's beautiful," she finally managed to say.

"Do you want me to help you put it on?" Riki offered.

"I...I...I guess you'd better," Lisa stuttered. "I don't want to leave it where anyone could take it."

"Wear it in good health," Tzachi commanded.

She was still wearing the new jewelry the following day when Shifra and Aaron came to the hospital to take her and the baby home. Lisa was happy to be leaving the hospital. It'd be good to sleep in a room without three roommates, to take a shower in her own bathroom, and to eat her meals when she wanted. It would be comforting to have Shuki close by and not have to speak to him on the pay phone down the hall. And it would be wonderful to have her baby to herself and not have to follow all of the nursery rules.

But when Aaron and Shifra helped her into the house, it was eerily quiet. Irene must have gone to nursery school to get Shuki. Lisa looked around, half expecting Kobi to materialize. He did not. Only then did Lisa realize that he was gone for good. She was a single mother and she was going to have to manage on her own. This time there were no tears, just a stubborn resignation.

CHAPTER

"Are you okay?" Danny asked as he held the car door open for his wife.

"My arms feel empty," Sondra answered, blinking back tears.

"Don't worry," Danny spoke lightly. "You have a whole fan club at home waiting to fill them."

Sondra nodded and turned her face to the window.

"She's going to be okay," Danny said gently. "You'll be back here tomorrow to visit."

Sondra sighed a sigh so deep that it seemed to come from her toes.

"The baby in the incubator next to ours is from Casa Grande. The father can't take off work and there's a four-year-old at home. The grandmother brings the mother up twice a week to see the baby. That's all. I'm really thankful we're so close by."

"I'm glad you're being positive." Sondra heard the approval in her husband's voice.

Helga drove her to the hospital the following morning while the children were in school and Yossi was at Goldie's. The two women put on special, germ-free hospital gowns and signed into the neonatal unit. They were able to slip gloved hands into the incubator to pat the tiny little girl.

"When she's a little bigger," the nurse said kindly, "you can begin holding her."

"How soon will that be?" Helga asked.

The nurse shook her head. "It's different with each baby. I hope soon."

"I hope so too," Helga replied. "I am leaving Sunday."

Sondra was grateful that her mother would be around when Danny named the baby on Shabbos. She couldn't wait to call Lisa Sunday morning and tell her all about it.

"So, how's little Gilit?" Sondra asked by way of greeting.

"Good!" Lisa answered. "She has two names: Gilit Shulamit."

"Oh, are you going to call her by both names?"

"Only when she's in trouble." Lisa laughed.

"What made you add a second name?"

Lisa took a deep breath. "Riki dropped by Thursday evening and informed me that it's a Sephardic custom to name the baby after the grandparents. No one said anything about Shuki's name because he was born in America, but Tzachi was hurt and she thought it'd be nice to name the baby after Shula to make up for it."

"How do you feel about it?" Sondra asked carefully.

"What difference does it make?" Sondra could imagine her cousin shrugging her shoulders. "It's only her middle name. I made my in-laws happy and I got the name I wanted. It was my last chance to name someone after Oma."

There was something in Lisa's tone that Sondra didn't like.

"But Kobi could show up any day," she said, echoing Lisa's hopeful statements from the past.

Lisa gave a mirthless laugh. "If he's not dead, then he has no intention of coming back. He knew when my due date was."

"Oh, Lisa." Sondra swallowed the lump in her throat. "You sound so angry."

"Wouldn't you be?"

"Yes," Sondra answered without hesitation, "I certainly would, but this is all going to work out in the end. I'm sure of it."

"I guess," Lisa spoke halfheartedly. "I know Hashem's looking out for me, but sometimes it's hard to remember. How's your baby doing?"

"I held her today." Sondra smiled at the memory. "I know Hashem's looking out for her too. She has a name now: Miriam Frayda."

"Beautiful," Lisa said warmly. They spoke for a few more minutes and then Shuki came in from the playground with his grandmother. Sondra turned the phone over to her mother so the sisters-in-law could talk. Although Helga was returning home that afternoon, it would be another week until Lisa's parents left Israel.

It wasn't easy for Lisa to say goodbye to them a week later. She waved from her front porch until the car taking them to the airport was out of sight. That evening, Shuki demanded that his grandmother give him his bath and put him to bed.

"Shuki, you know that Oma and Opa have gone back to America," Lisa explained patiently. "They're going to call us when they get home."

"I want Oma and Opa!" Shuki began crying and continued until Rivka, the National Service girl, walked in.

"I thought I should start coming again now that your parents left," she said simply.

Lisa wanted to hug her. With no nonsense, Rivka got Shuki all ready and tucked into bed with a story. When Lisa came in to say *Shema* with him, he was calm and ready for a good-night kiss from his mother.

Two weeks later, Miriam came into the store, obviously excited about something.

"There's going to be a play by women for women in Kfar Saba next month. The tickets aren't expensive and I want to try and get a busload to go. How about it?"

Lisa stared at her friend as if she had suggested they fly to the moon together.

"How am I supposed to leave Gilit and Shuki?" She moved to the cereal shelf and began straightening boxes that were already straight.

"I'm sure Rivka would be happy to babysit," Miriam said to her friend's back.

Lisa's face clouded over. "I take advantage of her enough as it is. Talk to the women who have husbands home to babysit."

"Do you really think my husband's going to babysit? He teaches that evening. Natan goes to the class, and both Myra and I have lined up babysitters. So has Elisheva."

"Well, none of you have a new baby at home." Lisa turned impatiently and stomped to the cash register.

"That's exactly why you should get out." Miriam followed her. "Gilit takes a relief bottle. Rivka's responsible. It'll be good for you."

"I think," Lisa's tone was icy, "I can decide what's good for me and what's not."

"I don't think so." Miriam leaned onto the counter and looked her in the eye.

Lisa just stared back at her.

Miriam took a deep breath. "You're spending too much energy feeling sorry for yourself."

"You know nothing about it." Lisa headed for the back room.

"Don't walk away from me," Miriam pleaded.

Just then the door opened and Boaz came in. Miriam groaned and censored herself for bringing up the topic with her friend in a public place.

"Can I help you?" she asked pleasantly.

"Where's Lisa?"

"In the back room checking stock."

"I just need some bread and milk."

Miriam took his money and watched him leave. She walked through the crowded shelves and found Lisa sitting on a crate with her head in her hands.

"Lisa," Miriam began, pulling up another crate next to her friend and putting an arm around her, "I'm sorry."

Lisa nodded.

"You're right. I know nothing about it. But I care about you. Just because Kobi left doesn't mean you have to stop enjoying life."

"I'm not the same person I was," Lisa spoke slowly, "before Kobi left."

"I miss my friend," Miriam said plaintively.

Lisa shrugged. Gilit began crying and Lisa went to tend to her just as the phone rang.

"Should I get it?" Miriam asked.

Lisa shrugged again, so Miriam grabbed it on the fifth ring only to hear a click.

"They hung up," she announced.

"Yeah." Lisa nibbled her fingernail.

"Does that happen often?"

"The number here is one digit off from the number of a car mechanic in Tel Aviv. I guess some of the men get nervous when they hear a woman's voice." Lisa managed a small smile.

The smile encouraged Miriam and she waited patiently until Lisa was finished with Gilit. Then she moved her crate so she could sit across from her friend, face-to-face. "You've been hurt a lot, but you're still Lisa and we love you and want you to be happy. I want to take you to the play because I think it would be good for you to get out. I don't want you to fall into postpartum depression. And I want your company. Can't you give it a try?"

Touched by Miriam's honesty, Lisa bit her lower lip. "I'll think about it," she answered slowly.

CHAPTER

Fifty-one

Little Mimi, as Naomi had nicknamed her baby sister, was five weeks old when Danny came home from the office agitated.

"Meir Rosen called today. They want to know when I'm going to sign the contract."

"That's a fair request," Sondra said. They were sitting in the den and the children were asleep.

"Yes, but I don't know what to tell them."

"Today the nurse told me there's a good chance they'll be moving Mimi out of the ICU by the end of the week."

Danny nodded thoughtfully.

"Sign," Sondra advised. "Let's have some faith that Mimi will continue to develop and be out of the hospital soon. Worst-case scenario," Sondra was matter-of-fact, "is that you'll go by yourself to Israel and I'll come later with the kids."

"That's a very big worst case." Danny raised his eyebrows.

Sondra convinced him, though, and he made reservations to fly east and sign the following Sunday. Sondra was looking forward to the signing. Up till now, afraid that things would fall through, they'd told no one except their parents and Debbie about their plans.

She'd let the secret slip out to her friend a week earlier when Debbie had dropped off a casserole for dinner. As always, Debbie's children made a beeline for the playroom, and while the children were playing nicely, the two of them settled at the kitchen table. Debbie reacted to Sondra's news in disbelief.

"I can't believe you're going to abandon me!" she exclaimed.

"Debbie," Sondra responded quickly, remembering how deserted she'd felt when Brachie Frisch had moved to Los Angeles, "you know you'll be leaving Phoenix in a year or two. With the experience Shraga's getting here, he's going to be grabbed up for a better-paying position in a bigger community. And then you'd be abandoning me."

"Maybe," Debbie had answered with a sigh. "Well, I wish you the best." She took a sip of iced tea and avoided Sondra's eyes.

"Thank you." Sondra stood and brought the sugar bowl to the table. Neither of them needed any more sugar, but she couldn't sit still.

"Do your parents know?" Debbie finally broke the silence.

"Well...," Sondra hesitated and then reminded herself that she was talking to her oldest friend. She lowered herself into her chair and faced Debbie.

"We sat down with my mother the day she left and told her of the possibility. I'd really wanted to tell her and my father together, but it was either tell my mother alone in person or tell the two of them together over the phone."

"I bet you didn't want to do either," Debbie said sympathetically.

"You're right." Sondra rolled her eyes.

"So how'd your mother take it?"

Sondra gave an uncomfortable laugh. "She said we were putting her in a hard position. When she prays for Mimi to get well fast, she now feels like she's praying for us to leave America."

"Oh, no." Debbie groaned.

Sondra twisted her wedding band around her finger and kept her eyes down. "Then she said she knew that was what we'd always wanted and so she'll try her best to support us. My father called that evening. He told us how much he'd miss us and wanted to know if there was anything they could do to help."

"Wow, that was good of him!"

"Yeah."

"They'll be able to visit you, no?"

"I don't know how easy that'll be, but Danny and I have made a commitment to each other that I'll see my parents once a year."

"What about Danny's parents?"

"Danny spoke to his father in the office the day after my mother left. He was supportive."

"And Shirley?"

"Don't ask." Sondra tossed her hands. "She acted very melodramatic. Now she's coming around and beginning to talk about taking the kids shopping, one at a time, to buy special things they can take with them."

"Well," Debbie stood up, "I guess I'd better get my kids home and start baths."

"Debbie," Sondra said, looking up at her friend, "please understand."

"I do," Debbie reached out and put a warm hand on her friend's shoulder.

"And," Sondra added as she covered Debbie's hand with one of her own, "please don't tell anyone."

"I won't even mention it to Shraga."

She'd kept her word and now she was the only one of Sondra's friends who knew why Danny was flying out Saturday night.

Debbie offered to watch the kids when Sondra went to the hospital to visit Mimi Sunday morning; afterwards they'd all go to the zoo together. It was a great plan, but Thursday Yossi began whining. Nothing seemed to distract him from pulling at his mother's skirt, begging for juice but not drinking it, and rubbing at his stomach. Finally, Sondra lifted up his top and, to her dismay, saw the beginnings of chicken pox. With a sinking feeling, she realized that even though Mimi had been moved out of the ICU, no doctor would let her come home with chicken pox in the house.

Fortunately, Sharon came through again as a babysitter and Sondra was able to get to the hospital Sunday morning. Debbie declared that her girls had their hearts set on going to the zoo with Batsheva and Naomi and she loaded all of them into her car for the outing. Zvi Chaim was invited to join in, but he decided to go play with Benny. Sondra had a full afternoon to give Yossi her undivided attention. Danny returned home after supper Sunday evening, red-eyed and exhausted, but beaming with satisfaction.

"Okay, guys," he announced once he'd finished hugging everyone. "Let's go into the den. I have an important announcement to make."

Yossi climbed onto his father's lap. Thankfully, his bout with chicken pox was far lighter than when the older three had had them two years earlier, but the medicine he'd been given to keep him from scratching kept him groggy and clingy.

"*Nu*, Abba?" Zvi Chaim looked at his father expectantly. He sat on the couch, flanked by his sisters. Sondra stood in the doorway with a big smile on her face and tears of happiness glistening in her eyes.

"Today I signed a contract, a special piece of paper, which means we're going to move to Israel this summer."

"Yay!" Zvi Chaim jumped up clapping.

Batsheva followed her brother's lead and Naomi smiled uncertainly.

"Are we going to live in Kfar Yonatan?"

"No," Danny answered, "we'll visit there a lot, though."

"We're moving to an absorption center right outside Jerusalem," Sondra explained. "We'll be with a lot of other families from all over the world who are also coming to live in Israel. There'll be a special nursery school for Yossi right there. Abba and I are checking out which schools to send the rest of you to."

"When we go?" Naomi demanded.

"After school's out for the summer."

"Can I tell Morah Yaffa?" Batsheva asked.

"You can tell whoever you want tomorrow."

"I want to call Sima now," Batsheva begged.

"Tomorrow," Danny repeated firmly.

He made his official announcement at the office the following morning, and the children told their classmates as soon as they arrived at school. Sondra knew all of her friends, with the exception of Bayla, would hear the news from their children. So on her way home from the hospital, she made a detour to Harold's office. Even though it meant losing a family from the community, Bayla took the news well. In fact, she insisted that she wanted to make a farewell party for them.

For the next three days, the three oldest children spoke nonstop about moving to Israel.

"I'm going to miss Sima," Batsheva confided to her mother the next evening at dinner.

"I know," Sondra reassured her. "And I'm going to miss her mother. I'll help you write a lot of letters."

"I can't wait to see Moshe!" Zvi Chaim exclaimed. "Don't you want to see Tzippie?" he asked his sister.

"Yes," she said hesitantly.

"When Grandma taking me shopping?" Naomi piped up.

"Are we going to take all our toys with us?" Batsheva asked.

"Of course," Sondra answered.

Finally, Thursday morning, she took Yossi for a well checkup. Together, they brought the letter from the pediatrician to the hospital. Mimi would be released the following day. If all went well, they would be together as a family for Shabbos. And they'd be able to move to Israel together as a family.

Full of excitement, Sondra began making phone calls to share her good news. The only one she didn't reach was Lisa. She'd just have to wait until Sunday to speak to her cousin.

Lisa buttoned up her jacket as she got off the bus and fell into step next to Miriam. The February nights were cool and there was a hint of rain in the air, but she felt a warm glow inside. She'd enjoyed the play and told Miriam so.

"I'm so glad," her friend responded sincerely. "By the way, I want to warn you, I'm making a really spicy cholent this week, a new recipe."

"*Oy*," Lisa gasped.

"What's the matter?"

"I forgot to tell you we're not coming for lunch this week. We're doing Shabbat together with Yael."

"I wish I'd known before I turned down Chava's invitation."

"Oh, no," Lisa moaned. "I feel terrible."

"Don't worry about it," Miriam answered quickly. "Yehezkel doesn't like going out for meals. I probably wouldn't have accepted anyway."

"I'm so sorry," Lisa repeated.

Again Miriam said not to worry. "But I'll miss your company," she said as they parted to go into their respective houses.

Yael and her husband had moved to Kfar Yonatan as newlyweds a year after Lisa and Kobi. A most unlikely couple, he was very proper, British, and newly religious. She was a sixth-generation Jerusalemite, impulsive, and far more interested in her jewelry business than running her home. Two years and one baby later, they'd had a quick divorce and he returned to England, leaving Yael to raise their daughter and make jewelry by herself.

Although she was impressed with Yael's talent, Lisa didn't think that she had much in common with her. That changed when Kobi picked up and left. Ever since Gilit was born and Lisa had come to the angry conclusion that Kobi had abandoned her for good, she felt that Yael could understand her emotions better than anyone else. The Shabbat lunch together had been her idea, but now she felt terrible. How could she have forgotten, after more than six months of eating Shabbat lunch week after week with the Gruenbergs, to let Miriam know her plans? She hoped she hadn't hurt her friend.

If Miriam did have any bad feelings, she didn't express them to Lisa. She continued with her normal dropping in, calling, and offering assistance. A week later, she knocked on the door with a new book in her hand.

"Lisa, you've got to read this. Yehezkel bought it for me yesterday and I couldn't put it down." Miriam laughed. "Don't ask how the house looks or about the backlog on my desk. Do you want to borrow it?"

"Well, I don't know," Lisa answered mischievously. "Maybe I'll forget to open the store tomorrow morning."

Miriam chuckled heartily. "It's good to have you joking!"

Lisa just blushed.

"How about coming with me to Israeli dancing tomorrow night?"

"I don't think so."

"Why not?"

"I'm tired in the evening." Lisa shrugged.

"It'd do you good to get out a bit and get some exercise."

"Am I getting fat?" There was an edge to Lisa's voice, but Miriam ignored it.

"You know you're not," she answered. "I'm green with envy that you already got your figure back."

"I'm glad there's something in my life to be envious of."

"Lisa, please don't be bitter." There were tears in Miriam's eyes.

"Why not?"

"I don't understand. For months you talked about giving Kobi the benefit of the doubt and that there would be an explanation for everything. What's changed?"

"I had a baby," Lisa said simply.

"So?"

"Kobi knew when my due date was. If he didn't make contact, then he's either dead or doesn't care."

"Oh, Lisa." Miriam reached out to put an arm around her friend, but Lisa pulled away.

"Miriam," Lisa's voice quivered as she spoke, "you have a great husband and a wonderful marriage, and there's no way you can understand what I'm going through. Even Elisheva doesn't have a clue. Avi was taken away from her. He didn't get up and leave."

"So," Miriam said softly, "the only one who can understand you now is Yael."

"You could say that," Lisa answered evenly.

"Listen to me, Lisa." Miriam shook her head. "There are a lot of things going on in people's homes that *you* don't have a clue about. Everyone has their challenges. Some are big and everyone knows about them like yours, and some are small and hidden, but eat away at people's lives."

"So what's your problem?"

"If it will help you to know," Miriam hesitated, "my mother-in-law and I haven't spoken for two years."

"You haven't?" Lisa was aghast. "Why not?"

"I don't want to go into it." Miriam waved her hand at the problem. "Suffice it to say I feel terrible about it and it has a big affect on everything."

"I'm sorry." Lisa was sincere. "But it's not the same as having your husband get up and walk out on you."

"Of course not," Miriam readily agreed. "But it's a real problem and," she repeated, "it affects everything."

The two women sat in silence.

Finally Miriam spoke. "Won't you come with me tomorrow night? I don't want to go by myself."

Lisa laughed despite herself. "There're a dozen women who would love to go with you!"

"But you're my best friend here," Miriam spoke plaintively.

"Really?"

"Well, you were. Do you still want to be?"

Lisa took a deep breath. "I don't know if I know how to be a good friend anymore, but I'll try."

CHAPTER

Fifty-two

"Yossi," Sondra smiled at her youngest son, "shall we look in the Purim box for a costume for you?"

He nodded enthusiastically. Little Mimi still had another half an hour before she needed to be fed and Sondra was eager to have some special time with him. Just as she pushed the box into the den, though, the phone rang. Assuming it was Debbie calling to discuss the Purim *seudah*, she grabbed it without a second's thought. Her friend would understand when she'd ask to call back later.

But it wasn't a local call; rather, it was a long distance one from Tucson.

"Sondra, it's Carol, Lisa's friend. I need to talk to you."

Sondra felt her stomach muscles tighten. The last time she'd spoken to Lisa's college roommate was after Kobi disappeared. Carol's reaction had been just what Sondra had been dreading. *You mean a religious Jew would do something like that?* Sondra had cut the conversation short. When Carol called several weeks later, Danny took care of the phone call. After that, Carol must have spoken to Lisa directly.

"Just a minute, Carol." Sondra put her hand over the receiver. "Yossi," she instructed, "look through the box and I'll help you as soon as I'm off the phone." She blew him a kiss and uncovered the receiver. "Okay, Carol, I'm with you."

"Good. Sit down."

"Is everything okay?" Sondra was in no mood for games.

"Yes, but sit down."

Sondra's heart began hammering as she dropped into a chair. "Is it about Kobi?"

"Yes, he's here, in the office, in the waiting room."

"Oh my gosh!" Sondra gasped. "How'd you find him?"

"I didn't," Carol said simply. "He found me."

"He found you?"

"Yes, he looked me up in the Tucson phone book and came here without an appointment. He refused to give a name to my secretary and insisted that I'd want to see him, as he was an old friend. So I skipped lunch and she sent him in and I almost fell off my chair."

"Oh my gosh," Sondra repeated, standing up and pacing. "What'd he say?"

"First of all," Carol's manner was professional, "he wanted to know how Lisa was and if she'd had the baby, whether it was a boy or a girl, the name — all those details. And he wanted my opinion about whether there's a chance that Lisa would take him back."

"Wow!" Sondra exclaimed.

"And," Carol continued, "he wants to know if he can come to Phoenix and speak to you and your husband."

"I...uh...um..." Sondra stuttered. "What do you think? Is he normal? Did he have a nervous breakdown or what? Is he remorseful? Is he safe?"

"Let's take the questions one at a time. He appears to be normal and safe. He's talking rationally. Regret is oozing out of him. Yes, I think he had a breakdown of sorts. He's lost weight and looks like he might have been sick. He wants to call Lisa and he's afraid."

"I don't blame him." Sondra tried to keep the sarcasm out of her voice. "And I don't think he should just call out of the blue. Someone there should break the news to her gently and then he can call."

"That's what he thought," Carol concurred. "He wants to come to you and call from your house. Apparently there's not much money here."

"How's he going to get here?"

"I can drop him off at the bus station."

"Okay, tell him to call Danny at the office when he gets in."

Sondra looked at her watch as she hung up the phone. It was already time to wake Mimi. Poor Yossi. She'd just have to feed Mimi in the den and do two things at once. Then she'd have to call Danny. Kobi turned up! A small part of her wanted to sing and dance in celebration, but the major part was full of apprehension and worry.

It was half an hour after Kobi had called him when Danny was finally able to leave the office, and it was a ten-minute drive to the bus station. Kobi was standing on the curb waiting, and at first glance, Danny thought he was one of the vagrants. His shoulders were slumped and his brown eyes were lowered. They wouldn't meet Danny's as he jumped out of the car and extended his hand.

Kobi's handshake wasn't as firm as Danny remembered it being. As he opened the trunk for Kobi to throw in his backpack, Danny spoke. "We were so worried about you." He hoped it sounded as nonjudgmental and caring as he wanted it to.

Kobi nodded silently and rubbed his temples. Danny saw that his friend was beginning to go gray.

"I've made a lot of mistakes," Kobi said softly as he closed the door and settled into the passenger seat. He lowered his head, and Danny digested the fact that Kobi was bareheaded.

"Uh, where, um, have you been all this time?"

"Payson."

"Payson?"

"I always liked the looks of Payson."

"It *is* pretty," Danny agreed. Then, even though he'd thought of all sorts of things to speak about on the drive over, he was tongue-tied.

Fidgeting behind the wheel, he bore no resemblance to the young, confident doctor who'd just left work. He wondered how well Sondra was prepared for Kobi's arrival.

* * *

Between adding an extra side dish to stretch their dinner to feed another person and taking care of the children, Sondra hadn't had much time to prepare herself at all. What could she say to the man who'd caused Lisa so much grief? The only thing she did was to tell the children that Kobi was coming. They were to be polite to him and not ask any questions whatsoever. Something in her tone made it clear that her statement wasn't up for discussion.

The greetings that the children gave their father and Kobi were very stilted. Their mouths were quiet, but their eyes and ears took in everything. They noticed that Kobi wasn't wearing a *kippah*, but he asked to borrow one before they sat down at the table.

Kobi washed his hands and made the blessing on bread just like everyone else. He was interested in the discussion at the table, mainly about what was happening in the Phoenix community. When Zvi Chaim repeated something his rabbi had taught him that day, Kobi paid as much attention as his parents did and even asked a question.

"It's not fair that he can ask questions and we can't," Batsheva whispered to her brother.

If anyone heard or noticed, they didn't say anything. The meal ended soon after. Sondra busied herself with the cleanup and Danny settled the younger children into bed. When he left for evening services, Kobi joined him and Zvi Chaim, and the *kippah* stayed on his head.

They returned to a peaceful house. Zvi Chaim was sent to bed and Danny took the phone off the hook. Sondra thought the only sounds that could be heard in the den were the ticking of the clock and the hammering of her heart. Now they would hear what Kobi had to say.

"I just had to get away!" The words burst out of Kobi. "I was afraid I was going to hurt someone — Lisa, Shuki, the *rav*, somebody. They made me so angry with all their 'it's all for the best' talk. I couldn't stand it! I wanted to punch them out."

Kobi took a deep breath. Slowly he explained how he'd spent the last seven and a half months of his life. He'd flown to America and, after several flights, ended up in San Diego. Sondra and Danny exchanged long looks. If only Danny had seen him when he and the children were there on vacation!

California was too expensive and noisy, though, and Kobi remembered how he'd liked Payson. He and Lisa had spent such peaceful outings in the nearby forest when they lived in Phoenix. So he took two buses, one to Tucson and then one to Payson. Of course he'd wanted to avoid Phoenix. He found himself a room in a boardinghouse, but he was running out of money and found a job in the supermarket.

"My father and my wife both own grocery stores," he said sardonically, "and I was a stock boy."

"I guess it covered your expenses," Danny responded.

Kobi nodded and admitted he'd had few expenses. His rent was minimal. He was entitled to a discount at the grocery store, but he didn't have much of an appetite. He had no car and walked everywhere he wanted to go. He did a lot of hiking in the woods or borrowed books from the public library. It was not that hard to support one person.

This was uttered with his eyes down, so he missed the expression on Sondra's face.

"I did a lot of thinking and I felt terrible knowing I'd hurt Lisa and Shuki, but I just couldn't face them or my life back there. I missed them, but I was so depressed. I did my job like a robot and tried to avoid people."

"What changed?" Danny prompted.

"Well, there was this man who came into the store a lot, an older guy, with, would you believe it, a *kippah*. I stayed far away from him. But I guess he heard me talking and heard my accent, so he came up to me and said *shalom aleichem* and insisted on having a conversation.

"He's quite an interesting character. His name's Motti. He and his wife, a really sweet woman, were living in Denver, enjoying their golden years, and then his wife's mother fell and broke her hip. You see, his wife's a convert, and her mother lives in Payson, and she needed help when she came home from the hospital. So they're in Payson for a while and making the best of it. He kept getting after me to come for Friday night dinner. Finally I ran out of excuses, so I went.

"Motti has these piercing blue eyes and it was like he could see into my soul. When his wife brought out the cake and tea, he asked me, 'Why are you angry with Hashem?' I hedged, but he wouldn't be put off. He told me it was clear after five minutes at his Shabbat table that I'd been observant and stopped. So I explained how I was angry with everybody."

"With Lisa and Shuki?" Sondra asked in a tight voice.

"With everybody!" Kobi repeated emphatically. "My brother died fighting in Sinai and then our government gave away all he'd captured. The *rav* went around saying, 'We need to work on ourselves to become better Jews.' I was really sarcastic when I told Motti that. I thought we'd been doing a pretty good job already in Kfar Yonatan. And then Avi..."

Kobi's voice faltered and he took another deep breath. "Avi was such a great person. All he wanted to do was serve Hashem and build the land, and he was murdered in cold blood. And everyone was saying, 'It's all for the best.' Well, I didn't think it was for the best. I thought it was rotten.

"And then Lisa announced she had good news — she was expecting. That was the last thing I wanted to do, bring another baby into this rotten world. And I was sick of trying to pretend with her and Shuki that everything was fine. So I took off my *kippah* and left."

"That's what you told this Motti?" Danny asked.

"He said he understood and that was it. He went on with the meal, singing and saying *divrei Torah*, as if I hadn't told them anything. But he asked me to come back for lunch. The food was good and he didn't seem like he would hassle me, so I went. And I went back the next week, and at that lunch, he and his wife began talking about how they lost their only child when he was just ten years old to leukemia. And they started telling me all the *emunah* stories." Kobi paused and swallowed hard.

Sondra stirred impatiently and Danny signaled her to stay still. "What stories?" he asked gently.

"You know, like how the back side of a tapestry is such a mess and that it's like life in this world and that we'll understand everything in the end. I've heard them all...

"But he said something else. He said that I can say Avi's murder was terrible. That giving away Yamit was horrible. That losing my brother was a big tragedy. And that doesn't mean I don't have faith, as long as I believe that in the end it will all turn out to have been for the good."

"That helped you?" Danny asked.

"Yes! I finally felt that I could talk about my pain and not feel like I'm a heretic. Then he told me that he thought I should have counseling. His neighbor is a retired psychiatrist from the University of Arizona and still sees a few clients on a sliding scale fee. So I started going to him.

"It's been two months, and he helped me realize I need medication and serious counseling. I think...I hope...I'm ready to face life again, even if I have to stay on the medication and go for counseling for the rest of my life. I want to put my *kippah* back on and come back to Hashem. And I want to go back to my wife and family, if Lisa will have me. I never stopped thinking about her. Every day she and Shuki and the new baby are on my mind."

"Believe me," Sondra snapped, "you're on her mind every day too. Wondering if you're dead or alive, if you've rejected her or..."

"Sondra," Danny's voice was soft but stern, as if he were speaking to one of the children. "Stop it."

"I can't." Sondra shook her head stubbornly. "Kobi needs to hear how his wife and son have suffered. Who does he think...?"

"Enough," Danny commanded. "Let's go in the other room for a minute."

"Never mind. I have to feed Mimi now anyway."

"You'd better calm down beforehand," Danny spoke quietly. "I'll go with you."

Sondra frowned but fell in step next to her husband.

"What do you want from him?" Danny asked as they walked down the hall.

"I don't know." Sondra wiped angrily at the tears coursing down her cheeks. "A better excuse than that his brother died. Lisa's brother died too, and she didn't go off the deep end."

"Lisa's Lisa. She dealt with Howie's death her way, and Kobi didn't cope at all. Obviously it was swept under the carpet and now he's paying the price."

"Lisa and Shuki are paying the price," Sondra muttered.

"Them too. Listen, Sondra," Danny said, guiding her into their bedroom and closing the door, "the man suffered and he's still suffering. Wait." He raised his hand to stop Sondra's retort. "Everyone makes mistakes, maybe not as big as Kobi's, but mistakes. Even you, Sondra Klein, make mistakes. Hashem gave you the chance to do *teshuvah*. If you expect Him to forgive you, then you have to forgive others. Holding grudges helps no one."

Sondra grabbed a tissue from the nightstand and wiped her face. "How's he ever going to make it up to Lisa?"

"That's between the two of them."

"She might not take him back."

"She might not," Danny agreed. "If she does, though, you have to be supportive."

"I have to feed Mimi." Sondra gathered up her used tissues and tossed them into the trash.

"Are you calm enough?"

"I think so."

"Then I'll go back to Kobi."

Sondra tiptoed into the baby's room and lifted Mimi tenderly out of the bassinet. Her feelings softened just by holding her tiny little girl, but her thoughts were about the implications of what Danny had said. Did she hold grudges?

Once Mimi finished eating, Sondra continued to rock her gently. She remembered all the times she and Danny had fought and it had taken her longer than she wanted to get over her anger.

Then there was that time Debbie had been so mad at her. Sondra had been quick to say she was sorry. Debbie had said she was sorry too.

Sondra didn't think she'd held a grudge. Yet she had to admit that it wasn't until she was the godmother at Debbie's baby's bris that she'd felt fully comfortable with her friend again.

And she couldn't forget the cold war she had with her mother-in-law.

Sondra respected her husband and she heard the truth of his words. Resolutely, she settled Mimi back in the cradle and made her way to the den via the kitchen.

"Can I get anyone some tea?" she asked in what she thought was an upbeat voice. She hoped the tray she held with the kettle, cups, and cookies would signal Danny that she was ready to be conciliatory.

"Great idea." He gave his wife an appreciative smile. "We're discussing how Kobi should contact Lisa."

Sondra looked at her watch. "It's a little after eight in the morning there. She's at the store now. You can't call her at the store."

"We know that," Danny replied patiently. "Kobi wants to call one of her friends to break the news and make arrangements for him to talk to her. He thinks Miriam's the one to call and wants to know if you agree."

Sondra took a sip of tea as she thought over the question. Finally she nodded.

"I think Miriam's the best choice. Do you want some privacy to call?"

"Not to call Miriam," Kobi answered quickly and then hesitated. "Before I call, well, I just want to say that this isn't easy for me, but I know none of this is easy for you, and, well, I want to thank you for everything. I'm going to make it up to everybody."

CHAPTER
Fifty-three

It was a good thing she'd had the flu two weeks earlier instead of later, Miriam thought as she made her way to the grocery store. If not, she was certain she'd have told Kobi to call Yael, Lisa's new friend, when he'd called earlier that morning.

However, she'd had the flu. And although Lisa had said a month earlier that she didn't know if she knew how to be a good friend anymore, apparently friendship was like riding a bicycle. Because when Miriam was laid low with fever for the same three days that Yehezkel had to be away, Lisa was there for her. Shifra arranged to send in soup each day, but it was Lisa, knowing that Yehezkel's mother wasn't going to come help, who took the kids and hauled the laundry hamper over to her house.

Later, when Miriam was back on her feet and had tried to express her gratitude, Lisa just waved her thanks away.

"It felt good to be able to give for a change instead of always taking," she'd responded.

Miriam thought it was Lisa's first step to returning to an emotionally healthy Lisa. Now she wondered how her friend would react to the news of the phone call.

It'd come right after she'd returned from taking her youngest to nursery school, before she'd even had a chance to pour herself a second cup of coffee. Sondra was on the line and Miriam hadn't been surprised to hear her voice. She was shocked, though, when Sondra dropped the bombshell that Kobi was alive, in Phoenix. Briefly she explained how Kobi had started medication and counseling, and wanted to come back to Lisa if she'd have him. And then Miriam had to talk to Kobi.

Although Sondra was adamant that Kobi was full of regret, Miriam's voice was cool and distant as she said hello. Kobi's was hesitant and uncertain, but in spite of everything, Miriam had to admit that he sounded sincere.

She entered the grocery store five minutes before closing and waited patiently until Lisa rang up the last order.

"Hi." She tried to sound nonchalant. "Let's walk over to pick up the kids together. There's something I want to talk to you about."

"What new project do you have in mind for me now?" Lisa sighed exaggeratedly, a gleam of mischief in her eyes.

"Well, um...," Miriam hesitated and Lisa realized that she wasn't in a playful mood.

"It's about Kobi, isn't it?" she asked slowly.

Miriam nodded.

"Is...is he alive?"

"Very much so."

As Lisa grabbed onto the counter, she felt the room spin. Miriam literally saw the blood drain from her friend's face.

"Lisa," she cried, "sit down!"

Lisa collapsed onto her stool and put her head down. Miriam grabbed a bottle of soda from the cooler case and instructed her to drink. It took a few minutes for the color to return to Lisa's face.

"Tell me everything," Lisa demanded.

"Well...," Miriam began. The door to the store opened. She turned and saw Yael standing there. "Lisa's closed now."

"I just realized we're out of bread," Yael begged. "I'll be quick. Okay?"

"Okay." Lisa gave a curt nod.

"Is everything all right?" Yael asked as Lisa rang up the purchase.

Lisa nodded shortly. Yael gave Miriam a searching look and Miriam just smiled politely. It wasn't her place to say anything if Lisa didn't want to.

"Well, I'll see you later," Yael said brightly and Lisa just nodded again. Miriam watched her leave and turned to Lisa.

"Why don't you lock up and we can walk the long way around. You can use the fresh air and I'll tell you everything."

Lisa strapped Gilit into her stroller numbly. Miriam, who had rehearsed what she was going to say, took a deep breath and began.

"Kobi came to see your friend, Carol, in Tucson, and she contacted Sondra, and he went to her and Danny, and then called me. He really regrets what he did..."

"Where was he all this time?" Lisa interrupted.

"In Payson, Arizona."

"Payson!" Lisa's face paled again as she remembered all the pleasant Sunday outings they'd had in the forest outside that little town.

"Yes, Payson. He began going for counseling there and started antidepressants. Apparently they're working because he wants to call you and ask for forgiveness. He wants me to ask you when's a good time to call. He's calling me back in a few hours to hear your answer."

Although it was a sunny day, spring had barely started, and there was a strong breeze. Lisa burrowed her hands in her coat pockets as she tried to reply.

"Maybe I don't want to talk to him," she finally said.

"You don't?"

Lisa stared at a kitten scampering next to the sidewalk.

"I don't know what I want," she spoke flatly. "I so much wanted to have a good explanation for his disappearance. Amnesia, kidnapping, something...," her voice trailed off.

"I think," Miriam answered carefully, "he was kidnapped by all his negative emotions and destructive feelings following Avi's murder."

She let Lisa mull that over and they continued to stroll in silence a bit.

"You know, I'll be happy to bring Shuki to my house tonight so you can talk to him uninterrupted."

"So you think I should talk to him?"

"Of course!" Miriam exclaimed. "Whether or not you take him back, you have to have some closure."

"I guess you're right," Lisa agreed halfheartedly.

Again they strolled in silence. They could already see the children waiting for their mothers on the playground at the nursery school when Lisa spoke again.

"Tell Kobi that he can call me tomorrow morning after eight. Shuki won't be home, and I'll get Elisheva to open the store for me."

"Okay, and if you need me for anything, you know I'm just a phone call away."

"Thank you," Lisa said. Impulsively she took a hand out of her pocket and squeezed Miriam's.

At two in the morning, when she got out of bed to feed Gilit, she realized that all she'd done for the last four hours was toss and turn from side to side. She began to regret her decision. If she'd let Kobi call that evening, it would be behind her and maybe she would have been able to get some sleep. On the other hand, she told herself, she'd had plenty of restless nights the last seven and a half months. What was one more night?

It was after three before she finally nodded off, and at seven she was awake for another feeding. Somehow she got Shuki out to nursery school and then waited with a pounding heart for the phone to ring.

She didn't have long to wait. At two minutes after eight, two minutes after ten at night in Phoenix, the ringing broke the tense silence of the house. Lisa let it ring five times and then answered.

"Lisa?"

How many times had she picked up the phone, hoping to hear his voice? Now it was soft and unsure.

"Yes." Hers was hard.

"I'm so, so sorry. I want to make it all up to you."

"Are you going to send me a *get*?"

There was a long silence.

"Lisa," she could hear the pain in his voice, but steeled herself against it, "if that's what you want, I will, but please give me a chance to make it up to you."

"How?"

"I want to come back to Eretz Yisrael and see you and Shuki and meet Gilit. I want to be there for you again. I want to return the money I took. I'm going for counseling. I know I was terribly wrong but please give me a chance."

"Kobi, that all sounds very nice, but I don't know if I can ever trust you again. You can do all of that, but please send me a *get* first. I don't want to be an *agunah* if you decide to disappear again."

"I see." His voice was incredibly sad. "Is it okay if I come back to Israel?"

"I don't own the country."

"Please, Lisa." Now his voice was pleading. "We had good times, remember? I wasn't always a bad husband."

"No, Kobi." Lisa's voice thawed slightly. "You were a good husband," she paused and took a deep breath, "until the last year."

"Please. Say you'll see me when I get there."

"I'll see you. But, Kobi, bring the *get*."

"I'll take care of it as soon as I get to Israel. I'm leaving as soon as I can get a ticket."

"Have a safe flight." This was said automatically.

"Lisa?"

"What?"

"I'm going to make it up to you."

CHAPTER

Fifty-four

Lisa had no idea how long it would take Kobi to arrange a flight to Israel. So it was quite a shock to answer the door on Ta'anit Esther and find her husband standing there. Part of her wanted to throw herself into his arms and cry out all her hurt. Another part wanted to slam the door in his face.

"Lisa, I'm so sorry."

She nodded, acknowledging his words, but had none of her own.

"Can I come in?" He seemed so unsure of himself.

Silently she opened the door a bit wider.

"Where's Shuki?"

"At a friend's." Her tone was icy.

"Can I see the baby?"

"She's sleeping." But she led him into the children's room.

"She's beautiful," Kobi exclaimed and his eyes filled with tears. "Carol told me you named her Gilit. It's a beautiful name."

Again Lisa nodded. She remembered how painful it had been to pick a name alone.

"Would you like a cup of coffee?" she asked mechanically.

"I'm fasting, but I'd like to sit and talk," he answered eagerly.

He studied the house as he made his way to the living room. "The place looks really great, Lisa."

"Thank you." Her whole body was stiff, not just her voice.

"I brought some presents." His tone was pleading, grating on her, as he reached into his backpack and pulled out a small jewelry box.

Lisa set it on the coffee table without opening it. When he pulled out three paperbacks by some of her favorite authors, though, she smiled in spite of herself.

"Bayla and some of the others sent baby presents, but I picked out a dress for Gilit all by myself."

Again his pleading tone bothered her. "Did you bring anything for Shuki?"

"Of course!" There was an uncomfortable silence. "Lisa, please, can't we try to work things out without a *get*?" he begged.

As Lisa stubbornly shook her head, the front door burst open.

"Ima," Shuki hollered, "I want to show Dov my..." He stopped short as he caught sight of his father, who'd risen to go to his son.

"Abba!" Shuki exclaimed as Kobi hugged him. "Is your heart all better?"

Kobi looked over his son's head at Lisa with a questioning expression.

"I explained to Shuki that you had a boo-boo on your heart because Avi died and maybe you'd come back when it was better. Do you have a better explanation for him?"

Kobi lowered his eyes.

Lisa turned to her son's friend. "Dov, this isn't a good time for Shuki to have guests." She watched him leave. "Maybe," she suggested to her son, "you'd like to take Abba for a walk and show him all the new things here?"

When they returned, Gilit was awake. Kobi held her and spoke softly to her. Lisa watched them silently. No matter what would happen, she knew it was good for the children to have their father back in their lives. Still, she was relieved when he left, she presumed for Beit She'an.

Unlike his mother, Shuki wasn't at all relieved. "Why did Abba leave?" he fretted. "Is he coming back again?"

"What did he tell you when you went on your walk?" Lisa adjusted his *kippah*.

"That he wasn't going to stay in Kfar Yonatan tonight, but he'd be back tomorrow."

"So I guess he's coming back."

"I want him to see my Purim costume tomorrow."

"I'm sure he wants to see it too."

"And I want to give Abba *mishlo'ach manot* tomorrow."

"Shuki." Lisa dredged up all the patience she had. "Remember, tomorrow isn't really Purim. It's just the party at nursery school. Then we'll have Shabbat and then it'll be Purim."

"Right," Shuki agreed solemnly. "Will Abba be here for Shabbat?"

"We'll see," Lisa answered wearily.

A little later, Rav Yehezkel called and asked to come speak to her. He arrived with his wife, and Miriam turned immediately to Shuki.

"Dov's mother invited you for supper. If it's okay with Ima, do you want to go?"

Shuki looked to his mother. She'd raised her eyebrows at Miriam's suggestion, but gave her approval. He was out the door in just a matter of seconds. As Lisa settled her guests in the living room, she was reminded of how they'd come over when Kobi first disappeared to get her organized. What was on their minds now?

"Lisa," the *rav* began, "Kobi came to the house and asked me to make up a *get*."

Lisa nodded quickly.

He cleared his throat. "I don't think the two of you understand what's involved here. It's not a one-two-three process. I can't do it. You need to go to the *Beit Din* in Kfar Saba."

"Can't Kobi do that?"

"He can get it started, but chances are that they're going to ask the two of you to try for reconciliation."

"What does that mean?" Lisa asked warily.

"Go for counseling to try and save the marriage."

"I did nothing wrong," Lisa declared. "Kobi's the one who needs counseling. I need a *get*!"

Rav Yehezkel's eyes were compassionate. "Kobi's willing to give you one. But the *Beit Din* will ask him if he wants to try to fix the marriage. You know he wants to make it up to you, so if he says no he'd be lying."

"Let him lie." Lisa's voice was belligerent. "He owes me that."

"She's right, Yehezkel," Miriam interjected. "The best way he can make it up to Lisa is to give her a *get*."

Her husband settled his chin in his hands as he mulled over her words.

"And what's going to prevent him from disappearing again?" Miriam continued. "If he can't handle Lisa's resentment — legitimate, of course." She gave her friend a reassuring nod. "Or if there's, G-d forbid, another crisis."

The *rav* sat silently, lost in thought. Finally he spoke. "I hear what you're saying, Miriam. I need to think this over and talk with my *rosh yeshiva*. The *Beit Din* won't be open now until after Purim. One way or the other, I'll call to make an appointment first thing Monday morning."

"Thank you." Lisa closed her eyes with relief.

The *rav* smiled. "In the meantime, I suggest you do a lot of praying."

Lisa's prayer book had become dog-eared from all its use the last seven and a half months. She turned to it over and over again during the following days, unsure of what would happen with the *Beit Din*. Kobi came back to Kfar Yonatan for Shabbat, apparently sleeping and eating at the yeshiva. He came to the house Friday night to read Shuki a bedtime story and took him to the playground Shabbat afternoon. On Purim, Shuki sat happily next to him for both Megillah readings. Lisa didn't know where Kobi was for the meal and she didn't ask.

Later that evening, when all the Purim mess had been straightened up and she was getting Shuki into his pajamas, he told her that his father was staying at Aunt Riki's.

"Why isn't Abba staying here?" he asked his mother in a whiny voice. "Did you ask him?"

Shuki nodded, pushing her hand away as she tried to help him snap his top.

"And what did he say?" Lisa prodded.

"That he has to fix some things before he can stay here."

"So," Lisa took a deep breath, "that's your answer."

"When will he get things fixed?" Shuki persisted.

"You're going to have to ask your Abba." Lisa's calm voice belied the tension his questions created. "Now pick out a story and I'll tuck you into bed."

That tension was just as strong the following morning as she opened the store. What had Rav Yehezkel decided? How would his conversation with the *Beit Din* go? The phone rang during the midmorning lull and Lisa lunged for it, expecting to hear Rav Yehezkel on the other end. Instead, she was rewarded with Riki's upbeat voice.

"So," she asked, "how did Shabbat go with my brother?"

"Uh, I didn't see much of him."

"No?" Riki was surprised. "He feels so bad that I thought you'd be able to patch things up."

There was silence from Lisa as she wondered what in the world she could say to her sister-in-law.

"You know, his old job took him back." Although she didn't continue with "why can't you," Lisa heard the implied rebuke and cringed. "He's staying with us, but I hope it won't be for long. We're going to need the guest room soon."

Lisa couldn't help but smile at that comment. After five years of marriage, Riki and Efraim were finally starting a family and they were telling the world. If all was well, though, they wouldn't need the guest room for another eight months.

Riki continued with her monologue to tell Lisa that Kobi was barely home. "All I have to worry about is having coffee and milk on hand. And I do his laundry. Someone has to do it. You should know, Lisa, that he feels terrible about leaving you."

"Yes, so you told me." Lisa thought she managed to keep the cynicism out of her voice. "Riki, I've got to go. A customer just walked in."

No one had actually entered the store, but Lisa was desperate to hang up. A few minutes later, someone did enter the store. It wasn't a customer, though, but rather Rav Yehezkel.

"I made an emergency appointment with the *Beit Din* for Wednesday morning. I spoke to my *rosh yeshiva* and he told me to listen to you. He had a similar situation last year, advised counseling, and half a year later the husband skipped out and the wife is an *agunah* again." Yehezkel hesitated. "If, though, during the next two days, you have any misgivings and decide you want to try to make a go of it, let me know."

"I don't see how I would ever be able to trust him again." Lisa shook her head sadly.

"I understand." Rav Yehezkel's voice conveyed only sympathy. "As hard as it is right now, try to remember that Hashem will make everything work out in the end."

CHAPTER

Fifty-five

"Lisa," Sondra's voice was a bit louder than a whisper, "how'd it go yesterday?"

"I've got my *get*." Lisa was matter-of-fact. "What time is it there?"

"I just finished Mimi's midnight feeding and I thought it'd be quiet at the store. I've been thinking about you all day. Did it go smoothly?"

"From what Rav Yehezkel said, I think so. I have custody of the children and Kobi has unlimited visiting rights. I also have the house and the car."

"They didn't give him anything?" Sondra was surprised.

"He took half the bank account, remember?" Lisa sounded weary.

"I do remember." Sondra rose from her easy chair in the den. "I'm glad the *Beit Din* took that into consideration."

"Yeah." Lisa sighed. "How are things there? What's doing with the move?"

"I'm at the sorting stage, what to put in the lift, what in the suitcases, what to get rid of."

"I guess you're doing Pesach at the same time."

"More or less, but I want to know what's going on with you. Are you relieved everything from the *Beit Din* is behind you?"

"Yeah."

"But?"

Lisa sighed again. "I hope I did the right thing."

"Of course you did." Sondra said firmly. "Kobi could pick up and take off again, and then where would you be?"

"I know, but some people think I should have tried for reconciliation for the children's sake."

"Maybe you'll still have reconciliation. If Kobi can prove that he truly regrets what he did and you feel you can trust him, you can remarry. He's not a *kohen*." Sondra hoped she sounded comforting.

"Well, he's done some changing. He spends his days at work and his evenings at a *kollel*. He calls every day and talks to Shuki. He's still going for counseling. He was in Kfar Yonatan again last Shabbat and I understand he's coming this one too. He brought me a bouquet when he came the last time."

"Anemones?" Sondra asked.

"How'd you know?"

"They're your favorite flower."

"Yeah."

Sondra heard the ambivalence in her cousin's voice. "Take your time, Lisa," she said gently.

"I will." Lisa sighed again. "Gilit is stirring. I should hang up before she begins crying."

"Okay. I'm so looking forward to seeing you in two and a half months."

"Me too."

Kobi was back in Kfar Yonatan the following day and brought another bouquet to Lisa right before candle lighting. He returned after the meal to tell Shuki a bedtime story, and afterwards, joined Lisa on the front porch.

By now it wasn't so difficult to remember what had first attracted her to Kobi. His eyes didn't look as defeated as they had when he first arrived. There was more confidence in his bearing and she caught glimpses of his sense of humor and sensitivity to her emotions.

He was full of concern for how the past seven months had been. Lisa tried to answer his questions without sarcasm or bitterness. She, in turn, asked nothing about his life in Payson. Instead, she questioned him about the *kollel*.

"I think the only way to combat my loss of *emunah* is to learn. Obviously I can't go to yeshiva full time, but I can learn in the evenings."

"I have to admit I envy all my friends who went to seminary."

"Lisa," he looked at her seriously, "with your self-discipline and determination, you know more than some women who spent years in Beit Yaakov."

"Well," she smiled, "maybe the ones who weren't good students." The compliment pleased her, though.

Natan and Myra strolled by and stopped to say hello. There was no expression of the rancor they'd felt toward Kobi when he'd disappeared. Still, Lisa knew her friends were there for her no matter what happened with her ex-husband.

After they left, Kobi and Lisa sat in silence. Lisa so loved the peace of Shabbat in Kfar Yonatan. There were no sounds of traffic and loud music. Instead, there was the singing of the boys coming from the *rosh yeshiva*'s house and the wind whistling through the trees. Sitting next to Kobi and dealing with all her conflicting emotions about him made her uncomfortable, though. Finally he said goodbye and she felt relief.

On Saturday night, when both Shuki and Gilit were asleep, Miriam came over. Ever since she'd told Lisa of Kobi's phone call, she came over as usual, to borrow books or sugar and to take Lisa to Israeli dancing, but she asked no probing questions. Tonight was no different. She'd come for Lisa's cordless vacuum cleaner. "I'm going to get started on the Pesach cleaning tonight, no matter what," she declared.

Lisa smiled, moving her laundry basket out of the way so Miriam could pass by. "This house will be cleaned of *chametz*, but I'm not doing any spring cleaning this year. Every spare minute I have needs to be at the store."

Lisa spoke lightly, but she was concerned. Each year the store took up most of her energy before Pesach. In the past, Kobi had been there to help out. Now she was alone, and she had an infant to take care of, besides.

She looked up from the laundry basket at her friend. "I'm so glad you're having us for Seder."

"I wanted to talk to you about that," Miriam said. "Don't worry," she soothed, seeing Lisa's concerned expression. "We're all set for you to come. What I wanted to know is, um…"

"Yes?"

"How do you feel about us also having Kobi at the Seder?" Miriam's words came out in a rush, as if she couldn't wait to have them said.

Lisa blushed to the roots of her hair. "It's your house. You can have whoever you want," she answered slowly.

"I know that." Miriam waved her hand impatiently. "I want to know how you feel. Would you like it or would it be uncomfortable for you?"

Lisa sighed. How she wished she didn't have to make any decisions concerning Kobi. Just let Miriam decide what she wanted to do. Yet she appreciated her friend's consideration.

"I guess," she answered thoughtfully, "it would be good for Shuki to have his father at his side at the Seder."

"Okay," Miriam decided. "We'll invite him." She made no mention of how Lisa had sidestepped an explanation of her feelings on the matter.

Two days later, both the yeshiva and the *kollel* began their Pesach break. Wednesday afternoon, Kobi called to say he would be on the six-thirty bus to help with Pesach preparations. Lisa was tempted to tell him that she could manage fine by herself, but the truth was that she didn't know if she could. As soon as he arrived, she handed him a list and left for the store. He returned the following evening, ready for another set of instructions.

Myra and Natan invited him for Shabbat. They asked Lisa if she and the children would still come Friday night and Lisa said yes. Tears flowed down her cheeks as she watched Kobi give Shuki and Gilit their blessings.

By Shabbat HaGadol, she realized that the community had accepted the fact that Kobi was back. She also perceived that they all knew he was courting her. No one, though, herself included, had any idea how she was going to react to his courtship.

On Erev Pesach, Kobi stopped by the store right before Lisa locked up.

"Would you like to go on an outing the first day of Chol HaMoed?" he suggested. "The four of us could go to Sebastia after you're done at work and have a picnic there."

Lisa's gut reaction was to say no, but then she thought of Shuki. All of his friends would be going on outings with both their parents.

"I guess so," she answered, somewhat ungraciously.

Later at the Seder, she tried to avoid eye contact with Kobi, but she couldn't help thinking about the first time she'd met him at Sondra's Seder in LA. What would her life be like now if she hadn't accepted her cousin's invitation? It was impossible to imagine and she didn't even want to try. Despite all the pain he'd caused her, they'd had more than six very good years together.

The store was only open for three hours in the mornings during Chol HaMoed. Lisa returned home the first day to discover that not only had Kobi kept the children happy, but he'd also packed the lunch, diapers, and changes of clothes. All she had to do was get into the car.

There were just a few other families at the ancient ruins. After they'd finished eating their picnic lunch, Shuki scampered on the rocks. Baby Gilit fell asleep on the blanket and Kobi turned to Lisa.

"Can I tell you about my time in Payson?" he asked hesitantly.

Lisa nodded, her heart hammering.

"I don't want to make excuses, but I want you to understand that I wasn't myself." He repeated the story of Motti and the psychiatrist. Lisa wrapped her arms around herself protectively, drawn in despite herself. "I know I hurt you and Shuki, but I also hurt myself. I…I almost tried to end it."

Lisa swallowed hard. "Are you serious?"

Kobi nodded as he handed her a cup of juice. "You should drink. I went for lots of hikes among the Ponderosa pines. There were some steep ravines, and sometimes it just seemed like it would be a good idea to jump and join Uri and Avi." He lowered his gaze, fixing it on the pebbles he was sifting through his fingers.

"What kept you from jumping?" Lisa whispered.

"I'm not sure. Maybe I still had enough respect for the mitzvot that I couldn't do it. Maybe I was too scared. Or maybe I realized that it would be the ultimate way to hurt you, and I didn't want to hurt you. I think the reason I chose Payson was because of all the good memories I had of being there with you. You don't know how many times I tried to call you."

Lisa gave him a skeptical look.

"Really." Kobi's eyes met hers almost defiantly. "I'd save up piles of change and practice how I was going to apologize to you, while I walked to the pay phone at the courthouse. Once the phone started ringing, though, I'd panic and hang up."

"So that was you."

Kobi hung his head. "I was too ashamed to even say hello."

Lisa didn't know what to say. "How's the counseling going?" she finally asked.

"It's helping." Kobi spoke slowly. "I'm beginning to believe that even if I'd gone on the hike, I wouldn't have been able to protect Avi. The doctor's cut back on my medication and I hope eventually I'll be able to go off it totally. I'm sorry I didn't go for help when you first asked me to. It would have saved us both a lot of heartache."

While Lisa was waking up in Kfar Yonatan on that first day of Chol HaMoed, Sondra was lighting candles for the second night of *yom tov* in Phoenix. She took a moment to contemplate their light, and then made a mad dash into the kitchen. Carmen, the cleaning lady, had come in that morning while she and the children had gone to shul. She'd straightened the house, washed all the dishes from the first night's Seder, and swept up all the matzah crumbs that could be removed with a broom. Seven hours had passed since she'd left and there was plenty to straighten up all over again. And now there was the food to warm up, lunch dishes to wash, and the table to set.

Last night, when they'd settled around the table for the first Seder, it had seemed as if the whole house shone. Now, well, Sondra comforted herself with the thought that this was the last time she'd have to worry about making a second Seder. *What a feeling of freedom*, she thought with a smile. Still, she didn't have much enthusiasm for this second Seder. She was anxious for the following night, when she'd be able to place an overseas call to her cousin.

Like Lisa's friends in Kfar Yonatan, Sondra was full of concern over how Lisa was handling Kobi's return and if she would ever forgive him. Danny, of course, was sure his friend had done sincere repentance. Sondra was waiting, though. If Lisa forgave him, she would too. If Lisa didn't forgive him, well, he'd have no need of Sondra's forgiveness.

CHAPTER

Fifty-six

"Sondra, honey, we need to go," Danny said.

"Oh," Sondra groaned, "just two more minutes?"

"Take five," Doc said, smiling kindly.

"Thank you," she smiled back, but her father-in-law didn't see. She was already down the hall on her way through the bedrooms, saying goodbye to their home in Phoenix. The house was empty and the new owners were moving in the following week, but now it was still full of her memories.

She'd had her share of goodbyes this last month. It began with the poolside farewell party Bayla made on Lag B'Omer. In the end, the party wasn't just for the Kleins. Tova and Yaacov were returning to Beersheva, and Debbie and Shraga were also leaving Phoenix.

"I can't believe you won't be here when we come visit!" Sondra had been shocked when her friend Debbie confided that Shraga had accepted an excellent job offer in Silver Spring.

"You're the one who told me we'd be leaving in a year or two," Debbie had reminded her.

They had their last get-together three days after Shavuos.

"I'm going to miss you so much," Sondra confessed. "You'll write me like you used to, right?"

"I hope so," Debbie answered. "Those days of having plenty of time to write are long gone, but we have to stay in touch. You'll write me too?"

"Of course! But your letters were always so much better than mine."

"You'll have such adventures to write about!"

"I got you a present." Sondra held out a thick package of aerograms.

"This is great!" Debbie hugged them to her chest.

"I'll let you know every time I'm going to visit my parents and maybe we can meet in Kansas."

"Oh, that would be really wonderful!" Debbie blinked back tears and the two women hugged each other tightly. Sondra thought it would be her hardest goodbye in Phoenix, but she hadn't reckoned with the parting from Shirley.

After leaving their home, Doc drove them to his townhouse, where they'd spend their last night before flying out the following morning. Due to the excitement, none of the children had an easy time falling asleep. Sondra was especially blurry-eyed the next morning. Apparently Shirley hadn't slept well either and was irritable even after her cigarette and cup of coffee. Sondra hadn't realized how irritable until they were at the airport and walking to their gate. Shirley placed a hand on Sondra's shoulder and pulled her back from the others.

"I hope you know," she whispered fiercely, "that you're breaking our hearts by taking our grandkids away from us."

Sondra had clamped her mouth shut to keep from responding with an angry retort. Plenty flew through her mind, though.

Why are you telling me and not your son?

What about the last five years we stayed in Phoenix for you?

Aren't you glad you have grandchildren in Chicago?

Instead, she managed a mumbled, "I'm sorry."

She really thought Shirley had come to terms with their move. She'd taken each of the children shopping, one at a time, to buy them a special toy to take with them. And she'd thoughtfully bought a collection of books for Sondra so she'd have English reading material in Israel. Was her comment the result of a bad mood or did she really harbor bitter feelings toward her daughter-in-law?

Sondra resolved not to breathe a word about Shirley's comment to Danny, but she thought of little else during the two-hour flight to Kansas. She was glad she was out when Shirley called Lincoln that evening.

The Kleins spent a bittersweet week in Sondra's childhood home saying goodbye to all the relatives, as well as to Sondra's memories. For years she'd wanted to move her family to Israel, but when the time came to part from her parents at the Wichita airport, tears welled up in her eyes. As she kissed her mother and father goodbye one more time, she felt tremendously guilty. How could she take their only grandchildren to the other side of the world?

Once on board the plane to Kansas City, the tears overflowed and didn't stop until they landed fifty minutes later. With just an hour to make their connecting flight, they scurried through the airport. Running to the gate, Sondra had no more time for tears. Besides, she reminded herself as she hurried her children along, they were the reason she was making the move. They were her future, not her parents. By the time they landed in JFK, she was calm.

They had a three-hour layover that was decidedly hectic with claiming and rechecking their baggage, getting seat assignments, and making sure none of the children wandered away. When Sondra returned from taking the girls for their last bathroom stop, she saw Danny at a pay phone with Zvi Chaim and Yossi at his side. He smiled at her as he hung up.

"One more goodbye to my parents," he reported. "They wanted to talk to you, but I didn't see you'd returned. They send their love."

"Thanks," Sondra said, smiling back. What a relief not to have had to speak to Shirley. Once in Israel, they wouldn't have a phone, so it might be months before she'd have to talk to her mother-in-law. With that comforting thought, she concentrated on settling her family on the plane.

* * *

After a long flight and several even longer hours in Ben Gurion Airport filling out forms, the Kleins were finally in a van on their way to the Absorption Center in Mevasseret Tzion. Danny sat in the front with the driver from the Jewish Agency, who kept a running conversation going, while Sondra sat in the back with the children, dazed from exhaustion and unable to believe they'd finally made it happen. They'd moved to Israel!

"Ima, I'm thirsty," Naomi complained.

"I'm hungry," Zvi Chaim announced.

"Didn't you have enough sweets in the airport?" Sondra asked him wearily, wondering where Danny got all his energy from.

"That was hours ago."

"When are we going to get there?" Yossi whined.

"It's just a few minutes away," Sondra answered, as they passed Ein Hemed.

Indeed, less than ten minutes later, the driver announced, "Here we are!" He exited the highway, passed a wooded playground, and made a left turn at a sign welcoming them to the Absorption Center. Soon they were pulling up in front of the office.

"Can we get out?" Zvi Chaim begged.

"Sure!" Danny was charged with adrenalin.

The whole family trooped into the office, where a middle-aged man sat at the front desk, the phone to his ear. After a few minutes of waiting, a tall woman emerged from the end of the hall. She took off her glasses and gave them a scrutinizing once-over as she welcomed them.

"You must get back into the van," she spoke in heavily accented English. "We'll drive to your villa."

The "villa" was a one-story duplex that smelled of fresh paint and cleaning supplies.

"Here," the woman pointed to the table in the large living room, "you have new dishes, silverware, glasses, and a chair for each of you." There were even new plastic plates and bowls for little Mimi.

"And here's the kitchen." The woman led them into a tiny room that held two gas burners and a small refrigerator.

"The freezer is about big enough for one box of ice cream," Zvi Chaim exclaimed.

"The grocery store is right behind you," the woman continued. "It's open from seven until two every day and from four until six, except Tuesdays and Fridays. Let me show you the bedrooms."

There were three of them, each with two beds, plus a crib in what would be the girls' room. Piled on each bed were white linens, a pillow, and a blanket.

"You must go to the office tomorrow and sign that you received all of this and that everything is in good condition," she instructed. "This," she pointed to the red switch on the wall, "is your connection for the hot water heater. You won't need to have it on for more than three hours a day. It's been on already for two hours so you'll have hot water." She shook her finger sternly at Sondra, "It uses a lot of electricity, so don't forget to turn it off."

Sondra nodded obediently as Danny and the driver unloaded the van and piled their six suitcases, twelve boxes, and seven carry-on bags in the living room, which no longer seemed so large. She couldn't help contrasting the whitewashed walls and the stone tile floor with the wallpaper and wall-to-wall carpeting they'd had in Phoenix.

"Okay." The woman put her hands on her hips. "Do you have any questions?"

Sondra couldn't come up with any, but she was so tired, she could barely think.

"Good," the woman said. "I stayed overtime to wait for you, so I'm taking off now. I'll be by to check on you tomorrow."

She and the driver left, leaving them alone.

"Where do we start?" Sondra fought a feeling of panic.

"I guess we should unpack pajamas and start baths," Danny suggested.

"I'm hungry," Zvi Chaim reminded his mother.

"Me too!" the other children echoed.

"Me too," Sondra agreed. "Danny, can you open up that box marked *kitchen*?"

"What are we having?"

"Tuna and crackers." Sondra ignored the disappointed looks on her children's faces and began rummaging through the box. She'd just found the can opener when there was a knock on the door and Danny answered it.

"I've been watching for you and then I had to pick up my daughter and I guess that's when you snuck in, but this is for you."

Curious, Sondra set down the can opener and came to see who was at the door and what she had for them. A rather heavyset woman with a blue headscarf and a wide smile was holding a large pot and a loaf of bread.

"Hi, I'm Rochel. Welcome to the *merkaz klitah*. May I set this down in your kitchen?"

"Sure," Sondra smiled, showing her left dimple and feeling decidedly more cheerful than she'd felt a few minutes earlier. "I'm Sondra. Thank you!"

"It's a pareve soup. No buggy vegetables, just potatoes, carrots, squash, sweet potatoes, and barley. I checked the barley well. You're probably famished and exhausted. We were when we came."

"How long have you been here?"

"Two months. We're from Baltimore. And you?"

"Phoenix."

"Wow, that's exotic. Well, I don't want to keep you. Eat up and get some sleep. I'm right across the way if you need anything."

"Thank you," Sondra repeated. She was smiling as she closed the door. Getting everyone fed, bathed, and into bed seemed less daunting than it had five minutes earlier.

She'd just placed her bowl of soup on the table when there was another knock at the door. This time Sondra opened it, and as she did, she let out a squeal.

"Lisa!"

The children jumped up from their chairs. Yossi knocked his over in the excitement and everyone gathered at the doorway. Lisa and Sondra were locked in an embrace with Gilit held between the two of them. Shuki stood shyly in the doorway, half hidden by his mother's skirt.

"Shuki, remember me?" Zvi Chaim was down on his knees.

Shuki nodded and allowed his cousins to lead him into the living room. Soon their mothers followed.

"Sit down, everyone," Danny suggested. He took the seventh bowl into the kitchen and filled it for Lisa and Shuki to share.

"You don't need to feed me," Lisa exclaimed. "Shuki, where's the cake?"

"By the door."

"And I have a box of some staples you'll need in the car," Lisa explained as she ran for the cake. "Oh, it's so good to have you here! You're coming to Kfar Yonatan for Shabbat, right?"

Sondra hesitated before answering, "Don't you think that will be too much for you?"

"Absolutely not." Lisa set the cake on the table, smiling. "I already have a house lined up for you and I started cooking last month. Right, Shuki?"

The little boy nodded his head.

"We'd love to come," Danny said decisively.

CHAPTER

Fifty-seven

"So, how's the *merkaz klitah*?" Lisa asked. It was Shabbat afternoon and the two cousins were settled comfortably on her living room couch in Kfar Yonatan.

"I think it will feel like home soon." Sondra hoped she sounded confident and not full of false bravado. After four days, they'd unpacked all their suitcases and boxes, but nothing felt like it was in its place yet. Maybe it would after their lift arrived.

Zvi Chaim and Batsheva had joined the children's activities at the absorption center enthusiastically and already found a group of English-speaking friends. Both Naomi and Yossi had balked at their programs, though. Sondra wondered if she'd be able to talk them into staying Sunday morning. Of course, Mimi stayed in the "villa" with her, helping her get organized.

Now Mimi and Gilit were sleeping, and the older children had gone out to see their playmates from two summers before. Kobi had come by, and he and Danny had taken the younger ones to the playground so their mothers could finally talk uninterrupted.

"Tell me how things are working out here," Sondra said. "Kobi doesn't look at all like the pathetic man who came to our house before Purim."

Lisa nodded slowly. "He's back in Kfar Yonatan full time, sleeping at the yeshiva and learning there in the evenings. He's still working, and he's returned most of the money he took from our joint account."

"That's good."

"Uh-huh. He's cutting down on his medication with his doctor's supervision and still going for counseling every week. He sees the kids every day."

"You too?"

Lisa nodded.

"And?"

"It's hard, Sondra. He's so apologetic. It's like he'll do anything to make it up to me. And, well, I kind of feel like I'm taking advantage of him."

"Like how?"

"Like I told him since I'm no longer part of his family, there was no reason for me to go to the family reunion they have every year on Yom HaAtzmaut. I wanted to go on Elisheva's hike, especially since this year she was making it into a memorial for Avi after the service at the cemetery. And I said we'd discuss who should take Shuki." Lisa took a long sip of her juice.

"So?"

"Kobi decided to go on the hike."

"I see." Sondra drummed her fingers on the side of her glass thoughtfully. "It was probably good for him to be at the memorial, though, wasn't it?"

"Sure, but he did it because of me. It's like it's all one-sided now."

"Well, he hurt you a lot."

"I'll say," Lisa exclaimed. "But you know, he hurt himself even more."

"Are you going for counseling too?" Sondra asked.

Lisa blushed. "Kind of. I've been talking to Rav Yehezkel a lot."

"Is it helpful?"

"I think so."

They sat in silence, a comfortable silence.

"I haven't told you," Lisa finally spoke, "Miriam's cousin made *aliyah* last month. He's in Ra'anana. He's divorced, no children, and I met him when he was here for Shabbat."

"Yeah?" Sondra sat forward eagerly.

"He wanted to go out with me."

"Are you going to?" Sondra's eyes lit up.

"I already did. Miriam and the *rav* encouraged me."

"And?" Sondra moved to the dining room table, ostensibly to fill up her glass of juice, but truthfully, she couldn't sit still.

"We have so much in common! He grew up in St. Louis, drove through Kansas a few times, knows Arizona. He took me out for dinner to a really nice place and we had so much to talk about."

"Sounds wonderful!" Sondra returned to her seat with a warm smile. "Did you go out again?"

"Yes." Lisa hesitated.

"What's wrong?"

"I keep comparing him to Kobi," Lisa whispered.

"And?" Sondra asked with a sinking feeling in her stomach.

"He doesn't make my heart sing." Sondra had to lean in close to her cousin to hear her soft answer.

"And Kobi still does?"

Tears trickled down Lisa's face. "I don't want him to. I want to close the door on him so he'll never be able to hurt me again, but I can't."

"Oh, Lisa!" Sondra put her arms around her cousin and let her sob.

"Do you remember when Tim dumped me?" she sniffled.

Did Sondra remember!

"I thought my life was over and I'd never get over him, but I did. Why can't I get over Kobi?"

Sondra took her time to form an answer.

"I think," she finally uttered the words that she'd wanted to say in Lisa's dorm room years ago, "your relationship with Tim was a leftover high school romance that didn't have much substance. He rejected you and you were able to get over it. But you and Kobi built a mature, solid marriage and," Sondra didn't want to give Kobi any credit, but she felt compelled to be honest, "it was a good marriage for the most part. He didn't reject you. He just didn't know how to deal with all his problems so he ran away from them, not from you. Plus, he's the father of your children."

Lisa thought over her cousin's words. "Everyone here knows he wants us to remarry, but I don't know. I...I don't know if I'll ever be able to forgive him, really forgive him with my heart, not just my head, 'cause I do forgive him with my head."

"Oh, Lisa," Sondra repeated. "I'm so sorry."

Lisa wiped her eyes and took a deep breath. "If only he could push a magic button and show me that he'll never go off the deep end again. That I can trust him never to abandon us even if the going gets rough."

Sondra wrung her hands, wishing she had some words of wisdom.

Lisa fingered the design on the couch and continued, "We learn that we never know if our *teshuvah* is complete until we're in the same situation we were in when we committed the sin and we can refrain from doing it again. This is kind of the same, but I don't want someone to have to die to see if Kobi's going to have a setback and run away."

"I'm so sorry you have to go through all this."

Lisa took a deep breath and wiped away another tear rolling down her cheek.

Sondra grabbed her cousin's hands tightly. "You know, this will work out, and in the end we'll be able to see it was all for the best."

"Yes, I know," Lisa took a deep breath. "I really do believe that Hashem is looking out for me. I just wish it was easier to know what I should do."

❀ ❀ ❀

Lisa remembered that conversation the following week when Riki made an early morning phone call to the store.

"There's no easy way to say this," her sister-in-law announced, "but Aunt Tirza died last night."

"*Baruch Dayan HaEmet*," Lisa said softly. She'd always liked Kobi's great-aunt, who was so glad her great-nephew was observant.

"Yeah, well, she'd been really weak this last year. It was time. Anyway, the funeral's today at four and I thought Kobi should know. No one called him last night. The pay phone at the yeshiva's always busy and he doesn't have a home with a real phone. Can you tell him?"

"I guess so." Lisa didn't even bother to ask why Riki couldn't call her brother's work number herself.

As she placed the call, she resolved that she would find a sitter for Shuki and go to the funeral with Gilit. She told Kobi of her plans.

"I'll get a ride to the funeral with Riki, but would you be able to drive me back to Kfar Yonatan afterwards?" he asked, his voice tentative. Reluctantly, she agreed.

When she arrived at the funeral, Kobi's family greeted her warmly and, too late, she realized that by coming, she was giving a message that she had no intention of giving. So instead of going back to the shivah house after the service, she decided to visit Cousin Leah and her family at their nearby kibbutz. It had been a while since she'd been there, and they were pleased to see her, extracting a promise from her to come back with Sondra and all the children.

As arranged, Kobi was waiting for her outside the shivah house an hour later.

"I'm tired," she told him. "Can you drive?"

"Was Gilit up a lot last night?" Kobi was concerned.

"The usual," Lisa answered shortly.

Kobi was glad to take over the steering wheel. He'd always loved driving, but since his return, he'd never even hinted at borrowing the car. Lisa never suggested that he do so either.

"Everyone appreciated that you came for the funeral," he said on the long drive home.

"Even though we're no longer married," Lisa replied crisply, "she was my aunt for a while and I really liked her."

"Don't you think we could change that?" Kobi asked softly.

"Change what?"

Kobi pulled over to the shoulder of the road. Turning off the motor, he faced her.

"Lisa," his voice was hoarse, "please, you see I'm better. I'll never let you down again. Please marry me again."

Lisa swallowed the lump in her throat. "How can I ever trust you again?"

"I care so much about you. I'll never hurt you on purpose."

"You cared about me before and you hurt me. You hurt me big time!" All of a sudden it felt good to let Kobi know the extent of her hurt. "You abandoned Shuki and me when I was pregnant with your child!" she shouted, her fists clenched. "How do you think I felt going to give birth and not even knowing if you were alive or dead? Do you have any idea what it felt like to have Rav Yehezkel name Gilit because her father had skipped out? Do you know how many questions Shuki asked about you? How many times he cried for you? How many excuses I made for you? How can I ever trust you again?"

Gilit, woken by the noise, began whimpering from her car seat. Lisa scrambled into the back to comfort her baby, ignoring the tortured look on Kobi's face. Once their daughter was calm and buckled back into her car seat, Lisa strapped herself in next to the baby. Kobi turned around and faced his ex-wife.

"I have no easy answers," he said. "All I can tell you is that you're the most important person in the world to me and I'm not going to give up on us. I'm going to continue counseling until you believe I'm all better. I'll wait until you're ready to trust me again. I'll wait for you forever."

Somewhere from the recesses of her mind, Lisa remembered once telling Tim, "I'll wait for you forever." She knew "forever" was a long time. Kobi took a deep breath and restarted the motor. They drove the rest of the way back in silence.

CHAPTER

Fifty-eight

"Lisa," Sondra stood outside the Absorption Center's office, clasping the pay phone and feeding special tokens into its hungry mouth, "I changed my mind. We do want to go with you to Cousin Leah's kibbutz."

"Great," Lisa answered. "What happened?"

When Lisa had first presented the idea, Sondra had adamantly refused to consider it. There was just too much to do: a bank account to open, health fund and National Insurance to sign up for, changing over their drivers' licenses, finding schools for the older children and registering them, to say nothing of unpacking and ulpan classes. Danny had started working a week after they'd arrived, so the bulk of the arrangements fell to Sondra.

"Everything's closing down next week for the whole month of August," Sondra moaned. "The day-care center, the nursery school, and the day camp. Everything!"

"I'm sorry," Lisa commiserated. "There'll be babysitters available, though."

"Maybe." Sondra spoke quickly as she dropped yet another token into the phone. "You said there's a swimming pool at the kibbutz?"

"Olympic-size, separate hours, and a lifeguard. We haven't been yet this summer, but we went once last year."

"Sounds wonderful! Can we go right after Tishah B'Av?"

"I'll check with Elisheva. If she can take care of the store, we're on. Meet you at nine-thirty at the Alligator Farm?"

"Love you!" Sondra hung up, grateful for their new van. She walked back to their villa, enjoying the night air and the fact that she felt perfectly safe walking by herself in the dark.

Two weeks later, Lisa was packing up her car in anticipation of their outing. Among the snacks, changes of clothes, swimsuits, and suntan lotion were Shuki's floaters. Unlike his cousins from Phoenix, the four-year-old didn't know how to swim. Lisa decided he'd have his first swimming lesson that day. Shuki was so excited about seeing his cousins and going to the pool that he didn't complain once as they sat in the parking lot of the Alligator Farm, waiting a good ten minutes for Sondra to drive up.

"I got lost leaving the *merkaz klitah*," she said sheepishly. "I guess you know the directions from here?"

"Straight on the Jordan Valley Highway until we reach the turnoff to the kibbutz," Lisa announced. She unbuckled Gilit's car seat and moved her into Sondra's van. Sondra helped her transfer Shuki, and Zvi Chaim got out to help with the bags.

"Can we see the alligators?" he begged.

"Maybe on the way back," his mother agreed, "if we're not too tired."

"We'll be too tired." The almost nine-year-old kicked at the gravel before he got into the van.

"Just let me double-check that I locked the car," Lisa said.

"I need the bathroom," Batsheva announced.

"We're never going to get there," Zvi Chaim complained.

"Slow down," Sondra cautioned. "If you're going to be crabby, then we won't stay on for men's hours and you won't go swimming."

Zvi Chaim flashed his mother a look of pure resentment, but didn't say anything more. Lisa brought out her thermos of lemonade and poured drinks for all, while Sondra took Batsheva to the bathroom. She offered some to Sondra and Batsheva when they returned.

"I hope we won't have to make any more bathroom stops," Sondra said as she climbed into the driver's seat. "That certainly was not a clean one."

Lisa laughed. "Don't worry; it'll all be sparkling clean at the kibbutz."

The children sang and then listened to a story on the tape deck. In less than an hour they were at the kibbutz. Cousin Leah came running to greet them.

"Welcome, welcome," she called happily. "Look how you've grown." She hugged Shuki and then introduced herself to Sondra's children. "Come inside. I have treats for all of you."

"When we go swimming?" Naomi asked loudly.

"After a while," Sondra shushed her.

"Oh dear," Cousin Leah frowned. "You're going to be disappointed, I'm afraid. The lifeguard is sick."

"No pool?" Shuki's shoulders sagged in disappointment.

"Well, it may open after lunch. They're trying to find a substitute. How about a tour of the kibbutz now, and after lunch, we'll see?"

"That sounds lovely." Sondra frowned slightly at the youngsters to indicate that the new plan wasn't up for discussion.

Despite the overbearing heat of the Beit She'an Valley, it was a pleasant tour. Leah kept them on shaded paths and made them stop often for drinks.

Zvi Chaim perked up at the dairy barn, which was similar to his grandfather's farm, although on a much larger scale, and he was able to ask some questions in simple Hebrew. Batsheva loved the sewing room. Leah's daughter was in charge of the laundry and her husband worked with the chickens. Gilit and Mimi both conveniently fell asleep in their strollers as the group made their way to the kibbutz dining hall. The children looked around the huge room in fascination. Leah and her family helped them go through the line, cut their chicken, and got them seconds.

They were just finishing when one of the kibbutz members approached their table and informed Leah that a substitute lifeguard hadn't been found.

"I'm so sorry." Leah smiled sympathetically at the disappointed faces surrounding her. "How about I go to the kibbutz store and buy popsicles for everyone? Then we can go to the petting zoo."

"I want to go swimming," Shuki whined.

"What kind of animals are there?" Batsheva asked, pacified already.

"All sorts. Ducks, a peacock, different birds, a baby goat, and even a grumpy camel." Leah chuckled.

"That'll be fun," Lisa told Shuki, but he wasn't convinced.

At that moment, both Mimi and Gilit woke from their naps, crying to be fed.

"Okay." Leah had learned through the years the importance of flexibility. "Let's go back to the house where it's cool. You can feed your babies, I'll go get the popsicles, and then we'll go to the zoo."

Once in her little house, she settled the children with puzzles and turned on the record player. Easy Hebrew songs filled the sitting room.

"You two go into my room," she instructed. "I'll be back in a few minutes."

"I want to come in with you," Shuki complained to his mother.

"No, Shuki." Lisa forced herself to be patient. "You'll bother the babies. Yossi's waiting for you to help him with his puzzle."

"I want to go swimming," he said loudly to his mother's back.

She ignored him and settled herself on Leah's bed with Sondra at her side.

"It's really frustrating to try and make a nice day and have him throw it back in my face," Lisa fretted.

"Tell me about it." Sondra sighed. "I thought we were making a great move for Zvi Chaim, and, boy, has he become a champion grumbler."

"What're we supposed to do?"

"Be patient, I guess." Sondra took a deep breath.

Gilit was a quick eater, and in a few minutes Lisa was back out with the others.

"Where's Shuki?" she asked. None of the children responded.

Lisa checked her cousin's little yard, but Shuki wasn't there.

"Zvi Chaim, do you know where Shuki is?" she asked.

He looked up from the comic book he'd brought with him and shook his head.

There was no place in Leah's two-room house for the child to hide.

"Batsheva?" Lisa fought her worry. "Do you know where Shuki is?"

Not taking her eyes from the puzzle she was working on with her sister, Batsheva said no, but Naomi looked up.

"He went swimming."

"No!" Lisa gasped. "When?"

"Now."

"No!" Lisa shrieked. Without thinking, she set Gilit on the rug and tore out of the house in the direction of the pool. *Please, Hashem, please let him not remember the way. Please, Hashem, let the pool be locked. Please let me find him wandering around, hot and disappointed.*

As she prayed, she ran, the kibbutz homes blurring around her. Breathless, she reached the pool area in just two minutes, where, to her horror, she saw that not only was the gate unlocked, but it was also wide open.

"Shuki!" she screamed. Fear gripped her heart as she entered the gate. A quick glance at the pool showed that her son wasn't there. She would go back to the chicken coop. He'd been fascinated by it. Before she turned around, though, she took a second look, just to make sure.

And then she saw him. He was floating face down in the water. There was a blue tinge to his body.

"Shuki," she cried and grabbed the little body out of the water. She pressed her mouth on his and breathed. Then she pushed on him, just as she'd seen done in the movies. Breathe and push, breathe and push. As she breathed, she begged Hashem to save her son, as she pushed, she screamed for help. The screams came from the depth of her soul.

After what seemed like forever, help arrived at her side. One of the gardeners working nearby had heard her screams and come running. He was a medic and took over. In just a few seconds, she heard her little boy crying. He was alive.

In a matter of minutes, they were surrounded by a crowd of people. Someone called an ambulance. The gardener got in the back with

Shuki and, without a second thought, Lisa climbed in front next to the driver. As they left the gates of the kibbutz, she suddenly remembered Gilit. She knew she could count on Sondra to take care of her baby. Meanwhile, she wasn't going to leave Shuki. She moaned and hid her face in her hands. The driver gave her a compassionate look and handed her a small book of *Tehillim*. She took it from him and opened its pages.

CHAPTER

Fifty-nine

"Lisa?" Kobi said softly.

Startled, Lisa looked up from the *Tehillim* in her lap. "How'd you hear?" she asked him in a shaky voice.

"Sondra called me. She told me everything. How's Shuki?"

"He's alive, but...," Lisa's voice broke and she swallowed, regaining control, "they don't know yet if there's going to be any complications or brain damage."

Although Kobi's face paled, he kept his voice strong. "If there is, we'll deal with it."

"We will?"

"Yes, we will."

"Oh, Kobi." New tears coursed down Lisa's face. "I'm so sorry."

She was a mess. Her skirt had gotten wet when she'd pulled Shuki from the pool and was now covered with all sorts of grime. Her hair was slipping out from under her scarf and her face was tear-stained and streaked with dirt.

She'd followed the staff as they transferred her son from the ambulance to the Intensive Care Unit, but she wasn't allowed inside. Unable to bear the inquisitive glances and sympathetic attempts at conversation from the other parents in the waiting room, she'd found a hard bench outside the double doors leading to the Pediatric ICU. She still held tight to the *Tehillim* the driver had given her, but the letters kept blurring and she couldn't concentrate on the words.

"Will you ever forgive me?"

"Lisa." Kobi knelt down in front of her. "You didn't throw Shuki into the pool."

"I know." She hid her face with her hands. "But I wouldn't let him come into the room when Sondra and I were feeding the babies."

She took a deep breath. "I don't think I'll ever get the sight of how he looked when he was floating in the pool out of my mind," she moaned and continued. "I didn't know if he was dead or alive when I pulled him out!"

"That must have been terrifying."

"It was!" Lisa was touched by Kobi's empathy. She closed her eyes, trying to block out the horrifying picture.

"Why don't you go to the bathroom and clean up?" Kobi suggested.

"I'm not leaving Shuki!"

"Of course you're not," Kobi soothed. "You're just going to the bathroom. I'm here. I'm not leaving."

She hesitated.

"Go," he urged.

She went. It felt good to wash her face and fix her hair.

"How'd you get here?" she asked as she rejoined Kobi on the bench.

"My supervisor drove me to Alligator Farm, Natan met me there with the car keys, and I came. I guess Hashem wanted me here quickly because there wasn't any traffic. Let's pray He'll heal Shuki."

Lisa gave a halfhearted smile. Unable to sit still, Kobi rose and began pacing. Lisa fingered the *Tehillim* but didn't reopen it. Both were silent, wrapped up in their own tortured thoughts until a nurse came out to speak to them.

"Are you Yehoshua Chazon's parents?"

"Yes!" Lisa jumped up. Kobi froze. "What is it?"

"He's stable. One of you can come in."

"Just one?"

"I'm sorry. Hospital regulations."

"You go, Lisa," Kobi said. "You need to see him."

"So do you," Lisa mumbled, but she followed the nurse.

Shuki was awake and connected to all sorts of tubes. He began crying when he saw his mother.

"Ima, I want to go home," he whimpered.

"Soon, Shuki, I hope." Lisa took his hand and squeezed it.

"Okay." He closed his eyes and drifted back to sleep.

Lisa smoothed his hair and kissed his forehead.

"It's a good sign that he recognized you," the nurse said kindly.

"Can I send his father in now?"

"Sure."

Kobi had just gone in when Sondra appeared with Gilit in her stroller. "Leah and her girls are watching the others," she explained as she hugged her cousin. "I thought you'd want to see Gilit and maybe feed her."

Lisa held out her arms to her baby.

"What're they telling you?"

Lisa gave a brief rundown of the little she knew.

Sondra pulled a plastic basket out of the back of the stroller. "Here's a bag of food Leah arranged for you. She's been wonderful. She has the whole kibbutz praying for Shuki."

"That's good." Lisa gave a half smile. "Can you call Miriam and tell her to do the same at home?"

"Sure. Yehoshua ben Liba, right?"

Lisa nodded.

"Also," Sondra hesitated, "Leah's made arrangements for Gilit to stay in the baby house at the kibbutz tonight. Unless," she added quickly, "you want me to take her back with me. I'm happy to feed her and take care of her. It's up to you."

"I want her as close as possible," Lisa hugged her baby to her.

Sondra handed her a blanket so she could feed Gilit.

"Thank you for calling Kobi," Lisa said.

"I was hoping you wouldn't mind. Did he call?"

"He's here. He's in with Shuki."

"I'm glad to hear it."

A volunteer strolled by with a cart of snacks, drinks, and sandwiches. Lisa couldn't imagine swallowing anything, but she saw that they had Kobi's favorite sweet rolls and asked Sondra to take one for him. Sondra stayed by Lisa's side until Kobi finally came out of the double doors. He looked as if he might have been crying, but he was smiling now.

"Lisa, he woke up again and asked for food. They let me give him some juice." He noticed Sondra and nodded to her. "Sondra, thank you so much for calling me."

She acknowledged his appreciation awkwardly.

"Did you bring Gilit?" Kobi asked.

"Yes," Lisa spoke up, "she's right here. Sondra's taking her back to the kibbutz for the night."

"Why don't we have her sleep at my folks?"

Lisa's eyes grew big with panic. "Do they know what happened?"

"Not yet, but it's not something we can keep a secret."

"They're going to hate me," Lisa exclaimed.

"They're not going to hate you." Kobi stood his ground.

"Please don't tell them," Lisa begged.

Sondra cleared her throat. "Can I say something?"

Lisa and Kobi turned to her. "You know we're not supposed to keep secrets about health from our parents," Sondra said firmly. "Kobi's parents have to be told. They'll find out one way or another. This is such a small country, and it's better coming from you, right?"

Lisa fidgeted uncomfortably, remembering the advice she'd once given her cousin a lifetime ago in a hospital in LA.

"But maybe," Sondra continued more gently, "you can wait until the morning and see how Shuki's doing then."

Lisa looked at Kobi and he nodded reluctantly. They both hugged Gilit goodbye as Sondra prepared to leave.

"I'll jot down the phone numbers by the pay phones at the end of the hall," Sondra said. As soon as she and the stroller were out of sight, Lisa took her place by her son's side.

An hour later, Dr. Shimshon, the head of the department, wanted to speak to them. "It's looking good. I want to keep him on the monitors overnight and, if all goes well, we'll take him off all the tubes tomorrow morning."

"And then he can go home?" Kobi asked.

"Well," the doctor hedged, "we should probably keep him an extra day to make sure he doesn't come down with pneumonia. He swallowed a lot of water."

Lisa winced and Kobi began pacing.

"Things look good, though," the doctor repeated. "You have a lot to be thankful for. Is one of you going to sleep here tonight?"

"Can't we both?"

"Of course." The doctor smiled. "There's a parent's room with chairs that turn into beds, and the nurse will give you some linens. As long as your son's stable, you can visit him as much as you want during the night, one at a time."

They spent the next six hours taking turns sitting by Shuki's side and answering concerned calls at the pay phones from their friends in Kfar Yonatan, Cousin Leah, and Sondra. Finally, at about midnight, they joined the other parents in the special room, though it was doubtful that anyone there slept much.

At five in the morning, Lisa woke with a start, wondering why Gilit wasn't crying. Then she remembered where she was and what had happened. Quietly she got up, tiptoed out of the room, and made her way to Shuki.

Instead of seeing her son sleeping peacefully, though, she was greeted with a frenzy of activity. An oxygen mask was being held to his face by a harried nurse and two doctors were standing over him as machines beeped and lights flashed.

"We were going to call you as soon as he's stable," another nurse spoke up as she readied a syringe. "The doctor will be out to speak to you soon."

Shaking with fright, Lisa collapsed on the bench outside the ICU. For a second she debated calling Kobi, but was loath to leave the double doors. Burying her face in her hands, she begged Hashem to help her son. Several minutes later, she heard footsteps and looked up. Instead of the doctor, Kobi stood in front of her.

"Why aren't you sleeping?" he asked, disoriented.

"I came to check on Shuki and he was having some kind of emergency. Two doctors and a nurse were working on him!"

He sank down next to her, and with a trembling voice, Lisa described what she'd seen inside the ICU. Kobi closed his eyes, trying to absorb Lisa's words. It was a good half an hour before someone came out to speak to them.

It wasn't Dr. Shimshon, but this doctor spoke with as much authority. "Your son has fluid leaking into his lungs. We've heavily sedated him and he's on a special respirator. It's serious, but I'm optimistic. I suggest that you spend as much time as possible by his bedside, talking to him and telling him his favorite stories. He won't respond, but he'll hear you.

"And," he added gently, "it would be a good idea to do a lot of praying."

CHAPTER

"Anything new from your cousin this morning?" Rochel asked as her shopping cart almost bumped into Sondra's.

"No, and it's so frustrating having to rely on pay phones. I have less than an hour free between Danny getting home from shul — he's always later on Thursdays — and him leaving for the office. When I called the hospital before coming here, one pay phone was busy and the other just rang and rang. And if someone else had answered, I couldn't have left a message for Lisa to call back. Where's she supposed to call me? I can't stand next to the *merkaz klitah*'s pay phones all day."

"It's a problem," Rochel agreed. "You know, there's a legend that once there were phones in our 'villas,' but the Jewish Agency took them out because no one wanted to leave and move to permanent housing."

Sondra gave her neighbor a skeptical look.

"Really," Rochel insisted. "For us, these houses might be tiny, but for the Eastern Europeans, they're luxurious, especially the ones with a yard."

"I guess so," Sondra conceded. "I've got to get going. Danny has tomorrow off, and if they don't discharge Shuki by this evening, he wants to go up to the hospital and talk to the doctors. I'm doing all my cooking today and hope to line up a sitter so I can go with him. I need to see Lisa."

"Come to us for Shabbat lunch," Rochel suggested impulsively.

"Really?"

"Sure, it will be less on your head and we'd love to have you."

"Thanks! That sounds great!" Sondra smiled and hurried to the checkout lane.

Kobi, meanwhile, was on the phone, having an emotional conversation with his parents.

"The doctor says it's serious, but he's hopeful."

"Why didn't you call us yesterday?" Tzachi demanded gruffly.

Kobi took a deep breath. "Yesterday was just so tense and there was no time to think clearly. We thought Shuki would be coming home today or tomorrow. I planned to call you this morning, after we heard how he was doing. This new complication developed during the night. I called as soon as I was sure I wouldn't wake you."

"He's our grandson, Kobi. We want to know what's happening."

"Yes, Abba, I promise to tell you everything."

"How can we help?" Surprisingly, Shula interrupted from the extension. "Do you need us at the hospital?"

"That would be great." Kobi sighed with relief.

"Okay." Tzachi's voice was kinder. "I'll call Shimon to open up the store and we'll be on our way."

When they arrived, they found Lisa sitting on her hard bench. She lowered her eyes, unable to meet theirs. Shula sat down next to her and put her arms around her former daughter-in-law.

"I'm so sorry." Lisa began weeping.

"Shh, shh," Shula soothed. "Kobi told us all about it. You did nothing wrong."

Tzachi watched the scene uncomfortably and cleared his throat. "Can we see Shuki?"

"W-when Kobi comes out, one of you can go in," Lisa sniffled.

He came out of the double doors just a few minutes later and, after greeting his parents, headed downstairs to the hospital chapel to pray. Tzachi took his son's place next to Shuki and Lisa was left alone with Shula.

"I understand Gilit's at the kibbutz."

Lisa nodded, her eyes still lowered.

"You must want to feed her sometime this morning."

Lisa nodded again, this time with more enthusiasm.

"How about when Tzachi comes out, he takes us over there so you can feed her, take a hot shower, and get an hour's nap in a real bed in your cousin's house?"

"Oh, I couldn't leave Shuki," Lisa protested.

"You have two children to be concerned about," Shula said firmly. "You have to take care of yourself for their sake."

Lisa began weeping again.

Shula took her hand and patted it. "Feeling guilty won't do anyone any good."

Lisa just stared at her.

"You think I don't know what you're going through?" This was a different Shula from the meek, soft-spoken woman Lisa had always known. "Believe me, I know what guilt is. I lost a son, remember?"

"He was in the army," Lisa whispered.

"And how do you think he got into combat?"

"Like everyone else?"

"No." Shula's face was contorted with pain. "Uri could've had a job serving behind the scenes somewhere. His medical profile was low because he was born with a heart murmur, but he wanted to be on the front lines. When he was five, the heart specialist said his murmur was functional and he didn't need to go for any more checkups. Uri asked me for the doctor's letter in order to raise his profile. I should have..." Shula's voice trembled, "I should have told him I couldn't find it. I should have torn it up. But I didn't, and he went into battle and he died."

"Oh, Shula." Now Lisa patted the older woman's hand. "I'm so sorry."

"I knew then," Shula wiped at her eyes impatiently with her other hand, "that I could either try to make a normal home for Kobi and Riki or I could dwell on my guilt and lose all my children."

"You made the right decision." Lisa bit her lip nervously.

"So we'll leave Kobi in charge for an hour or two so you can take care of Gilit and yourself?"

"Kobi needs to sleep too."

"We'll take care of him next."

Later, after both of them had taken short naps and Shula was sitting with Shuki, Kobi pushed Lisa to call her parents. She groaned, knowing he was right, and made her way reluctantly to the pay phones.

He followed her over. "Do you want me to stay with you for moral support?"

"I guess so." She dialed the operator and recited the familiar number. On the fourth ring, she heard her father accept the reverse charges.

"Lisa, you're still by Cousin Leah?"

"Uh, no. How'd you know I was there?"

"I tried to call you at home and at the store. Your friend said you'd gone there."

"Yes." Lisa hesitated. "Why were you trying to call?" It was Thursday, not Sunday.

"Oh, honey, I'm sorry, but Mom's in the hospital."

Lisa moaned, her fingers tightening on the receiver. "What's wrong?"

"It's minor," her father reassured her quickly. "We thought at first she was having a heart attack, but it's an infection around the heart wall. She's on medication and should be coming home in a day or two. I just wanted you to know."

"Oh."

"So, tell me about your visit."

"It was really nice, Daddy."

Kobi stared hard at her and shook his forefinger. Lisa got the hint.

"Uh, Daddy, I'm not at the kibbutz. I — I didn't get your message. There was an accident with Shuki. Um, he's alive, but it's serious."

"Oh, no!" her father exclaimed, slipping into German. "What happened?"

Lisa took a deep breath and briefly explained the situation. "I'm so sorry, Daddy," she concluded. "You have enough to worry about now without this."

"No, we're under control here. Everything's going to be okay. You take care of Shuki." His voice broke. "I'm not going to tell your mother anything about this until she's feeling better. But," he took on his voice of authority, "I want you to call me every day at least once and tell me what's happening. I want to know every change, good or bad. I don't care whether it's the middle of the night or high daytime rates. You call me collect. Understand?"

"Yes, Daddy."

"Okay, you pray for Mom and I'll pray for Shuki. We'll get through this."

Although Sondra had gotten her Shabbat cooking done, she hadn't been able to speak to Lisa all day. It took every ounce of patience she had to entertain her children and fend off their questions about Shuki. As soon as Mimi woke up from her afternoon nap, Sondra loaded her in her stroller and took the younger ones out for a walk, with the goal of checking her post office box in the Absorption Center office. Her heart began beating quickly as she entered and spotted a pink message slip in number 157.

Grabbing for it, she saw immediately that it wasn't from Lisa or Kobi, but rather her parents. *Please call as soon as possible.* She read the panic between the lines and made a U-turn with the stroller.

"Zvi Chaim," she spoke quickly, "please, I need you to watch everyone at the playground while I make a phone call to Oma and Opa."

Zvi Chaim put down his comic book without complaint.

"Do you want me to come too?" Batsheva asked.

"That would be helpful." Ever since Shuki had disappeared the day before, her children had been on their best behavior. No one was even whining to talk to Oma and Opa.

As expected, only her mother was home, and Helga made no attempt to hide her distress.

"Since Aunt Irene is in the hospital, Uncle Herbert has not told her..."

"Aunt Irene's in the hospital?"

"It isn't that serious. It's being treated." Briefly, Helga explained what had happened. "If she knew Shuki's life is in danger, she would want to be on the first plane out."

"Shuki's life is in danger?" Sondra cried out, her hand flying to her throat.

"I thought you were there with them yesterday."

"I was, but —" Sondra began pacing as far as the short pay phone cord would allow her. "They said that as long as he didn't get pneumonia, he'd be going home in a day or two."

"Well, something new developed," Helga said. She repeated what Herbert had reported to her.

"Mom, listen." Sondra took a deep breath, forcing herself to stay calm. "Danny and I are going to the hospital tomorrow. I'll call as soon as I know anything."

CHAPTER

Sixty-one

No one was sitting on the hard bench outside the ICU when Sondra and Danny arrived at the hospital Friday morning. They found Lisa inside the waiting room, playing a game of checkers with a middle-aged Yemenite woman. Seeing them, Lisa's face lit up and she excused herself from the game.

"Thank you for coming!" She hugged Sondra.

"How's Shuki?" Sondra hugged her back.

Lisa exhaled deeply. "He's heavily sedated, but they've lowered the amount of oxygen they're giving him. His heart's good, *baruch Hashem*."

"Where's Kobi?" Danny asked.

"In with Shuki."

"And the doctor?"

"Around here somewhere." Lisa waved her hand. "Do you want to talk to him?"

"That's why I came."

"So let's go to the hallway and I'll look for him." Lisa turned to her checkers opponent and said in Hebrew, "We'll try another game later, okay?"

"Okay." The woman packed up the pieces.

"I never knew you liked to play checkers," Sondra commented.

"I don't," Lisa answered with a shrug, "but Mazal was going stir crazy and asked me to play, so I said yes."

"You look a lot better than you did Wednesday." Sondra sat down next to her cousin on the bench.

"Miriam and the *rav* came last night, and Miriam brought me some fresh clothes. Yesterday I wore a dress from the kibbutz."

"I didn't just mean your clothes," Sondra laughed. "You look a lot calmer."

"Well, the shock's worn off," Lisa admitted as the doors to the ICU opened. "Oh, Danny, this is Dr. Shimshon." She stood up. "Doctor, please meet my cousin, Danny Klein. He's a pediatrician and just made *aliyah*."

"Pleased to meet you." The doctor held out his hand. "I guess you'd like to be filled in about Shuki."

"I would," Danny answered. The two men excused themselves and strolled down the hall, talking seriously.

"Where's Gilit?" Sondra asked.

"Right now she's at the kibbutz, but Tzachi and Shula will be bringing her soon."

"So Kobi called them?"

Lisa raised her palms in resignation. "You were right. He had to. And they've been..." She paused midsentence as two medics ran toward the doors of the ICU, pushing a stretcher with a small child on it. A young woman with a tear-streaked face followed close behind, clutching a teddy bear.

"That's probably how I looked Wednesday," Lisa said as the double doors swung closed.

Sondra squeezed her hand. "Shula and Tzachi?"

"They're being supportive."

"I'm glad."

"Me too," Lisa said. "I was so scared to face them. Tzachi was upset that Kobi hadn't called right away, but Shula calmed him down and now he's really coming through. He has a friend who lives a block away from the hospital, so he and Shula are going to stay there with Gilit for Shabbat. I'll walk back and forth to feed her."

"I brought you some challah and cake for Shabbat." Sondra motioned to the bag she was clutching, all but forgotten in the tension of the moment. "I didn't know if you'd have a place to refrigerate food. If you do, I'll go to the supermarket for you."

"There's a fridge in the waiting room, and we put our names on things. I feel like I'm back in the dorm." Lisa smiled ruefully and Sondra chuckled at her description. "But," Lisa continued, "I don't need more food. Mazal told me that there's a Chassidic family who comes every Shabbat with all the food anyone needs for three Shabbat meals."

"Wow!" Sondra exclaimed. "No one ever did that at Atkins Memorial back home."

"*This* is home," Lisa declared, "not Phoenix. And this is one of the many reasons we live here."

* * *

As Lisa lit candles in the spot the hospital provided in the ICU parents' room, she felt almost as if she was standing in the lobby of the UN. Besides Mazal and herself, there was Henia, who had come from Hungary as a child, Elana from Russia, and an Arab woman. The Arab woman didn't light candles, but showed with her hands and help from Mazal as a translator that she was willing to help the Jewish women out if they needed anything done on Shabbat. Now that she had let her defenses down, Lisa found the other women to be unfailingly polite and supportive of one another.

The food provided by the Chassidic family was simple, but tasty, and there was plenty to eat. Tzachi and Shula observed Shabbat with them, something they wouldn't have done if they'd been home. They, Lisa, and Kobi took turns sitting by Shuki's bedside throughout the day.

After lunch, Lisa had just finished telling her son the story of Choni, who begged Hashem for rain. Weary from sleeplessness and stress, she couldn't think of another single story. As she closed her eyes for just a minute, the doctor's words echoed in her mind. *I suggest that you spend as much time as possible by his bedside talking to him and telling him his favorite stories. He won't respond, but he'll hear you.*

Summoning energy she didn't know she had, Lisa softly began to sing "The Wheels on the Bus." She was feeling decidedly foolish when she reached the verse, "The mother on the bus says, 'Shh, shh, shh.'"

At that moment Shuki, eyes still closed, put his finger to his lips.

Unable to believe her eyes, Lisa sang the verse again, and again he put his finger to his lips.

"Shuki," she couldn't keep the excitement out of her voice, "it's Ima. Do you hear me? Squeeze my hand." He squeezed it. Tears flowing down her face, Lisa tried another question. "Shuki, how old are you?" The little boy slowly held up four small fingers. Then he let his hand drop.

The nurse who'd watched it all put a kind hand on Lisa's shoulder. "That's fantastic progress, but it looks like it wore him out."

Lisa wiped away her tears. She softly sang Shuki's favorite lullaby and then left to share the good news with Kobi and give him his turn.

After Shabbat was over, Kobi sat down next to Lisa in the parents' room. "We need to talk about tomorrow. Let's go for a little walk?"

"Okay," Lisa agreed.

They walked slowly down the corridor. Most of the rooms on the floor were dark, the children inside them already asleep. From a few, they heard the crying of ailing babies and frightened toddlers.

"I'm so thankful that Shuki's making progress," Kobi clasped his hands together.

Lisa nodded, not trusting herself to speak.

"Do you think that you could manage tomorrow morning with my parents' help if I go to work half a day?"

Lisa swallowed. "Probably, but how are you going to manage driving and working on the little sleep you get here at night?"

Kobi raised his eyebrows at her concern, so different from her coldness of the last several months. "Maybe, if everything's going okay here, I'll stop at the dorm and take a nap."

"If you do," Lisa hesitated just for a second, "maybe I'll give you a key to the house and you can pick up some of Shuki's things?"

"You don't mind me going into the house by myself?"

Lisa shook her head slowly.

* * *

Their week fell into a routine of sorts. Tzachi brought Shula to the hospital each morning and then took Lisa to the kibbutz. From there he'd go to his grocery store for a few hours, and then pick up Lisa again and drive her back to the hospital. Once Kobi arrived, his parents would leave together for the store, and after they closed up, they'd drive to the kibbutz and collect Gilit to see her parents.

Each day, Shuki's condition stabilized more. On Monday, he had his eyes open for most of the day. Wednesday, Dr. Shimshon decided to take the breathing tube out. Shuki was able to talk a bit in a strange, hoarse voice.

"We're going to start giving you real food," the doctor told him. "Would you like to eat some ice cream?"

"Can I?" Shuki's eyes lit up.

"Sure, and jello and applesauce and mashed potatoes."

Friday morning, he was disconnected from all of the wires and tubes. Dr. Shimshon lifted Shuki off the bed and set him down on the floor, while the staff and Lisa held their breath to see how his large motor coordination had been affected. Shuki took a few normal steps with the doctor holding onto his hand and then began to stagger.

Quickly, the doctor scooped the little boy up and settled him back onto the bed. "He's weak," he explained to Lisa. "But I'm going to move him into the regular pediatrics ward. We're going to feed him well and fatten him up, and when he gets his strength back, I think he'll be going home."

"*Baruch Hashem*," Lisa whispered with a full heart. "Shuki," she kissed her son, "I'm going to go call your Abba and tell him the good news."

Being out of the ICU that second Shabbat made everything different. There was no limit on the number of people who could be by Shuki's bedside. Lisa and Kobi brought the food provided by the Chassidic family into the room and ate their Shabbat meals together with their little boy. His roommate was a young girl from the kibbutz Riki's husband, Efraim, had grown up on. She'd had her appendix removed and was healing nicely, so there was a definite Shabbat atmosphere. That changed a bit, though, when Riki and Efraim walked in.

"Don't bite my head off," Riki said, anticipating her brother's annoyance. "You're not the one who drove. You didn't tell us to come. For all you know, we could have been here all weekend and walked over. Ima called yesterday, and when I found out that Shuki can finally have visitors, I told Efraim I had to come. Shuki's my nephew, you know." And she gave him a hug.

Lisa just smiled at Riki's harangue.

"Efraim!" the father of the little girl from the next bed exclaimed. "How are you?"

"Ronny! I don't believe it! I haven't seen you since the army! What are you doing here?" Efraim sat down on the other side of the room to catch up with his childhood friend, while Riki motioned to her brother to join her in the hallway.

"Is Shuki going to be okay?"

"We think so."

"No brain damage?"

"*Baruch Hashem*, no."

"When's he going home?"

"In a day or two, it looks like."

"That's excellent news." Smiling, Riki returned to the room. "Shuki, we didn't bring you a present because of Shabbat, but we want to buy you something. What would you like?"

"A train?" Shuki looked at his mother uncertainly.

"You got it!" Riki exclaimed. "Now," she turned to her brother and Lisa, "I want you to give me some time alone with Shuki. Don't worry, I won't turn on a radio or anything. You two go relax together."

Lisa knew it was hopeless to argue with her. "Kobi, why don't you walk me over to see Gilit?"

"Don't stay cooped up in that apartment," Riki instructed. "It's really nice out and there's a park around the corner. Go get some fresh air."

Fresh air sounded perfect to Lisa, and twenty minutes later she and Kobi were seated on a shaded park bench with Gilit sitting on the grass at their feet, chewing on a teething toy. They sat in silence for a few minutes, unwinding from the tension of the past week. It felt good to watch healthy children playing, hear birds chirping, and feel the breeze on their faces. Lisa was the one who finally spoke.

"Kobi, I'm so thankful that Shuki's going to be okay," she said, biting her lip. "But I'm so sorry that I didn't take better care of him. Please forgive me."

"There's nothing to forgive. You're a wonderful mother." Kobi's brown eyes smiled into hers. "It was an accident that could have happened to anyone, and you saved his life by finding him in time. You've got to stop feeling guilty. Please, Lisa. Can you forgive yourself?"

Lisa twisted her hands as she considered his words. Could she forgive herself? She thought about what Shula had told her, about the other mothers from the ICU, Rav Yehezkel's talk on faith in G-d.

"Yes," Lisa spoke resolutely. "I can." She took a deep breath. "And I think it's time to forgive you too."

"Can you?" he asked, looking at her steadily.

"Yes, Kobi." She met his gaze. "I can."

CHAPTER

Sixty-two

At six Sunday evening, Sondra dialed the number of the hospital pay phone, just as she and Lisa had arranged on Friday. Her cousin picked up on the second ring.

"Sondra," she said happily, "if all's well, we're going home tomorrow."

"*Baruch Hashem!* Did you speak to Uncle Herbert already?"

"Yes, and Mom too. She's home from the hospital and taking it easy for a couple of weeks, and then," Lisa paused, "they hope the doctor will let her come for a visit."

"Wow, that's fantastic news! I guess they really want to see Shuki."

"Yes." Lisa hesitated and then let her words out in a rush. "They want to come for the wedding. Kobi and I are getting married."

"You are?" Sondra gasped at the abruptness of the announcement. "I mean, mazal tov," she caught herself. "I'm not surprised, I know that he's been great during everything with Shuki, but, Lisa, do you really feel you can trust him?"

"I only trust Hashem," Lisa said, her voice firm and confident. "But, remember the conversation we had that Shabbat when you were by me?"

"Which part?"

"How I said we never know if our *teshuvah* is complete until we're in the same situation we were in when we committed the sin and we can refrain from doing it again, but I didn't want someone to die to see if Kobi would go off the deep end or not."

"Yeah," Sondra nodded into the phone.

"No one died, but Shuki almost did and Kobi didn't run away or freak out. He hung in there. He's back. The old Kobi is back. Sondra," Lisa's voice cracked, "be happy for me. Please."

"I am, I am," Sondra responded quickly. "Mazal tov," she added weakly. "Um, so what are the plans? Are you going to the rabbi's office in Kfar Saba?"

"Absolutely not! We're having a real wedding in Kfar Yonatan with Kobi's relatives, our Kfar Yonatan family, Cousin Leah, and everyone from the kibbutz who helped us so much, and," Lisa faltered for a second, "I hope all of you."

"Of course!" Sondra exclaimed. "If all's well," she added hastily. "Lisa, I'm really happy for you!"

She hung up the phone, remembering Danny's words the night Kobi had reappeared in their lives. *If she does take him back, you'll have to be supportive.* Slowly she left the office courtyard. Instead of going straight home, though, she strolled around the long way. Twenty minutes later, when she opened her front door, she had a big smile on her face.

"Guess what!" she announced. "Lisa and Kobi are getting married."

"Mazal tov!" Danny grinned widely. "That's marvelous news!"

"They're not married?" Naomi asked, confused.

"They were divorced," Zvi Chaim used his best big-brother, know-it-all voice, "because Kobi ran away. But now he's come back and he's sorry and he wants to be a good Abba again."

"I guess that sums it up," Sondra said softly to her husband.

Danny just smiled.

Later, as they cleaned up the dinner dishes together, Sondra cleared her throat.

"Yes?" Danny asked.

"Um, maybe..." Sondra hesitated. "Maybe I'll go with you when you call your parents tonight." She concentrated on drying the plate in her hand. "I'd kind of like to say hello."

"That would be really nice." Danny flashed her a warm smile and Sondra smiled back, grateful that he'd never questioned her avoidance of his parents since their arrival.

Shirley's voice was warm, with no trace of the rancor she'd expressed at the airport. Only six weeks had passed since then, but those six weeks seemed like an eternity.

"We miss you and the children."

"We miss you too." As soon as Sondra said it, she knew it was true. "I really enjoyed the books you gave me, and I'm sharing them with some of the women here."

"That's nice. You're making friends?"

"Yes." She paused and swallowed. "I really miss the Sunday evenings you used to have us over."

"We miss them too." Shirley's voice was husky. "Did Doc tell Danny that there's a medical conference in Israel in the spring? We're thinking of coming."

"We'd love that!" Sondra exclaimed. "I'm giving the phone back to Danny so my friend who's watching the children can go home. We love you!"

The warm glow of the conversation lasted through the following day. At six o'clock, she made her way to the pay phones again. This time she dialed Lisa's house phone and was rewarded with the welcome news that Shuki was home. After a short conversation, she checked her mailbox and found a puffy manila envelope with her mother-in-law's handwriting on it, addressed to her. On the outside were the words "used clothing."

Intrigued, she tore the package open and found a beautiful hand-knit sweater just her size. Folded inside it was a note in Shirley's handwriting.

Dear Sondra,

I'm so sorry for the mean words I said at the airport yesterday morning. I regretted them as soon as I said them and there's no way to take them back. Instead, I'm sending an apology with a present for you. It's brand new from Saks Fifth Avenue. My friends at the support group for parents with children in Israel told me that if I took off the tags and marked it as used clothing, you wouldn't have to pay taxes on it. I hope it fits and you like it.

Love,

Shirley

As soon as the children were settled down for the evening, Sondra grabbed an aerogram and began a letter to her mother-in-law.

Dear Shirley,

The package came today and the sweater is beautiful. It's just right for the chilly evenings we've begun having here.

It was so good to talk to you yesterday. I looked at the calendar and saw that the conference is right after Pesach. Maybe Doc can take some extra time off and you can be here for Seder. We can't imagine having it without you.

She continued with news about the children and signed the letter, "With love, Sondra."

Her days were hectic, getting everyone set up for school, kindergarten, and nursery school, and beginning her own advanced ulpan course. Before she knew it, the day of Lisa and Kobi's wedding arrived. Danny left the office early and she and the children, all dressed in their Shabbat best, loaded into the van. They arrived in Kfar Yonatan right on time and went straight to the lawn outside the synagogue.

It was a clear day and they could see the hills of Mount Gerizim and Mount Eival in the distance. No one was paying attention to the scenery, though.

Sondra spotted Riki, dressed in a long, flowered maternity dress, deep in conversation with Myra. Miriam greeted Sondra with a one-armed hug. With the other arm she held Gilit, dressed in the frilly pink dress Lisa's parents had brought from the store in Lincoln. Shuki was also dressed in Apple's finest, fully recovered and adorable in his blue suit. His friend Dov, standing at his side, was quite a contrast in his normal nursery school clothes.

Rivka, the National Service girl, picked up her flute and the music began. Kobi made his way to the *chuppah*, flanked by his parents, both smiling proudly. Herbert and Irene were far more somber. Sondra saw Irene squeeze her daughter's hand tightly as they made their way down the aisle. Lisa, dressed in a white suit reminiscent of the powder-blue one she'd worn to Riki's wedding, lifted the bouquet of anemones nestled in her arm and inhaled deeply.

Sondra watched Rav Yehezkel perform the marriage service through a haze of tears. As she looked at Lisa's serene smile, Sondra realized Lisa was no longer her little cousin. Rather, Lisa had grown into her role model and mentor. She prayed that they'd stay close, and no matter what Hashem sent the two of them, they'd be able to continue to pass His tests.

Acknowledgments

Writing this book was very much like raising a child. It wasn't a solo act and it obviously never would have been accomplished without the support of the Almighty. I thank Him for all the special helpers He put in my life.

Like Lisa, I grew in Torah observance while living in Arizona and am forever indebted to the many teachers and their wives who left thriving communities to come live in the desert and reach out to their fellow Jews.

Like both Sondra and Lisa, I came from a warm, loving family, and I grew with my cousins. I'm grateful to all of them. A special thanks to my parents, who always encouraged me to write, my in-laws, who treated me like the daughter they never had, and my Uncle Max, who helped me publish this book. May their memories be for a blessing.

Once in Israel, my family and I were blessed to make our home in Shilo. There are no words to express the appreciation I have for all the Torah teachers, both in Shilo and Jerusalem, who continue to enhance my life.

Shifra Devorah Witt's writing group with Mirel, Judy, Gladys, *z"l*, and Zipporah Malka pushed me to make my characters come to life.

Chaya Baila Lieber, a sensitive and talented editor, helped me move the book forward.

Rabbi Doron Kornbluth and the rest of the Mosaica staff decided to take a chance on *Growing with My Cousin*. It was a pleasure to work together to come up with a good title, lovely cover, insightful editing, and good proofreading.

Ellen Portnoy filled me in on being a medical student's wife.

Susan Baum shared details about the workings of department stores.

Nurses Yoella Weiner and Sharon Brem, z"l, gave me information about premature babies and infertility.

Yona Myers helped me with all sorts of history about the beginning of Israeli villages.

Rabbi Moshe Berliner, noted counselor and director of Machon Netivot, assisted me with facts about mental health.

Rabbi Dov Berkovits and Rebbetzin Holly Pavlov helped me with issues concerning Jewish law.

Dr. Amir Sheinberg, a pediatric pulmonary medicine expert, approved the details of Shuki's hospital stay. He also gave me a wonderful son-in-law.

His son, my other sons-in-law, daughters-in-law, and, of course, my children and grandchildren continue to inspire me.

Most important is my husband, Avraham, my best friend and fan.

It is my prayer that this book will help readers to deal with the many challenges Hashem invariably sends all of us.

Glossary

AGUNAH: woman unable to remarry according to Jewish law.

ALIYAH: to move to Israel.

BA'ALAS (BA'ALAT) TESHUVAH: formerly non-observant Jewess who returns to Jewish practices.

BARUCH DAYAN HA'EMES (HA'EMET): blessing said upon hearing of a death.

BARUCH HASHEM: thank God!

BEIT DIN: Jewish court of law.

BEIT HAMIKDASH: the Holy Temple in Jerusalem.

BEIT KNESSET: synagogue.

BIRKAT HAMAZON: blessing after eating bread.

BENTCHER (Yiddish): booklet containing the text for the Grace after Meals.

BENTCHED (Yiddish): having said the Grace after Meals.

CHAMETZ: leaven that's forbidden on Passover.

CHEDER YICHUD: private room for the bride and groom following the wedding ceremony.

CHEVRAH KADDISHA: Jewish burial society.

D'VAR TORAH: short teaching on a Torah subject.

EMUNAH: faith.

ERUV: enclosed area that allows for carrying outside on the Sabbath.

GET: divorce according to Jewish law.

HAKADOSH BARUCH HU: the Holy One, blessed be He.

KABBALAT SHABBAT: service to usher in the Sabbath.

KIDDUSH: blessing to sanctify the Sabbath, usually recited over wine or grape juice.

KIPPAH: skullcap.

KOHEN: member of the priestly tribe and forbidden to marry a divorcee.

KOLLEL: yeshiva of advanced learning for adult and mostly married students.

KRISTALLNACHT: massive pogrom carried out throughout the German Reich on 9 November, 1938.

LASHON HARA: harmful speech about another person that is forbidden by the Torah.

LECHAH DODI: opening words of the song in the Friday night prayer service that ushers in the Sabbath.

MAZAL AND BRACHAH: good fortune and blessings.

MERKAZ KLITAH: absorption center for new immigrants.

MIKVEH: special pool of water for ritual immersion.

MISHLO'ACH MANOT: gifts of foods given on Purim.

MOHEL: trained man who performs ritual circumcision.

MOTZEI SHABBOS: after the Sabbath.

OMA (German): grandmother.

PARSHAS HASHAVUA: weekly Torah portion.

PIDYON HABEN: ceremony of the redemption of the firstborn son.

RAV: rabbi.

REBBETZIN (Yiddish): rabbi's wife.

ROSH YESHIVA: head of Talmud academy.

SEUDAH: festive meal.

SEUDAH SHLISHIT: third meal of the Sabbath.

SHALOM ALEICHEM: traditional Jewish greeting.

SHALOM BAYIS: marital harmony.

SHALOM ZACHAR: Ashkenazic celebration on the first Friday night after the birth of a boy.

SHEITEL (Yiddish): wig.

SHEVA BRACHOS: seven blessings recited at festive meals held the first seven days after a wedding.

SHOCHET: Jewish ritual slaughterer.

TANACH: the Bible.

TEHILLIM: Book of Psalms.

TESHUVAH: repentance.

YOM TOV: Jewish festival.

Z"L: a Hebrew acronym for "May his/her/their memory be for a blessing."